UNDISCOVERED
TERRITORIES

ALSO BY ROBERT FREEMAN WEXLER

In Springdale Town

Circus Of The Grand Design

Psychological Methods To Sell Should Be Destroyed

The Painting And The City

The Silverberg Business (forthcoming)

UNDISCOVERED TERRITORIES

(stories)

ROBERT FREEMAN WEXLER

Published in November 2021 by PS Publishing Ltd. by arrangement with
the author. All rights reserved by the author. The right of Robert Freeman
Wexler to be identified as Author of this Work has been asserted by him
in accordance with the Copyright, Designs and Patents Act 1988.

Publishing history appears at the end of the acknowledgements.

Experpt from "Only One Sky" by Jack Hardy. Copyright © 2000
Jack Hardy Music (BMI). Used by permission. All rights reserved.

FIRST EDITION

ISBN
978-1-78636-589-7
978-1-78636-588-0 (signed edition)

Design and layout by Alligator Tree Graphics.
Printed in England by T J Books Limited.

PS Publishing Ltd / Grosvenor House / 1 New Road / Hornsea, HU18 1PG / England

editor@pspublishing.co.uk / www.pspublishing.co.uk

CONTENTS

CONTENTS

For the memory of my parents, Shirley and Seymour Wexler

"There are still, depend upon it, quaint undiscovered countries and continents of strange extent."
    —Arthur Machen, "The Novel of the Black Seal"

PART ONE

in the undiscovered
city

TALES OF THE GOLDEN LEGEND

Prologue: Bread

Remnants of the previous week's snow, hard and blackened, lay in crusty mounds on the sidewalk. An endless flow of pedestrians crunched between the piles. Crossing the street, a man held his hand to his head to keep the wind from removing his hat. The morning sun sent a shaft of light through the windows of the Italian food store; the round semolina loaves, lined up and stacked on the chrome rack, glowed. In their shadow lay rows of baguettes, bagels, rye, and whole wheat. Farther left sat a company of prosciutto, rosemary, and provolone breads. Several varieties of focaccia rested below on a shelf of their own.

In front of the shelves, a young, hawk-faced woman with pale skin and blue eyes stood at the cash register. A strand of rusty hair hung over her eyes. Her father, the fat owner in his white apron, had just unlocked the door and flipped the sign from closed to open. He moved behind the opposite counter to guard his sausages as the first customers of the day entered the store—a pair of women in their mid-seventies carrying wicker baskets.

"Parmesan," one of the women said.

"Romano, Romano," the other said, shaking her basket for emphasis. "Anna Felina always buys Romano."

The hat-holding man came in and stopped in front of the bread. He gazed at the loaves, entranced, as though he had sleepwalked into the store and awaited a signal to act. Several minutes passed before he lifted his hand from his gray felt hat and removed his black leather gloves. His hair was dark, like pumpernickel, his skin light like the plain bagels. The hawk-faced woman asked what he wanted.

Seeming not to have heard, he stepped back to allow the women to pay for their cheese.

"And a Tuscan bread," the first woman said to Hawk Face in a demanding tone.

"Not that one, too small," the second woman said when Hawk Face chose the nearest loaf.

The man appeared to be listening to something; he stared at the loaves as if they could help him. Finally, after a minute or so, during which time Hawk Face ignored him, he pointed to a round loaf of semolina. All of the semolina brightened, glowing like moons; the other varieties grew darker.

"Did people bake the first bread, or did bread bake the first people?" the man asked Hawk Face. She punched the cash register keys. She looked at him, then at the loaves, and held out her hand for his money. The man paid and left the store. Now smiling as though at a private joke, Hawk Face watched him leave through the door; he put his hand back on his hat and crossed the street.

The Bread Dialogs

It was morning, a month since I discovered I could talk to bread. I sliced a piece from a loaf of rye and spread some butter. The tea had steeped enough; I tossed the bag and added milk. Bit into the bread, began wrapping the loaf in plastic.

"You're not going to finish me?" the loaf asked in a musical tone. Because bread is a collective organism, it speaks in a chorus-blend of male and female.

I stopped wrapping and looked at what remained of the loaf. "Not now, I'm full. Maybe later."

"But you have to. I'm getting old."

"Everybody gets old."

"Then put on some music."

"I'm about to leave for work." Bread can be demanding. Its age gives it a sense of superiority—there has been at least one loaf of bread existing in the world for 10,000 years (since the beginning of agriculture, though maybe longer, the bread isn't sure).

"If you won't put music on, I'll sing."

I slipped into the bedroom for a shirt and the bread began singing a song about making a sourdough sponge.

"Yeast is in the air.
Bread is everywhere."

I returned to the kitchen. "I'm late for work," I said, interrupting the loaf's singing.

"So what? Your job isn't vital."

Bread is right. I keyboard text for a company that publishes books on real estate tax law. I could die and nobody would notice.

I looked out the window to check the weather. Gray drizzle. I wound a plaid scarf around my neck. My over-warm apartment always made me forget it was still winter outside. I took the rest of the loaf with me to finish for lunch. The bread kept talking to me on the train to work. "As the protein chains grew in the primordial sea and became the bacteria base of all life, that bacteria was yeast. Yeast was the first being on a planet of rocks and sea. Therefore all life is bread."

This was the second time the loaf had explained bread history to me. I know that yeast is really a fungus, not a bacteria, but didn't feel like arguing. Besides, I'm always careful not to talk to bread in public.

The first bread ever to speak to me was a loaf of golden semolina that I bought in the Italian food store after the final argument with Susan, whom I'd been seeing for close to two years. When I took the loaf out of the bag and put it on a cutting board, it asked me if I was planning to toast it.

"I never toast fresh bread."

"Okay, just checking. You seem upset."

I began telling the loaf about Susan, about how I had found out she was having a fling with an English chef at the French restaurant where she worked as a waitress. The semolina said it would let me know if it heard anything from the baguettes in the restaurant, but I said it didn't matter anymore.

Since then, I've talked to over a dozen loaves. Each loaf is different. Heavy varieties, like olive breads and anything with meat or cheese, have little to say. White breads are the least interesting, whole grains the most thoughtful. Perhaps because of the holes, bagels don't make much sense. Bread has told me that maybe one out of five million people can understand its language.

On the way home from work, I stopped to buy bread at a bakery near the office. I tried not to be overwhelmed by the myriad conversations. The fat loaves of country white complained about the skinny onion baguettes, while a basket of whole wheat rolls laughed at its own jokes. I selected a loaf of something called struan. The label said it was made from wheat, corn, oats, brown rice, bran, buttermilk, and honey. The struan laughed and talked at the same time, a lusty, world-loving voice full of confidence and mirth. I heard it entertaining the other loaves, whistling like the sound of a baroque flute.

During the subway ride, the struan didn't talk (though it hummed a Bach flute sonata). However, it complained when I stopped at DiPalo's for fresh mozzarella.

"You don't need cheese with me," the loaf said from within the bag. I ignored it. We can't always do what bread says.

At home, I opened my newspaper and scanned a few headlines, then turned toward the loaf and asked: "What's going on in the bread world right now?"

"In the Negev, a Bedouin has just pulled a fatir from a sajj and handed it to a guest at his tent. In Austin, no, that's boring. Oh, here's a good one." The struan laughed, then continued. "Six blocks from here. A woman just whacked her husband on the side of his head with a long, stale baguette. He's crying, saying: 'She's nothing to me, I love you honey, I was weak, it was just a fling, trust me, please.' Ha ha ha."

Bread has told me that the mass-produced loaves found in supermarkets are not alive, not real bread. Injected sponge, it calls them. A fact that should surprise no on. Bread only comes to life with the slow-rise method. Mix, knead, let rise. Punch down, let rise again. "Each loaf is interconnected through its yeast culture," bread has said.

I recently saw a man talking to himself on the train. He spoke with great animation, gesturing to the air in front of him. I thought: is that what it looks like when I talk to bread? The man's hands were empty, but how could I know whether there was something seen and understood by him alone?

The Sound of Crust

I was born at 350 degrees in a small, white, gas oven. I first became aware inside this metal box while the yeast died, screaming silently within me. I lay upon a baking sheet, in darkness relieved only by the pulse of flame visible through round holes in the bottom of my oven-box. I burned with life. I was alone. Time meant nothing. I had being, I had substance. I wondered, is this life, this metal womb?

A sudden light: the door swung down and oven mitts reached toward me—Mother?

My creator, a young woman with hair golden like corn flour, pulled me from the oven and slid me from my baking sheet to a wire rack. As I began to cool, I exulted in my newness, stretched the limits of my crust. At this point I had no notion of those who came before me. I was the universe. Then, The Awareness overcame me—the knowledge of all bread. What can I say about the flames that catalyzed my birth that better loaves have not already said? Potatoes are always potatoes. Water boils, cheese melts, but bread alone transmogrifies. Yeast is one form of life, bread another. From bread all life begins and is sustained.

Unfortunately, bread-baking is not a genetically acquired skill, and I, a round loaf of buttermilk white bread, am the young woman's first attempt. I dwelled too long in her oven. I lack the air pockets that indicate well-risen dough, and my crust is far too thick, too chewy. I know I don't have a rewarding life to look forward to; when she realizes the extent of her failure, she will lose her desire to eat me, and I will mold.

Because gestation continues out of the oven, bread should not be sliced for twenty to forty-five minutes after birth. Fortunately, she knows this. So I sit on the rack, awaiting my fate. I can sense her impatience while she paces in front of me. She stops several times and stares at me, unfocused, as though looking out from a dream. Her face is soft and round, like a hamburger bun. She smiles at me, touches my crust lightly, bends over to smell me. When she leaves the room, I relax.

I hear her on the phone. Then I panic. She is inviting someone to come over and share me. I wish the poor woman could understand our language, for I would tell her of her failure. Will she be embarrassed when, with anticipation flooding her senses, watched by her friend, she slices into me? The knife will struggle through my outer shell. She may flatten me if she isn't careful. Then she will see the dense interior.

As a white bread, I am sweet but not deep. Yet I have feelings. And I carry the weight of centuries of bread knowledge, bread awareness. I know the ovens of our past as well as my own birthplace. We have a fondness for brick, for the artistry of a loaf made without controlled temperatures. Sometimes, we think that bread's time has passed. People's lives move too quickly for us, and we do not travel well.

She's pacing again. I wonder how far away her friend lives. In ten minutes, I will be ready for slicing.

My crust will make me difficult to eat. Perhaps they will dig out the soft flesh within. Perhaps the young woman's friend will be polite and eat me with feigned enjoyment and much butter. Oh! A horrible thought has come to me—what if they can't recognize that I'm not a good loaf? What if they have no concept of what bread should be?

I just realized I haven't seen her knife. I hope she has the right kind. The edge must be serrated. Pulling a loaf apart with the hands is a natural act, but mutilation with the wrong knife is agony. I fear I will be crushed beneath the clumsy pressure of an inexperienced hand and an improper blade. What will happen to me, I wonder, after these initial slices, while I, still warm, am the center of their food world? All bread grows cold, changes in texture. A mediocre bread becomes worse. Will I sit, forgotten on the shelf until I turn rock-like? Or, into her too-small freezer to chill the life from me? Like trying to tell time from a sundial left in the shade, bread is useless if not eaten.

A knock at the door, and she runs to open it. I hear their kiss. They enter the kitchen. He makes dutiful compliments about my appearance. I'm worried now. The first slice is always difficult. The waiting and . . . the cutting. Where is the knife? I must see it.

Good. They have a real bread knife. It's new. Twelve inches long with a seductively curved wooden handle. I palpitate. I wait. He takes it out of the cardboard packing, runs tap water over it, dries it. He's ready. The expectation is killing me. He hands the knife to her. No, she gives it back. Please, please, I'm ready. Let me feel the blade.

Finally, he begins the first cut. The arm comes down, knife edge presses my crust. Ah, he's experienced—he turns me on my side. I can't breathe, I can't think. His hands, delicate, like those of an artist. I wish he would hold me forever. The new knife bites. I feel it. Back and forth, back and forth. He saws with precise strokes. Yes, yes . . . I feel the blade. I can't take it. I don't want it to end. Oh oh oh. I can't I don't I can't. Ahh. It's over now. They're eating. I can rest.

Epilogue: Bread Aria

In the sky, a lone cloud slid across the blueness, borne along by the breezes of the young spring. The late afternoon sun shone just over the tops of the buildings. A man coming out of an apartment building squinted and probed his shirt pocket. He pulled out a pair of sunglasses and slid them over his eyes. On the way to the crosswalk he sidestepped a puddle of rusty water that had accumulated from a dripping fire hydrant.

Inside the Italian food store, Hawk Face watched a boy in his mid-teens bring several fresh loaves of ciabatta from the cooling rack. She pushed a few bâtardes aside to make room. The ciabatta thanked her for giving them a spot near the cash register; she didn't respond. She stood leaning with her elbows on the counter, staring at the cheeses and sausages in the glass case opposite her. Few customers had come in that afternoon; she kept looking at her watch. Her eyelids, colored a metallic blue, drooped over her pupils. Her chin kept bobbing, losing her fight with afternoon drowsiness.

Behind her, the new ciabattas, their voices purring like cats, chatted with their neighbors. They discussed the corn muffins in the basket on the counter; one loaf described them as sweet nothings of negligible nourishment. The focaccia, always pushing their pedigree, spoke in haughty tones about the quality of the mushrooms baked into their tops, while the prosciutto bread, sated by its own flavor, said nothing.

Hawk Face continued to stare at her watch, and without lifting her head called out once to the fat man behind the cheese counter, "I'm so damn bored I almost wish a bus would drop a load of tourists at our door."

A woman with a green scarf over her head came in with a young girl; Hawk Face stood up straight and smiled.

"Either that or ice cream, but only ice cream with chocolate chunks," the girl said to her mother. "Not chocolate ice cream. Or maybe an apple turnover *and* ice cream."

"I'll get you something sweet, but you can't have it till after dinner."

"Fine Momma, but I don't want eggplant again. We've been having egg-plant all this long winter, and I'm sick of it. Sick of it, sick of it."

The man with the sunglasses entered; he dropped the glasses back into his shirt pocket. The breads greeted him by name: "Steven!" they said. He smiled, but walked to the back of the store, where he selected cartons of milk and orange juice. When he returned to the bread, the multigrain was singing the part of Tamino from *The Magic Flute*.

"O endless night! Wilt though never pass?
"When shall my eyes behold the light?"

The ciabatta, in chorus, answered, "Soon, young man, or never!"

While the woman with the scarf paid for a focaccia and an apple turnover, the girl stared at the bread and giggled. Her mother and Hawk Face apparently couldn't hear the singing, which was so loud now it would have drowned out their comments about the weather. The girl began humming along with the bread, and continued humming as her mother led her out. The man stood looking at the bread; the loaves stopped their singing. He idly played with a strand of his dark hair. The semolina bread whispered to its neighbor that they knew the man would pick one of them; the multigrain, in a commanding tone, told them to hush.

"Well, order something already, before I fall asleep," Hawk Face said. She smiled.

The man smiled back. He continued to stand before the bread, which began asking in turn, "Choose me—What about me?—Am I the right flavor?—Choose me." The semolina glowed when he asked for one of them.

The man left the store. Hawk Face turned to watch him through the window. He crossed the street, walking back toward the building he had left a few minutes ago. The remaining loaves resumed their singing. For a moment, as Hawk Face watched, the man paused to allow a taxi to turn in front of him. With a pile of baguettes between her and the window, his head seemed to be connected to the bread. The loaves became his body. She shook her head as though emerging from a dream.

SUSPENSION

My name is Quatrain Brauner. Look at me, six foot six inches, four arms, and 320 pounds flat in the snow at Grand and Center. I fell on my back with my arms outstretched. If viewed from above, the indentations my four arms made in the snow would resemble a giant dragonfly.

An icy sidewalk caused this tumble. My feet flew up as though propelled by their own will, my body thumped down, all four hands grasped air. What is it like to slip in such a manner? The unexpectedness, manifested as a dull, abdominal stab; the impact with the pavement and its treacherous topping—a shock felt throughout my body. My sudden crunch through the snow forced an exclamation, but the sound cut off in mid shriek. The seconds beat into hours; my heart slowed to normal; my shoulder throbbed. Calmness settled. New flakes dusted my forest-green wool coat.

Each moment, each breath, brings forth a new present, leaving behind the previous moment, relegating it to a past soon clouded by the inaccuracies of memory. Each day leads us to a multitude of possible futures, realities based on: mood, actions, choices. Perhaps, had I fallen another day, I would have popped up and walked away, but I like it here, lying in the snow. The flakes whisper to me, though what they say makes no sense.

People walk past. Their comments amuse me: "Do you think he's dead?" "Lookit the size of him!" "Shouldn't we do something?" Ignoring them, I think instead of the texture of snow and sky. I am the wind. I scour the cliffs, freeze the bones of the exposed and unwise, push the clouds across the sky. I savor the swirling darkness. Follow me, I say to no one. Follow me, I say to all.

A sudden pressure in my leg as an old Chinese woman walks over me. I pull in all my arms before she can injure them. A sleeve and a red bag from the produce stalls pass through the edge of my sight, and her footsteps crunch away. I admire the old Chinese women. Although my size allows me to walk the streets with a serenity felt by few in this over-crowded city, I always move aside for the old Chinese women. Though some are barely four feet tall, on the sidewalk they defer to no one. Not even a 320 pound man with four arms. They walk with such determination that I know I would be the injured one if a collision occurred.

"Sir?" Someone speaks to me. I turn my head to see a thin woman with a pointed nose and tufts of brown hair splaying out from under her knit cap.

"Sir, do you need assistance?"

"No thank you." Such a nice lady. The only one to stop and show concern. I hear a continuous clip-clop of steps passing, and I wonder how long it will take before anyone else addresses me. Will it be a policeman? Fireman?

There's a fire house a few blocks uptown. I prefer firemen to policemen. They seem goodhearted. I often see them in the nearby grocery store, joking and calling out to each other while they choose their produce. I've pictured the communal meals they prepare at the station house while waiting for their next call.

Myself, I could miss a few meals. It's hard for me to admit that I have a weight problem, but I've been exercising. Since the beginning of autumn, I've lost 50 pounds; on me that amounts to nothing. A body like mine hides a lot of weight. In college and many years after, I carried a normal weight for my age, height, and appendage number, but ascetic ideals have no appeal for me. I surround myself with intelligent conversation and its companions, food and drink. And where is the harm in that?

Life, for me, is often a pleasure: music, scholarship, witty companions. Yet, some see me as a monster; I've witnessed the nervous looks, the attempts at vague deference, the fear. I usually wear a cloak to hide my arms. Though nothing can hide my size. I am peaceful, gentle, but people so often associate a large person with violence and a brutish temperament.

I breathe, I desire, and I hide nothing. What would my life have been with two arms? Four is what I have; as a four-armed man is how I've lived. As a child, while I played with my two-armed peers, I used to wonder how they survived with such a handicap. Besides, two or four, we all live in a state of punctuated equilibrium, where instability and catastrophe are inevitable.

However, my four-armed life suffers from, has always suffered from, the absence of love. In college I had a few dates, but most women weren't comfortable around me, especially alone. We would be having a wonderful time until the kissing started. My dates all had the same reactions: when I began touching them with all my hands at once, they would grow alarmed. They said, the ones willing to talk about it, that the feeling was too intense. Freakish, one said. Another said she thought she was being gang-raped. There are, of course, people interested in sexual perversions. I met enough of them to remove my virginity, but I want more than sex.

Romance, love—finding it may be unlikely, but an unlikely event is likely to happen because there are so many unlikely events that *can* happen. So I never stop searching. My resilient nature doesn't allow me to give up, though the years of rejection have built layers that weigh upon me, thick, dark, and lifeless.

Recently, I saw a magnificent production of *Cyrano*, a translation true to the spirit of the text and an actor believable as poet, lover, and swordsman. It's a role that I, for obvious reasons, empathize with. The play is a testament to the power of poetry, living poetry that can smite down evil, a poetry almost lost today.

Infinite worlds of sight, smell, and sound lie beneath every surface, but few have the power to excavate them. I wonder, do I, here in my cloak, my white cloak, have the will to seek them? Above me flow the lives of the others, those with whom I am nothing but a shape, a four-armed reminder of their frailty. Look up to the stars, I say to them; the stars see all, no one can hide from them. Lasers, they bore into our thoughts, our bodies, our senses, even into the worlds beneath.

From where I lie, I can see little without turning my head. I see only edges. The side of a brick building, parked cars, a light pole. No, it isn't true that I can see little, or rather, it's the truth of humanity that I only ascribe being to that which is made by human hands. For above me rises the sky, and what more is there? The sky holds everything, every color and texture of the universe. The sky forms the window onto distant worlds. Here in the city, stars, the moon even, are difficult to see. Had I fallen on a country lane, I would have vast stretches of stars to contemplate, come nightfall. Oh, how the city circumscribes everything! I close my eyes to make it vanish.

"Spawn of Satan," someone says, a shrill, male voice. He stops near my head, as though waiting for a reaction. I can hear his breathing, ragged in the cold air. I don't bother looking. What point would there be to acknowledge those who spit and spew? Religion has never been a friend to differences. My kind must represent something, some moral lesson about the alleged demon within.

Over the centuries, I wonder how many four-armed infants were left outside to die, alone in the night. If a she-wolf ever rescued one and raised it as her own, no report came back, no legendary four-armed wolfman of the forests. I'd like to think it happened though, that a fierce, yet kind, maternal she-wolf, having perhaps just lost her own cubs to accident or hunter's bullets, would have taken and cared for an abandoned infant, given it a chance at life in this unfeeling world.

Will I be able to see the moon? Tonight is the full, the shining pearl, an emblem, a magnet. The sky clears; no more snow to dust my resting place. Four arms outstretched, I embrace the night, the darkness behind which I hide. Sometimes at night, when I'm home, alone, I open the windows wide to let the darkness rush in.

Someone shakes my shoulder, and I hear a voice, a voice speaking Chinese with a few words of English. No, it's two voices, two Chinese women. I look at them and smile. Both small, black-haired with gray streaks, one slim, one stocky. They nod to me, and I wonder if they are prepared to lift me from the snow. But I'm not ready yet. I shake my head at them, smile, say no thanks, I'm happy here. They look at each other and talk about it. Language is such a maze of visual and notational elements. I wish I could understand.

The two Chinese women pick up their bags of produce and walk away. The sky grows cloudy again as the hours meander along their predetermined path. I prefer the blue, but find the present situation acceptable. The passing voices continue to provide a sense of drama. "How can the dust be responsible?" "I prefer the alchemy of the visual image." "Daddy, is that a person? Daddy, Daddy, that *is* a person lying in the snow."

The worst thing about my position is the lack of scents, though the smell of snow has a pleasant flatness. At an archeology lecture a few years ago I learned about the layers of buried civilizations, the bones of which we walk upon. In this city alone, many civilizations rose and fell. I've read that some of the early inhabitants formed small communities based on cooking techniques. This area had been full of stone hearths, stewpots, and people who ate many varieties of root vegetables. The legend says, four times the people rose and four times they were put down. The fifth time rang triumphant, fire fell and touched the sky. And myself? I stretch across the gulf, a suspension bridge from the buried past to the future, where my kind walk hands in hands to the spring.

Flat in the snow at Grand and Center, flat, but how flat really? As flat as a 320 pound, four-armed man can be, more like a sleeping cow shrouded by snow. I recently told a group of people gathered around my long, farmhouse table, that my problem is simple: because of my four arms I eat so efficiently and quickly that I tend to overeat, especially when I am with other diners—because I don't like to finish first, I keep eating. I gain weight, then I have to exercise. And my exercise takes longer because I have to work out all of my arms. Some of those present actually laughed at me, and one said he had never heard such a ridiculous explanation for obesity, that extra hands couldn't make me eat more without an extra mouth to go along with them. For a moment, I considered tearing off his head.

Ah, but here in the snow, none of that matters.

In the snow, I occupy my time with reverie and wait for life to resume. I observe the snowflakes—each one identical and perfect. Snow has always fascinated me. I was born in the south, in a place where snow came rarely. This snow, a living beast, aware yet ignorant, comforts me. Its blanket holds me with the gentleness of one whose great strength is restrained by moderation and maturity. I listen to its music, progressions of notes in a minor key. Its voice surrounds me.

Is solitude such a bad thing? More and more, I am finding the answer to be no. Solitude is better than the company of fools. Alone is where I find comfort.

As a child, I often hid in the laundry hamper. I liked to stretch my four arms against the sides, feeling comforted by their proximity. In the hamper, the safe, dark hamper, I rested undisturbed. Darkness is a spice known to only the few, great chefs of the world. A pinch of darkness and a handful of time, the saying goes. Or is it thyme?

Now everything has turned—darkness, friend, betrays me. I am caught in a thick black net. Viscous fingers search my pockets, my sleeves. Please, I hide nothing here. It is only me, only me. The fingers vibrate, laughing. Cold seeps from them, drills into me. I cry out.

My eyes cannot pierce the leathery blackness. Gasping, I thrash the snow with my arms. The snow is now the blackest ash, the sky and everything around me black also. Where does the snow end and the rest, the non-snow cars buildings people street begin? Blackbirds settle on a branch, black feathers, black eyes. Black sky black sky, its suffocating mass pins me. I stop my thrashing . . . take short shallow breaths . . . heart a train rushing . . . I close my eyes. With eyes closed, the blackness is worse, more total, annihilating. Where is my white bed? I have to see.

But I don't open my eyes. I lie still, waiting for the darkness to pass. Even when the starbursts come, I lie still, and sensation returns in gradual waves. When I open my eyes, the snow has become white again. I reach to touch it.

Sometimes, I get lost in my own words, in the dark maze of processed thought, in rows and rows of unseen objects. Then I hunger for simplicity. The scent of frying food invokes comfort. The sight of yellow makes me cry. No one comes here anymore. No one cares. Those faraway places are lost forever. Now I hear them, the dreamers, calling my name. Their perseverance gives me hope. They hover nearby, ionizing the air with their collective will, changing things grain by grain, particle by particle.

The fluttering sound of wings surrounds me, but I see no birds. Above, only a gray-blue sky. I turn my head, and the flutter-sounds become voices speaking Chinese. The two Chinese women have returned, joined by another woman and a man, both older than the original pair. The man bends over me; his silver hair falls across his forehead, and I stare at his lined face. What joys, what horrors has he seen while crossing the decades of life? Furrows fan out from his eyes and mouth, furrows hiding more than the ocean's deepest trenches.

The old woman, her face lined as deep as the man's, leans over me. She reaches down, and before I can raise an arm to block her, she pinches my cheek just below my right eye. Something must have pleased her because she lets out a cackle and says something to the others. They nod and each of them grabs one of my hands. What machinations are they attempting here? I think about asking the question aloud, but hesitate, curious to see what occurs next. The old woman chants, and my arms tingle as though massaged by invisible fingers. Something else is happening. They're pulling me, and while they pull, the old woman maintains her chant. Up I go, without a choice in the matter, lifted by the quartet whose combined weight probably falls short of my own.

Suddenly I am on my feet. I stand among them, unsure how to react to the sight of the street and sky from this new position. The quartet, none of whom come up higher than my chest, stand near, laughing, proud of their success at raising this snowbound whale. Around me, the peaceful streets have emptied of traffic. Banks of snow line the pavement. The place where I had lain is a trench dug deep into a white world. Now, I too begin to laugh—a slow ripple cascades from my stomach.

A Chinese boy appears with a thermos. He hands it to one of the younger pair, the slim one, who loosens the top and pours into a cup. The liquid steams and the scent of tea washes into the air. She hands the cup to the old man, who sips and passes it on to me. "Lung ching," he says and smiles.

I thank him, thank them all, and sip the finest tea I've ever tasted. Now nothing can hold in my laughter. It flows from me, flows from all of us. I reach out with all four arms and take the hand of each of them, my quartet. With their free hands they grasp each other's and we dance, spinning around and around, a laughing circle in the snow. We trample through my former resting place, churning the snow, filling in the gap left by my body until no trace remains.

INDIFFERENCE

Brown's wife left—when?—already two or three months ago. He had explored her geometry so thoroughly in the three-room apartment that he still found her superimposed over everything. In the mornings, her face covered the walls, and landscapes of thick hair draped the furniture; evenings, her voice taunted him. She erupted from his ears in pink and green surges. He could do nothing. She arose, unwanted. Yet, what feeling did that squeeze from him?

Indifference.

Nights were the worst. He got into bed and sleepless hours passed. He would chant, silently, over and over: I am a man with an indifferent heart. But even his indifference was a failure, for one would think that a man with an indifferent heart would be able to sleep. One night, he crawled out onto the fire escape and howled with laughter at the absurdity.

Food became inessential. Water served as breakfast. A mid-afternoon snack of two glasses had to carry him to the next morning. He couldn't work. A five hundred page art history manuscript he had been hired to copyedit remained on the table with the rest of his mail, unopened.

Sometimes, the phone rang, but he never answered. It wouldn't be for him. All calls had been hers.

On a rainy day, he sat on the fire escape; on a sunny day, he sat inside. Then for a time, he sat outside on a sunny day and inside on a rainy day. His apartment had two fire escapes. One overlooking an airshaft, the other above the street. Sitting on either one suited. He ignored the layers of smells rising from the Italian restaurants: frying calamari, baking lasagna, and later, after closing, wine from broken bottles, and rotting food.

Some say humanity is easily crushed by circumstances. Others laud a person's ability to survive. In 1840, a group of Comanche attacked and wiped out the small Gulf-Coast Texas settlement of Linnville. A 42-year-old seamstress named Emma Golden, who had recently moved from St. Louis and had never before lived outside of a city, escaped and walked over one hundred forty miles to San Antonio, with no food and only a small canteen of water.

When she reached the town, limping, holding herself up with a branch found in a dry stream bed, she claimed to have been helped by the disembodied head of a woman. This head, she explained, appeared on her second day, hovering motionless, staring to the west. It showed her the ten ways to survive, she said, and she never spoke of it again.

When the temperature dropped toward freezing, Brown wore thermals to sit on the fire escape. He had learned long ago the layering techniques needed to maintain comfort in a variety of elements. One evening, as he sat on the street-side while sleet fell, he pictured his wife and her new lover walking below, hand in hand. They went into Di Francesca's. How easy it would be to climb down the fire escape, enter the restaurant, and confront them. Consider a crime of passion—what jury would convict him of killing his wife's lover?

But Brown felt no passion. What would be a crime of indifference?

There had been a time, after they first moved into their Little Italy tenement, when they had made love in every room, on the living room floor, the kitchen table, in the narrow entryway. He had expected this life to continue. They had been close, he thought. She called him her *copain*.

Brown's wife took an older man for a lover. This man had not been the first to profess his love for her while she and Brown had been together. Her need to be loved was a desperate thing, and to fulfill it she had perfected an ability to comfort people, to make them feel worthy of admiration. They assumed this attention existed for them alone, and worshipped her for it. This had never bothered Brown, for she loved him, not these others. Though after she left, he realized he had merely been a long-term project. When she said she was leaving, his tears surprised her. She had told him that he didn't care. When she left, his tears stopped, proving her right.

He took out his dictionary and turned to indifference. His favorite definition: Absence of compulsion toward one thing or another. That described his life perfectly. Thirty-five years—why had it taken so long to figure out? Aloof, detached, not showing feeling or interest, apathetic. He possessed all those things. The next entry was Indifferentism: the belief that all religions are valid. Yes! That was he. He had often said either everyone is right or everyone is wrong. Indifferentism had no color. He was an Indifferentist.

The universe is alive, each particle unique yet connected. The Mona Lisa and nuclear waste, baseball and rain, dogs and fear. Where did Brown fit? After a time, he came to believe that his life resembled a progression of notes on a piano. He had only to find his melody.

1. Thirty-five years
2. Uncomplicated
3. Kisses

On a Thursday, a man's head materialized in the middle of Brown's living room. Brown knew it was Thursday because his watch showed the day.

He needed to know the day; an event as significant as the arrival of a head in his living room must be marked, but he hadn't looked at his watch in so long that finding it took hours. What felt like hours, of course; he had no way of telling exactly until after he found the watch, and by then it was too late. Time had passed.

But what of the head? It appeared in the morning, in that instant when the ascending sun splattered the wall outside with gold. Brown was sitting on the sofa, having finally begun to copyedit the book (the people for whom he worked had told him to return it or finish it). He looked up from the pages, and there was the head, hovering in his living room. Though not hovering exactly—that indicated an absence of body, whereas this head acted as though it connected to an unseen body.

When the head made this unexpected appearance, Brown sucked in his breath and stared. His red pen fell from slack fingers. The head faced Brown's sofa and the windows. It occupied the center of the living room. Brown didn't move, and neither did the head. When it occurred to him to look for his watch, he got up, and when he determined that the watch wasn't in the room, he walked past the head to reach his bedroom. He flattened his body against the wall, keeping far from the head, but the head made no acknowledgement of Brown's passing. Brown could hear the breath flowing through the head's nostrils, an even rhythm that he found soothing.

Brown secured the watch to his wrist and returned to the sofa. He sat, admiring the head—its thick nose, cleft chin, hair and sideburns shot with gray, long hair pulled back in a ponytail. This was no ordinary head.

The head stared forward, as if concentrating on something in another place, somewhere other than Brown's apartment. Perhaps that was where its body existed, in some faraway land unreachable by current means of travel. Brown liked to travel, by car, plane—less than a year had passed since he and his wife had taken that trip to London (where she met the man who was to become her new lover). Now, there was nowhere he wished to go.

The head shimmered sometimes. Eighty percent here, he thought, thinking back to the graphics work he used to do. Like an eighty percent screen applied to a photograph. A little fuzzy but mostly there. The head possessed an aura of command, and he deferred to it, waiting, so patient in his waiting that he forgot to drink his afternoon water until his throat constricted from dryness.

But the time came when observation was insufficient. He wasn't the type to sit quietly while a head dominated his life. So he stood. If the head did indeed connect to a hidden, standing body, the person would be a couple of inches shorter than Brown. He approached the head and shuffle-stepped to his right. Was there an eyelid flicker? He tried a quick step the other way, nothing. What would happen if he touched it? Reaching out with both arms extended, like a cartoon sleepwalker, he moved toward the head, a half-step at a time. Somewhere among his steps and half-steps, he observed that he was no longer making forward progress, though the action of walking proceeded without impediment. He measured his range of motion against the knob of a cabinet—one step with his right foot carried him beyond the knob, then the left joined the right, but when he tried another step he found himself starting again from the same place. The head remained inches from his outstretched fingers.

No more of this tentative half-stepping then. Brown lunged for the head. With a thump, he hit the floor. His fingers were even with the knob. He closed his eyes and rested his forehead on his arms.

After a time, he got himself back to the sofa and sat, panting, surprised at how exhausted the attempt had made him. He looked at the head. Why didn't it speak? His failure made him think of his wife. She wouldn't have been surprised. Would have expected it, another proof of his indifference. So little control here . . . alone . . . inert. But such things can't trouble an Indifferentist. He stood, turned his back on the head, and went out onto the fire escape.

The morning sun gave way to clouds, drizzle, but it cleared toward sundown. As he sat, it occurred to him that his wife's lover might have sent the head to torment him; this was a troubling concept. He had heard the voice of his wife's lover on the phone once, a message left for her as though Brown didn't exist.

"You are my wildest dreams. Missing you hopelessly but full of hope," the lover had said.

"Unfortunate" was the word Brown's wife had used (via note) when he told her (also via note) about hearing the lover's message.

Brown's wife acted, in plays, TV commercials, films. The lover had directed her. Her face would soon appear in advertisements for their forthcoming film. The anticipation of this event should have filled Brown with dread, with loathing for his pitiful position. Instead . . . indifference. She had told Brown that he was all those things: detached, unfeeling, aloof. Her words revolved through him while she packed, emitting silver geysers of dismay and fear, like streams of discursive neon glue. The weeks of her packing were the black time, the period of disbelief, before. . . .

But she had meant to hurt him with her words. That didn't make them true. He hadn't always been those things, not thirty-five years of indifference. Now, yes.

1. Who am I?
2. I am here to serve.

Such a fatherly head. Brown appreciated its silent presence, and though he hated to break that silence, he needed to talk. "I wasn't always this indifferent. Did you know that my wife left me? It's up to me to change. I know that. But I don't know how. And sometimes, sometimes I like this indifference. I don't think that makes me irresponsible, or cold." He continued in that vein, but one-sided conversation exhausted him—He longed to hear the head speak.

How would its voice sound? Dramatic, to match its sideburns? He had learned long ago that people's voices rarely correspond to their appearance. In a past job, he had gotten to know many people over the phone before meeting them, and they never looked the way he had envisioned them from the sound of their voices. He supposed the same was true of him. But there was one whose appearance matched her voice, and she had such dark eyes. Jane McDonald. He hadn't thought of her in years. *She* should have been his lover. With her honest voice, she would have prevented onset of this indifference that eliminated his passion.

He took his breakfast water onto the street-side fire escape. He felt bad excluding the head from his company, but he didn't need to share every moment with it. The head would understand. They had worked out an easy relationship so far, and the head wasn't bad, as roommates go. He took up little space. Someday though, Brown might want to invite a woman home, and how would he explain the head?

Little likelihood of that. He didn't know any women and didn't know how to meet one. What had he done before he met his wife? He must have had friends, but he couldn't remember any names. He thought about Jane McDonald again, but years had passed, and she lived halfway across the country. She had no doubt forgotten him long ago. *Not that an Indifferentist cared.* He sipped his water.

He looked at the head through the open fire escape window, then glanced away, embarrassed, but the head gave no indication that it had read the lie in Brown's thoughts. "I do have friends," he said. "I checked my messages this morning. Kit asked how I was doing, and Frank. So did Kari. Danvers called yesterday. But I can't talk to any of them right now."

Mathematics lives in a land of mystery and wonder, a universe oblique to our own. Its explorers win few accolades from popular culture. Those who need to refine and enrich the concept of number find their rewards in the work itself. Consider Bernardo Bolzano. He entered the University of Prague in 1796; he studied philosophy, mathematics, and physics.

Bolzano liked to say, "My special pleasure in mathematics rested particularly on its purely speculative parts . . . I prized only that part of mathematics which was at the same time philosophy." Bolzano is best known for his work on infinity. He argued that the most promising approach toward an analysis of the infinite is mathematical. In *Paradoxes of the Infinite*, he asked: "Who, for instance, would not agree that the length of the line which is unlimited in the direction aR is infinite?" His paradox involved the idea that not all infinite sets can be considered equal with respect to their multiplicity. "Instead, some are larger (or smaller) than others, that is, one can encompass the other as a mere part (or, conversely, one can be a mere part in another)."

Bolzano also speculated on the connections between mathematics and beauty. He originated formulas tied to hair color and computed the likelihood of beauty, both male and female, coming from a variety of economic and educational backgrounds. His theories on beauty, along with his socialist and pacifist views and criticism of religious doctrine, led to his being barred from further teaching. Late in life, he began to work in clay, sculpting busts of men and women based on his mathematical models, rather than from life.

At times, Brown wished for a female head, a head of such startling beauty he would sit in awe, and not the typical beauty of film or fashion, but someone special, with features that mesmerized. What would he like in a female head? Red hair. He had never dated a woman with red hair.

One morning, as he sat contemplating the head, he realized that it might be hungry, and he felt ashamed for having neglected its needs. He found his watch. Friday. What did Friday mean? Instead of returning to the head, he opened the window and stepped onto the fire escape. Such a lovely view of the airshaft today, and the opposite wall. Friday. He would prepare a Sabbath meal for the head. He had never done that on his own, though he had grown up with Sabbath meals prepared by his grandmothers, sometimes by his mother. What should he cook? Chicken, always chicken, perhaps roasted potatoes, salad, green beans, and of course, challah. He would light candles too. He still remembered the prayer. The things memorized in childhood forever remained.

But he needed groceries; it had been so long since he had gone out.

Now that he had made this decision, he dreaded what he would find out there. So many people, up and down the streets they walked on missions that defied his understanding. They pushed aside anyone blocking the sidewalk. Something occurred to him—feeling, he felt dread—his first post-indifference feeling!

The recognition of his dread gave him the necessary strength. He could *go* outside.

The familiarity of Met Foods calmed him: the wilted produce, narrow aisles crowded with boxes, the cashiers chatting in Spanish. Everything he required could be found here. Forgetting his diet, forgetting he had come for Sabbath meal ingredients only, he darted up and down the aisles, filling his shopping cart. He read labels, squeezed tomatoes. He stood in front of the canned tuna, trying to decide which variety to add to his cart, but no no no, this wasn't right. Up and down the aisles again, returning everything but his Sabbath meal items.

Throughout Brown's life, cooking had given him pleasure. Cooking transformed him. He lost his inhibitions. He risked the life of his meal in search of the greater good flavor. He crossed the boundaries of ethnic seasonings without fear. Dust now gathered on the tops of his spice jars.

These were his most-used spices (aside from salt and pepper).

1. Oregano
2. Cumin seeds
3. Rosemary
4. Jalapeño flakes

A month or so before his wife left him—before his life changed, before he knew it *would* change, for there had been no warnings of change approaching—he had gone away for a week. When he returned, he noticed that a jar of whole coriander had appeared on the spice shelf.

His wife had never used it before; her cooking consisted of tomato sauces seasoned with an Italian spice mix. He wondered why she had bought the coriander. When she left, it was the only spice she took.

Back home with his groceries, Brown glanced out the window. Snow had begun to fall. He opened the jars of his favorite spices and sniffed each in turn. Once, each separate scent would have elicited an emotional response: oregano-wistfulness; cumin-contentment; rosemary-sexual passion; jalapeño flakes-inquisitiveness. All these months, the spices had been dead to him. Today, he thought, something might be returning.

He squeezed lemon onto the chicken, crushed oregano with rosemary and salt and rubbed the blend into its skin; happy now, this new happiness engendered more, until he laughed at his former indifference.

He felt gratitude toward the head, which had brought this happiness into his life, and focused his energy on preparing the meal. Soon, the aroma of roasting chicken filled the apartment. Lacking the necessary oven space to roast potatoes alongside the chicken, he decided to boil and mash them. He blanched the green beans, then sautéed them in olive oil. He set candlesticks on the coffee table. When everything attained its optimum of readiness, he fixed plates for himself and the head and carried them into the living room. He recited the prayer and lit the candles. Was this prayer supposed to be done by a woman? There must be allowances for meals involving one man and one mute head.

Contrary to Brown's usual cooking style, he had refrained from tasting during his preparation; after going so long without solid food, he had waited for this moment, with everything finished and arranged on the plate, as though he had become two different people. One who prepared the meal and one who consumed it. He lifted a chicken wing to his lips and bit into the crunchy skin; texture and taste rose through him, petals flowered outward into realms untouched by clash or despair. This was how to prevent the end, to beat back the forces of indifference!

One of the candles sputtered; wax dripped down its side. He glanced at the head. Its food would remain untouched, a prophet's plate waiting, forever ready.

An air of mystery surrounds the life and artistic career of Hart Meisner. Many things are known: the deprived early childhood replaced as a teenager by an ascension into high society when his widowed mother married the industrialist Bernard Levy; his aborted attempt at a career in professional baseball; his apprenticeship with Robert Henri. But so much remains unchronicled. No photographs exist. Fortunately, there is the art itself, and his few comments regarding it.

Meisner painted cityscapes. Angles fascinated him: clean edges, abrupt breaks. Formlessness terrified him. He determined that because representation of organic matter dominated the art world, he would refrain from painting it. He thought landscapes and portraits to be arrogant, a form of appropriating the natural world. In a lecture he once said, "Vanity causes us to lay claim to earth and trees when architecture should be trumpeted as our greatest achievement." On March 2, 1924, while painting a collapsed warehouse in Trenton, New Jersey, he cut himself on a jagged scrap of iron. Tetanus resulted. Death followed. No clean edge there.

Brown carried the dishes into the kitchen. On his way back into the living room, a sharp object jabbed his heel. He sat down and raised his foot to look—a glass sliver. Months ago, he had shattered his wife's picture, slammed it down on the desk where it stood. Glass flew everywhere; most he had found and disposed of. He removed the splinter and stared at it, as though it held the key. Then the head spoke, its voice a raspy thing, vocal cords scored by time and trauma, a voice that demanded an audience.

"The flame fans the fates, darkness infests your sight."

Outside, the snowfall had stopped, snow draped the window ledge and fire escape railing. The sofa, the uneven shapes in the old plaster walls, flowed in and out of focus; they reshaped themselves into his wife's image. All this time he had sat, indifferent to her absence, yet obsessed with traces of her presence.

They had met three years ago this day, he realized. They had danced amid the shapes of others, oblivious to all but themselves, and from there, life became a fairytale existence in which she, in her flowered dress, played the part of star. He wondered whether he would ever know what had been real.

1. Sex
2. Oak
3. Rent
4. Departure

The head spoke again. "Rain consumed the burning holes and soothed the edges. The clash of armies could never haunt us as it did that night of tattered refugees. Your heart opened, gushing expressions of black and silver. Your undulating nature allowed respite. Smooth clouds swelled along the horizon, obscuring hill and plain alike."

The head knew him better than his wife ever had; Brown opened his mouth to tell the head that, but changed his mind. His earlier attempts at conversation had brought forth no response. The source of this break-through lay elsewhere, in his cooking perhaps. He lay on the sofa with his back against an armrest, where he could see both the snow outside and the head.

"Two brothers farmed their father's land. One loved the land and honored it; one preferred the sea but feared change. And which worked the harder?"

"Not the one who loved the land, but the other, for his fear of change drove him to desperation and made him seek his father's approval over his brother's."

Brown looked down at the candles, thinking through the head's words.

"Rain falls regardless of whether the garden needs it," the head said, then its gaze returned to that faraway point.

Knowing that the head had finished for the night, Brown blew out the candles and walked into the bedroom. So much had happened this day that he didn't think he would be able to sleep, but it seemed that the head's phrases had contained a powerful metatonic, for sleep claimed him as soon as he lay down.

He woke later, calling out in the night, and lay in bed with his heart thumping. A nightmare, was all, but one so startling he forgot it immediately. He got up and walked past the head to the sofa, where he lay with his eyes open. The only thing he could recall of the dream was the sight of his wife's face filling the horizon, formed by sky and cloud. Brown remained on the sofa, closing his eyes, and eventually he slept.

Brown sat on the sofa, looking out the window. He had finished the art history manuscript and was preparing to take it uptown, to the office of the publisher. Heavy snowfall had mounded on the window ledge and fire escape platform. He leaned closer to the window to see the sidewalk, now buried beneath the white sheet.

What would his wife be doing now, in this snowstorm? He hadn't thought about her so concretely in a while. Now he felt a sudden urge to call her, but what would he say? As a teenager, he and some friends occasionally spent their afternoons making crank calls, dialing the numbers of popular girls in the school and pretending to be someone else. He picked up the phone and punched in her number.

"Hello?" she said. Brown couldn't believe he heard her live voice. The whole time they were together, he had never reached her when he called, only her voicemail. What would she be thinking now? Wondering who was calling, wondering. . . . "Hello," she said, louder. Brown hung up. He glanced back at the head, wondering what it thought of his prank.

Half an hour later, he pressed redial. Again, she answered. He held the receiver up to the head and waited, but the head did nothing.

"I know it's you," she said. "I've got that thing that gives the number of the person calling. If you're not going to say anything, don't call me." She clicked off.

She knew. Brown started crying. He hadn't cried when she left, but now sobs tore through him. He pushed his face into the sofa's pillows. Unable to stop crying, he breathed through his sobs. Nothing had been fair . . . what did she want? He couldn't exist to fuel her needs. *He* had needs. But what could an Indifferentist need? No, he wasn't that. He had lust, and fear, and . . . what? What did he have besides lust and fear? When he looked up again, the head spoke.

"Where have we been, in this field of stone? Once there were more of us. . . . " The head scrunched its eyes closed as though attempting to drive out images it feared. "Once. . . . " Its voice faltered. Brown waited. "You," the head said, and its eyes popped open, staring into Brown's. "You must never!"

Brown waited, but the head said nothing more. Its eyes gazed into its private distance.

Brown left his building. He had called the publisher to tell them he would bring the manuscript in tomorrow, after the snow had been cleared. It had taken intense concentration to leave the necessary voicemail message, but having done so pleased him. Now he was free for the day. He walked west through the snow. He had never seen so much snow in the city. No taxis roamed the streets, no pedestrians, no open stores. He traversed the streets alone. The mounds of unplowed snow made walking difficult, but the cleanness of it all, the fluttering whiteness, thrilled him. He walked through the undulating landscape of snow-covered cars. His footsteps crunched the loose, dry snow, and he concentrated on the sound, step-crunch, step-crunch, loving the texture. Turning a corner, he saw four Chinese—three women and a man—grouped around something in the snow. Together, they reached down to grasp it. Brown walked on, step-crunch, away from them.

He stopped walking. Around him, snow silenced the streets. With so many ways to say goodbye, Brown had chosen indifference and a frozen life. Contrary to what his wife had said, he had cared about her, had wanted their future together, but his life with her had numbed him in a way he had only now begun to break out of. He started crying again, though not last night's painful sobbing. All around him, people lived and died. He had always known that, but today it had more significance. Significance over indifference.

On his way home, the winter world took on varied aspects: the glitter of sun on snow, people emerging to dig out cars or shovel sidewalks, the fluttering of pigeons nonplussed by the weather.

Soon, the world would begin again.

THE SECRET BAG

A band of sunlight shooting through the window crossed my eyes, awakened me. With an effort that seemed to take hours, I focused on the white squares of ceiling tile, seeing in their surface a relief map of the ocean floor. The tiles—they were new to me. I twisted my head to the left—a window, blue, cloudless sky, brick buildings topped with water towers like fat rockets. I tried to panic, but felt too numb to do so.

Eyes closed again.

I turned my head to the right, opened my eyes a bit, then a bit more, saw two green chairs and a counter. These items appeared to have been arranged to serve me, and I felt grateful. Again, I looked up at the ceiling tiles. I smiled at them. When I turned my head to the right once more, farther this time, I saw a bag on the counter. Immediately, I felt relief, for I thought I recognized the bag.

Was it mine?

I stared at it. White plastic, stiff enough to hold itself upright. What secret did it hide? The design on its side must have some significance. Red shapes, some straight, some curved, held I thought, the key to my situation. Each shape told a story, some happy but most sad, though I could remember none of them. I tried to make one up—a gray cat slept on a sofa as a man and woman argued. The woman accused the man of loving the cat more than her. But that must have been years ago. Concentrating on the bag gave me a headache; again, I closed my eyes.

Evening now. The water towers glowed in the fading light like distant candles. Murmurs filled the air around me, like the thrumming of bird's wings. I listened, discovered that I could understand them. Two women talking. One, with a voice like apples, said something about grogginess. The other voice I knew and tried to associate a name with it. "Susan," I said. She turned and touched my face. I smiled and fell asleep.

In darkness, I thought to try my legs. Though they were stiff, and pain shot through them when I moved, I felt compelled to test them on the floor. I raised my body and pivoted, dropping my legs over the edge of the high bed. This activity and a throbbing in my ribs exhausted me, and I lay back, crosswise on the bed. Despite the pain in my legs, I must have slept again, because when I opened my eyes it was darker. No one had disturbed my position.

A sense of urgency consumed me. I pushed my body up again. With my stiff fingers, I gripped the edge of the bed. I pulled myself forward. My feet were only a few inches from the floor. All I had to do was slide off, and I would be there. I did it in one swift movement and yes, I was standing! I glanced at the bag as though taking a compass reading, but as I did so I collapsed. A howl burst from my throat and my body fell to the floor.

I awoke on my back, in bed, with a thin sheet pulled up to my chest. In the sunlight the bag looked innocent. The red designs meant something—I was positive. I felt weaker than before and closed my eyes. I knew I must reach the bag soon. Someone pushed a straw between my lips, and I sucked down a cool liquid that satisfied a thirst, until now unrecognized. I concentrated on the tactile—the straw, the liquid, the pillow supporting my head. I felt the straw being withdrawn, and someone dabbed around my mouth with a napkin.

Hearing the bird's wings again, I concentrated on them as though they were words. I listened, thinking they must be a message from the bag. They subsided before I could decipher them. Then, darkness surrounded me.

I could no longer move my legs. For hours, I think, I strained against invisible bonds. I cried out an agonized gibberish and tried to beat the bed with my arms. They felt heavy, as though filled with sand instead of blood. Forgetting about my legs, I concentrated on arms. My right arm didn't want to bend, but my left did. I touched my chest with my left hand, found it covered with a tight band of fabric. A similar band of fabric covered my right elbow and a tube ran from my hand to a sack of liquid on a pole.

The room was now darker than before. Somehow, the bed's headrest had been elevated, putting my head at a higher plane. I looked toward the secret bag, hoping that this new angle of sight would reveal something previously hidden. Yes—I recalled something about the bag! I saw it being carried by a woman with dark hair, high, angular cheekbones, and a wide mouth. I thought she must be someone I knew well, and this realization calmed me. I decided to close my eyes and wait, hoping that while I did so, the bag would help my legs regain their mobility.

Again, someone eased a straw into my mouth, and I wondered whether it could be the woman whose face I associated with the bag. I considered opening my eyes to find out but imagined the effort to be too daunting. I remembered something I usually did with other people—I opened my mouth. I tried to ask: "Who are you?" but the only sounds that emerged from my mouth were tree bark and cobwebs. Cool fingers—the woman with the straw?—touched my face. The murmuring resumed, and I wondered if there were birds in the room. If it was indeed the bag trying to communicate with me, I wished it would be more direct.

The birds flew around the room. I could see them so well through their sounds that opening my eyes became unnecessary. I smiled at them; they hovered nearby, feathering me with comfort. When they returned to the bag, I waved good-bye, hoping soon to join them.

I awoke to discover that I couldn't move my arms. My breathing accelerated. Soon, I was gasping. I knew I must stay calm. I must. I said this to myself, tried to repeat it aloud but my throat was too dry for speech. However much I tried, I couldn't open my eyes.

Was there an injection? Years ago, I thought, when I had my wisdom teeth removed. But I must have left the hospital afterwards, must have lived another fifteen or sixteen years since then. The bag would help me understand. I forced open my eyes and stared at it, willing it to reveal its secret. I was now sure that the red designs were a message.

I could rock, and did so. The pain was less now. It was a strain, using my neck and back muscles to move the rest of my body. Even if I did remove myself from the bed, I wasn't sure how I would reach the bag. Perhaps it would help me when it saw what I had attempted. I slipped closer to the edge of the bed. One last, mighty heave. I tumbled over the edge.

Inside the bag, I found myself ascending an endless circular staircase that reminded me of when I had climbed the leaning tower of Pisa. Could I be inside one of the water towers visible through my window? That would be ridiculous. On my left, the bag's white plastic side, on the right, darkness. I climbed and climbed, knowing that if I looked over the edge of the stairs I would fall. I thought I heard music above me, perhaps a saxophone screaming like a child in pain.

I climbed, moving ever higher into what I envisioned to be the bag's cloudless stratosphere, but soon wearied of the upward struggle.

Though happy to have regained, finally, the full motility of my body, I now desired to be somewhere else—say, standing in a field of sunflowers or even sitting in a subway car. I slowed, moving my feet ever so deliberately across each step as though waiting for it to be my last. I stopped, sat on a step. Thinking of Lebesgue's theory of measure, I decided to take the number of steps I had so far climbed and divide it into the amount of steps I climbed per second, then take that number and do the same, repeatedly, and use the results to compute the distance to the top of the stairs. Or perhaps Hasen's theory on the volume of cones and pyramids would be more applicable.

My eyes began to water from the odd, purple light, which changed, swiftly flowing through a spectrum of green until it stabilized at a hue resembling the surly green-gray of the Gulf of Mexico after a storm. It was at this point that I decided to act. Perhaps because of the resemblance of the void to the ocean, I jumped.

But did I plummet? It was difficult to be sure, because I experienced a sort of sensory deprivation. It wasn't merely that I didn't immediately feel the sickening, free-fall rush of my body plunging into the void. I felt nothing. I went from the scrape scrape of my boots over the worn marble staircase bathed in the ever-changing spectrum of light, to nothing. Not just a body hanging motionless in the air, but a body without sensation. It wasn't that I couldn't open my eyes, or that they were open to subterranean blackness—it was as though I had no eyes at all. Nor arms, legs, lungs, stomach. And in this state, I had no way of knowing whether I did, in fact, lack those attributes of arms, legs, eyes, stomach. I possessed nothing but awareness. I felt nothing in a most complete way, in a way that the nothing I felt became something, became the only something I had. Nothingness became my being. I considered whether this is what a god might feel, floating alone in a void prior to inventing a world to play with.

Thinking of gods, I thought I might invent myself a meal, though I would need to re-acquire a mouth and stomach to process it. The concept of mouth distracted me . . . teeth fill a mouth, do they not? Teeth chew the food that enters a mouth. I tried to recall the last meal that my teeth had eaten. I remembered a large, round table and many laughing companions. At what were they laughing, I wondered, for I couldn't recall anything save their faces and the food on the platters in the middle of the table. I concentrated on the platters. The one closest to me consisted of a bed of thin noodles and bits of meat and vegetables. I could now see it quite clearly before me; when each item came into focus, I identified it.

The concentration left me suddenly exhausted, and I allowed the image of the food to dissolve, though the faces of my companions remained. Directly across from me, or at least my point of vision, whatever that point was, for I still had no body, sat a woman wearing a large straw hat with purple flowers. I recognized her as the woman I had associated with the bag. She kept looking at me, smiling and winking, and I wondered why we didn't sit closer to each other. I felt a sudden longing to brush my lips across her body. Her mouth moved. Having never been able to read lips, I concentrated on sound.

"You shouldn't be eating the rice noodles, lovey. They're made out of fat, rice fat."

At the top of the stairs, I stood in a circle of reddish light ringed by a black mist. The mist stirred, as though disturbed by writhing limbs. Whatever the mist hid threatened me. The red air around me felt thick. It resisted my movements, gagged me when I breathed. I tried to run, but the air clung to my ankles. I kicked against the top step, trying to free my feet. A viscous tendril of the dark mist loomed above me. I pounded and pounded its manlike shape with my fists, crying at it to leave me alone. "You can't hurt me!" I heard a voice scream into my brain. I closed my eyes and lunged for the shape, knowing that if I could catch it, I would triumph. We rolled on the grass, struggling for the bag. He tore it from me, and my chest burned. I collapsed against the ceiling tiles.

My awareness floated upon winds that I couldn't feel, and I began to suspect that I would neither emerge from the top of the bag as once I had hoped, nor discover its origin and purpose. I wished that I was again trapped in my bed overlooking the water towers, for then I at least possessed a body, however defective. For then I knew that I could at last rest undisturbed.

THE BAKER

The baker stood in the empty room, as he had done in a dozen other empty rooms. He stared at walls that might once have been white, and saw ovens of brick, glass, and blue enamel. In place of the garbage bags, he conjured a marble counter for kneading, beside chrome racks where the dough would rise. When he closed his eyes, the leftover smells from the trio of dogs that had inhabited the storefront with their owner became herbs, yeast, loaves in the oven. In the chill of a vacant space with no heat or electricity, he surrounded himself with the warmth of baking.

He opened his eyes to reality, but smiled; soon, this emptiness would become the one place he felt at ease.

The realtor entered, stopping several feet from the baker. "Perfect, isn't it," the realtor said. He glanced at the baker with a quick movement of his eyes while keeping his face angled away, as though afraid to look directly at him. He had shown the same behavior throughout their two-month relationship.

The baker continued to walk around the room. The realtor maintained a perfect three-foot space between them.

Because of his size (six feet six inches), scars, reputation from his football past, and what had been referred to in the sports pages and talk shows as a "penetrating lifeless stare," the baker knew he appeared menacing, crazed even. But his only violent act, aside from football, had been to break a baguette over a man's head, a baguette that the man had just used to hit his own wife in the face. The wife screamed at the baker for hurting her husband, and the baker—at that time an amateur bread maker and only a customer of the bakery—had been asked to leave and never return.

What does bread look like when you're sad? Only those who have loved can know. Bread makes everyone dream. Moldy bread makes everyone dream in hallucinations and nightmares. Shadows splotch the crust, darken the corners of rooms, and in those corners lurk the devourers. It's a long way home if you don't know the way. Finding a path through the maze of loaves, loaves of maize. . . . But it crumbles, bread does. Bereft of hope, bread and dreams turn stale and dry, then ignite. Bread calls to him . . . but . . . not the bread . . . the dough. Ingredients, the alchemy—taking wet and dry and combining to create a new element. And the transformation of texture—feather-dust of flour to massiness of dough. He savored the finished product, its scents and tastes, but it was the making that brought him peace.

When someone walks into a good bakery, their demeanor changes. Conflict and trauma remain outside. In a good bakery, neither could survive. Most of the time . . . what had caused that man to attack his wife? Sickness persisted, some aberrant strain of yeast or rancid flour.

"I'll build a glass wall so the customers can see the ovens," the baker said, finally acknowledging the realtor. He spread his arms (and the realtor stepped back a few more feet). "There's room here for a display case, and by the window, a long counter with stools. People can sit and look out." He resumed his pacing, re-arranging the furnishings in his mind.

Dronings and questions from the realtor, costs per square foot, leasing terms. . . .

"Please leave," the baker said, too loud perhaps, because the realtor jumped. The baker smiled, hoping he looked warm and friendly. "I need to be alone here for a few minutes, that's all."

The baker sat on the floor, allowing his ideas to form around him.

Soon after being drafted in the second round and moving to the city, the baker had rediscovered bread, an interest abandoned in childhood. One summer, when he was eight, his day-camp took a field trip to the Soft Crust bread factory. The huge, churning vats of dough fascinated him. Soft Crust—what a contradictory and ridiculous name. His mother had baked, and as a child he joined her. Perhaps that was what compelled his uncle, the junior-high coach, to push him into football, after some long-ago family gathering at which his mother proudly told the relatives that he had helped bake the bread. The uncle hadn't approved of a woman raising a boy without a father.

There had been no real bakeries in the town where he grew up, nor where he attended college. But here. . . . He moved to the city in summer. Before training camp and rookie season stole his leisure, he explored, long walks through different neighborhoods, the parks, the Craphouse District. He sampled bakeries, many bakeries. Chief among them was Donovan Street Bakery, run by Nicholas Allard.

Donovan Street Bakery was on 15th street. The street named Donovan existed only in Allard's mind, taken from a recurring dream in which this and other cities connected by streets radiating from a strange and mysterious city-center, a place both ancient and modern. In Allard's dreams, he visited a bakery on Donovan Street. The bakery had no official name, but everyone called it Loaves, from the painted sign over the door.

And why not name a bakery from a dream? Bread *is* dream, the stuff of wonder and delight.

After the baker's rookie season, he began bread-making experiments. He took a historical perspective, trying to recreate early baking conditions to make the most primitive of loaves, flatbreads with hand-ground flour and no yeast. He built a fire on the balcony of his high-rise apartment and set a flat stone in the middle, for baking upon. Later, he brought in buckets of soil to shape an oven of mud. And onward, up bread's evolutionary road. Later, after football, he worked at Donovan Street, apprenticing with Allard.

He had thought that when he found his space, he would reprise his baking experiments, as consecration, but decided that would be excessive. Everything he had learned would go into his current work. His bread practice was as much a part of him as the yeast was to the finished product.

From the lunch counter where the baker sat, he could see, across the street, the exterior of his future bakery. The counterman approached him with a menu, and the baker ordered coffee and a bacon and egg sandwich. Brown paper covered his windows, shrouding interior preparations. The baker meant to keep the identity hidden for a time, revealing a new detail every few weeks, a series of drawings of loaves, leading to a final unveiling of the name painted on the glass, The Golden Legend (after the Magritte painting of flying loaves), set in an arc over a circular, braided loaf.

On the sidewalk, people passed as usual. One day, some would stop, enter his bakery. Who would they be, his future customers?

Soon, he would post a help-wanted ad in the paper and begin interviewing. He had learned, from his apprenticeship at Donovan Street, the importance of well-trained staff, people who were able to follow instructions *and* work independently, initiate if initiation was required. Too much authority and no one would do anything without his consent; not enough control and no one would work when he was absent. He needed to find his own version of Rose, the little one, from Donovan's.

What does it mean to be wrong: the wrong size, the wrong demeanor, the wrong dreams? An atheist and non-participant in his teammates' frequent prayer meetings, the baker was both shunned and proselytized by the evangelicals who dominated his team. If he hadn't quit, he likely would have been traded someplace less concerned with player's souls, as the team's ownership actively tried to assemble what they called a Christian group of players. He never understood how he had slipped thorough their filter.

Unable to participate in his teammates' easy camaraderie, he drifted deeper inward. Practice and games—those he enjoyed, but the rest of the time he tried to forget football.

Long before quitting football, he had become a regular visitor in Allard's kitchen. Their friendship began with a discussion of sourdough. The baker had read about sourdough and had tried several recipes, but he had been unhappy with the results.

"It's the city," Allard said. "Too much dirt and smog, too many people. Your air conditioner filters out some of the muck, but you lose yeast too. It's not that you *can't* create a starter in the city, but it's best to begin away from all the cars and noise. Once it's alive, you can feed it in the city, keep it going.

"You can always, *always* taste a city-born sourdough."

Allard talked to the baker like he was a regular person. He never commented on the oddness (if it was odd) for a football player to be interested in bread-baking. Possibly, to Allard, it was more odd for people to be uninterested in bread.

The baker accepted Allard's gift of starter, but kept at his experiments.

Allard's encouragement, his confidence in the baker's abilities, helped shape the baker's eventual decision to quit football. And he hadn't been wrong to quit, despite what the commentators said, "squandering his talent," "throwing away burgeoning all-pro career. . . ."

The baker was able to present Allard with something in return, when the owners of the building that housed Donovan Street filed for bankruptcy. Worried that the bankruptcy would threaten the bakery's existence, he assembled a group of teammate-investors to buy the building, even writing terms into Donovan Street's lease that would prevent unfair rent hikes (he didn't trust his football-player partners or their business advisors). After the sale was finalized, the baker remodeled the building's fourth floor to make it his home, another area where he differed from his teammates, as none lived in the city, preferring oversized houses in the suburbs.

Pushed by his uncle, football had been something he never questioned. He enjoyed the game, relished the impact with opposing players, forcing turnovers, sacking the quarterback. But it lacked, and, it was a game to him, always a game. He wanted to win, but not to the point where winning dominated his life. He had always disliked coaches, the way they treated the players as if they were machines, child-machines unable to think for themselves, told what food to eat, what drugs to take.

When asked by the media why he quit, he said: I want to open a bakery.

But he knew that reaching his baking dream required more training. He needed Donovan Street, needed to learn more from Allard, the other employees, and from the customers. Even now, despite the hours spent on preparations for his own place, he still worked at Donovan Street a few mornings each week.

A woman examined the contents of the display case, taking time with each item, ignoring the line that formed behind her. Two men, college students, talked with loud voices as if they were the only people there, or at least the only ones who mattered. They commented on the woman's slowness, but the baker refused to rush her.

"I'd like a cinnamon roll and a baguette," the woman said.

"Remember that cinnamon roll chick from our workshop . . . what was her name?" one of the students said.

"She was raped by a ferret," the other student said. "Swear-to-God—her older brother had this ferret and one night it got into her bed. . . . "

"The way she unwound and lapped up those cinnamon rolls did have a ferret-like quality."

"Exactly."

They ordered a focaccia topped with Parmesan and yellow peppers, and asked him to cut it into fourths. "Hey, you're the guy used to play pro football," one of them said. "What the hell are you doing here? Can't you do broadcasting or something?"

"I'm learning to bake bread," the baker said. "So I can open my own bakery."

The two paid. "Concussions," one of them said on their way out. "Too many."

"Assholes," Rose said, having approached during the exchange. But the baker considered whether they might be right.

"I'll take over," she said. "Boss wants you in the back, Ogre."

Well before Rose began working at Donovan Street, the baker had been a customer and friend of Allard, but as customer he had never been able to breach Rose's indifference. Once he began his apprenticeship, she adopted him as mascot, considering him simple and in need of guidance. She called him Ogre. She told him she had been referring to him that way since the first time she saw him. He had been talking to Allard. When he left, she said: "who's the ogre?"

From her, he didn't mind. Only five foot one, seventeen inches shorter than the baker, but she commanded his respect. She was one of those people whose presence has the effect of making them more imposing than their actual size. He had known football players like that. Already large, physically, their confidence and attitude enabled them to over-whelm other players, even those the same size or larger.

The baker walked into the kitchen, past a rack of sourdough rolls and whole wheat batons ready for transport to restaurants. Allard cut a thick slice from a golden loaf. He passed it to the baker. "Experiment. Potato flour and coarse-ground cinnamon."

The baker chewed, swallowed, took another bite. "Nice," he said. "Maybe more honey. Or molasses, but you wouldn't want to darken the loaf."

"Excellent idea." Allard spread butter on another piece and bit into it. "Now listen . . . something I haven't talked about with you."

Allard's normal voice was quieter than a football coach, but loud enough to be heard over kitchen clatter. He lowered it to the murmur of a scoop dipping into flour. The baker leaned his ear closer to Allard's mouth.

"Bread . . . you know it's alive? All bread is alive. Not just yeast. Yeast dies in the oven. Yeast dies and bread is born. It's talking to us all the time. Most of us can't hear it. I can't, you can't, but some can. Not many, and none of them will admit it. Bakers know this, but bakers. . . . "

A woman from the delivery service came in to get the loaves. The baker helped her load them into her van.

"It must be something genetic," Allard said when the baker returned. "Whatever makes someone a baker cancels out whatever makes someone able to hear bread. I had a customer who I'm certain of. The way he stood . . . his body . . . when he was in line and before he ordered. He was doing more than looking at the selections. He was *listening*, like he was waiting for the right loaf to talk to him. I couldn't get him to admit it. I think I pushed too hard. He stopped coming in. Remember that— watch for them, but don't scare them off. If they buy your bread . . . that means your bread is *worth buying*."

Remodeling proceeded, interior stripped to brick and bone. Today appeared to be sawing day—the screech of blade into wood drove him back onto the sidewalk. The bakery was on a corner, half of a larger building; his co-tenant was a hardware store. To promote neighborhood camaraderie, he intentionally bought supplies there, and asked his builder to do so as well.

The desire to bake bread, to open his bakery—those drove him, but then what? He wanted to provide good bread for those who appreciate it. He didn't care about clever marketing, psychological methods to sell. His was not a bread that would shout out from the rooftops. His was subtle bread, bread meant to be savored. Flour, water, yeast, seasonings—everybody used virtually the same ingredients, and many had skills equal to or exceeding his, but he was confident that if he infused his bread with his imagination, his uniqueness, the bakery would succeed. Perhaps it would take longer. Attention might first go to flashier places, but his would endure.

Any marketing consultant would have told him to use his football past, name the place "First Down Bakery," with poster-sized action shots from his career and giant television screens with a continuous flow of game action.

Doubts began to harass him: what made him think that he could open a bakery? He felt a sudden absence of the coaching that had controlled his life for so long, the absence of orders given and followed. He couldn't be a grownup doing grownup things . . . running a business, hiring people . . . those were far beyond his abilities. He thought each day that someone, some official person, would notify him that he wasn't qualified.

A kitchen emerged, ovens. . . . ovens that worked! The baker stayed late, testing the ovens' moods, finding their perfect spots. In retrospect, the problems began with the sourdough starter, left on the counter overnight. Chemicals—paint fumes, glue, varnish—invaded the dough, infected the yeast. He had meant to return the starter to the cooler-closet they had built for keeping flour near the ovens and mixing area.

Calendar dates peeled away, pointing ever closer to the opening. Nightmares haunted the baker's sleep. He woke from one, coated with sweat, and lay staring at the ceiling. He had been in Allard's dream-city, had recognized details from Allard's descriptions: the bowel-shaped municipal center, the spire-topped buildings that jutted into the river.

But Allard's dream-city was always a welcoming place, mysterious and different, but not threatening (no more than any other city). The baker entered along the Riverwalk, at the base of an almond spire. Haze obscured the other side of the river, a pink and crusty haze that sent swirling fingers toward his side. Pedestrians moved along the sidewalk; none showed signs of unease. Were some of them residents and others dream visitors like the baker? Disliking the insistent haze, he followed a street away from the river.

At a corner, he stopped, reading street signs. The intersection, the cross street . . . Donovan. Farther along, he saw a painted sign hanging over a door, golden loaves. He went in and joined the line. Unfamiliar loaves shaped in seven-lobed stars were arrayed on a shelf. A large man—larger than the baker—stood behind the counter, resting his thick forearms on the glass top. He had odd, deep-set eyes and pale skin. When the baker's turn came, he pointed to a loaf with a dark crust speckled with pale yellow seeds. The large man ignored him, took the order of another. And another. The baker slammed his fist on the counter.

"You shouldn't be allowed around bread," a voice behind him said. He turned, recognizing the woman whose husband he had hit with a baguette.

"That's not true," the baker said. He knew his voice was too loud, but he couldn't change it. "I'm a baker. I am." The counterman laughed, and all the loaves turned their backs. Without the support of the loaves, he fled.

Awake, he walked into his kitchen and began mixing a dough, mixing and kneading until peace returned.

Another night, the baker returned to Loaves. The pale giant with deep-set eyes bagged a loaf for a customer; the customer left. The baker pointed to a dark oblong. It was labeled Surfeit. "What's that?" he asked.

The pale giant stared forward as if the baker wasn't there. The man's lack of response unnerved the baker.

"What grains? I'd like a loaf, please."

The giant turned his face toward the baker. "You have no right to bake bread. *You are not a baker.*" His voice boomed at the baker, pushing him through the door. He sprawled on the sidewalk. The giant stood over him, pointing a long finger down at the baker's face.

Days turned clattery, all sharp angles and jittery sounds; his sourdough starter grew sullen and bloated, as though disapproving of the surrounding activity. He fed it flour, water, and a bit of apple juice to reduce pH.

The simple day-to-day pleasure of mixing and kneading offset by the requirements of staffing. He would base his operation on Donovan's—no need to experiment with that. His first hire, Timmy, had worked at Donovan's for a year and a half, left town, came back; with no openings at Donovan's, Allard sent him to the baker. Perhaps not dependable as a long-term employee, but good to start with. And Timmy liked to make espresso drinks, something the baker had no interest in but recognized as a useful thing to offer.

Hire two: Langston, age 30, returning to town after living in the west. She had never worked in a bakery but was a friend of Rose; with such a reference, not giving her a job would have been imbecilic.

Rose came to inspect his progress. "This is going to be a great place, Ogre. I'm really happy for you."

They stood in front of the new counters. It was a Saturday, and the construction workers were off. The baker hadn't wanted to show Rose the place amidst the din of remodeling. Even more than Allard, he wanted her to approve.

"Boss says I can come work here for a few weeks, to help you open."

For a moment, the baker couldn't speak. Their generosity, so different from what he had learned in the world of football, where the weak and vulnerable were attacked and devoured. "Thank you," he finally said. "That relieves all my anxieties."

"If you say so, Ogre."

He woke with his cheek in a wet mess of dough. More dough coated his legs. He pulled off his apron and dropped it on the floor. With each step, the dough pulled the clogs from his feet. He hadn't brought a change of clothes. At the sink, he splashed his face and cleaned himself as well as he could, and left.

Distracted by the drying and congealing dough, he made a wrong turn somewhere and entered a multi-lane avenue with a wide, tree-covered esplanade. Few cars passed. Yellowy mist clung to the air and coated the streetlamps. He crossed to the esplanade. A sidewalk curved amongst the trees. Weariness tugged at him. The dough pressed into his muscles. A bench appeared from the mist, and he sat, not minding the damp. What was a little dampness on top of his doughy skin? After a time, he felt rested enough to continue. He walked up the nearest cross-street. A few blocks on, he reached a familiar corner. The next intersection brought him to 15th, four blocks from where he lived. He soon passed Allard's bakery, now closed, and entered his building.

The starter outgrew its bowl and splayed over the sides until the container became lost somewhere within the quivering mass. It gave off a sickly odor, more chemical than yeast. It bubbled, then rose in a pulsating column; thick globs flowed upward from the base, adding to its height. Behind the dough-torso, Allard stood, face split by a jagged grin. "Sometimes it all goes splat in your face," he said. "Splat in your motherfucking face!"

He laughed, roaring and cackling. The dough-torso grew a head with a wide mouth that emitted a wet echo of Allard's laughter.

The baker let himself into his bakery. Leaving the lights off, he sat facing the ovens. He dozed. Waking, a band of light from the cooler-closet splashed the floor. He got up. The door had been closed when he arrived—he would have noticed the light. The sourdough starter had expanded, pushing against the door. The baker lifted an edge of the towel that covered the bowl and deflated the contents.

"I'm going to have to throw you out," he said. He shut the door, and . . . a throbbing shook his legs—had he fallen back asleep? The starter . . . it had pushed open the door again and flowed from bowl to floor. An elastic band squeezed his ankles, a grip so tight it sucked out his breath. He dug his fingers into the starter and yanked. Pain seared his hands. He yelled and jerked them free, then kicked and stomped till the dough subsided; it cowered at the base of the counter, buzzing like a wasp's nest. He plunged his hands into cold water. Red welts appeared. The sourdough—too much acid. He dried his hands and applied burn ointment.

The phone woke him. He lay on his sofa. Sunlight rimmed the closed blinds. Rose calling, from his bakery, from inside, having used her key to enter.

"Where are you, Ogre? We're supposed to be training with Timmy and Langston."

He muttered an apology and hung up. What had she found there? He could still feel the snake-like hold of the starter. His hands were tender, but the welts had faded. At the bakery, all appeared normal. Rose said that Timmy and Langston were on their way. A mop stood propped against the counter. She saw him looking at it.

"I had to buy that at the hardware store. Dough all over the floor here." She pointed to the area in front of the cabinet door. "Rancid starter? Smelled worse than month-old cat litter."

He opened the cabinet, glad he had a companion. The starter had subsided into a reddish slurry. He dumped it in the sink. "I'll have to start over. I have some mother in my refrigerator at home. From Allard."

His home starter appeared to be fine. He took part to his bakery, used it to make a bread dough, baked it when it had risen. But when he sliced through the crisp, dark crust, an acrid wind exhaled. He gagged, then vomited onto the loaf and counter.

The next day, he stayed home. He told the builder he was sick, and convinced himself that it was a good time to avoid the bakery. The interior was nearly finished. They were starting to paint the walls (a color called semolina). Best to let the fumes dissipate before resuming any baking. He took out his starter—his home starter, not tainted by. . . . Tainted: was his bakery tainted? He refused to accept that. The routine of bread-making, scoop out starter and mix with flour, feed the remaining starter. The day passed, the loaves turned out sublime.

The starter that he had poured down the drain returned. It had grown in the pipes, grown and pushed its way out of the sink. It expanded—a dough-wall arose between him and the door. He howled, howled and ran at the dough, charged as he had once charged the opposing line. The starter swallowed him. His bakery vanished. The world vanished. Nothing existed outside this landscape of wet, stinging dough.

The baker unlocked the door and let Allard enter before him. He was surprised at his nervousness, sharing his space, his dream, with his friend and teacher. Allard didn't speak. Ignoring the front room, the displays, he walked straight to the kitchen. He opened an oven and pushed his head in; eyes closed, he rested his head on a rack as if it were a loaf.

The baker waited, nerves fraying with the escaping moments.

Allard looked in the cooler-closet, the refrigerator, he removed lids from containers and sniffed. Back at the cooler-closet, he took the metal bowl of starter and held it toward the baker.

"This isn't what I taught you." He spoke in his loudest kitchen voice, and for emphasis he dropped the bowl. It clanged against the concrete floor. He kicked it at the baker. "Garbage! Begin again. Go away. Go to my country place. Start again . . . restart your starter. . . . " He laughed, a howling cackle. "Restart your starter!" He bent over, hands on knees, cheeks red, laughing and laughing.

The baker ran from him, ran from his dream.

Blocks on, the street narrowed, became a twisting lane where buildings of brick pressed close. Upper stories overhung the wisp of sidewalk and third floors nearly met over the street. The day waned. Light faded quickly, blocked by the crouching brick. The sidewalks were pedestrian-free. There were no shops, no signs at street level to tell him what he

passed, private home or storefront. Windows were few and uninviting—
a street that shunned outsiders.

Life was unwelcome here.

The sidewalk sloped upward, a gradual rise, but with the overhanging
buildings he had no way to know where it led, what lay at the top of the
hill. Where he longed to be—with a jolt that surprised him—the Congee
House, in the Asia District. It was the other end of the city from his
bakery. And . . . how to find his way there from . . . ? The street ended
at a brick wall. To his right was an alley, really, a gap between buildings.
His shoulders were too wide. He slipped in sideways, preferring to keep
moving forward rather than return along the cheerless street that had
brought him here.

He regretted that choice immediately.

Walls pressed in on him, their touch clammy and glutinous. Daylight
fled. Hoping for at least a sliver of evening sky, he tilted his head back, but
the overhanging roofs blocked everything. He wasn't even sure whether
he was still outside. The walls . . . hard-baked dough. They squeezed him
onward. Now, the path descended, and the walls pushed him, faster—
his foot struck air. He tumbled. And was deposited on another sidewalk.
He got up and limped toward a red awning. His right hip and shoulder
throbbed. *This* sidewalk carried pedestrians; they passed around him,
giving extra space, like his former realtor. Under the awning, he stopped
and looked in a window—a bakery window! Inside, the pale giant with
deep-set eyes. The baker hesitated, but why? He had a right, the right of
a bread creator. No one could deny that, not even Allard.

"Please serve me," he said. "I'm a baker."

A voice behind the baker called out—"I would like a loaf of Surfeit."—
a voice he knew without turning to see its owner. The giant handed her
a loaf. He was as large, compared to the baker, as the baker was to Rose.
Beside this baking giant, she looked like a child. She took her loaf and
walked away.

"Rose . . . wait . . . Rose!" He turned back to the giant. "Allard said this
city is a wonderful place, but all I find here—"

"Allard . . . Allard is a baker" the giant said. "You must leave."

The giant reached toward the baker and pulled him up, over the counter. He carried the baker out a back door and slammed him into a wet and stagnant trash heap. Garbage enveloped the baker. He sank into a doughy soup. His body wanted him to kick, to struggle, to push his head up and up to where sweet air waited. What of these survival urges? They reside in our oldest genetic code, always aware, watching, an internal alarm system that resists sedation, but . . . the brain can sometimes counteract such primitive impulse. How nice to sink, explore the depths of this cesspit. And why not? The surface world had rejected him.

He hovered over a barren and blasted landscape where once a forest had thrived. Stumps like broken fingers pointed upward, condemning the world for destroying them. Nothing lived, down among the tattered forest, and no bacteria to bring life back. He lay upon a stump as large as a parking lot. Above, an orange glow marked the surface, and somewhere past it, the giant in *his* bakery. Let him keep his precious loaves.

Thoughts of loaves stirred the baker's mind, tugged at his ancient impulses. He rolled onto his belly and looked about. The muck at the base of the trunk reminded him of the mud-pies of youth . . . mud-pies or . . . mud-loaves? He wormed himself to the edge and dug fingers into the muck. Its consistency revived him. He worked the muck, mixed and kneaded, then set his dough to rise, covered by his jacket. When it had doubled, he pulled off a clump and shaped a round loaf, then a pair of oblong loaves, a ring; he experimented with forms—a loaf can be anything that will hold a shape and bake evenly. He composed a complex Snyder twist and let it rise. When he was satisfied with its contours, he lifted it, gentle touch to keep it whole. Then he leapt toward the distant orange.

He came ashore on a rocky coast. The orange light had given way to blue, as if filtered through burnt crust. The rocks jabbed his bare feet, shoes lost somewhere in the depths.

The scent of smoke tugged at his nose, drew him toward it despite pain from the million rock-teeth. The giant crouched before an oven built of piled stones and mud. Seeing the baker, he growled. The baker growled too. He lunged and slid his loaf onto the bakestone before the giant could block him. Then, hands free, he slammed both fists into the giant's face. The giant's nose crunched like hard-crust roll struck by a mallet.

Pain made the giant roar; he tried to stand, but the baker kicked him in the belly, in the ribs, and again, breaking through the brittle crust. The baker dug his hands in and pulled out gobs of undercooked dough. These he flung out into the darkening landscape. A frenzy of scavengers screeched and fought for tidbits.

With much of his interior gone, the giant collapsed. The baker stomped on the remains. Satisfied, he sat, and waited for his bread to finish baking.

THE GREEN WALL

Erickson had not been sleeping well. For ten days every September, the Italian street festival engulfed his lower-Manhattan neighborhood, block after block layered with food vendors and carnival games. Drunken tourists gathered to sing themes from gangster movies. After midnight, the noise faded, but the stench of beer, onions, and greasy sausage remained, permeating his sixth floor apartment. He would lie in bed, unable to banish images of the crowds that had flowed under his windows like herds of braying goats, and when he did sleep, the sausage invaded his dreams, leaving him with mental indigestion. But Wednesday morning, a rain forest, green and overpowering, appeared on the brick wall opposite his windows.

His apartment was a two-room tenement at Grand and Mulberry. Every morning, before going to his job at the Rezinsky Gallery on Spring Street, he would wash and dress while his coffee brewed, then fold the sleeper-sofa and sit, drinking coffee and watching the play of sunlight and shadows on the brick wall. Sometimes he would read a book or finish the previous day's newspaper. Now the wall had become a giant movie screen, displaying a shadowy jungle filled with hidden dangers and undiscovered beauty. Monkeys danced through the foliage. An end-less snake flowed down a branch. The projection had to be part of the festival, though he couldn't imagine how the jungle had any connection to the patron saint of Naples. The scene appeared so real that he cringed when the snake whipped across a branch to trap a monkey. The sound, if there was any, didn't reach him through the glass.

Forests, camping, outdoor activity, those had never interested him. City- (or at least suburban-) born, his pursuits took an inward turn, art, books, and food. Of sports, boxing drew him the most; of course, it was primarily a sport of the city, and performed indoors. But something about the canvas of green in front of him stirred unexpected desires. Its shadows beckoned like visions of past selves.

On his way down the stairs he met Mrs. Venturi, carrying up a loaf of bread. A widow somewhere in her sixties who never smiled, she lived two floors directly below his apartment. Though he had often carried her grocery bags up the stairs, he never knew what to say when they met.

"Carlo," she said as he passed her. Unable to pronounce his first name, she approximated. "It's hard, Carlo. People out there, no room."

"I know, I know." Erickson looked away from her pained expression and continued down. Even the Italians in his building hated the festival. Few Italians actually remained in the neighborhood, an aging population unable or unwilling to flee to the suburbs. Although Little Italy (now little more than a few blocks of Mulberry) always conveyed an aspect of festival, luring weekend visitors to its bland array of restaurants and souvenir shops, this ten-day period was the worst.

Erickson trudged toward the street door; he could see through the glass that the tourists had already begun their inundation.

Once outside, he squeezed around a booth selling Italian pastry and fled the neighborhood by the quickest route. By the time he reached the gallery, he had banished thoughts of the festival. He unlocked the door and walked through the ground floor exhibition space and down the stairs to the office. Each day amplified his revulsion for the job. The owner, Hannah Rezinsky, was often drunk and insulting. The chaotic way she ran the gallery, the never-ending contradictory orders, wore him down. Without the art, he could never have lasted. Eight years now. He had taken the job a month after withdrawing from his art history Ph.D. program.

Erickson turned on the computer and sat. Beside the monitor, the telephone answering machine blinked. The first message was from Rezinsky.

"Won't be in till 12:30. You finish the letter to Michelson, do the press releases for the Joss, Nevill, and Camelminder show, and pack up von Sem's. . . ."

He turned down the volume on her harsh voice. The festival had left his nerves jagged, and this grace period relieved him. Having to deal with her so early would have been too demoralizing. Once . . . but there was little point thinking about that. Here he was, and if he wanted to change his situation, move to a more congenial place—if such a place existed—he would have to work to find it. Resumé, letters, hope . . . possibly leaving the city, but he loved the city, its flux of life and clashing cultures, even loved his apartment when the festival wasn't invading the landscape.

The second message was the voice of an unknown woman. With the volume low, her words sounded like the hum of beating wings. He couldn't understand anything she said, but the tone of the voice thrilled him.

During the first two hours only one person visited the gallery. Per Rezinsky's orders, Erickson wrote the press release and designed an ad for the show. At noon, the phone rang—Rezinsky, telling him she wouldn't be in till after two. He sat at the front desk and leafed through the newspaper. An article in the science section explained the climactic changes in the last ice age. Another described a hallucinogenic orchid found recently in the rain forests of New Guinea. The author quoted a botanist, the discoverer of the orchid, who talked of vast possibilities from yet-to-be-found rain forest plants. Like Erickson's green-wall forest—what lay hidden inside its mass of vegetation?

The door opened and a woman in a green overcoat—tall with a gliding walk—led a line of five girls in similar coats. The children's ages ranged from about five to twelve, and they walked in order of height, tallest to shortest. Was the woman their mother? Guardian? He enjoyed speculating about gallery patrons. These didn't look like the usual visitors. Probably filming a television commercial outside, or shooting a fashion spread. The neighborhood around the gallery attracted fashion models, though they never came in. He often saw them in the cafés, eating their miniscule portions on oversized plates. She had that look, the high cheekbones and underfed face. The children were obviously her props. Erickson smiled a greeting at her, but she never looked his way.

Rezinsky's current show featured two artists—a painter and a sculptor. In the front half of the gallery, mounted on four-foot-high pedestals, Jacob Lerner's sculptures, curved and twisted bronze rods welded together at odd angles, like cages, or the skeletons of bizarre animals. Paintings hung in the rear of the gallery, giant abstracts made up of lines and patches of color, like a landscape viewed from an airplane.

The green woman pointed at one of the sculptures; the children grouped around her. He should ask them to sign the guest book. The green woman's name would be something musical, like Annabelle. She, along with four of the girls, moved toward the back; the smallest remained. She began climbing one of the pedestals.

"You can't climb on that," Erickson said. The girl ignored him. He got up. "Young lady," he said more loudly, "you must not climb on that."

With simian ease, the girl scrambled up the pedestal before he finished the sentence. She stood on top, squealing with pleasure. "I need to get you down from there now." When he put his hands around her waist to lift her off, she gripped one of the bronze rods and screamed.

"What are you doing to her?" the woman said from across the pedestal, startling Erickson, who hadn't seen her return to the front room. He released the girl, who hopped into the middle of the sculpture and clapped her hands. The woman moved between him and the pedestal; she was a couple of inches taller than he. Thinking she might push him, he stepped back.

"The girl can't climb up there," he said. He felt his voice fading, unable to push against the might of her authority. " . . . she . . . might get hurt."

"You shouldn't leave dangerous objects out in the open."

The woman stepped closer, and he backed toward the desk, stopping when he felt the edge against his thighs. She stopped too, a few feet away, as though waiting for him to say something. Her face showed no emotion. Her arms remained at her sides, relaxed, hands unclenched, and she spoke with the relaxed manner of an art history lecturer. He looked at her green eyes, a green so brilliant he thought their intensity had to be caused by a reflection of the light on her coat. A sudden desire to put his hands on her waist and kiss her possessed him.

"I'm sorry," he said. He looked away, afraid she would sense his thought. "But this is an art gallery. Shouldn't you tell her not to touch the art?"

The woman turned around. A clip in the shape of a monkey's head tied her hair in back.

"Come down from there Cedilla, we're leaving."

The girl jumped into the woman's arms, and the other girls followed her out.

Two hours later, Hannah Rezinsky stumbled in, smelling like a winery. Erickson was sitting at the front desk. She leaned her face too close to his. "Look at you, you don't even shave," she said, slurring the words. The press releases lay on the desk; she berated him for not mailing them. He reminded her that mailing them was impossible unless he either closed the gallery or found someone to stay there while he was gone.

But she turned away from his explanation and plodded downstairs to the office for the rest of the day. During the remaining afternoon, between brief conversations with the few people who came in, he fantasized the return of the tall woman, without the children. Alone, talking to her would be easier. He took her sudden appearance as a sign of imminent change, a promise of romance or adventure. He hadn't been involved with anyone since Kari, a former intern at the gallery; their relationship hadn't lasted beyond her departure.

After work, he planned to go straight home; then he remembered the festival. Between Rezinsky and the festival he had no peace. Likely he would snap at the first fat tourist blocking his door (visitors to the festival often sat on the steps of his building, their reluctance to give way likely caused by their belief that no one lived there, the whole area having been set up as a massive Italian-kitsch theme park for their entertainment). He turned and walked uptown, angling eastward, thinking he would stop at St. Marks Books to see if his friend Jeremy wanted to get some dinner.

Rezinsky's gallery hadn't always been such a desperate place. When he started working there, she employed a full staff: director, assistant director, receptionist, interns. At that time, the gallery included the second floor. During his interview, he had fallen so in love with the paintings on exhibit that he had thought it charming when Rezinsky, before even hiring him, sent him eight blocks away to Chinatown, to buy shrimp for a party she was giving that night. But years passed. People left. She rented the second floor to a coat distributor. Now she ran the place in her drunken, indiscriminate way, treating Erickson as hapless tool. He should quit. But where would he go—another gallery, another Rezinsky?

The man at the St. Mark's Books cash register told him that Jeremy had left early. Erickson wished that he had made plans for the evening, but the festival numbed him, kept him from thinking beyond the moment. He needed to start carrying his address book—to do something with a friend tonight would mean plowing a furrow to his building, carrying himself up to the sixth floor to call, down again through the suffocating crowd, then eventually home to the same.

He selected a book and carried it to the register. "Jeremy gives me his employee discount," Erickson said. The man nodded and rang it up.

East then, 6th Street, to one of the Indian restaurants, where he sat with beer, matar paneer, and book. At the next table a woman kept leaning across to kiss her companion. Their happy talk irritated him. He hadn't felt so alone in years. So hard to meet people in this harsh city, and without anyone else at work to help him share the daily burden of Rezinsky, he found himself speaking less and less to the friends he *did* have, not wanting to bore them with his constant, disgruntled talk.

He would have to convince Rezinsky to let him find an intern or two to help him. Six months had passed since the last one left. Rezinsky liked interns. They cost her nothing. But there had been problems—the last had complained to his dean about Rezinsky forcing him to act as a waiter at one of her parties, and it was doubtful that the school would allow anyone else to intern with her. Fortunately, there were other schools, both in the city and the outlying areas, and if nothing else about the gallery was attractive, some of her artists still meant something.

Erickson returned to his apartment and went to bed. Night sausage-dream entwined with the green wall, liana-wrapped trunks and branches shooting skyward, burning sky, but his shaky flight couldn't bring him above the treetops. Leaves slapped him. Frantic straining against their pull, against gravity, against the drowning silence of the trees, shelter and swelter, airless dank humid creatures pulled him to the forest floor. He woke shivering. On the television, sitcom reruns, then eventual return to sleep.

Morning, with the dream still fresh, the green wall saluted him. He wanted to sit and watch the forest, but he had overslept. He decided to look for books on rain forests, and an errand for Rezinsky in the afternoon gave him enough time to go to the library.

Walking home after work, he ploughed across Mulberry on Spring Street and continued to Mott, then down to Grand, a direction that gave him less exposure to the festival, which commandeered all of Mulberry from Houston down to Canal but only extended a short way into either side of Grand. And this part of Grand, with its familiar flux of Chinese, helped prepare him for the chaos surrounding his front door. He stopped to pick up dinner at Grand Sausages, a combination Chinese meat market and take-out food counter across the street from his apartment building. One of his favorites, he especially liked to give it his business while the area swarmed with festival-goers, oblivious to anything that wasn't Italian.

He crossed Grand to find his stoop possessed by a seated herd of tourists, four across, clutching bags of Italian pastry, effluence from hero sandwiches dripping down their wrists; their bulk blocked his way. And none of them moved, not when he mounted the first step, not when he said "excuse me," not when he kicked through them to his door. "People fucking live here," he said, and shut the door behind him.

Safe inside his apartment, he laid his food out on the coffee table and sat, eating and watching the wall. The pile of food comforted him. He had over-ordered, purposely, having decided that enough leftovers for another meal or two would reduce the need for carrying groceries over the throng.

The sun set, but the film played on, showing a dense jungle night. The racket from the festival distracted him, the constant thrum of talking, yelling, singing. He picked up one of the rain forest books and read about the noises of the forest, for which he would gladly trade, and watched the film as the day creatures gave way to those of the night. One book said that although rain forests cover less than six percent of the planet's total land surface, three-fourths of the world's plants and animals live in them, and over seventy percent of rain forest life is in the trees.

The next morning, Erickson woke two hours early to give himself more time to watch the wall. He went downstairs to the Italian Food Center for milk and a loaf of bread. The sausage and souvenir booths had yet to open, but festival-goers had already begun to trickle past. Deciding to see how the rain forest film looked from outside, he turned down Mulberry. The door to his building was on the opposite side from the wall of the neighboring tenement where the film appeared. An architectural oddity separated his building from its neighbor—the ground floor of the next tenement was a restaurant, and part of the restaurant extended into what must once have been an alley between the buildings, leaving a gap that began at the second floor.

He stopped in front of the gap and looked up at the wall. From that angle, all he could see was green, a flat green that gave no indication of the forest. No projection equipment, no sign of anything having to do with the jungle film.

Once again inside, ensconced in the comfort of his sofa, the forest still played. He ate bread with Piave cheese and watched the wall. Monkeys as usual, a small, camel-colored variety. Probably marmosets. He hoped that they wouldn't become a snake's breakfast. Their prehensile tails told him that the forest was in the western hemisphere. At first, he had assumed that the movie played in an endless loop, but realized instead it always showed the same place, as though someone had set up a camera and filmed continuously. Maybe not a film at all, but a live broadcast. He thought of the tall woman from the gallery—her green coat and monkey hairclip. The children were her monkeys. He pictured her below, walking along the forest floor, unafraid of lurking beasts. Green of eyes, green of coat, thick slabs of green leafy forest . . . she would be at home under the trees, attuned to the strange ways of branch, vine, and creature.

Surprisingly, Rezinsky was already at the gallery when Erickson arrived. Downstairs, he paused in the office door. Rezinsky emerged from the storage closet at the opposite end of the basement. "Where's my passport," she said, her voice an agonized squeal. She clumped toward him, one shoe dangling from her hand. Discontent oozed from her haggard cheeks. What creatures lurked behind her bloodshot brown eyes? Even at their first meeting, Erickson had sensed the cracks forming in the façade of her absolute control.

"Where's my passport, you dumb-ass?" she said, and leaned against him for support while she re-shod herself.

"If I'm a dumb-ass, how the fuck would I know where to find your passport?" He backed into the office, and she slumped against the wall, a more reliable replacement for his shoulder. She froze there, apparently unwilling to risk further movement, while he unlocked the file drawer, reached into the back, and removed her passport. He pushed it into her unresisting hands and walked up the stairs. Some minutes later, she followed him. She announced that she would be leaving for London in an hour. He would have to run the gallery alone the rest of the day and all of the following week. To keep him from protesting, she sent him out to the printer's to pick up brochures for the next show, and on his return handed him a list of duties. Then she left.

The afternoon lasted an eternity. No one came in between noon and four. Without Rezinsky there to watch him, he considered closing early and returning to his apartment to watch the forest. How would it feel to touch the tree trunks? Massive dark fertile green—so alien to this city. He had just read that rain forests provide most of the world's oxygen, with the canopy, that dense mass of leaf and branch, being the richest part, full of seething life. According to one book, there was a rain forest in Washington! Forget equatorial swelter—here was a place he might actually be able to visit. The book reprinted a creation myth that said trees gave birth to humans:

> An elder of the Makah told this story. He said it didn't come from his people, but was older, given by the ancients to all who followed.
>
> First, came the oceans and the mountains, then the trees and minor plants, then the animals of the forest. Of the trees, the conifers were the greatest, and because they were the greatest of the trees, they were the masters of all. No animal could harm them. But they grew haughty in their power and tried to shut out everything else from their realm.
>
> They covered the sky, and all plants watched by the sun were forced to retreat. The only being strong enough to stop the advancing trees was the mountain, for it was decreed that nothing could cover its head but cloud and snow.
>
> Blocked from advancing to the mountaintops, the trees

reached toward the heavens, casting their branches high. They charged tribute to all who would pass, to the sparrows and hawks and marmots and elk. Only the lowly mushroom could defy them, for it needed no sun to fuel its life.

One day, the voice of the maker echoed from the branches, foretelling the emergence of a new being, soft of skin but with the power to fell forests. If the trees did not heed this warning, and cease their arrogant behavior, they would suffer.

The trees laughed. For what soft-skinned creature could harm mighty cedar or hemlock?

Seasons passed. The trees continued as before. Then one morning, in the densest part of the forest, where lived a fir of girth so great it laughed at the wind, there came a crash and flash, and the clouds parted. Living fire struck the mighty fir's crown, splitting its center. The halves tumbled, flattening the forest for miles, from the mountain to the sea. And from the split stepped a creature, then a second, creatures no plant or animal had ever seen, creatures that walked upright. The first creature was the being we now call woman, and the second, man.

When they emerged from their birth-tree, the woman spoke the words of the maker: not until all trees who lived before the birth of woman and man are replaced by their descendants will the trees know peace. The trees will become the slaves of woman and man, will provide them with shelter, means of travel, fire to cook their food, paper to write their words. And so it has been.

Now would be the ideal time for the green-coated woman to reappear. Erickson would question her about the ways of the forest.

He looked out the window at the street. Plenty of people there, seething life like the rain forest canopy. Why didn't any of *them* come in? Despite Rezinsky's decline, Erickson still believed in her artists and their work, still felt the thrill of hanging a show or viewing a new painting, but he lacked the energy to change the atmosphere of the place. The draining menace of Rezinsky shaped his life, fetid rot of the forest floor seeping into everything.

Why did Rezinsky keep the gallery open? Few clients came in and fewer bought anything. Obviously, this place wasn't her main source of income, but it did serve to form a superficial gloss over her coarseness. She owned rental property, including the building containing the gallery and a Lower East Side tenement rumored to have been her birthplace.

No, he *could* do something. Rezinsky's mailing list was right here, on the computer, including contacts at various art history departments. He called them, telling each person or their voicemail that the gallery was seeking interns. Companionship here would help, though he would have to take care with the applicants, prepare them for Rezinsky's abuses.

At five—nearly closing time—a group of German tourists came in and stayed for half an hour asking him questions about the sculptures. Normally, he would have relished the contact, the opportunity to pros-elytize art, especially Lerner's—his dynamic forms invaded Erickson's blood like a drug—but today the wall dominated all thoughts. As soon as the tourist left, he locked the door and hurried home, alone again amongst the milling hordes. But stopped in the middle of Mulberry. He had forgotten to cross and go down a less-crowded street. Booths over-whelmed the sidewalks, giving the street over to rank upon rank of pedestrians. Sometimes, to avoid the festival-walkers, Erickson would squeeze between the rear of the booths and the buildings, but obsta-cles abounded there as well. He found himself hemmed into the crowd along the west side of the street. The mass of bodies constricted, giant boa wrapping him tight, suffocating, pressing into his flesh, his psyche. Trapped, panting, he cried, wordless bellow exploding from his constricted lungs, and with the bellow, flailing arms struck out, clearing a space into which he fell. Stillness descended, city noises silenced. Noble trunks stretched skyward, not marred by branch for many yards. Understory of smaller trees and shrubs enclosed him, pressing him to the mulchy forest floor. But soon, footfalls penetrated the silence, drawing closer, and he looked up to an advancing herd of brown, droopy-snouted creatures snuffling stamping, their stench reaching him before their hooves. They kicked and trampled, taking their usual watering path as though he didn't exist. With the jabbing pain of their hooves, the ground beneath him returned to pavement, a pavement traversed by hordes of festival-goers, who parted to allow his still-flailing arms space while he struggled to his feet, but otherwise gave him no attention whatsoever.

His body ached. Home, he opened the hot tap of his claw-foot shower-bathtub, which occupied the space in his kitchen between sink and toilet-closet. Soaking in the tub drew out his tension, soothed the bruises along his thighs and torso. For a moment, he had been there, free in the forest; he longed to return.

He reheated leftovers from yesterday's Chinese take-out, and the rest of the evening, he sat, entranced by the swaying branches and hanging vines, the birds with their colorful feathers. How did the projection achieve such depth and clarity? Tree trunks stood out in such detail it was as if he gazed at a real forest. The greenest parrot he had ever seen sat on a branch. It stretched its wings, then flew toward him.

If he could reach the wall, he would be able to touch the trees.

Not bothering to unfold the bed, he slept on the sofa cushion, and woke to another rain forest morning.

Saturdays, the gallery opened an hour and a half later, giving him more time with the wall. A light rain fell on the street, but the forest looked dry. He noticed an open space at the base of the trees. The forest's floor was even with the rooftop below him. He opened the window, took off the screen, and leaned out. A faint path led from the edge of the scene into the trees.

Of course—that was where they had set up the camera. There must be a clearing. Where did the path lead? Into the brick, into the green wall, into the next building, the next world, the next life? He pictured himself among the trees, walking with the tall woman from the gallery. She would whisper forest secrets to his starving ear.

The festival would end tomorrow.

At four o'clock Monday morning the crash of booths being ripped apart would wake him. And the green wall would be gone. He would miss the forest, miss the purpose the dark trees gave him. He couldn't allow the end to come without an attempt to get closer. Touching the wall on which the film projected would reveal the answers.

In the shower, he thought about ways to get down to the roof of the neighboring building to see the forest from its ground level. A ladder wouldn't reach. A rope maybe. But his apartment was so high—a long way to climb down a rope. One of his rain forest books described how scientists used mountaineering gear when doing canopy studies. He sat on the sofa with the phone book and a pad of paper and called a store that sold camping and climbing equipment. He told the woman at the store that he was writing an article for a journalism class. With her help, he made a list of the necessary equipment.

1. 150 feet of 11-millimeter static rope
2. climbing harness
3. 6 yards of nylon webbing
4. two prusick devices for ascending
5. a figure eight for descending
6. carabiners
7. gloves with leather palms

After work, he would go to the store to buy everything. Sunday, his day off, he would use the equipment to climb down. He sighed, not wanting to leave the wall. But he had to get to work. It was still raining outside, and the temperature had dropped. Too bad the skies had remained sunny during the bulk of the festival. A few days like this would have kept the tourists away. He hated walking to work in the rain. Forget the gallery—the damn place could stay closed today.

That would teach Rezinsky to treat him so poorly. He felt suddenly powerful.

The store that he had called was down near City Hall. If he had to go out in the rain, let it be for something *he* wanted.

Back in the apartment, Erickson spread his purchases on the floor. The pile confused him: nylon webbing (green of course, to go with the forest), rope, ascending devices (two metal gadgets with pulleys and a locking mechanism). Along with the equipment, he had bought a book that showed everything—how to make a chest harness out of webbing, how to tie all the necessary knots . . . but the task was hopeless—he would never get it all put together.

He opened the window and leaned out, trying to breathe rain forest air. His plan would work. Concentrate on the diagrams in the book until the method coalesced, became logical.

Returning to his task, he held an end of the stiff rope over the diagram, as if he could will the rope into the required shape. He formed a loop, but the result looked nothing like the book's example. He tried again and again, frustration building with each failure.

After another attempt he flung the rope away and leaned his head on the sofa's armrest.

But forced himself to resume. Once more, he fumbled with the unfamiliar materials, but eventually worked with increased assurance. Perfecting the knot took him another hour. He looked around the living room for a place to tie the rope. The book said that a rope should always have two secure anchors, but he couldn't think of anything besides the radiator. Already four o'clock. His legs stiffened from sitting on the floor. He hadn't eaten since morning. But he had to try today. The forest would soon be gone.

On to the chest harness then: create a loop with the webbing (securing the ends with something called a water knot—surely that was too soft a name for something meant to support a person's weight!), and twist the loop to form an eight . . . and and . . . what was this for? Going up? The other system was for down. Down was all that mattered. The roof below him was only one floor up from the street. He could easily get down the rest of the way and return to his apartment by the stairs.

He picked up his rappelling device, called a figure eight for its shape, and stared at the dull metal surface. It looked too small to support him. The rope went through the larger hole, then over the end that clipped to his harness. Though the woman at the store had shown him how to put on his seat harness, it took a while for Erickson to sort out the confusion of straps and buckles, slip his legs through the correct loops, and secure everything.

He pushed the rope out the window and watched its snakelike fall. *When rappelling into the unknown*, the book said, *always descend with your ascending gear ready in the event that you have to ascend unexpectedly*, but his articles of ascent remained scattered across the floor. He stepped onto a chair, then to the window sill, and ducked his head. Once standing outside on the ledge, he glanced down. The rooftop looked farther than he had thought. He was supposed to control his speed by pressing the rope between right hand and thigh. The window ledge was similar to the protruding edge of a cliff. The book said that the hardest part was getting over the edge. You had to ease yourself down until the rope rested secure. If you stepped off, you would fall a couple of feet; when the rope caught the edge you would slam into the cliff (or building, in his case).

Someone was supposed to stand at the bottom and hold the rope—belaying, as it was called. If the person coming down slipped, the belayer would stop them from plummeting by pulling the rope taut.

Erickson slid his right foot off of the window ledge and onto the wall, testing the slickness of the damp brick. He held the rope tight against his thigh, then let the rope slide a little. The slithering rope burned his hand. Gloves? On the floor, mixed in with the unused ascending gear. He squeezed, stopping his descent a few feet below his window.

His fingers soon cramped from the grip. He couldn't keep holding the rope so tight. The book had made everything seem simple. He had been a fool to try. He lowered himself to the window ledge of the floor below his and leaned against the glass. There was just enough room to stand with his feet sideways. Resting on something solid relieved him, but his hands were shaking. He tried to relax his fingers. The glass felt cold on his cheek—he wondered if anyone was inside. Blinds covered the windows. How could anyone close their blinds to the glorious sight of the green wall?

He turned his head enough to see the trees. From a branch, a monkey stared across at him. Another joined it. He waved to them with his free hand. Their grunting barks made him smile. If he went down slowly, he wouldn't need his gloves.

A fevered wind blew through the chill September air. The musky forest smells filled his lungs. He would swing through the branches with the monkeys, walk among the hoary trunks. A blue and red bird flew from a branch to alight on a nearby window ledge; it examined Erickson, first with one eye, then the other.

Determined to continue, Erickson stepped off the ledge and walked his way down the wall. The next room down belonged to Mrs. Venturi. Though he was afraid of burning his hands, he had to let out enough rope to get him to her window ledge. Slowly then, a little rope at a time, and. . . .

A shriek sounded from inside and something struck his legs. Keeping his right hand on the rope, he swung his left down to protect himself. Mrs. Venturi shouted something in Italian. He tried to move away from the window but his foot slipped, and he pendulumed back toward the glass. Mrs. Venturi leaned out her open window. She rammed an umbrella into his stomach. He screamed and let go of the rope.

Adrift, motionless, eyes filled with deafening silence. A dark glow cradled him. Warm and cold, and the rain filled his mouth. As he drank he wept. So hot near the wall, heat of the forest pushing out, pulling him in. Trees surrounded him, mute with expectation. Contours of sound seeped from the air, unexpected bursts scented with spice, with a rainbow shower of green. Dark layers of rainforest earth beneath his cheek contained universes, pyramids of light and color. The far-off walls of his building, the dangling rope, Rezinsky, all receded like an unnecessary dream.

He smiled up at the tall woman from the gallery. Around her, the air shaped itself into a violet-tinged corridor. She lifted him, holding him gently in her powerful arms. The fibers of her green coat swelled and hardened, re-aligned themselves, forming a cradle to support him. Now she returned his smile, her expression broad as the forest. The sky called. Higher she lifted him, bark and branch extending, but part of him remained below, penetrating the roof of the building, pushing downward. Finding soil, his stiffening toes dug deep.

She cast him loose, and he stood beside her, branches reaching out toward each other but never touching.

PART TWO

in the undiscovered territory

TRAVELS ALONG AN
UNFURLING CIRCULAR PATH

The man found himself at the entrance to a grotto so vast that its envelope of darkness swallowed the glow of his flashlight. His muscles ached from the long, twisting cave-crawl that led to this spot, far from sun or moon or leafy branch. Sweat soaked his shirt, and the exhaling cavern cast a chill. Veering from a pool of dark sludge, he crept forward. To his left, a shape emerged, a pillar of white rock clothed in moisture droplets that sparkled where his light struck; he stopped before it, seeing in its folds of stone a sculpture depicting unimaginable gods.

A sudden explosion of radiance blinded him.

Afraid to move, he froze beside the sculpture. Floor-wall-pit . . . swallowed whole by mountain, by solid dark. Whose voice, this cry of anguish?

His own, bouncing from the distant ceiling.

When his vision cleared, he saw three figures moving toward him, tall, far taller than he, with elongated bodies and drooping arms. Their gait was so fluid, their approach so silent, they seemed to make little progress. The figures stopped. Each pulled a mud-colored ball from a pouch at their waists, and the nearest threw its ball. With a wet-sounding crack, the ball smacked the stone floor near the man's feet and vanished, cave mud returning to what spawned it.

No longer bemused, the man turned and ran, but couldn't find the narrow crack where he had entered the grotto. Something impacted with his shoulder, then his leg. He flopped onto his stomach. Thumping feet sounded from behind. He rolled onto his back and tried to sit up, but when he did, another ball struck his chest. He cried out, an agonized wail that reverberated from the stone walls. The figures crowded over him, each holding another of the balls, but he could do nothing to stop them.

Coruscations of sunlight shook the man, pressed glowing fingers deep. Brightness suffused the air, vibrating and pulsing. The man's rapid blinking fanned the light into dancing, emerald swirls. He lay in a pile of feathery leaves beneath an orange tree. Globes of ripe fruit hung over him; others littered the ground. In the light, everything appeared hard. The branches, fruit, leaves, all glowed with such sharp focus he feared moving. Great shards of brightness snapped off and drifted in the seven directions, floating over the branches, which shimmied at their passing.

Lying on his side, the piles of leaves and grass, so close his eyelids threatened to touch, stood taller than sequoias. He stared into them, letting his gaze separate each leaf into its world of cellulose and decay. Microscopic insects traversed the veins of the leaves as though they were the highest mountains. Must and mold flooded his lungs, but he was content to lie there, entertained by the unfolding dramas. Seasons could pass, with him becoming as much a fixture as the surrounding fruit and leaves.

There was an odd sense of being newly activated, but at the same time, sun, fruit, leaves, defined a world he felt he had always inhabited. The carpet of leaves formed his cradle, the sun his tutor, and the fruit his nurse. He examined his palms, thinking that the valleys contained there might offer a story of his origin. His hands carried a heavy look, thick with callous. His clothes were clean and pressed—their creases echoed the lines of the orange tree. A shadow passed and he shuddered, but the shadow was internal. The sunlight remained crisp, a surrounding warmth and brightness both comforting and confusing.

His clothes—blue jeans and jersey—held a faint scent of detergent, as though they had been recently washed . . . and here, he experienced a perplexing sense of repetition. The branches whispered to him, humming a familiar melody.

Perhaps he was dead. Death could be this . . . awakening. But if he was, let us say, newly born or reborn, would not his palms be new as well? Smooth, rather than these pads of thickened flesh?

Now, he was restless and claustrophobic, wanted to be somewhere other than this comfortable zone under the tree—the comfort was beginning to take on the aspect of a trap—but at the same time, he hesitated to attempt departure. Maybe a compromise, perhaps a move to a sitting position, so that he might take in what he saw before him on a grander scale than that of the world inside the grasses and leaves he loved so dearly.

This change in perspective gave him confidence—the sharp-hardness of sun and leaf that had loomed so threatening now softened, presenting an invitation to explore. Life thrummed around him, crawlings and buzzings. Near his orange tree stood several others, and beyond those, tall grasses.

The tall grasses, he decided, were actually a wheat field, and beside it was a path.

Had he traveled that way? He was confident that he had been here, at this orange tree. Though looking around at the other orange trees, he thought, could he be positive that this was the same tree? Everything— the oranges, leaves, wheat—haunted him, puzzle-pieces of memory, though the pieces floated in and out of view, disparate meanings that he couldn't bring into focus. But the perfume of the fruit soothed, softened this other sense, this repetition.

He was ready to stand.

A shadow cast by one of the orange tree's branches pointed toward the entrance of the path. Trusting the tree's guidance, he decided to follow the path. To one side of the path was wheat, but the other side was a choking of grasses, low shrubs, blooming wildflowers of yellow, red, and blue. Their scent, honey-like, floated on the wind. He stepped onto the path, which was packed down by myriad animal tracks. Bending closer, he noted deer, raccoon, and wolf, but no trace of human. A pile of pungent droppings, probably deer, marked the entrance.

The walking invigorated him—sun warming his head, leg movements enhancing his circulation. His feet were shod with leather boots that rose a few inches above the ankle. They were quite comfortable for foot travel. Their treads gripped the grass and dirt, but he tried not to let his heavy feet disturb the tracks. Sounds followed him, hidden animals swishing and rustling amongst the wheat. He stopped and parted the stalk wall, but beyond was only another row. When he continued along the path, the tops of the wheat whispered to him, a faint sound resembling an unfolding bedsheet.

Ahead, he glimpsed a thatched roof, a cottage, a place with a familiar feel, though not the warmth of home, something else.

A friend's?

His approach was from the back, or side perhaps—the cottage was square, with small square windows. On one side was a woodpile and a kitchen garden where flowering squash vines stretched out in neat rows. The path wound around to another side, perhaps the front. Yes, it was the front, and someone, a boy, sat on the stump of what once must have been an impressive tree. The boy, maybe eight or nine years old, played with two carved wooden eagles. He flew them, holding each by the legs and swooping them through the air.

Seeing the eagles made the man smile. He believed they represented some aspect of his past. Another puzzle piece.

A branch snapped under his approaching feet, and the boy jumped. The man stopped.

"I'm lost," he said to the boy. "May I rest here for a while?"

"I can feed you," the boy said. "Mother always says to help travelers. These are my eagles."

The boy extended both hands. The eagles were impressive, the curve of their beaks, glaring eyes. Individual feathers were etched in astonishing detail. The boy led him through a door that hung on rawhide hinges.

"We have bread and turnips. You can have bread and turnips. I eat bread and turnips myself, all the time. I don't like wine. My father makes it. You can have some."

They entered a kitchen, with a pine table, four chairs, fireplace, washstand, and cupboards. The room smelled of sage and coriander, with briny undertones. Turnips hung in a basket under the window. A curtain divided this room from the back.

"You can sit at the table," the boy said. "I'll get you something to eat."

Splinters from the crude chair bit the man's thighs, and he squirmed to find a comfortable spot. The chair had not been shaped by the same person who crafted the eagles.

The boy brought him food: half a loaf of dark bread, a turnip, and an earthenware jug. Part of the turnip's stalk remained, and dirt clung to its roots. The boy handed him a small knife, which the man used to trim the turnip and cut it into wedges. He pulled the bread apart with his hands and drank the tart wine. He hadn't thought he was hungry, but with the simple food before him, he immersed himself in eating.

Some time later, he pushed aside the remaining bread and asked the boy how far it was to the nearest town.

"Did you enjoy the food? My mother says always make sure a guest is comfortable."

The man assured the boy that he was quite satisfied, and again asked for directions.

Taking up his birds, the boy flew them around the cottage, voicing shrill screeches as they swooped and dipped; he speared the stub of bread with one of the bird's claws and flew the birds into the room behind the curtain.

The man lowered his face to the table. The rough pine massaged his cheek. Its knots formed a map he couldn't decipher. When he closed his eyes, he saw deep into the wood fibers, where colors burst, many shades of red, a tinted shower scattering across the landscape, pursued by shadows. But these shadows had teeth, millions of razored spears, splayed at wild angles, curved and barbed and dripping. The shadows erupted in metallic waves, rushing toward him, penetrating. With a jerk he pulled back from the table, and the chair in which he sat fell backward, tumbling him onto the floor.

He pushed himself to his feet. The boy must still be in the back room, though the man couldn't hear him. Guided by a puzzling familiarity with the shack, he opened a cabinet to reveal another loaf of bread, and on the shelf below, several burlap sacks. Near the door, a few feet of thin rope hung on a peg. The man took the rope and one of the burlap sacks. The boy still hadn't emerged from the back. Calling out a quick thank you, the man left.

Outside, he sat on the stump, where he cut and tied the rope, making straps he could use to carry the sack over his shoulder, and into it he put the jug of wine. Feeling some guilt at taking a portion of the cottage dwellers' limited possessions, he went to the woodpile and picked up the ax. The exertion filled him with energy, the suppleness of his swing and the solid chunking of the ax into the wood. He chopped enough firewood for several days' use, then resumed his journey. Having left the wheat field, the path now meandered through a sunflower forest. He walked and walked, not liking the crackly feel of the surrounding stalks or the still air. Over his head, the heavy blossoms swayed, but on the path the air was stagnant and humid, with a mustiness that made him cough. Though the plants blocked the sun, the heat was intense. Sweat slicked his arms and forehead.

Crows called from somewhere to his right, then from behind. He tensed—a wail of crows from right, rear, then left forebodes doom.

The wine bottle bounced against his hip, and he stopped often to adjust the length of the carry-rope. Farther along, the path declined and widened, until finally the flowers receded, and he came to a creek. At his intrusion, a deer drinking on the opposite bank looked up and bolted.

Though still sunny, it was cooler by the stream, a relief after the closeness of the sunflowers. He knelt at the water's edge and tickled the surface. Several perch that were pecking at the body of a drowning insect flipped away, disturbed by the movement of his fingers. The man stripped off his clothes and slipped into the water; submerging, he shook his hair out in the current, surfaced, and floated on his back, watching the drifting cloud-shapes flitter across the blue. He stayed immersed long enough to feel the cold encroaching, such a counterpoint to the heat of the trail. Then, naked, he lay with his head on a rock to nap. With his eyes closed, his view changed. Perhaps he no longer lived, perhaps his real body sprawled cold somewhere while his mind, his unconscious consciousness, wandered nonexistent in his patchwork memory-land. There was once a man named Whitcomb, seller of spores, or onion skin, who came to the restaurant. They argued, over buttons, or furtwanglers, or some other comestible. Perhaps he had struck Whitcomb with a blanching iron, crushing the base of his skull. Though how did that explain his own death? Events must have unfurled in a different manner. That bastard Furtwangler—he had likely avenged Whitcomb's death.

The prickly feet of ants traversing his body awakened him. He sprang up and brushed them off. His clothes lay out of the ants' path, but he gave his pants a vigorous shake before dressing. He unstopped the wine bottle and dumped the contents onto the ant hill, then refilled the bottle from the creek.

A branch lay on the bank near him, driftwood really, sun-bleached, bark shed long ago. The shape was familiar: thick on one end, tapering to a shaft around which he could wrap his fingers. Grasping the narrow part, he held the branch with his right hand on top, left below, the thick part raised high, keeping his right elbow up and his left close to his body. He swung the branch out with a level motion, as though trying to connect with an approaching object. The shape and feel of the branch pleased him, stirring more echoes. It would make a useful tool for trekking off into the wild.

He swung the club-branch again, liking the weight of it.

Using the creek as his guide, he set off upstream, the club-branch resting on a shoulder. The music of the flowing water whisked along beside him, a soft song of comfort. Above, far above, a hawk flew. He

sang, softly, "Feather of a hawk/my love I give to you. . . . " There were
few clouds, and the sun was behind him, casting a band of shadow over
the opposite hills. The contrast of sunlight and shadow pleased him.

Needing to relieve himself, he left the trail, not wanting to be so close
to the creek that their streams would mingle. He pushed through the
low-growing evergreens and into a bowl-shaped depression. Not until
he had unbuttoned his fly and all was ready did he recognize the plants
lining the depression as poison ivy—its trios of leaves stood as a silent
threat, but his unexposed skin was safe from them. He would have to
be careful of his boots though. If any of the poison clung, touching them
could spread it to his hands.

Back at the trail, he rubbed his boots in the dirt to cleanse them.

Farther on, the banks rose, and the path grew steeper. Willow trees
leaned out over the water, and from their tops came bird songs, a sort
of "see-see-see" sound. He passed through a mat of wild thyme, and its
perfume stayed with him. The creek ran faster here; its music altered
as the flow accelerated. He reached a place where the water, with a
crashing of spray against the rocks, surged from a cleft in a wall of white
limestone too steep to climb. Perhaps traveling downstream would have
been a better choice, would have carried him to habitations, but he preferred sources to endings.

A mass of colder air pushed at him, a dramatic change in temperature,
as if he had stepped into an invisible glacier. A path veered from the
creekside, and he followed it to an opening in the rock, out of which
came the flowing air, a current cool and powerful. The cave drew him,
promising comfort, but a gate set in the rock blocked the entrance—hor-
izontal metal rods spaced about eight inches apart. He tapped one of the
rods, which emitted a hollow sound. Seeing no way to enter, he turned,
but stumbled in the uneven ground near the entrance, and fell onto his
stomach. From his position on the ground he could see dig-marks below
the bottom rod, where an animal, perhaps, had scrabbled at the dirt to
force its way inside. Still on his stomach, the man eased his head and
shoulders beneath the rod.

Leaving the club-branch resting on the lowest bar so he would be able to pull it in after him if his entrance was successful, he extended his right arm and kept his left close to his side, which narrowed his shoulders enough to fit.

He pushed himself into the cleft.

Something caught on the bar, stopping him.

He had forgotten about the burlap sack at his waist. The carry-rope rested on his right shoulder. His left arm was still at his side, his right stretched out. Cramped by the contour of the floor, he couldn't bring his right arm down or slide the left up. He attempted to push himself backwards, out of the hole, but had inadequate leverage. His breath came in bursts, ragged and painful. He pulled and pulled, trying to force the bottle through, but there was no room, not with his body there. The only way to free himself would be to raise his left arm. He ground it against the side of the depression. The dirt there was hard, packed, with little give. Using his legs, he pushed his body to the right, allowing his left arm more space for maneuvering, and somehow, with a painful wrench, he freed his arm. Then he was able to reach the carry-rope and slide it over his head. He slithered the rest of the way into the cave and sat up, gasping, spitting dirt that had piled onto his face when he freed his arm. His left arm throbbed and his elbow hurt to bend. He retrieved the sack and gulped water, which turned the grit around his mouth to mud; wiping his face with a sleeve made it worse, because the sleeve was covered with dirt too. He poured water over his face, letting it dribble down his chin.

Relieved to have his mouth free of dirt, he glanced about the cave. Chisel marks scarred the walls around the steel door frame, showing that the entrance had been modified to fit the bars, but the rest of the space appeared natural. Outcroppings of stone showed through the dirt floor. The bones of a small animal were scattered on one of the rocks. A few feet from the entrance was a plastic box with a symbol about the size of both his hands, two perpendicular, bisecting red dashes in a white circle. He went to the box and opened it, finding a packet of bandages, batteries sealed in an air-tight bag, and three helmets with lights attached.

A passage extended inward, and from it a scent washed over him, an underground smell unlike any other—the earth's blood.

He stood for a moment, eyes closed, inhaling, slow deep breaths, then slipped one of the helmets onto his head and tightened the strap. The passage stretched before him, straight, wide, and high enough for him to walk upright. Its sides curved like the interior of a pipe, bulging at about hip level. He started walking, leaving the helmet lantern switched off until out of daylight's range. The passage curved to his right and continued. Though its height remained fairly constant, the hip-level bulge varied, sometimes narrowing to a point where he had to lift himself and crab-walk in the upper section, though there was also room below to crawl, if he chose to do so.

His passage split into three. The right branch went more steeply up, the left downward, and the middle, straight.

Taking the left path, which emitted a dank odor, he descended through a series of crawlways and shallow pits. Crawling with the club-branch in his hand was difficult, and his left elbow was still sore, but the activity helped relieve the tightness. On reaching the edge of a muddy pool, he stopped. A foot or so of space remained between the surface of the pool and a maze of stalactites. He stared at the water, on the surface of which floated bits of desiccated grasses, leaves, and clumps of something dark and soggy. A foul smell pushed at him and, declining to challenge the rank water, he returned the way he came.

Back at the trifurcation, he attempted the middle. A faintness of incense emanated from the room, sandalwood, or perhaps sage, and a repulsive, heavier smell. The entryway was low; he bent at the knees and shuffled under a rough, overhanging stone for several feet until the ceiling rose. His light caught something on the far wall, and he drew closer, discovering a monstrous bull's face carved out of the rock, with the horns of a real bull, each about the length of the man's arm, set into the stone. The bull's red-painted eyes were level with his own.

With so many myths that describe bulls, he had no way of determining which this might represent. In the baptism in bull's blood, the devotee of Attis descends into a pit, which is then covered with a wooden grate.

A bull is driven onto the grating. Its throat is cut with the sacred dagger. The steaming blood pours out to drench the devotee. But here there was no pit.

Below the bull-face, something protruded from the wall at waist level—a stone shaft, a foot or so long, not quite as thick as his wrist, with a flaring, rounded tip. The shaft extended from the wall at an angle. He leaned over to examine it more closely. The tip was splotched with something dark, as was the shaft and floor around the base.

Panic welled upward, thick onslaughts fraught with pain and the memory of pain, worse, the anticipation of pain-to-come. Breathless, unable to stop the shaking quaking. Surrounded by merciless stone. He scurried from the bull room and tried to return the way he had come, but around the next bend, a stone curtain blocked him, standing between him and the exit, between the outside sun and air and this inner desolation. He slid to a sitting position and held his face in his hands.

Caves don't block themselves. He must have turned a different way, but there *was* no other way. Dry sobs shook him, but he would not allow himself to give in to despair. After a time, he forced himself to stand. With no apparent choice, having tried left, middle, and the way he had entered, he continued into the right branch.

The passage sloped upward and remained a fairly uniform size. Its walls were smooth, but the ceiling was honeycombed by constant seepage. This cave had obviously formed from flowing rather than dripping water, a stream that forced its way through the rock from some higher point. The water, having backed up in the downward section, then flowed outward till it passed into open air. Some other shift could have occurred, deeper, which resulted in the creek's current exit point.

On one side, creamy white formations parted to shape an alcove, and in the alcove: a snub-nosed figurine with an elaborate headdress. Given its muddy color and rough shape, the man could easily believe that the figurine had coalesced from the surrounding clay.

Past the formations, the ceiling dropped, forcing him to crawl on hands and knees, then onto his stomach. The burlap sack scraped the ceiling and he had to push the club-branch along the floor. After a few

more feet, he stopped and slid the sack off, then crawled onward with
its cord wrapped around the thinner end of the club-branch, pushing
both before him.

He was glad for his helmet, which kept his head from bashing against
the ceiling.

His muscles burned from the effort of crawling, but he didn't want
to stop, not until he was free of this mountain pressing on him. The
cave filled with silent fireflies, so bright he could see them with his eyes
closed. He turned off his light, and the sudden darkness startled him.
Not fireflies after all, his tired brain creating illusions to let him know
he was over-taxing himself. He tried to laugh, but in the close passage it
sounded pained.

Despite his desire to carry himself away from this intestinal passage,
he knew he must rest, the which he did, laying his head on his arms and
closing his eyes. *This isn't bad, here in the low passage*, he thought. Though
some would find such a space claustrophobic, the closeness of the walls
comforted him. The womb had been similar. He slept, dreaming of
the sound of a closing door, of trees, cascades of images. If they could
lose their muteness, these oaks and maples could show him many
things . . . he dreamed on, under the mountain's weight.

When he awakened, the last thing he remembered of his dream was
crawling through four-leaf-clover while sheep grazed.

Rested, he continued, and countless body lengths farther, the tunnel
widened until he could stand, and he realized that he had entered a vast
cavern. He glanced in all directions, a hard stare, as though his eyes could
force the light to penetrate farther. All was quiet save for the dripping
from the damp walls and the echo of his steps. Then a burst of light shattered the darkness, blinding him.

He stood, off-balance from his blindness, using the club-branch as a
crutch. Without vision, he concentrated on sound. Ahead of him, something breathed. By fixating on the breath, he determined its location
relative to his, and separated the *über* breath into three sets of lungs.
He tensed his legs, lifted the club-branch, and hurled it at the nearest
breather. He heard the branch collide with something fleshy and,

simultaneous with that sound, came another from the same location, a drawn-out wail of pain.

Meanwhile, his vision had begun to clear. He discerned three figures, about twenty feet away. The middle one—not the closest, as he had thought—was prone, motionless. The figures appeared to dwarf him, but that wasn't true—it was their bodies, narrow, oddly elongated, and the placement of the light behind them, which gave them an illusion of height. They were actually somewhat shorter than he. Their narrow bodies were augmented by fur vests, which made them look massive, but their waists looked narrow enough that he could encircle them with his hands.

Upturned noses reminded him of the earthen figure in the alcove. Did they live here, subterranean home deep under the pressing mountain? Without sun, rain, snow . . . and while observing these beings, whose appearance was both startling and expected, he had an odd thought that everything he had encountered—path, boy, oranges, these beings—existed only for him, unfurling as he drew near, dissipating on his departure.

His attack, his accurate hurling of the club-branch, appeared to have surprised them, though their hairless, triangular faces showed no expression.

He rushed them, howling so loud the force of it tore his throat.

Pulling the paring knife from his pocket as he ran, he was ready when he reached the first one, and slashed downward at its face. The knife skidded across his foe's jaw and imbedded in its neck. Up close, the limestone-pale skin under the vest appeared luminescent.

The bloodied knife jerked from his hand as the figure fell. While reaching for the handle, he checked on the position of the last figure and stopped, distracted by the breasts showing from behind that one's vest. Though the figure's appearance—narrow body, snub nose, and metal hat—matched that of the others, those breasts could not be mistaken for a male's.

She pulled something from a pouch that hung at her waist, a ball of some sort, dark like the mud of the cave.

She hurled it toward him, and he ducked.

The mud-ball thing struck nearby. She charged him, pulling another mud-ball from her pouch. His club-branch was within reach; he groped for it, lifting it in time to deflect her thrust.

Stepping back, she raised her arm to throw the thing, and the movement of her right arm pulled back the vest on one side, showing roundness of breast and nipple.

The man, though he held the club-branch ready, couldn't bring himself to hurl it. But when she threw the mud-thing, he reacted, swinging the club-branch out, connecting with the mud-thing and sending it back at her. Impact snapped his club-branch and his still-sore left arm went numb. A foot or so of handle remained in his hand; the rest skittered into a pool of sludge. The female dodged the mud-thing, but in doing so she toppled. He lunged at her, swinging his hand with what was left of the club-branch down to bash her head, but she was too strong. She grabbed his wrists and forced him up. He dug his knees into her stomach, but it was like pushing the cave wall. She rolled him over, pinned him with his arms on the cave floor.

The sack was now beneath his hip, and pain jabbed him where the water bottle dug in, but despite the pain, seeing those unlikely breasts brushing his chest, feeling their weight, aroused him. Her scent, thick, like the first, wet smell of the cave, filled his nose. He laughed, hysteric now, crazy . . . he was going to be killed . . . and this . . . this lust was all he could manage? But she felt his erection and stopped fighting, instead pulled at his pants buttons and bared his crotch.

Screaming, he kicked her away from him. She flopped onto the cave floor with a look of surprise, but before she could react he jumped up and pushed her into the pool of sludge. Her body made a sharp sucking sound as she broke the surface, then sank. Clouds swirled, and the cries of birds sprinkled the air. From far off emerged the sweetest memory, abstractions of ploughed land and warm breezes. Mountains rose to starry nights, and from their tops came gauzy beings redolent of cinnamon and air. But the images deserted him . . . left arm throbbed . . . stomach rumbled hunger . . . back bruised by water bottle pain.

He reached into the sack. The water bottle was unbroken despite his having landed on it. He drank, wishing he had saved the wine. His heartbeat slowed. Eventually, he pulled himself to his feet and buttoned his pants.

Doubting that he could return the way he had come, he searched the perimeter for another outlet. On his third circuit, he spotted a ledge about ten feet above the floor. The rock provided ample juttings and indentations to support feet and hands; he wedged his boot into a crack and pushed upward. Once on the ledge, he needed to rest again before crawling onward.

Though the opening was only high enough for him to squeeze through on his stomach, the section widened after a few feet. He crawled on his belly, then hands and knees, up to a crouching walk, and finally, upright again. This new passage was formed from a type of porous rock, with many fissures and outcroppings. He moved with care, afraid of a twisted ankle, or worse. The walls and floor gradually became smoother, and he hurried over the even surface, eager to reach the outside, but the corridor turned into a cul-de-sac, ending at a double-door made from dull metal. Light emanated from fixtures set in the ceiling.

The doors had no handles. To the right, about four feet up from the floor, two round buttons protruded from a metal plate set in the wall, one button a few inches above the other. The buttons were made of green plastic with black arrows in the center of each. The arrow on the top button pointed up, the other down.

He pressed the top button, which caused it to glow, and waited.

With a pneumatic hiss, the doors popped open to reveal an eight-foot-square room occupied by two people: a gray-haired woman with a road map of wrinkles around her eyes and a young woman wearing a pink dress. The gray-haired woman held two packages. The younger woman smiled; her teeth were straight, though small. His reflection, from a mirror covering the rear wall, confronted him. His light was still on and his hard-hat was caked with mud from the cave, which also smudged his face and clothing. There were other, darker smudges. Blood, most likely, though not his.

To the left of the doors was a panel of buttons similar to those outside except with numbers on their surface. He pushed the highest number, 126, and peered at the wall above the doors, where there were three rows of numbers. Numeral six was glowing. Of the buttons by the door, 36, 54, and now, 126, also glowed.

The doors closed and the room lurched, then crept upward. Its ascent was smooth, though numerous rattles and screeches sounded from some-where outside the walls. As the room rose, the lighted numbers above the doors flickered. The room stopped at 18, and a young woman holding a baby entered. She was about the same age as the pink-dressed woman. Upon seeing the baby, the pink-dressed woman smiled and moved closer to the mother. The mother pressed number 63, and the doors whispered shut.

"Oh he's so cute," the pink-dressed woman said. Her voice was high and child-like. The gray-haired woman, whose lined face seemed locked in an eternal frown, muttered something and moved into a corner.

"He's a darling," said the mother. "Never a problem, so easy going. I wish they could all be that way."

The pink-dressed woman nodded. "My nieces—one's like yours, such an angel, but the other, oh my word, you just can't please her." The baby extended a hand to the pink-dressed woman, and the mother held him out for the pink-dressed woman to take. The pink-dressed woman brought the child close, making nonsensical noises into his face.

From the rear of the ascending room, the man watched. His lips rose and fell as he fought to maintain his detachment. The gray-haired woman's lips formed themselves into a smile, stiff, unaccustomed to the position. The man experienced an urge to say something, to coo at the infant, to say how much the child reminded him of pictures of himself at that age.

"My grandson . . . my grandson," the gray-haired woman said. "Before my daughter moved so far away, before that bastard her husband took her from me, the times we had, just me and the little guy." Tears formed at the edges of her eyes and started their way down her cheeks. She reached to touch the baby's head, brushed her fingers through his sparse hair.

When the room stopped at number 36, neither the gray-haired woman nor the pink-dressed woman left or acknowledged the opening of the doors. The man's assumption had been that the illuminated buttons meant someone was planning to disembark at the indicated floor, but perhaps the button had been pressed by mistake.

The gray-haired woman dropped her packages and the pink-dressed woman handed her the baby. "You *are* like my little darling grandson," the gray-haired woman said.

The doors opened at 54, and the gray-haired woman, her face momentarily returning to its former glum expression, glanced up at the number and took a wavering step to the door.

The baby made a happy gurgling sound, and the gray-haired woman's smile returned.

She stopped.

The doors closed.

The man sensed the danger, and readied himself. When the ascending room arrived at 63 and the door slid open, the mother retrieved the child from the gray-haired woman and exited. The pink-dressed woman and the gray-haired woman followed her.

And why not? The young mother would take them all to her quiet apartment, serve them tea while the child napped. And the stories they would tell of their travels. The man felt tears forming. For so long he had yearned for these promised comforts. He stepped after them, moved a foot over the threshold, but no—he *won't* be made to follow. He slapped the wall and backed away from the exit, to the rear of the room. The doors closed. The gray-haired woman's packages remained on the floor, discarded. A trace of the mother's floral perfume lingered.

When the room reached 126, and the doors wheezed open for the final time, the man exited, finding himself near the top of a mountain. The ascending room had stopped in a vertical rock face, with a slender ledge in front of the doors and a path leading down. Below, lay a valley between the mountain on which he stood and another range that rose opposite. The air up here, after so long in the cave, invigorated him. It carried the scent of friendship and ginger.

He stepped onto the path. The sun was setting, and he had to take care of his footing in the reduced light. Its batteries drained, his headlamp was too faint now to help. Some ways down, he met a man herding goats and offered to help the goatherd drive the animals home in return for a place to sleep. The goatherd's house was near the base of the mountain.

Knowing the path well, the goatherd stepped as nimbly as his animals. The man followed, watching where the goatherd placed his feet.

Once they had secured the animals in their pen, the goatherd gestured to a structure of shiny metal. The rear of the structure sat on two dark, circular objects. A pile of stones propped the front. Three steps rose to a door, and inside was a narrow, carpeted room with a cot and shelves filled with jars of green beans, tomatoes, and corn. Dust ruffled the tops of the jars, and an odor of mold clung to everything, but the man was too exhausted to care. He flopped onto the sheets and closed his eyes.

In the morning, the man woke confused about where he was. He eased in and out of dreams; in one, he strolled along a familiar sidewalk, with cars on one side and a park on the other. Though the terrain was level, walking, for some reason, was difficult, and he found himself scrabbling with his hands at the tufty grass to propel himself forward. He reached a street with stores, a café, and a vegetarian restaurant, and movement became easier, but the light faded into a myopic dimness, and shapes of people and buildings passed in and out of focus.

Fully awake, he sat up and watched dust particles floating in the light that sliced through the grime-streaked windows. His back was stiff from yesterday's exertions, but not too painful. A morning this fine defied the aches of mortality. He reached his arms out over his head, then brought them down to his side, stretching and loosening the muscles. In doing so, he bumped the muddy helmet with his left hand. He shuddered, looking at it, thinking back to the cave and his battle there with the elongated beings. He hadn't had a chance to react. Now he found himself afraid to depart this warm bed, fearful of what dangers he might encounter on the path today.

But the scent of frying meat reached out to him, and he left the boxy room.

The goatherd's dwelling was nearby, a structure built from concrete and scraps of metal. Its walls were uneven, bulging here, concave there. The front door was set in a turret-shaped protuberance embedded with smooth rocks that formed the silhouette of a long-necked creature, a cross between rabbit and giraffe. Half a dozen steps led to a porch where the goatherd's bony wife laid out a place for him. She served him fried strips of meat, goat perhaps, with dried apple and an oval of flatbread dusted with nutmeg and pepper. This food, after yesterday's ordeal, tasted better than anything he had ever eaten. The new day bloomed sunny and clear, and all these things, the food, the weather, he took as signs of good fortune.

The goatherd returned carrying a bucket of milk, which he left in the shade of the overhanging eave. A breeze blew cool. The climate here was different than the land of orange trees and sunflower path. The evidence—high hills, decreased temperatures—pointed to his being a great distance from that sun-filled starting point.

They chatted, he, the goatherd, and the goatherd's wife.

"Once, my people came from across the sea," the goatherd said. "More of us then, in my grandfather's grandfather's days. None left now but we two."

The man considered this statement and the sounds of the words. Though the words appeared to originate in a language not his own, he had no problem understanding.

"River cuts through, southwest. No road this side. Cross, other side, follow to the city by the sea," the wife said.

The goatherd stared off at a distant ridge. "Goats are cynical creatures," he said.

The man thanked the goatherd and his wife, then set off down the valley. However, before he had traveled more than an hour, he clutched his stomach. Spasms flooded his body. He collapsed onto the path, moaning, and retched violently, spewing the remains of his breakfast. Footsteps approached. The goatherd and his wife stood near, watching him, their faces calm, unfeeling. The man motioned to them, his fingers outstretched, pleading, until he no longer had the strength to keep his arms raised, but they made no move to help. He writhed on the ground, attacked first by fever, then chills, in ever increasing waves of pain until fetid darkness overcame him.

Sunlight surprised the man, warm and succulent, filled with unspecified promises and the lure of danger. Each day the sun rises and begins a journey from which none can dissuade it. Glowing fingers beckoned, stirring the man from his bed. He lay half-buried in damp leaves. Above him extended the branches of an orange tree. Sunlight tickled him, particles flowing unhindered between the branches, forcing their way through the filtering leaves. The trunk was near, stolid and as firm in its desire to stay as the sun was in its need to travel.

The man reached for a fruit hanging low above him, removed the spongy outer layer, and ate, a segment at a time. He peeled and ate another. Then he stood and moved to his left, where he saw a path of reddish dirt.

SIDEWALK FACTORY: A MUNICIPAL ROMANCE

*Lord Mayor's Proclamation and Municipal
Dispatch #21025: The Sidewalk Factory*

The new sidewalks of our city are to be molded from discarded felt hats. This revolutionary new formula will provide a surface congenial to all forms of footwear and walking styles. The new material's pliable resilience is stronger than concrete and more comfortable than a grassy meadow. The factory for manufacturing the sidewalks was built on two square blocks of newly leveled and disinfected slum housing. Though the method was developed in one of our coastal towns, the regents of that town insisted that the factory be located in the city, affirming their patriotic duty of bringing new jobs to our island.

In an elaborate ceremony at the opening of the plant, the Lord Mayor took off her hat and waved it to the gathered multitudes. With a cry of "prosperity to all!" she tossed it toward the intake chute. Next, the city council members and our most prominent business leaders removed their hats and dropped them into the chute.

"This is the modern age and we welcome it happily," the Lord Mayor said, and everyone cheered. She proclaimed a new era of economic growth for our great and wonderful city.

It was early February, and the Lord Mayor's breath misted as she spoke. An aide placed a new hat on her head to block the chill east wind. The dignitaries soon retired to a cozy reception at the Lord Mayor's palace.

May the Lord Mayor Grant Order and Prosperity to All!

Exclamations for the city's glorious future filled the next week's newspapers. Omitted from the reports was how I had to clean up the mess in the intake chute. The system hadn't been activated, so all the hats did was jumble around at the bottom. The way it works is, the hats go down the chute to a vat of chemicals that soften them and puff out the fibers. Then the hats are pushed through a micro-shredder. The shredding process turns the hat pieces into puffy little spirals, which move along a conveyor belt to six-foot by two-foot by sixteenth-inch compacting receptacles.

I had gone to the colony town where the process originated to assess their production methods. While there, I had a brief affair with a shipping clerk named Myra. I only mention this because it's not the sort of thing I normally do, but I was lonely, and she had that kind of dark spirit I find intriguing. I met her when arranging for several crates of samples to be shipped to my office at the Ministry of Technology. My last night, we had dinner at a nearby restaurant.

"Ours is a crossroads cuisine," Myra said. "Influenced by years of control by others, and of course our own fascination with halibut. I spent a summer working on one of our halibut farms."

"Indeed," I said, expecting her to go on.

Our fish arrived, raw slices of halibut the thickness of notebook paper, laid over a mound of barley hash. Myra picked up a small ceramic pitcher decorated with purple lilac blossoms. "Pour this over the fish," she said, and I did. The fragrance of cloves, butter, and lemon arose from my plate.

"Now let it sit for a minute. Between the barley hash and the hot butter and lemon, the fish will cook as much as it needs."

I thanked her for introducing me to her native town's specialties, though I doubted that the dish had truly originated here, for everyone knows that my city is father and mother to a vast range of cuisine, and that prospective chefs from all of the colonies venture there to learn the trade.

"I wasn't always a shipping clerk," Myra said. "It's a job that affords me freedom and anonymity, and gives me access to the intricacies of all the various shipping services."

"I see."

"Being invisible has its benefits. As long as I do what's needed, no one notices me, leaving me free to conduct my true work."

"Halibut farming?" I asked, hoping to steer her back to that topic.

Dinner over, we took a streetcar to the Ink-Maker's Quarter, where she had a two-room flat on the third-floor. Upstairs, the scent of brewing ink floated under the eaves, a promise of books, memos, proclamations. I sat on her sofa, and she poured me a cordial of a locally made liquor flavored with henna and marjoram. Its strength surprised me.

After handing me the glass she paced the room; I tried to judge her mood but could only assume that she was debating whether to take me into her bed. She stopped in front of me.

"You know we were independent once, with a history older and more grand than your city's."

Her words surprised me too.

"First, we were forced to do business with your city. Then, our ruling body was replaced. Now our people lack basic freedoms, and your government—"

"The city is prosperous," I said. "And free. The Lord Mayor provides—"

"The Lord Mayor," she said, much louder than before. "Your Lord Mayor controls what the *people* provide."

"There are elements that need to be controlled," I said. "Elements that would upset the stability of the city. It was different once, but the world was different. Enemies were scattered. The Lord Mayor only takes control of what is needed to keep us safe. And that other thing you said . . . that isn't true. The city is the most ancient in the world. None others preceded it."

She walked to the window and looked out. I could see past her, to the apartment across the alley, where a family sat down to dinner, a young couple with three small children. Myra waved to them, then lowered the blinds, leaving a gap for the ink-scented air. Turning from the window, she said: "I know it's harder to recognize something when you're in the middle of it. From here, it's obvious how circumstances have been manipulated to magnify threats and justify your Lord Mayor's actions. There were those here who wished to follow her example, but they've been ridiculed and ignored. At least we still have the freedom to do that."

She approached the sofa and lowered herself to my lap. "But that's enough talk for now."

I woke in the morning on a rocking, wooden floor. Dryness had invaded my mouth; I sat up, and the floor twirled, emitting a rainbow that shot skyward, flared out, and dissipated. From this position I could identify my surroundings: not a floor—a deck. The deck of a ship, far from shore, though I had planned to take an overland route back to the city, save for the usual ferry ride across the river. My cheeks were scored and prickled with splinters; I could only surmise that I had been dragged along the deck.

Cries of "take in sail!" punctured my stupor, and I managed to raise myself to my knees and peer out at the wide expanse of living water. But that motion only served to make me notice my seasickness. I vomited over the side, and as the contents of my stomach (last night's dinner with Myra?) flowed outward, the noxious bits transformed to swans, miniature swans, which flapped horizonward, leaving me with a vague sense of having forgotten some task that had previously required my attention.

There was a door on one end of the ship (I'm not sure what it's called, though I do know that everything on a ship has some term or other assigned to it). Feeling better after getting rid of all those birds, I decided to investigate. What I found was a lecture hall of perhaps 200 seats, only a third occupied. A blue and gold banner hung across the back of the stage. It said: PROFESSOR FENSTER MODERN MASTER.

The World of Professor Fenster

"Language over meaning," said Professor Fenster. "I care not what you say but how you say it."

I took notes. I copied each word with reverence. Professor Fenster was a Fellow of the Academy. The tuft of white hair on the top of his head bounced as he spoke. He smiled a smile that included everyone in the lecture hall.

Professor Fenster talked of eggplant. The color of its skin, he said, personifies beauty. "Eggplant's strength and wisdom are legendary, yet its flesh is the most sensitive of lungs."

I laughed. A man on the row ahead of me turned and frowned. I didn't care. I think Professor Fenster was happy to hear someone laugh.

"Laughter is dust settling on a window," he said.

I felt as though he spoke to me alone. I stopped taking notes, allowing his words to massage my brain. The man who had frowned at me was sleeping. Professor Fenster banged a wooden spoon against a cast-iron skillet; the sleeping man grunted and looked around.

"Noises are beauty," Professor Fenster said. "I have recorded a combination of found sounds. Streetcar klaxons blaring, my ex-wife yelling at me from the second-floor window, rain falling through pecan trees, prostitutes laughing, the sound a male fox makes after sex with its mate. Each is recorded separately and combined to form the voice of the planet."

Professor Fenster played the recording. Mesmerized, I found myself holding my breath. When it ended, half an hour later, applause and excited conversations darted through the hall. (I wondered if he was recording . . .)

He held up a hand and all talking ceased. "The world speaks in complex symbols of which only a few are apparent." He placed a hat on his head, a felt hat with a brim the size of the lecture hall. Its shadow covered the room. Shielded in darkness, he left the podium.

The audience applauded, cheered, stomped, but the professor did not reappear.

I left with everyone else, down the gangplank to the dock and out along sidewalks flashing neon butterflies.

The Temple

Walking inland down the avenue that begins at the Lord Mayor's Community Waterfront Recreation Park (where all citizens are welcome), I passed the ruins of a temple that had been preserved as an icon of the city's origins. Superimposed on this relic was a flickering image of its former self, giving me glimpses at its history (a vision no doubt emanating from the effects of Professor Fenster's talk).

In a grove of date palms that stood before the portico, several women picked fruit for the priests. The newly quarried limestone walls glistened. This was opening day and everybody was nervous. The Lord Mayor would be making an appearance and perhaps commit an act of violence that would give the peasants something to talk about during the long summer. Once (so it was said), a bee stung her on the cheek. Enraged, the Lord Mayor hacked out several holes in the chest of the most convenient priest. The blood fed the orange trees which fed the bees which had stung the Lord Mayor.

I watched a date-picker place a fruit in her mouth. The supervisor saw and struck her with the Rod of Obedience.

"These dates are sacred," the priest said. "None may eat but those blessed."

"Blessed, what is blessed," the woman said. "If I eat blessed fruit then I too am blessed. Why would I care to be blessed? I don't even like the way the word sounds. It's the noise a sheep makes." She spat the pit onto the hard (but blessed) ground.

Lord Mayor's Proclamation and Municipal
Dispatch #21058: Wrist Measurement

All citizens of this city, aged eighteen and older, are to have their wrists measured by a new process! This new process and the results thereof will replace all old processes and results. According to Barnard Smith, the Lord Mayor's Director of the Ministry of Communications: "Statistically speaking, a trend chart of our citizen's wrist diameter is a far more useful tool for urban planning than anything but the most exhaustive comparative study of rainfall and its relationship to body-mass density." He assures that all measurements will be recorded and catalogued anonymously and will not be used as a means of determining viability for service in the city's Diplomatic Defense Corps.

There is no reason for anyone to think that the wrist measurement plan has or will have a military application.

The new measurement process is accomplished by means of two devices hereafter called "wrist scanners." Wrist scanners are attached to steel rods and can be adjusted to fit each citizen's height. The citizen is to stand with elbows resting on a padded cradle, wrists extending into the scanner's measuring field.

Citizens unable to stand will be accommodated.

The wrist scanner is a technological marvel. It projects across a gap three separate beams of light that are set sixty degrees apart from each other. On the opposite side of the gap, sensors record the beams; when a wrist is placed in the gap, it blocks the light, and the sensors record the absence of light. This absence of light is then translated into a measurement for a citizen's wrist.

Advances such as these have propelled our great city to prominence!

Though some may ask: Do the poor care about the data compiled from measurement of their wrists? We, as their stewards, must set the tone. The poor may only see what's on the plate in front of them, but we must think of the next plate, and the next after that, and on, infinite plates for infinite generations, all of whom fall under the care of our illustrious Lord Mayor.

As a show of solidarity, municipal employees are to be the first-measured.

Desmond Spangler, our Lord Mayor's Minister of Technology, released a statement vowing that the light emitted by the device is in no way harmful to the skin or internal organs of those whose wrists are placed within its measurement field.

The wrist-scanning device was developed by one of our own citizens, who, aided by a Lord Mayor's small business grant, formed a company five years ago with the aim of developing products that would innovate the way measurement is done. That is, in fact, the company's motto: *Innovating the way people do measurement and the way they do life.*

May the Lord Mayor Grant Order and Prosperity to All!

Walking home from my wrist measurement session, I admired the blooming redbuds that dotted the sidewalks of my neighborhood. Spring!

How can one be truly depressed when blossoms lighten the air? If only I had a lover or a family with whom I could share the season . . . but I spend my days either in the dank and crowded municipal concourse, or visiting factories in the city or colony towns—it would not have been appropriate for me, an honored inspector, to have a sexual relationship with even the lowliest receptionist at a place under my jurisdiction. Which is why my defiance of protocol with Myra was so unexpected yet welcome.

Perhaps I will marry on retirement, if I still have the energy. My municipal pension would likely be more attractive than my eventually graying, sagging body.

But is that fair?

Even a loyal, diligent municipal worker like myself deserves the attentions of another. My career, previously with the Ministry of Library Resources and now eight years as an inspector of manufacturing facilities for the Ministry of Technology, has put me into contact with the broadest swath of our citizens, but none who could someday become my mate. Perhaps if I still worked at the library. . . . In that long-ago period I spent my time around books, around the readers of books. Then came the Lord Mayor's decree that technology would raise our city from decadence and torpor; I was transferred from the library, books being deemed of lesser value.

But Spring drives away all such melancholy!

Around the corner from my flat, two buildings border a gap, a missing tooth in the line of brick structures. This is the site where Burnside Turner, our city's foremost warrior-artist, was born and lived the first decade of his life, before he entered the Academy. The building was disassembled and relocated on the grounds of the Lord Mayor's palace, and here, a park now fills the gap, at the center of which stands Burnside's statue, showing him in his usual artist's garb, sword, woolen trousers, and vest.

I often stop to sit by the fountain in the evenings and watch fireflies emerge.

Today, my usual seat was occupied by a red-haired woman who

appeared to be of an age near my own. I hesitated, but the lady smiled at my approach.

"My name is Penelope," she said. "I've only just moved in upstairs from here."

"How fortunate to live beside such a landmark," I said.

"It was my mother's apartment. Her funeral was yesterday. And now, here I am." She bowed her head, and I remained silent. "I'm sorry," she said, raising her gaze to meet mine. Her eyes were the green of the daffodil shoots that lined the beds around the fountain. "I hadn't seen my mother for many years, having been away, captain of a small trading vessel. But I've grown tired of the sea; this will be my refuge for a time."

"I was at sea recently," I said. "But my recollections of it are fragmentary. I don't think the experience agreed with me." I paused, considering her green eyes and the sturdy wrists that poked out from the sleeves of her tunic. "Would you allow me to be your guide to our city? I'm sure much has changed in your absence. My own family once lived near here also, but my parents have long since passed, and I have no close relatives."

I sat beside her and we talked more, of Spring and sunshine. I learned why she had despaired of her waterborne life, a story too long and sad to relate here. Evening approached, as it always does. Her hands were strong and coarse from years of work at sea, but guided by a gentle nature.

A Day in the Ministry of Technology. . . .

This morning, I submitted a report evaluating a new development in the fabrication of cardboard flaking. Sadly, I can think of no useful purpose for the material that is produced other than, perhaps, dollhouse construction, but such toys have fallen out of favor with the current generation of children, obsessed as they are with towerblocks and blow-worms. Then, back to work on the technical manual for the sidewalk factory. The manufacturing process is simple, but it requires a set of procedures enacted in a specific order. I like to include explanations and drawings for each step, so that the operators will gain more of an understanding for the entire concept, even if all they really require to complete their task is a list of what to do and when to do it. My supervisor has been critical of my methods, but has yet to contradict them.

Although I have three times requested permission to visit the factory and sketch the equipment so that I can diagram the steps, I have received no answer, which I find odd but doubt that it is due to anything beyond normal bureaucratic sluggishness.

At lunchtime, I walked down to the port to have a bowl of clam soup with Penelope. Refreshed by her months ashore, she has been refitting her ship and is planning to leave soon for a short voyage. Despite my previous experiences (or whatever they were) at sea, I would like to accompany her someday. To do so would require a variety of travel permits, or a reclassification of her captain's charter to include either: transport of municipal workers on municipal business (if my business were to coincide with hers), or: transport of passengers, a license that is difficult to acquire.

Despite having known each other a short time, we have become quite close. Yesterday, out of curiosity, I made an appointment with someone at the Ministry of Municipal Employee Requirements to find out how I could change my status to cohabitator (should we decide to proceed in that direction), and I discovered that a clause buried deep in my contract forbids cohabitation between captains of trading vessels and employees in the Ministry of Technology. Had I still been based at the library, there would have been no restriction.

"You can, of course, request a transfer," the man said. "But then the whole reason for your transfer *away* from the library was due to municipal needs, and those needs haven't changed. At best, if a transfer were granted, you would face a steep reduction in salary and benefits as a penalty."

Penelope laughs at such rule-following, but I find I cannot easily stray from responses learned over a lifetime in the city; she would be less cavalier had she not spent so much time in command of her own ship. The rules of the sea, I am told, often supersede those of the land.

Lord Mayor's Proclamation and
Municipal Dispatch #23011: Defense

The Lord Mayor announced today that only one out of every eight men and one out of every twelve women between the ages of seventeen and twenty-five will be chosen to serve in our city's Diplomatic Defense Corps. This is a dramatic reduction from the previous plan, which would have been announced yesterday. In that plan, one in five men and one in nine women ages seventeen to twenty-six would have been chosen.

"The one way we can placate our enemies is a firm commitment to military preparedness," said defense ministry spokesperson Creighton Packard. "Though not as large a commitment as we had hoped for, this induction will still enable a broad range of our youth to serve their city."

The Ministry of Defense is issuing flyers with a list of benefits that will be available to those inducted (after completion of service) or to the families of inductees who are unable to survive their term. Inductees will be distributed among the seven branches of the military and, as usual, those who enlist, rather than wait for their induction notice, will be given first choice for the elite units.

Reports of deterioration of our current, all-volunteer Diplomatic Defense Corps are false.

But a larger Diplomatic Defense Corps will provide the Lord Mayor with the much-needed flexibility to perform her civic duties. One of the chief benefits of service will be choice of housing in, or farmland outside of, provincial towns, should it become necessary for the current residents of those places to flee during the process of redeploying our Diplomatic Defense Corps to secure (or expand) our borders. Once those towns have been cleansed of possible radicals, residents are free to return, but their houses may no longer be available to them.

"We're not saying that there *are* dangerous radicals in any of the nearby towns," says Creighton Packard. "But all possibilities must be investigated to ensure the freedom of our citizens. Enemies abound."

There will be a formal ceremony honoring the first inductees. Each will receive the Lord Mayor's blessing.

The Lord Mayor wishes to remind all citizens that, while our city has remained untouched by hostile forces, a volatile world always carries the threat of attack, and therefore, stabilizing as broad an area as possible is of utmost importance. "Our wealth and freedom are always targets," she said. "And although our technology has made it possible to keep our borders secure with a smaller Diplomatic Defense Corps, there comes a time when its flexibility quotient degrades."

She also informs us that although there have been no more overt attacks on our frontier outposts, a group that had recently infiltrated our city has been apprehended. More are likely on the way! These radicals must be stopped, and anyone who harbors such groups will have an eye removed and will then be relocated to a provincial factory to labor until their demise.

May the Lord Mayor Grant Order and Prosperity to All!

A young man from my department, a junior technology-processing assistant named Blevins, was one of the first designated for enlistment in the Diplomatic Defense Corps. I had assumed that municipal workers, especially those in technology, would be exempt. Apparently, he did too. His eyes, his expression . . . the range of emotions that the human face and eyes project is impossible to describe, but in his twitches and dilations I saw dread and despair. I saw no hope, no joy, no quest for glory.

And I am glad to be beyond draft age.

Some complimented his good fortune, some assured him that his expertise would exempt him from combat and that he would likely be given an important position in a Diplomatic Defense Corps' technology unit. After all, there were sufficient laborers and, of course, the unemployed, to fill front-line quotas.

I wasn't sure what to think. Since my encounter with Myra, I have begun to doubt our leaders. The questions she posed to me, her statements about the city's history, its control of our lives . . . though rejected at the time, they have since stirred my brain. Perhaps it's true that women are more perceptive, for it was Myra, and now Penelope, who have helped my understanding grow. Having been away for so long and seen distant lands, Penelope has brought a new perspective on life in our city.

Of course, the Lord Mayor is a woman too, but no one said that she isn't perceptive, or that woman aren't ambitious.

This current military action . . . continuous threat from unseen enemies . . . should the need arise, Penelope's ship could take me from the city, to a new life for us elsewhere.

I was called into the offices of Desmond Spangler, our Lord Mayor's Minister of Technology. My departmental chief (a man the rest of us call "Mr. Nearly There") escorted me. I had never been to Spangler's office or even known its location. Besides Spangler, three others waited for us: a man who began asking me questions as soon as I entered, a woman who took notes of the proceedings, and another man who was not identified and who said nothing, but stared at me the entire time, as if penetrating my skull to assess my honesty. I was forced to stand throughout the interview.

I learned two things: the factory that was reputed to be manufacturing sidewalks from hat fibers is in reality using the material as lightweight, protective clothing for members of our Diplomatic Defense Corps (which explained my difficulty gaining entry to document the machinery), and that Myra, whom I had met at the manufacturer's home office, was one of those arrested recently for "conspiring to commit harm to our city and/ or its people."

"Did Myra try to recruit me for her plots?"

"We had a sexual affair," I said, knowing that although our government officials publicly decry lewdness and sex, in private they are very much in its favor. "It occurred the last night of my factory inspection. We talked only of food, then other activities eliminated speech."

The staring man whispered to my interrogator, and I was directed to return to my department.

Though the interrogators seemed satisfied with my answers, I fear that my ordeal is only beginning. What had happened, after Myra? The ship, Professor Fenster, the temple—were these true events, not dreams, not random wanderings through the interior of my brain? Likely they were a form of communication from Myra, disguised as dream to protect me from interrogation. Did I reveal anything during my interview? The staring man—his part bothered me the most.

As time passed, the dream faded, but details emerged, details indicating a web of intrigue that threatened to engulf me, and I rode along, casting aside thoughts of my comfortable life and future municipal pension.

Lord Mayor's Proclamation and Municipal
Dispatch #25006: Geography

As everyone knows, our city occupies an island where the mouth of a river gives way to a vast, sheltered bay; this location formed the means of our ascendancy. The bay and the river give the city's merchants access to trade in all regions, and what few conflicts arise are quickly settled by our city's Diplomatic Defense Corps, whose advanced weaponry is held in awe by our neighbors.

Though only two and a half miles at its widest point and thirteen miles long, the island provides ample room for our citizens. Were it not for the want of farmland, we might never need venture to the mainland. It is in our agricultural communities where we are most vulnerable. During the first decade of the Lord Mayor's reign, steps were taken to secure our agricultural colonies, and these lands continue to provide abundant foodstuffs to the greater metropolis. And in fact, settlements on the mainland have grown, and serve as distribution centers, taking goods from the city and bringing in the wares of the country.

The Lord Mayor's Director of the Ministry of Distribution governs these settlements with fairness and generosity. While it is true that residents of these settlements exhibit a more lawless nature than their brethren in the city, they are accorded the same rights and freedoms as those on the island. But the island is, and will always be, the center of the world. The Lord Mayor has in fact never left our shores!

And why should she?

Up and down the coast and in the hinterlands, there are other cities, cities with unusual customs and indecipherable languages, cities dominated by repressive religious doctrines, even cities with some semblance of our system. But none of these cities is as great as ours!

The Lord Mayor often entertains delegations from these cities. All are welcome here. Let them come, let them see the wonders we hold. We have no reason to hide behind our vast walls of stone that none have ever breached.

Our international district abuts the central port, and it provides color and entertainment for our citizens. Though many of these foreigners' customs are questionable, and some are indeed banned, there is no reason why the curious shouldn't be allowed to investigate. Research has shown that it is healthy to give people an outlet for their frustrations or inhibitions. Hence, the occasional brawls and other activities in these port-side taverns are not punished as thoroughly as those few altercations within the city proper. After all, where is the harm if a few foreigners are injured?

News reports of a squabble involving our Lord Mayor's grandnephew, Sir Lucius, are true, though they overstate the damage caused. Off-duty from his post as liaison to the Ministry of Internal Communications Defense, he chanced to overhear a conversation relating to a group of our citizens inquiring about sea-passage to another city. While not specifically a crime, such passage is regulated, and when Sir Lucius asked those involved to explain the nature of their journey (in order that he might determine whether it fell within the bounds of the five approved criteria), one of those persons attempted to flee the tavern, thereby proving the guilt of the entire party. Sir Lucius was merely exercising his right, and the right of all true citizens, to defend our city's interests and reputation.

The Lord Mayor's Council is debating a moratorium on all trade and travel by citizens away from the safety of our island. Let others bring their goods to us! True citizens have no reason to leave our shores!

May the Lord Mayor Grant Order and Prosperity to All!

These proposed travel restrictions have both strengthened my desire to leave and increased my anxiety at attempting to do so. Because of the interrogation, Penelope and I thought that waiting would be prudent. I went about my municipal duties, was even sent to one of our settlements across the bay, to a factory where lumber was milled to make handles for agricultural tools but would now be converted to the construction of clamp bushings and other implements for our growing military.

It is possible that sending me there was a test, to see with whom I interacted. I had one odd encounter with a seller of whalebone, who tried to interest me in an investment scheme involving tubular asphalt. I informed him that, as a municipal employee, such would be inappropriate.

A similar visit has been added to my calendar for next month, a facilities inspection in the same colony town where I had met Myra.

Penelope and I decided that this would be the time to act.

Penelope has journeyed widely, even beyond the bay, beyond our colony towns to other cities, even some cities where ours is but a vague rumor. It is one of these distant towns that we plan to visit, perhaps settle in. The extent of her travels surprised me, for I had thought such ranging was forbidden.

"There's official policy, and there's what the Lord Mayor needs for the city to maintain its power. Someone has to follow world events. And seek new markets and resources."

She had accepted a commission for a trading venture, carrying a cargo from the city to an agricultural village. From there she would sail to the town where we would meet. Over a period of weeks, she had taken bits of my things to her ship, but I would have to abandon most of my possessions. She sailed two days before me.

On my departure day, I boarded the official Lord Mayor's packet that carries mail and Lord Mayor's Directives to the colonies. I had packed as I normally would for a brief commercial visit. I would be spending one night on the ship, which made stops at other towns along the way. The day was the sparkling kind, diamond-waves and cloudless sky. I stood on deck, joined by Hoban, an engineer newly attached to our Ministry; Hoban was a thick-necked man who had shown off his strength his first day in the office, carrying unassisted several filing cabinets, in turn, from the records office to his own. Hoban's specialty was glass extrusion, and together we were to evaluate a new technology for pliable glass.

Years ago, I had noticed that most innovation originated elsewhere and was then appropriated by the Lord Mayor. The city creates nothing—instead, it brings in what others produce and converts it to money, to commerce. And from commerce all life flows. This concept formed the basis of my upbringing. In my youth, I had never questioned its principles, but over time I have begun to see the city as a parasite. It is true that a form of art flourishes here, and music and literature. But the art has become nothing but a paean to itself, devoid of imagination, praised by self-satisfied functionaries from the Ministry of Artistic Endeavors and their ilk.

Penelope and I went to a play . . . but I would rather not think back to that evening.

On the deck of a ship, even if it wasn't Penelope's, on a fine day . . . the bleakness that had grasped and circled me now receded. I turned to my companion. "Let us go down and claim our breakfast," I said.

After a meal of eggs and flatbread, he asked me some troubling questions.

Did I ever feel constrained in the city, did I ever feel an urge toward a more simple life in one of the colony towns?

Such questions and impulses are not specifically banned, but if someone were to express them publicly it would generate the assumption that they were unsatisfied with their position in the city, and dissatisfaction—that *is* a crime. But the city, wise and just, would grant the dissatisfied their wish. They *would* be allowed to leave, but their destination would be forced-labor at a farm or factory. Only after survival of their term would they be allowed to settle in the colony of their choice.

"No," I said. "I love the city; I can't imagine a better place."

What else could I say? Though emboldened by my imminent departure with Penelope, I was not yet on board her ship, and many obstacles could still arise.

"I agree with you of course," Hoban said. "But in my field, I can't help noticing that inventions originate elsewhere, and *that* observation leads to certain logical questions and extrapolations." He gazed out at the bay. In our present position we were equidistant from the mainland and our island home. "Out there,"—he pointed in the direction we were sailing—"The people are technically citizens the same as we are, but the colonies are allowed a certain laxity. It's our walls. They protect us, but they also stifle. If I had an idea for something, say a new way to process metalized concrete, and wanted to work on it, I would first have to apply for permission to take the time from my assigned duties, and then, if permission were granted, I would have to re-apply monthly, giving evidence of my progress. Intolerable!"

Turning away, he stared back along our wake, where seabirds darted, fighting for the remains of our breakfast; I had the impression that he was now uncomfortable with having expressed his opinion. And who could blame him? Many citizens would have turned in a relative for similar statements (often profiting by inheritance of said relative's house and possessions).

"I will keep your statements in confidence," I said. "After all, we are at the moment closer to the colonies than we are to the city. But if you were to speak of this while in ministry offices, I would have no choice."

A thunderstorm attacked the next morning, sending both myself and Hoban to our cabins, and all day the rain and winds persisted, as if adhered to our masts. Meanwhile, the ship continued on its business, docking as planned at several coastal settlements, which provided us a chance to emerge on deck for a time. I suppose I needed to accustom myself to such weather—once Penelope and I left the relative shelter of the bay for the open ocean, a storm such as this would seem minor. Although, I am happy to say, the conditions bothered me less than they did Hoban.

Open ocean! The very words hold magic. I know that other lands, other nations, present their own difficulties, but with Penelope's ship (providing I can adjust to life aboard), we will have a nation of our own.

At one of our stops, we took on another passenger, a slim, well-dressed man named Fowler, who claimed to be an inspector for the Ministry of Agricultural Purity.

On reaching our destination that evening, Hoban and I moved into a hotel in the business district, the same hotel where I had stayed my previous visit. As usual, we had to leave our citizenship and travel papers with the local office of the Ministry of Travel Control. I hoped to be able to retrieve them before departing—the thought of being without something that had always been mine by right of birth sent quivers through my stomach.

The plan—its totality—had begun to seep into my being.

There would be no return to the city of my birth, except, perhaps, disguised as a trader from another land, which would leave me quarantined in the merchant's quarter, with no access to the rest of the city. Even if I did recover my citizenship papers, they would show my departure date, and such a span of time away would attract unwanted interest. Though it was likely that somewhere, should I desire it, I could find a forger . . . my brain was obviously over-working itself. I needed to have my dinner, rest, and prepare.

The storm had washed through this town also, scattering a wake of leaf and branch along the avenues and bringing a temporary crispness to the air that had been steady in its march toward the fullness of summer. I took a long walk to enjoy the weather, passing the docks to observe that Penelope's ship had indeed arrived, and then to the restaurant where I had dined with Myra. Having returned to the scene of what I consider to be a pivotal moment in my life, I had an urge to re-create a portion of the experience, though I was unable to remember how to get to Myra's neighborhood. And what of Myra? Had she truly been arrested by city authorities, or had telling me that been part of some ridiculous loyalty test?

On the way back to the hotel from dinner, I spotted Hoban and Fowler walking ahead of me. They were too far off for me to reach them easily, and in any case I preferred solitude.

Despite my anxieties, I was able to descend into sleep without difficulty, thanks in part to the cool evening air caressing me through the open windows.

Lord Mayor's Proclamation and Municipal
Dispatch #26333: On the Subjects of Travel and Labor

To all Colonies and Provinces . . .

The Lord Mayor hereby states that travel to the city is now under control of the Investigative Board of the Ministry of Naturalized Citizens. New forms and procedures will be made available. Certain classes will be forbidden access—details will be made available. Certain age groups will be forbidden access—details will be made available.

Production needs dictate that a greater number of unskilled and semi-skilled laborers will soon be relocating to facilities in the city—details will be made available. Those chosen will not be permitted to bring families, as there is limited housing in the city and costs are high. Rent will be removed from paychecks as needed.

Please be assured that the Lord Mayor loves and cares for her provincial citizens, and their welfare is of utmost importance. All other provincial life will continue in the normal manner. As usual, anyone chosen to relocate has the option of enlistment in the Diplomatic Defense Corps with all its inherent benefits.

May the Lord Mayor Grant Order and Prosperity to All!

At breakfast, I asked Hoban if he had enjoyed his freedom after being confined on board ship; he replied that he had felt ill and had not left the hotel. Surprised by his lie, I chose not to reveal that I had seen him out with Fowler. I should have taken more care, but I was preoccupied by the realization: tonight, I will be aboard-ship with Penelope! And so, overwhelmed with anticipation for later . . . I couldn't keep my mood hidden. Hoban remarked on my demeanor.

"My paramour is here," I said, and instantly regretted having revealed such a privacy, private even if we hadn't been planning what might be referred to as an unauthorized excursion. But having done so, I had no choice but to go on. "She is a ship's captain. We had hoped our schedules would coincide. She had a trading venture down the coast and stopped here to visit me before returning to the city." Hoban could make of that what he might—he had certainly revealed more to me than I to him.

"I see," he said. "So she didn't have authorized business here?" He paused, as if waiting for my reply, but I gave none.

"From what I understand, the proclamation received here this morning specifically bans such activities. I'm afraid she is in serious violation."

"She's been at sea—how can she be in violation of something that didn't exist when she departed the city?"

He shook his head and rose from the table. "I'm afraid ignorance is not an excuse. She may face a grim reception on her return."

I followed him to the glass facility.

We began our tour in a room far enough from the production floor to allow us to hear each other. The process engineer gave us a demonstration of some of the extruded glass products. The engineer brought out a coil of glass as fine and supple as hair and set it in a sample-bowl. He put on a pair of protective gloves. For an example of the glass-coil's strength, he tied an end to the drawer of a filing cabinet and then, from across the room, pulled the drawer out with a yank. Then he looped the strand around a thick candle and pulled both ends; it cut through the candle and the separate ends fell to the floor.

A thicker strand could hold great weights without cracking. I tested a sample, snapping it out as if using a whip; the end gouged a furrow in the plaster wall, a few feet from where Hoban stood. He had been facing the other direction and, startled by the impact, he jumped forward, then turned to give me what I took to be a baleful glare. After his earlier comments, I have to say I took some satisfaction at his discomfort.

"Please be careful," the engineer said. "Some of these samples can be dangerous if mishandled." He motioned for us to join him in another part of the room. "Here, as you can see, sheets of it are possible. Supple and nearly impervious."

Despite being at the end of my life as a municipal worker, I found myself drawn to the explanations and demonstrations, and jotted down many details on my ministerial notepad. At some point, I realized that, along with my notepad, I still held the glass whip-coil. I slipped it into a pocket.

The engineer handed us burn-retardant cloaks and elbow-length gloves, and we made our way down an increasingly warm corridor to the factory floor, where cauldrons of glass bubbled, and heated gravity-bell pumps sent molten rivers to the extruders.

We moved on to the laboratory, where they explained how the temperature of the cauldrons (500-rate higher than for normal glass-work) combined with a chemical compound to activate molecules that, once set in motion, maintained that state in perpetuity unless subjected to extreme heat or cold (with high temperatures the molecules moved too fast, and the material stretched; with too much cold, the molecules became dormant and the material crumbled). The controlled motion of the molecules is what gives the glass its flexibility.

Other demonstrations followed. When the day ended, Hoban told me he wished to explore the town and would meet me later at the hotel so we could discuss what we had seen and make our decision about bringing the process back to the city.

"And I assume you wish to see your paramour before she sails," he said.

Though his words were delivered in a tone of collegiality, after his statement from this morning I didn't trust him. I was of course pleased that he wouldn't be accompanying me back to the hotel, because I had planned to linger only long enough to pack. The which I did, transferring my belongings from the trunk that had accompanied me there to a duffel that I could sling over my shoulder.

Professor Fenster Rides the Streetcar

It should have been a simple matter to take the stairs down from my third-floor room, leave the hotel, and walk to the docks, but when I reached the second floor landing, I found that I had somehow entered a narrow corridor with rows of four seats separated by an aisle.

The building lurched!

Hugging a metal pole for support, I glanced around. The room was in motion, was in fact a streetcar, one of the many that traversed this town. I had apparently entered through the rear door. Shaken, I lowered my duffel into the nearest empty seat and sat beside it. The other occupants seemed unperturbed. I caught fragments of conversations of a genial tone; nothing to indicate surprise at their situation.

A milky gray coated the windows, giving the world the look of an unfinished painting, a cityscape of shadow and outline. Block followed upon block, far more streets than I had thought existed in this town. As we went along, the buildings—what I could see of them—became more scattered, eventually giving way to a terrain of cactus and scrubby trees, instead of the expected wooded hills and farms that lay inland from the harbor-town. The monotony of the landscape invaded my brain, and I longed for Penelope's ship. I stared through the glass, trying to determine whether we were nearing the docks, but the windows were even less penetrable than before.

Then we stopped, and the front doors creaked open. Several people boarded. One of them was Myra. She took a seat beside another passenger.

The streetcar resumed its course. I got up to walk toward Myra. A man on the front row stood and faced the other riders. I recognized him . . . my fellow ship's passenger—Fowler—from the Ministry of Agricultural Purity.

"Please be seated," Fowler said, looking directly at me. "And now, back from his tour of the wide reaches of forever, Professor Fenster."

The other passengers applauded, and I had no choice but to return to my seat.

Fowler lifted his arms to the audience as though conducting the applause. Professor Fenster rose, and shook hands with him; Fowler sat.

"Welcome to my rolling lecture series," the professor said. "And please, no applause. Applause is a rock dragging a body down into the ocean, down and down to where the ancient realms lie dormant, waiting for their time to rise again and complete the cycle. And yes, I have walked their streets." He paused and raised his hands to embrace all of us, his audience, his acolytes. The audience nodded, a few called out phrases like "oh-yeah" and "tell it brother."

Impatient, desiring only to join Penelope, I took no notes.

"Words emerge, they emerge fully formed on the lips of children. I have compiled them into lists, each list a layer of meaning that will shape the foundation stones of future cities. Imagine!"

Professor Fenster's words floated out among us, rose petals silhouetted against the stars. I tried to watch Myra, but her seatback and the other passengers obscured her.

"Imagine the heights that the new city will attain with such a foundation!"

And outside the milky glass, a city arose from the desert, vermilion spires, golden towers bathed in sunlight.

Professor Fenster talked of building techniques, materials . . . carbon fiber coiled around wooden poles and then dipped in foaming lye to give them unimagined strength, the strength to push towers into the clouds and beyond. Despite my restlessness, I couldn't keep from being drawn into his vision. Professor Fenster, Fellow of the Academy, traveler to hidden realms, shared his secrets with all who were willing to listen.

The streetcar stopped.

Professor Fenster again raised his arms to his audience. "Thank you, and good night," he said, and walked out into the desert. The streetcar resumed its journey. Through the windows, the professor's shape dwindled and faded.

I got up and walked to the front, but the woman I had thought was Myra carried a different face, flat and tired and old.

"Hoban has been looking for you," Fowler said. "He wants to talk about the glass."

"I'm through with that life," I said.

Fowler took a pouch from an inner pocket of his jacket and held it out for me. "Unwrap it," he said.

Sharp, slithering animals paraded through my skull. I groaned and opened my eyes to the glisten of carbide light. From beyond the glare, a voice spoke. "Oh, there you are."

The light extinguished, then another arose, more ambient, less painful. The animals in my head rested. I was sitting in a chair, slumped against a table. Straightening my body, I tried to look at what lay around me, but mist obscured the details. For a moment, I thought I was still on the streetcar, gazing out the clouded windows, but a heavy rocking from beneath made me think of the sea. My right arm lay at an awkward angle; when I tried to move it, pain shot up from my hand.

"I wouldn't move that one," the voice said, and with those words came familiarity. "This stuff cuts like a rime scalpel."

My eyes began to focus, first on my right hand—a strand of clear material, as fine as a hair, attached my pinky finger to a table leg. Wooden pegs connected the table to the floor, the floor was the deck of Penelope's cabin, and the voice that spoke belonged to my traveling companion, Hoban, who occupied a chair a few feet away.

Hoban pointed toward the wall nearest him. "It seems your paramour has agreed to transport us back to the city."

On board ship, Penelope's clothing, her uniform, consisted of loose canvas trousers that allowed needed freedom of movement. These she now wore. But from the waist up, she was naked. Her arms were roped to iron rings set in the wall, holding her upright. I have always admired her breasts, first as mystery beneath her garments at the fountain when we met, and later, skin to skin in her bed or mine. A strand of the same material that secured my finger to the table looped around one of her breasts, with an end trailing off to hang from Hoban's gloved hand.

Her only other garment was a band of fabric covering her mouth. Her gaze shifted back and forth, from me to Hoban. I faced her, trying to communicate something with my eyes, something to give her . . . comfort? . . . hope? . . . but I felt unable even to reassure myself.

"Quite a conundrum. To free oneself or one's lover. A perfect example of the Hala Strana principle. One body part severed, one remaining whole . . . but which, but which." He dropped the strand, letting it rest on the arm of his chair. Then he rose and walked toward the back of the cabin, where the stern windows overlooked the night.

"I don't understand," I said to his back. "What are you doing? When did. . . ."

My words trailed off, overwhelmed by the vehemence of his reply: "Will you sacrifice a finger so that she might keep her breast?"

He kept his back to me, perhaps waiting for a response, but I had none to give. My breathing, echoed by Penelope's—ragged through the confining cloth—reverberated from the cabin walls. From above came sailor-songs and the thump of their feet on the deck. Why didn't someone come down here? Surely Hoban couldn't have overpowered the entire crew.

Finally, he interrupted the silence.

"Perhaps if you make a sacrifice, the Lord Mayor will sanction your departure. Perhaps. Everyone must make sacrifices for the greater glory of the city. The costs of citizenship. Everybody pays something."

"All my life," I said. "All my life I've been a loyal citizen, never questioning, changing jobs as ordered by municipal needs. . . ."

"Yes yes, always loyal. As if that entitles you to special treatment. And where was your loyalty when I told you of my longing to leave the city? You should have reported me as soon as we docked. Now I think I've changed my mind. You both lose. You both must bear the scars."

He went on, statements about civic duty and the greater glory of the Lord Mayor, a litany of self-righteousness as only the most rabid of followers can produce. Who was he, really? Not just an engineer . . . likely an operative from the Ministry of Municipal Obedience. Not someone who would relent. The whip-strand nestled in my right pocket, but I couldn't reach it. I needed force, momentum. To sever bone. . . . With my legs I pushed out from the table, over-balancing the chair. Its weight tumbled me backwards. The razor-glass sliced through my finger.

Hoban turned at the sound of my chair crashing to the floor.

Before pain, before thought, I reached into my pocket for the whip-strand. As I had at the factory, I lashed out with it, this time not at a wall but at the advancing Hoban. The strand slashed collarbone and chest; a gray undergarment showed through the tatters of his shirt, gray blending with red. Blood also flowed from my finger, dripping down the whip-strand.

Hoban took a few steps, his body not yet registering the damage, then stopped. He pulled his shirt open, staring down at the tear in his under-garment, which I recognized as the fabric body-armor fashioned in what was supposed to have been the sidewalk factory.

I rushed to Penelope and tore the loop from her breast and the rag from her mouth.

Hoban slammed into me from behind, knocked me to the floor. The impact jarred the whip-strand from my grip. His knees pressed into my back, keeping me down. I couldn't turn to fight. He twisted my arms behind me and held them.

"Now get up," he said, and removed his knees from my back but kept my arms locked. "I'm going to tie you up again, but this time you'll have to sacrifice more than a finger if you want to escape. Then I'll start cutting on your woman—that's what happens when you turn against the city."

I made a noise, not words, but a cry of despair, and my legs gave way. He yanked at me, but something—all I saw from the periphery was a blur—something struck him. He let go of my arms, and I tumbled face down.

Dazed, I turned onto my back and sat up . . . Penelope . . . in pulling me up, Hoban must have moved closer to her. She had locked her legs, her sailor-strong legs, around his neck. Blood covered the front of his chest, but he still struggled, punching her legs. She called out to her crew in a voice I had never heard her use on shore, a trumpet-tone of command.

I got up and kicked Hoban in the stomach. His arms drooped. Penelope squeezed harder, then released him. His body crumpled.

And later, much later, I awoke, my body stiff but resting in the soft swaying embrace of a hammock. A bandage covered my finger. Someone approached and pressed a hand to my face. Penelope.

"We're at sea," she said. "We set off immediately, as soon as my crew cut me loose. We treated your hand, dumped that man's body in the ocean. That man—him and a man in a prim-pressed suit—they carried you aboard, said you'd taken ill. The prim-pressed man left, then this one knocked me out with mist from a little spray bottle. Who was he?"

I reached for her hand with my good one. "The city," I said. "He was the city and now he's gone. We're gone."

She held my bandaged hand. "My sail-maker reattached your finger and the carpenter fashioned a splint to keep it from moving. The end may rot and fall off, but it was worth trying to save it."

Pain from my finger jabbed at me. This room, its recent events, clawed outward, screeched and whistled like a collapsing building. I needed to move, escape the grasping cocoon of hammock. "Out," I said. "I want to go on deck."

She helped me from the hammock and guided me up the ladder. On deck, I held the railing with my good hand, eyes closed, overcome by the throb and fighting back an urge to vomit. Gone, gone, poor finger, expelled from my body, from the city. The heart of the city pulsed, a fat, slavering beast that refused to moderate its hunger . . . I would not let it control me. The wind luffed my hair, a breeze that said: onward. And as I stood, fingers embracing the wooden solidity of the rail, the city-throb waned, replaced by the slap and caress of water against the hull.

MOUNTAIN STORY

Over the past week, rumors have drifted into our capital that a new mountain has arisen in the lands beyond the Unreasoning Forest. The Office of the Grand Patronage immediately dismissed these reports as fabrication or illusion, the sort that explodes into public consciousness and dominates conversation until another fad replaces it. Last year, for example, we had the hysteria over log-dwellers hiding in municipal parklands, which turned out to be a simple infestation of ground marmots. But this morning, a man walked into the Department of Parks and Justice, a man with mud-caked clothing and a gashed forehead, a man who claimed to have proof. Park stewards brought him to the Director's office, and the rest of the staff assembled.

The mud-caked man described himself as an itinerant photo-engraver who traversed The Expanse, stopping in villages to capture portraits. He said that he would have brought prints, but his developing chemicals had been destroyed, and he lacked funds to purchase more. The Director asked the photo-engraver for details, to help her determine whether we should commit Department resources to purchase his prints, or behead him for fraudulent claims.

What followed was a tale of thunder and destruction.

The photo-engraver had stopped at a mining camp beyond the Unreasoning Forest. Late his second night, a tremor woke him. He sat up, thinking that someone had shaken his cot. The earth screamed. Outside the window, night turned green. The walls of his room flowed, then crumbled. He regained consciousness in pre-dawn darkness, lying in the ruins of his lodging house. Others were near, some alive, some not. He saw the mountain . . . its peak lost in cloud. Indeed, the mining camp rested on what were now the mountain's lower slopes. Before bed, the photo-engraver had returned his apparatus to its padded containers, as was his usual practice. To prevent thievery, he always slept tethered to the containers.

Though bruised and dazed, the sight of the mountain spurred him to activity. He assembled his devices and cataloged the scene until he had used all his photo-plates. Which is when he realized that the jars containing his development chemicals were shattered and lost.

A debate arose on the merits of the photo-engraver's story. He received compliments on his telling, which had cemented the attention of all who had gathered. The Curator from the Shrine of the Everlasting Current decreed that the mountain had emerged as punishment for delving into the earth and rock—because only the Everlasting Current has the power to alter the natural landscape (which is why mining is conducted along the River, in places where the water has eroded the banks). The Director reminded the Curator that a Tributary of the Everlasting Current flowed past the camp, thus mining had been sanctioned. The Director was inclined toward immediate disbursement of Ministry funds, so that the Department could view what the photo-engraver had described.

However, the Assistant Director for Budgetary and Prosecutorial Matters opposed. "I concede that *something* occurred," he said. "Therefore, we will Authorize an exploratory Commission, outfitted for whatever terrain might be encountered, but I see no reason to commit funds for development chemicals and photo-engraver paper *and* an exploratory

Commission, if the result of seeing the rendered plates is that we will Authorize the Commission. Meanwhile, we will hold his photo-plates in a Secure environment."

All agreed to the merit of his words (not that agreement was required—the Grand Patronage appoints all positions in Budget and Prosecution, therefore conveying to them full Patronage authority). Budget and Prosecution would meet separately to determine what personnel would be eligible for the exploratory Commission. The photo-engraver protested the keeping of his plates, but had no recourse. Park stewards removed him.

Then, to my delight, I was selected to lead the Commission.

In the evening, the Director honored me with an invitation to the Director's Club for dinner. The Club overlooks the River, near the Grand Patronage shrine to the Everlasting Current. From our seats on the terrace, we could use the railing-mounted telescopes to view the water and, through intermittent gaps in the mist-wall, the desolation of the distant opposite shore, home to noxious vapors and strange creatures. We chatted about past Commissions and, of course, inter-Departmental intrigue. "This expedition will be different for you, Viburnum. Leadership is a lonely charge. You will have to support group camaraderie yet remain aloof."

Viburnum is my Department name, reflecting my duties as a Parkland specialist. My parents named me Amelia, but I've quite forgotten how it sounds to be called anything else.

Our dinner arrived, steamed river prawns with fern sauce, and we drank a toast to my Commission. The Director reminisced about past Commissions, as member and leader. "Once, when was it . . . The Year of Tatters? Dissidents stole the Grand Patronage barge and attempted to cross the Everlasting Current."

"Cross!" I said, unable to keep from interrupting. "How can anyone be that stupid? The barge must have simply broken from its moorings."

"A manifesto," she said. "Dissidents with a manifesto. Park stewards found the text scrawled on the stone mooring posts. We attached a tether to a maintenance barge and rowed out into the vastness. We never found the Grand barge of course. Crashed on the Shrieking Drop, no doubt. It took all of us, hauling the tether against the current, to return to the Capital."

I absorbed her story, reading in it a warning not to underestimate the dangers that might assail my Commission. Dinner ended, and we parted. On a cool autumn night such as this, when the mud and stinging manta flies of summer have abated, the River District is the most pleasant part of the Capitol. I walked home along the Avenue of Wares, thinking that I might shed a coin for good fortune. I settled on sturdy goat-hide boots, suitable for traversing terrain both rocky and otherwise.

Let me talk here about the geography of The Expanse. The Capital was founded along the Everlasting Current, (as were most towns of The Expanse). The Everlasting Current flows north to the Shrieking Drop, which marks the end of The Expanse. Beyond the Drop are the Lowlands, distant and inaccessible. Forests and farms lie near the banks of the Everlasting Current. Beyond the agricultural belt, arid lands stretch for unmapped distance, lands carved by wind, held together by ironwood and reef-grass, populated by nomads who can thrive in such an environment. Caravans ply routes to scattered oases, where settlements of hardy malcontents maintain a quasi-independence from the rest of The Expanse.

To the south, The Expanse ends at the Black Swamp.

The Capital is of course the seat of the Grand Patronage, and the center of art, culture, and business. The Capital is the northernmost city. Southward lie other towns, large and small. All towns must deliver Patronage taxes. A system of post-roads connects the towns, some following the course of the Everlasting Current, some cutting across the land in the places where the meandering of the Everlasting Current necessitates a more direct route.

No living resident of The Expanse has seen a mountain. Geophilosophers have speculated the presence of mountains below the southern horizon. No modern expedition has ventured far enough, though records exist, accounts from the great Explorer-Captains of years past, from an age of enquiry. The most exalted of these Explorer-Captains was the great D. H. Tinker Von Sem. Born into a wealthy cart-building dynasty, Von Sem displayed a taste for adventure at an early age. At thirteen, while on an excursion with her family to Boulder Lakes, she organized the residents to repel an incursion of giant stoats. And that was merely the start to a life of daring that took her across most of The Expanse, culminating in an expedition during the Grand Patronage's second Triarchy to reach the fabled land of Ulaan Khol.

Although Von Sem died returning through the Black Swamp, one of the few surviving pack bearers saved her journal. Von Sem's map was of a scale none have deciphered, but it clearly shows a broad and terrifying range of peaks, through which she was unable to pass. Someday, the Department hopes to retrace her route.

There are legends that mountains once defined the southern border of The Expanse, but the Everlasting Current wore them to nothing. Some say that the Black Swamp formed after a collapsing mountain diverted a portion of the Everlasting Current, trapping it in a low-lying area, where it spread and pooled. The *idea* of Mountain—the rock against which the Current battles—has led to many fanciful stories, which is why reports of a mountain were discounted so quickly (and may still prove to be mass hysteria).

Not only was this was my first time leading an exploratory Commission, it would also mark the farthest I have ever gone from the Capital. During the wait for our list of approved personnel, I fantasized, I invented scenarios (no doubt influenced by the adventure tales of my youth), scenarios in which my Commission discovered wonders heretofore unimagined.

I was confident in my Director's ability to assemble Commission members without help from Budget officers, however experienced they are with monetary procedure. Such thoughts verge on punishable offense, and are especially improper for someone about to undertake leadership of a Commission. Disagreement with Grand Patronage decree, even contemplation of such, could result in exile. But I was eager to be off! I forgave myself for my few mental indiscretions, and . . . finally . . . Budget and Prosecution released the list of qualified personnel. The Commission would number four: Hamell, a low-level worker in foliage reconciliation; Belo, who had, until recently, been part of the Grand Patronage fauna preservation group but now worked in the second sub-basement sanitary facilities; Carson, a sketcher of justice offenders; Hays, a parkland excursions guide; and myself, Viburnum, manager of parkland resources.

An Officer from the Department of Claims would accompany us, because, if there proved to be a mountain, it would need to be annexed to Grand Patronage domains.

In addition, the usual park stewards and bearer/cart drivers would provide their services. Though attached to the Department of Parks and Justice, park stewards belong to Grand Patronage security forces. Conflict does not exist in The Expanse, but if disagreements arise between individuals, businesses, or even towns; a Conflict Retribution Group is dispatched to end all confrontations and assume full Patronage control over the Assets of those deemed at fault.

I held several preparatory meetings with my new Commission members, and led them through the recommended series of twelve interdependence-building exercises. They exhibited common group behaviors: some immediately became friendly, relating life experiences, while some maintained reserve. No personality discrepancies arose—yet—though I knew that some would be unavoidable. Belo displayed a contrary nature that I assumed came from his former duties, which kept him out in Grand Patronage fauna preserves for much of his time. He was missing a fingertip on his right hand—the punishment for a minor infraction of fauna management rules.

Familiarity and trust grew, but I maintained detachment. As my

Director had reminded me, a Commission leader must, of necessity, remain aloof. Command is therefore a lonely undertaking, but one I was prepared to follow.

Moving on from classroom exercises, we set off one morning for Patronage Park, which marks the southern border of the Capital. The Park stretches inland from the River for six leagues, and south for another ten. Access is normally limited to the Administrative class. Each of us carried a pack with personal articles and Department-issue lantern and log book. We loaded tents and cooking materials onto a hand cart and took turns pushing it, in pairs. Well-maintained paths cross the park, passing through bogs, fields of swank-grass, funnel tree groves. Wildlife abounds. Belo pointed out the droppings of antelope and other creatures. We heard an oracle sloth keening from the canopy of an evergreen tower.

"I recommend we stop here," Hays said, when we reached a meadow bordering a stream that wound its way toward the Everlasting Current. He handed me his Parkland guide, and I agreed.

Of the group, Belo, Hays, and myself had experience setting up tents. After raising mine, I assisted Hamell and Carson with theirs. We built a fire and prepared our evening meal. Before daylight failed, Carson had us sit close for a group portrait, which she sketched with great speed and skill. She drew herself in with us.

During our meal, we told stories. I described my prior Commission, to the rye-fields of Plover, the town just south of us. "We surveyed the parkland to determine which parts should be converted for cultivation."

"After the Roiling Winter?" Belo asked, and I nodded. "Should have been done sooner," he said. "A lot of hungry people that winter. Not enough grain."

"The Grand Patronage provides ample for all," I said, shocked by his words. "My recollection is that someone in the Department of Consumption mismanaged Supply, allowing too much grain for drink production and not enough for bread."

Belo grunted and turned away. The others maintained a respectful silence.

———————

I woke in the early dawn glow and left the tent to relieve myself. At a discrete distance, I found a comfortable spot, away from grasping, scratchy shrubs, where I lowered my dungarees, and positioned my cone—that wonderful invention of the last great Explorer-Captain, Serena Honeyman-Carter. After finishing, I rinsed the reusable cone with water from my canteen and walked back toward the tents.

Hamell stood outside, lighting her pipe. "I always smoke at first light," she said.

She was the youngest of us, being only three years out of Secondary, and would be a pleasant expedition-mate. We chatted for a few minutes, then I woke the rest of the crew. Though I worried that Belo might damage group cohesion, I was quite happy with the other Commission members. After our parkland exercise, I was even more eager to be off on our journey.

Delays and endless meetings sapped my spirit . . . then . . . the day arrived! Because our departure happened to coincide with the Harvest celebration, our Commission would take part in the annual Promenade through the city-center to the Grand Patronage barge. All festivals begin with the barge moving from one mooring, downstream or upstream, depending on where it started, to the other mooring. At the barge, the Grand Patronage would present us with the Rod of Free Passage, which required villages to provide food and lodging and exempted us from having to present Identification documents at each stop.

On reaching the staging area, I was thrilled and surprised to find that we had been granted use of a Grand Patronage water-engine dray. I had previously only seen them from afar, at ceremonial events. Not all shared my enthusiasm. Belo complained of their size (necessary for housing the machinery) and cumbersome pace, and said that their noise frightens wildlife. But Carson bounded up to the rear compartment to examine the water-wheel, exclaiming about its workings. She took out a sketch-book and drew, something I was to find she did often.

The engine carts are built much like a standard oxcart, though much larger, and enclosed to cover the machinery, with a load area in the rear and a passenger deck on the roof. They move by means of gears and a water wheel. Water from a tank pours into wheel-buckets, the weight of the buckets rotates the wheel, and the wheel turns a system of gears; another gear operates a pump that returns water to the tank.

Bearers loaded our supplies into the cart, and we mounted the ladders to the roof-deck. And then, with a creak of its wheels and clashing of gears, the cart moved into the line. During Promenade, the various Commission members chatted, speculating on what we might find. None had ever traveled far from the Capital (none farther than the Filtered Lakes region), and there was some trepidation. Rumors abound of strange creatures and eccentric villagers. But I dismissed such stories, because all are governed by our illustrious Grand Patronage, and they provide goods and workers to maintain the Capital's needs.

Nearing the barge, silence overcame us, and we stared with expectation and awe. The Grand Patronage raised the Rod of Just Obedience, and the Director of the Department of Interior Relations spoke of our bravery and the need to maintain order over all the land. He read a Grand Patronage dispatch:

> My fellow citizens of The Expanse: Let us praise our Department of Parks and Justice, which on this day sends out their most Exceptional on a mission of Exploration and Discovery in the spirit of Monde and Tinker Von Sem.
>
> Though the age of the great Explorer-Captains is past, The Expanse fully mapped, and even some of the Wastes examined, we, on occasion still need those who are willing to venture into the unknown. Our new band of Explorers will traverse the boot-prints of those greats who came before. Dangers may be many, but these Citizens have agreed to press onward to

unearth what mysteries they might find. May they return to us with tales of Honor and Glory!

Let us praise them again.

The Officer from the Department of Claims who would be joining our Commission left the barge, bringing the Rod of Free Passage. On his chest he wore a pendant with the Grand Patronage interlocked GP, showing that he was part of the administrative class.

We resumed our Promenade. At the end, where the tree-bordered main avenue ends at the Department of Industry's factory district, the engine cart stopped near an empty oxcart. Bearers began to unload our provisions.

"Hold that," I said to the nearest bearer. "Why are you removing our supplies?" The bearer continued as though I hadn't spoken.

"Don't you see?" Belo said. "It was all for show. The water wagon. Just for Grand Patronage show. They wouldn't waste it on an expedition to nowhere. These things cost far more than our yearly salaries combined."

I stood dumbstruck. Deception . . . the slap of rebuke . . . at the outset of my first commission . . . Belo was right. Inaction clawed at me, someone should protest, should . . . but the leader . . . the leader is me . . . the leader has to show confidence. Loyalty.

"An oxcart is more suited to the roads we will be following. You said the same yourself, Belo. And an ox's pace keeps a person close to the land."

On our way out of the Capital, we passed through the paper-maker's quarter, a neighborhood of artists and writers. The buildings are some of the oldest in the Capital, brick, mostly four to six stories, clustered around squares containing moss-wrapped fountains and wide-boled flop trees with their characteristic drooping branches. The water cart was soon forgotten, and everyone pointed out landmarks, some of which we had only read of in our grade-school geography lessons: the Hexagon, Acacia Park—home to the Grand Patronage buffalo herd. Carson attempted to include in conversation the Officer from the Department of

Claims, but he only told us his name, Burton. He had the trimmed beard and light complexion of the administrative class. His lack of congeniality was not unexpected—those of the administrative class do not generally consort with other classes.

Toward sundown, we reached the nearest of the outlying agricultural villages—dwellings for farm workers and the shops that attend to their needs. A gray had spread across the northern sky, the gray of trampled ground and spurned lovers. But gray at day's end is much preferable to gray at the start.

We had ridden on the cart with our personal belongings close, and when we stepped down it was natural for us to take our own bags. But Burton, on alighting from the cart, ordered a bearer to follow with his bag. The bearer stumbled while stepping down from the cart; the bag thumped to the ground. Metal flashed. Burton swept out a knife and stabbed the bearer's hand, pinning it to the side of the cart. Heedless of the bearer's cries, he twisted the blade, pulled it out, and walked away, bag in hand.

The other bearer began shouting, but the chief park steward silenced him with a slap to the back of his head.

Carson wrapped a cloth around the hand of the injured bearer. "Did you see that? she said. "Violence, off-handed violence. I can't continue in the company of such a person."

"It's beyond my power to expel someone from another Department," I said, knowing that I would look weak.

"Only a bearer," Belo said. "He should have taken more care."

"Even a bearer is entitled to fair treatment," Carson said.

"I agree," I said. "But there is no recourse."

Much subdued of temper, we made our way to our lodgings. I presented the Rod of Free Passage to the dormitory warden, who provided us beds and our evening meal. I was relieved that Burton did not join us for dinner. Later, I learned that he had dined with the Grand Patronage's Governing representative.

In the morning, the injured bearer failed to appear, and I attempted to hire a replacement, but all workers were pledged to their farms. I hoped that we could find one at the next settlement. Our remaining bearer hitched a new team of oxen to the cart, and we set off. Last night's gray-ness had given way to clear skies, accompanied by a crisp breeze that prophesied early winter.

None of us besides Hays, the parkland excursions guide, had traveled so far in this direction. "The road returns to the River in a short while," he said. "And later, we will reach a town located where the far bank is much closer than what we have in the Capital. The effects of the River mists have resulted in practices that might seem quaint to us. For one, they seal their doors at sundown—they say that in darkness, rabid, winged creatures with fierce cutting beaks take flight."

"Then I hope we're well past by nightfall," Carson said.

But Hays said that would be impossible. Not far beyond town, the Unreasoning Forest begins, and no one wanted to stay the night inside its borders, where fearsome beasts roam, creatures that we *knew* exist—unlike the townspeople's alleged nightwings—because specimens have been exhibited in the Capital: the blotchhog (a pig-like thing with wide, fanged jaws and patches of spiky gray fur alternating with thick green hide), the gudgel (with its sucking pucker-mouth at the end of a snake-like snout), and others.

Despite the presence of these beasts, the prospect of seeing the Unrea-soning Forest, even that small portion that we would pass through, excited me. Plant life there is sparsely categorized; indeed, a full explo-ration has never been attempted.

As before, I presented the Rod of Free Passage. The administrator informed me that a fresh ox-team might not be available. I lectured him about Grand Patronage authority embedded in the Rod. He acqui-esced. He also agreed to find us a bearer to replace the missing one. We proceeded to dinner, which was a local delicacy: spratling, a fish large enough to feed our entire party, grilled whole and served with a tangy sauce of woodberries. The fish was of a type new to us, having a wide head and mouth, and a tall, fan-shaped fin. Our hosts said that they catch them far from shore, where the depths and current are unimaginable. They row out in boats tethered to a winching system, and communicate via notes passed along a smaller line. In the Capital, we harvest fish from pens built along the shore. The only craft that go in the water are the Grand Patronage barge and a few maintenance barges. We were incredulous that these people could brave the Everlasting Current. Even in the times of the great Explorer-Captains, no one is known to have done so.

After our meal, several of our hosts accompanied us back to our lodgings. They lofted torches that emitted an acrid odor. "These repel the nightwings," one said. "If we must go out at night, they are indispensable."

"But far better to keep indoors," another said.

Burton had once again dined separately. In the oxcart, he had sat apart from us, talking little, save for a long conference with the park stewards. And, connected to this, I don't think I've commented on the number of park stewards accompanying us—eleven. Why so many? Any Commission needs stewards. The Expanse is a peaceful land, but once away from the Capital, out of the close orbit of the Grand Patronage, it *is* possible to meet outlaws and other unruly elements. For a Commission such as ours, I would have expected two to five, but no more. Though nominally under the control of the Commission leader (myself), when in company with a representative from the Department of Claims (Burton), that authority supersedes the Commission leader.

I have quickly grown to resent Burton's presence—I believe that would have been true even without the knife incident. The rest of us, being fellows of the same Department, have more to draw us together. I worried that he would diminish the trust and cohesiveness that we had worked to build. I could already see Belo aligning himself with Burton; he defended the stabbing of the bearer and sat near Burton in the cart.

The night passed without incident, but in the pre-dawn morning, a cry awakened me. I rushed to my second floor window, which looked out onto the street, and saw a figure on the ground—human-sized, perhaps larger, but with an outer surface (fur?) that writhed and flowed. A fist-sized shape detached and flapped away! Then another, and another, leaving the mutilated body of Hamell, who had gone outside for her early morning smoke.

I pulled on clothing and fled the room. But found the front door barred by a heavy beam secured with a lock through an iron latch. I stood for a moment, bewildered—for how could Hamell have gotten out?

Sounds from a nearby alcove drew me. A man sat, doubled over, holding his face and sobbing. He looked up at my approach.

"The warnings," he said. "Why didn't she heed? My charge is to bar the door, but none of us need the bar. We know, we've seen it . . . we forget about travelers. You've been warned, but you can't *know*. Not the way we know."

The others soon joined us, voicing fears and questions. The doorman returned to his sobbing, and I was unable to rouse him further. I explained what had happened, what I saw. My tale silenced the group. We residents of the Capital are not accustomed to the arbitrary nature of life in the provinces. The Capital has its violence, its brawlers and criminals, but those are easily understood, normal even. The thought of flying creatures that can incapacitate and devour a robust adult. . . .

Reluctant to separate from each other, we sat in the lounge. Someone brought us tea. We spoke little. The sun rose as usual, brightening the room and lifting enough torpor to prompt us to go and gather our belongings. Burial workers retrieved Hamell's remains and placed them in a pyre basket. We held a brief ceremony. Being from disparate parts of a large Department, none of us had known her well, but she had been an amiable companion. I read from the Articles of Departmental Conduct, as was required. After, we made our way to the cart and loaded our bags. Carson stood nearby, bag at her feet.

"I'm returning to the Capital," she said.

I asked her to walk with me. The main post-road, along which the town was arrayed, intersected with another, which led us toward the River. We passed several houses, larger and more elegant than those we had seen around our lodgings, and at the River we stopped at the local shrine to the Everlasting Current. Water-sparkle glinted through the morning fog, which stretched from the terrible loom of the mist-wall. From the bank came the calls of nesting river loons.

"I don't know that any of us retains much of our ancestors' love for exploration," I said. "We live content in our city. But when I look at this"—I waved my arms at our surroundings—"I see new and wondrous experiences that wouldn't have been possible had we stayed within the walls of our Department."

"My normal duties," Carson said. "Nothing prepared me. I sit in the Halls of Punishment, sketching the proceedings. I see the offenders and hear the details of their crimes, I witness the carrying out of sentences . . . beheadings, dismemberment . . . but everything follows the Rules of our System. Out here. . . . "

"Please, come a bit farther with us," I said. I also reminded her that abandoning the Commission would mean an end to her service at the Department. As penalty, she would likely be assigned menial tasks in a dank sub-basement. I didn't want her to suffer that fate, and . . . I was forming a quiet attraction for her. Her presence cheered me. Is that selfish?

We talked more. Eventually, she relented. We returned to the cart and set off.

A few leagues on, the forest swallowed us. The air thickened with color: the soft green of new growth, the dense, dark brown of trunks that had occupied this space for centuries, feathery green of moss clinging to rock and root. Forest noises resonated from all sides—birdcalls, rustles, barks, and murmurs. It always amazes me to hear the ominous din caused by a fist-sized brown squirrel as it scrambles through leaf-litter. The road meandered, having its origin in paths taken by animals, by fallen trees. Some amount of clearing has been done, lest the forest choke out all passage, but the razing of these grand trees is difficult.

"Game abounds in these woods," Belo said. "If we had time to set traps I could catch us a nice supper."

The deeper we infiltrated, the more the color-drenched air hampered breathing. Leaf mold and spores attached themselves to throat and lung. Vines dangled; branches met over the road, giving the impression we trundled through an endless tunnel. My mind drifted into memory . . . a Commission to catalog flora along a streambed just north of the Capital . . . my companion (long since transferred to a provincial town) and I, nights spent with her in furtive embrace. . . . The stopping of the cart brought me back. A tree, or rather a great bough, had fallen across the road. I stepped down to inspect. The bough was too large for our simple tools to cut. We could try to burn the obstruction, or unload the cart and haul it over. But even with our new bearer, unloading and reloading the cart would take hours.

We set to work, all of us (all of the Commission—Burton and the park stewards stood apart, alert for possible dangers, they said). I put most of us to unloading the cart, while Hays laid kindling along the branch—I chose to follow both of our options, to see which would result in quicker passage, and to keep our party busy, lest idleness bring on morbid thoughts. Even I, an avowed optimist, had begun to have doubts about our Commission. How I wished that one of our long-passed Explorer-Captains could return to guide us! But the responsibility fell to me.

The branch, despite its girth, proved to be old, with a hollow rotten heart, and the fire caught well. With about a fourth of our supplies remaining on the cart, I stopped the unloading. Carson and Belo went to help spread the fire, while the bearers and I hastened to reload the cart. The supplies remaining in the cart included two crates just behind the driver's bench, that I hadn't previously noticed. They took up near the width of the cart and were sealed with padlocks.

Overhanging boughs trapped the smoke, casting a vagueness to our surroundings, and our oxen became alarmed at the fire; one bearer took them down the trail, to where the park stewards loitered. I followed. "If you must guard," I said to the park stewards, "guard our oxen so that the bearer can return to reloading the cart. It would also help to have some of you assist us. I would like to leave these woods before dark." Not waiting for a response, the bearer and I returned to the cart.

A few minutes later, Burton joined us. "Those are not to be moved," he said, indicating the two large crates. He watched for a time, then, apparently satisfied with the condition of the crates, returned to his place with the park stewards.

In time, the branch reduced to coals, some of which we swept aside and some we piled into an iron pot to aid in setting tonight's cookfire. We mounted the cart and resumed our journey. But night in these dense woods approaches swiftly. Our carriage lanterns did little to stave off the encroaching darkness. "The road is reasonably smooth and level," I said. "We can continue until our normal stopping time. If that doesn't free us from these woods, we will have no choice but to camp."

With dark came an increase in forest noises—various snortings, the crackle of claws on wood, the baying of toads. And then the time came when the bearers announced that further driving might injure the oxen. We stopped. These woods, this dark, narrow road, suppressed our mood. Again, I thought it best to keep everyone busy. Belo distributed tents. Carson and I removed lanterns from a crate. I was glad for the practice we had taken, our easy night in Capital parkland. Some of us placed our tents on the road; some, myself included, set ours under the branches, on a soft floor of leaves. We worked in pairs, holding a lantern for each other. Hays and Belo gathered firewood, abundant enough near the road's edge for immediate needs. Later, we would have to look farther into the trees.

From deep in the woods came a high-pitched whine that silenced conversation.

"Blotchhog," Belo said, affirming what none wanted to hear.

"They won't come near our fire," I said, hoping that was true. "But we'll take turns as sentinels, with park stewards in each group."

Myself, Carson, and two of the park stewards took the first shift. Carson and I set out to collect more firewood. I suggested limiting our search to the west side of the road, because that was the direction in which the woods eventually ended—the thought of probing deeper into their vastness made me uneasy. As we searched for wood, we talked about what had happened that morning. "It already feels long ago," I said. "I'm glad you continued with us. The forest is like nothing else in The Expanse. I would love a chance at longer study."

"The mountain draws us," she said. "I think I hear it."

Strange shapes appeared in the gloom, as if, once free of the sun's watchful gaze, trunk and branch transformed into new configurations. A motionless figure standing in a small clearing startled us. Our hail met no response. Drawing closer, we realized it was an immense pillar of moss, about Carson's height but taller than me. The sides were thick with cedar-like fronds.

Carson laughed. "I was so sure I saw it move."

Standing on my toes, I held the lantern over the top of the moss. I assumed that the moss had grown over the remains of a tree, but the top had a rounded edge, or lip, encircling a deep cavity. The interior held a darkness that my lantern couldn't penetrate. I cut a frond sample from the side for later study, storing it in a muslin specimen pouch. The frond left a sticky residue on my fingers. I wiped them on my trousers.

Our shift ended, and I settled into sleep. Deep in the night, howlings and drummings shocked me awake. I looked out of my tent to see a phalanx of blotchhogs engulf our encampment, trampling tents and scattering the fire. The air clanged with cries of fear and surprise. I sat, frozen, watching. I swear I saw one enormous brute take a burning log in its jaws and thrust it into a tent. Then I ran.

Some distance on, I stopped, spent. My lungs cried for breath. A few trees away, something crashed past. I tensed, thinking it was one of those beasts, but the screech I heard was human. A lantern-light wavered. I ran over, finding Hays with an arm consumed by a gudgel's snout, sucker-teeth clamping into his flesh. His lantern lay on its side, capturing the creature in its beam.

"Kill it, kill it!"

I had slept with my belt on, folding knife in its case. I pulled the knife out and snapped open the blade, which was about as long as my hand. I stabbed the gudgel's snout. Blood spurted. The gudgel screeched and released Hays. The creature swayed and staggered, recovered, and fled into the dark, leaving a moment of silence.

Hays screamed. I spun to face him, thinking that another gudgel had attacked. He was looking down at his injured hand. It dripped. Flesh, melting like wax, fell to the ground in viscous globules.

"I have to cut off your arm above the bite," I said. "Stop the poison. Stop it from digesting your flesh." . . . leader, must help . . . must save. . . . No one told me what could happen. Training manuals—they don't work out here. Take the breath of Calmness, and again . . . what would help? Starflower plant all around us. Fibrous leaves. Fibers used for cloth. I used a leaf to clean my knife. Knife! Cut off an arm? No choice. Digesting him . . . more globules fell. "Lie down. I have to put a foot on your arm. I have to hold it still."

He did as I asked, but when I pushed the blade into his arm, he flung me off and bolted. I called out in vain. His lantern lay where he had dropped it. I picked it up and followed. Which way was the road? And did I wish to find it? I didn't want to return to the blotchhogs, but I didn't want to lose myself in these woods either. The sounds of Hays' flight vanished. Perhaps he fell. I continued but heard and saw no sign of his passing.

Stopping, I shined the lantern around. Two more of those moss-pillars stood nearby. On seeing them, my hand that had been smeared by the specimen tingled. To my over-heightened mind, the moss-pillars appeared to lean toward each other, as though conferring. Thick vines draped from several trees and encircled the trunk of one. Using the vines as a ladder, I climbed. I would wait for daybreak aloft. Safe from beasts. The lower branches were broad enough for me to lie on, resting my back against the trunk. I snuffed the lantern. Night flowed. I slept, fitful dream-darkened sleep. Tramping woke me—blotchhogs! I held my eyes shut, with the irrational hope that I would remain invisible to them. Safe in my perch . . . but how could I know? Their tusks might chew this tree to the ground.

Reason prevailed. I opened my eyes. Below, Burton and several of the park stewards, garbed in outfits patterned in irregular shapes that blended with forest gloom. Faces streaked with dark paint. They held compact versions of the firearms used by horse guards on Grand

Patronage Day celebrations and for executing criminals. They fired their weapons at the pair of moss-pillars; shreds flew everywhere, dusting the ground and the park stewards. Pain stabbed my hand; I passed out.

Morning light made me doubt my nighttime visions. I descended from my branch-refuge. Back on the ground, I found no traces of Burton and the park stewards. What I had thought had been a pair of moss-pillars proved to be one, no doubt multiplied by shadows cast from my lantern. The moss-pillars reminded me of the much (much!) smaller cluster-moss that grows in the Grand Patronage botanical garden. If these bodies reached such proportions, what behemoth roots lurked underground?

During my nighttime flight, I had forgotten to check the compass I kept on a cord around my neck. After consulting it, I set off, maintaining a course as north-westerly as I could manage around the trees; I hoped to intersect the road. My Expedition map showed that the road passed through a tapering finger of the Unreasoning Forest, the bulk of which continues along the River as it bends eastward. When we stopped for the night, we were likely two-thirds of the way through. I had camped on the west side of the road, and had not crossed it in my flight. At worst, I would walk straight into the finger, with the woods narrowing and thinning as I went. The mining camp was but another day's travel farther. Survivors of my party, if any, wouldn't linger for stragglers. My best hope to find them would be onward.

If not for the disastrous blotchhog attack, my stroll through these marvelous trees would have thrilled me, but botanical curiosity had waned, offset by worry about my companions. I wanted only to leave the wood behind.

Recognizing, as I walked, several species of edible plants, I was able to postpone hunger (and by edible I mean not-poisonous, rather than good-tasting—taste being a minor need compared to hunger). Passage was sometimes difficult, through tangles of late-summer growth, but in general the span of trees choked out lower-story plants, except those requiring minimal sunlight.

In early afternoon, I came to a place where a wall of moss-pillars had colonized the spaces between the great-oaks, blocking me. I turned, searching for a way to bypass the moss-pillars. The air blurred, thick with particulates, thicker the farther I went, blinding-thick. The stuff . . . spores . . . pollen . . . caught in my throat. To ease breathing, I tied a cloth over my mouth, but I couldn't see past the hand that held the compass. Luminescent shapes fluttered, always at the edge of sight. My steps drew me no closer. The shapes pulsed, larger, larger, then reduced to nothing. Flared again. At their brightest I had to shield my eyes. When I turned to my right, the fog eased; it remained always thicker to my left, as if herding me. I returned to the place—or another like it—where the moss-pillars bunched. A movement startled me . . . an arm, a flailing human arm, extended from the side of a moss-pillar. With a loud snap, a section of the pillar split, revealing Hays' face.

I screamed and ran in the opposite direction, ran into the spore fog. Branches whipped my arms and face. I kept going. Past a line of shrubs, the earth parted . . . a ravine . . . down which I tumbled.

When I regained consciousness, night had returned. Dampness clung to my right side, dampness that pulled and stretched when I lifted my arm. The dampness smelled of earth and rot. I sat up, and the damp released me with a viscous exhale. My eyes adjusted to the darkness. Stars were visible between breaks in the tree canopy. I had landed in the muck at the edge of a stream. Cheeks and exposed skin stung from cuts I must have acquired during my panicked flight through the woods. My neck twinged when I turned my head to look around. The lantern was a few feet away, broken in the fall. The ravine's sides were too smooth and steep to climb. Onward then, along the stream.

Walking, my mind constructed scenarios: companions trampled into bloodmash, survivors lost like me in the woods, stalked by blotchhogs, gudgels, or worse. Dawn, welcome dawn, emerged, a gradual lightening that lessened the dread that had pressed upon me in the dark. I climbed up the streambed and back amongst the trees, the all-encroaching trees. A consultation with my compass showed me the direction. Some ways ahead, I spied another of the moss-pillars, but, as I drew closer . . . not moss . . . Hays.

"Your arm!" I said, unable to hide my surprise. My first thought had been partially correct—although the figure was indeed Hays, his arm—the arm that I had attempted to cut off to save him from gudgel poison—had been replaced by moss-flesh. When I drew close to him, he started walking.

"Are you . . . what do you feel?" I couldn't tell if he was aware of his condition. His movements reminded me of the clockwork automatons used in Grand Patronage punishment ceremonies. I remained a few steps behind, observing, trying to discern where moss ended and flesh resumed.

Full daylight came. The temperature had dropped, and I wished for the warmer clothing in my bag. And where was my bag? My other companions? I stopped, unable . . . unwilling to keep walking. Hays stopped as well. In the brighter light, I could see lumps under his shirt. One rippled out from his collar, raised a green protuberance that swiveled in my direction. He turned to face me and reached with his moss-flesh hand. I jumped and sprawled backwards over a dwarf juniper. His expression . . . not blank . . . but something inhuman. Staring at him while he hovered there, plant-still, I realized that instead of hair, fine tendrils, like those covering the sides of the moss, extended from his scalp.

He remained still until I got up, then turned and walked away. I followed.

I don't know how long we walked before the change in the terrain penetrated my dulled and tired senses. I passed a fallen tree, upended from the roots, then another. And the ground on which I walked . . . the ground rose. I trod upon the slope of a mountain!

Now I understood the reason for the fallen trees—even they, despite their age and sturdiness, had not been able to withstand the earth's upheaval. The photo-engraver had surmised that the mountain encompassed a portion of the Unreasoning Forest. The incline was so gradual at this point and the remaining trees so large that I couldn't gauge the entirety of the mountain.

Hays was several strides ahead. It occurred to me that if I angled across the slope rather than ascending, I might soon find the road . . . and the others. Calling out to Hays, I set off to my right. He turned to look, then continued. The relief on parting shamed me—he was under my command and care, but his . . . condition. Being with him disturbed me, froze whatever compassion I should have felt.

He passed from sight. Soon, with a finality that surprised me, the woods dissipated into scattered trees, shrubs, and knee-high waif-grass. Away from the overhanging boughs, I felt suddenly vulnerable. My pace slackened. A night of fitful sleep, followed by a day of insufficient food, a fall, and constant movement had exhausted me, but I couldn't stop, wouldn't stop. Eventually, I came to the road. Though bent by upheaval and layered in leaf and splintered branch, the presence of the road gave me hope.

With no way to know whether my companions were ahead or behind, I chose to continue upward. What choice did I have? The mountain summoned me. Deep below my feet, I sensed the rumble of its stone heart. Creatures dwell in the earth's depths, beyond reach of the Everlasting Current. Alien to surface-dwellers. The unanswerable, blind in the cold darkness, jagged teeth, they wait for lost travelers. Nursery rhymes to frighten children into their beds.

Sunlight dimmed, blocked by the mountain, and with sundown, the air chilled even more. I worried about finding shelter for the night and wished I had saved the striker from my broken lantern—I could have used its sparks to make fire. A shape appeared, a shape that coalesced into the ox-cart, one ox dead in its trace. Hoping for additional clothing, I discovered only torn and empty food sacks and a blanket. I cut head and arm holes in the top and sides of the least-damaged sack and pulled it on. Then I cut strips from another to use as a belt. Most important, in one sack, someone had left a package of travel-bread.

Burton's locked crate was gone.

Remembering another storage place, I looked under the driver's seat, to find a full water bottle and a bag of nuts and dried fruit. Satisfied, for now, I unrolled the blanket in the cart-bed and lay down.

But sleep, sweet sleep, eluded me. I longed to know who remained, who had survived and reached the mountain . . . the mountain! A mountain in The Expanse! And on its thighs I lay. Even the stars looked different here, with my viewing angle changed. I gazed on the Traveler's Star, asking for guidance.

Weariness scored its inexorable triumph, a victory that lasted until the rising sun met my face. With no desire to linger, I rose and gathered my supplies. For daytime, I refashioned my sack-shirt as a pack and set off. Ahead I hoped to find . . . Belo . . . Carson . . . even the bearers. If my tree-perch vision could be trusted, Burton and his park stewards had survived and armed themselves. Them, I had no wish to find. And what of Hays? His path up the wooded side—would it converge with mine again, somewhere above?

The aroma of roasting meat tugged at me. I came upon a group gathered at a cookfire. The people—a mix of men and women—wore clothing unlike any I had seen in The Expanse, blanket-like shawls in many colors, loose-fitting white trousers. None of them acknowledged my approach, even when I stood amongst them. They cut sections of meat and ate them with flatbreads, which they also used to scoop beans from a pot. If I was invisible, my hunger wasn't. I reached for a bread-disk and wrapped it around a piece of meat. The fatty juices of the meat popped into my grateful mouth. I chewed and swallowed. And still, no reaction from any of them. I looked down. The piece of meat that I had eaten remained on the plate. A woman took it.

I staggered back.

Unknowing . . . the depths, the depths of the Everlasting Current, its bottom far beyond human understanding. I swam in choked-black darkness, arms and legs thrashing, hoping to butt against something . . . bot-

tom . . . embankment. Involuntary cries, plaintive and feeble, tore from
my throat.

My ascent took me past other groups, most oblivious to my passing. A
few . . . I swear could sense me, some peripheral awareness of another's
presence. The people's appearance: hair, clothing, body type, varied, as
if the mountain was a meeting-place of those from different lands, each
group only able to see its own kind.

My body ached, from my fall, from the constant climbing. And the
air changed . . . thinner in my lungs, insufficient bulk to sustain me. I
rationed the water and travel-bread. The weak air grew colder, and I
stopped to put on my sack-shirt. Late in the afternoon, I came upon the
remnants of the mining camp. Vines of smoke climbed skyward, and
the air reeked of burnt flesh. The survivors had erected shelters, ragged
tents strung from poles, wall fragments, and fallen trees. Around them
people worked, dragging rubble to the perimeter. Paving stones, chunks
of brick wall, and splintered tree trunks were being used for a barricade
that appeared to be gradually encircling the camp.

I called out to the nearest workers, fearing—after the long day of
phantom encounters—that no one would see me: "Greetings—have
you seen a party from the Capital?" One man stopped and looked in my
direction, then another. Heartened, I spoke louder: "My party . . . I don't
know how many may have reached here . . . in the forest we were set
upon by beasts, our group scattered."

"No stopping! Labor on, all of you." The command came from someone
behind the workers. One of the park stewards came into view. She wore
that mottled clothing I had seen in the woods. She pointed her weapon
and shouted at me to state my name and reason for being there.

I knew that I looked different, covered in my sack-shirt, my hair
matted with leaves and dirt, but I was still technically their leader. I
said who I was, but she kept the weapon rigid and told me to stop. I did.
She removed a hand from the weapon, raised a whistle to her lips, and
blew once, paused for a twenty-beat, blew again. A signal I knew was a

medium-urgency call for support from other park stewards. And so was not surprised when another came trotting out from somewhere else in the camp.

"Take this one to the detention center and let the Commissioner know," the first park steward said to the second.

The second moved behind me and pressed his weapon against my back.

"Don't you know who I am? Why—"

The man pushed me. "No talk."

We entered the camp. As the photo-engraver had warned, the devastation was shocking. Much of the camp had been temporary structures, but even buildings of brick had fallen. We came to a pair of cellar doors sealed with an iron rod through the two handles. Nothing remained of the cellar's building except a debris-covered floor. The steward pulled out the rod. "Open the doors," he said. "Down."

When I reached the bottom of the stairs, he slammed the doors over me.

I stood, blinking into the darkness. From the depths, my name emerged, first as a cracking whisper, then again, louder. "Viburnum!" The speaker appeared, rushing toward me.

"Carson!" I shouted her name, overjoyed to see her. We embraced. Her words poured out, fast and compressed, as if squeezed by the weight of the earth above us, by the mountain's bulk. . . .

"I knew you were dead. Not there after the blotchhogs . . . they . . . they trampled our camp into nothing. Bearer and two park stewards dead, crushed. Burton outfitted the rest of the stewards for conflict resolution. Morning came. No waiting for you or Hays—have you seen him? Burton forced us to load the cart and leave."

"Hays," I said. I didn't know what to say.

"One ox dead, torn apart, blood everywhere. The other pulled the cart till it died. Burton sent park stewards ahead for bearers to carry his weapons. That's what was in those crates. When we reached the camp,

he imprisoned me down here. Our surviving bearer is helping build the
wall with the camp survivors. Belo . . . he's with Burton . . . he'd always
sided with him. I don't know what they're planning here. They didn't
want me around. And I wouldn't help them anyway, I wouldn't."

We clung to each other. My eyes adjusted to the gloom. Fragments of
light pushed through a gash in the ceiling. Water dripped. A jumble of
crates surrounded us: mining supplies, bags and tins of food.

"I'm famished," I said, looking at the crates of food.

"Of course. They haven't starved me, at least. There's a stove down
here." She lit the stove and reheated a pot of beans.

I spooned some into a bowl and sat on a crate to eat. "Burton," I said.
"Whatever distaste we have for him, he represents the Grand Patronage.
He has the right to be treated *as* Grand Patronage-by-proxy. With full
Patronage authority. Think about what happened: Mountain—an outside force, an unknown force—manifested here, damaging a mine that
provides vital ore to the Grand Patronage. And, knowing nothing about
what caused the mountain, we don't know that it can't appear in other
places, in the Capital. . . ."

"Then they're operating out of fear," Carson said. "But . . . when we
first heard about the mountain, no one seemed concerned. They didn't
send a company of park stewards. They sent us."

I got up and walked around the cellar, looking for, I don't
know . . . another way out? Weapons? Carson followed. "Likely they
didn't believe it was real," I said. "Why would they? And now they know
it is. Now they know."

Carson grabbed my wrist, pinching her fingers into my skin. I pulled
my arm away.

"I'm sorry," she said. "You haven't seen Burton here, since the blotchhogs. He's paranoid, he's—"

I opened a crate containing mining supplies: assorted sizes of pry-
bars, chisels, picks, shovels.

"I saw him in the woods, with park stewards, shooting at the moss-
pillars, shooting and shooting until they were covered with bits of
shattered moss. And there's something in that moss. Not a moss-spore

narcotic or, maybe there is a narcotic, but there's also. . . . Hays . . . I told you, I haven't told you, he's part moss-pillar now." I described the gudgel bite, his arm, the protuberances. After I finished, we sat together on a crate, silent.

A scrape from above startled me—I found I had slumped against Carson and apparently slept. The doors opened. Light rushed in. A male park steward and a woman wearing the brown uniform of mining camp patrol descended. They told me to accompany them. They walked me to a shed made from mismatched wall sections leaning into each other, gaps covered by canvas. Inside, Burton sat at a folding table over which spread a map of the camp. I stood near the entrance, the park steward behind me. Burton wrote in a notebook, pen scraping across the pages, leaving smeared ink and vague characters. His hair sprung from his scalp in oily tufts, and stains marked his clothes, the same splotchy-green shirt and trousers that all the park stewards were wearing. Stubble prickled his once-smooth cheeks.

"Field report," he said without stopping his attack on the paper. After another page, he closed the notebook and slipped it into a leather bag. "Do you know why we're here?" he asked.

"I came to explore," I said. "To turn unknown into known, or at least part-known, to scavenge meaning from natural forces, however impossible that may be. That's my understanding. And I'm in command of the Commission."

"The manager of the mining camp died in the Attack. That indicates Conspiracy. Assassination! Transgression against a Grand Patronage official as well as a critical mining operation. Anarchy will not be tolerated. Not in The Expanse. Not *anywhere* in The Expanse. Did you see the photo-plates? Worse even than the site itself. NOT tolerated!" He retrieved the notebook and wrote more, talking as he wrote. "When the wall is finished, we will continue upward. No one else will be allowed in or out. The mountain is ours now. By the Authority of my position, I claim it for the Grand Patronage. We must ascend to the top and plant the GP. And soon, a monument to the Grand Patronage will anoint the heights, projecting from the topmost point in all The

Expanse. A sign to Anarchists and Assassins that we will root them out."

The higher we climbed, the colder it grew, and breathing became more and more difficult. Our party included Belo (who avoided me), Carson, Burton, some former mine-workers as bearers, and most of the park stewards (a few remained at the camp, augmenting the force of mining camp security officers). Of Hays, I saw no sign, but assumed he was far ahead, perhaps at the top already. And for what purpose?

Snowfall began in the afternoon, light at first but increasing. I had been allowed to reclaim my pack (and I thanked Burton's bureaucratic mind, which kept him from abandoning Grand Patronage property—it must have pained him to leave our tents); I wore my quilted jacket and new goatskin boots. Carson and I had stowed pickaxes from the box in the cellar. We were each allowed a small lantern. Even with bearers, we had much to carry, and the thin air, combined with snow, cut short our day. At our evening meal, Carson and I sat apart from the others. One loud-voiced park steward talked of an incident in the Capital from a few weeks ago. He and another had discovered an indigent woman sleeping in Patronage Gardens. Rather than take the trouble of escorting her to a center and submitting a report (proper procedure), they kicked and beat her, leaving her unconscious and bleeding.

"She wanted to stay there, and we let her," the steward said, and laughed; the others joined him.

I looked at Carson and she at me. It was well known what type of citizens worked for Grand Patronage security details. Many were con-scripted, though some volunteered, generally those with no hope for employment other than street cleaner or other menial services. The thought of our being under their control was sobering.

The bearers had set up tents scavenged from the mining camp. Carson and I were made to share, and with the unexpected cold we put our blankets together. We slept, but the wind and the slap of snow on the tent kept awakening me. At some point, having rolled onto my side facing Carson, I found her awake as well, studying my face as if trying to interpret my features to know my thoughts. Or, so I fancied.

"I have a lover in the Capital," she said. "A man, a cartographer in the Department of Streets and Population Control. But . . . " She inched closer and kissed my lips, touched a hand to my belly. As Commission leader, I should not have allowed such to happen, but the circumstances were not those of a normal Commission. Whether a supervisory court would agree was irrelevant. But our intimacy stopped at a kiss, kisses, embrace. Neither of us was comfortable enough for more—we didn't want our pleasure overheard by park stewards.

In the morning, chilled, sun just touching our cluster of tents, we were jolted awake by shouting. I wrapped myself with a blanket and looked out. Overnight, a moss-pillar had emerged, at least twenty feet tall and far thicker than those I had seen in the woods. Burton ordered the park stewards to form a line and fire their weapons at the moss-pillar.

With an explosive crash, the weapons spewed their projectiles. The pillar burst, expelling a fine and glittery dust.

I pushed Carson back into the tent and closed the flap. "Cover your face. Broken moss dust—shouldn't breathe it." I wound her blanket around her head, then wrapped mine. I kept talking, unsure whether she could hear through our muffling fabric layers. "The moss . . . spores? . . . narcotic. But what effect? . . . stay covered . . . let it settle." We held hands and waited. The spores would dissipate, and, I hoped, their potency would decrease.

The mass of percussions continued, faded to a scattered few, and stopped. My mind slipped into a zone between sleep and hyper-awareness; some moments I thought I walked across a sticky plain, a blue sun searing my naked skin, which flaked and fell around my feet like black snow. Then I would be back in the tent lying beneath Carson, our limbs tangled in frantic embrace—when this vision began to slip away, I grasped at it, willing it to remain, but it shattered. A moss-globe replaced her head and moss fronds advanced down her body. I screamed, my scream echoed by hers. We both tore off our head coverings and stared at each other's faces, our breath dry and ragged. She was the first to rise, and I followed her outside. No Burton, no park stewards—no one in sight. Snow and moss bits covered the ground. Tracks led from the tents, upward. We scavenged food for our packs and followed.

The area beyond the mining camp was arid and rocky grassland that few had traversed. The grass had fared better than the woods, adapting itself to the mountain's slopes. "I wonder," I said, my breath a cold mist, "did the mountain push up through the earth, retaining the same surface that has always been here? Or will we find something new as we continue?"

We stopped to eat. Carson opened her sketchpad. She sat on a rock and drew me, with backdrop of rising terrain, my head capped by clouds. I laughed when she showed me. "I didn't know I looked so serious," I said. I sat on her rock; our legs touched, the contact warm and pleasant.

"You smiled more when we first met, in the Capital. We all did."

"Well, as Commission leader, I'm responsible for your emotional well-being." I reached to kiss her but pulled back before our lips met. "I'm sorry. Those visions we had in the tent . . . moss. I know it was just the spores, but Hays . . . you haven't seen him. I'm afraid of that happening to me, to us."

We passed signs of Burton's party: trampled patches of snow, food wrappers, even an entire pack, which we stopped to check, finding a water bottle and a book of verse dedicated to the Everlasting Current. I wouldn't have thought they were so far ahead, but was happy enough without them.

Air wrapped its fingers around our bodies, transporting us to a realm where nothing existed but the gasping cold, clumps of faded grass, and our steps, one stride after another. We were too winded from cold and altitude for conversation. I tried to reconcile this twisted landscape with The Expanse, but couldn't. The land I knew was gone, replaced by a skewed plain that stretched into the clouds, defiant, merciless. Did time continue along its normal path, or had the mountain warped the

Current? The Department of Plausibility once released a paper theorizing this, citing, as an example, observations that the Everlasting Current runs faster or slower in different parts of The Expanse.

The only thing I was certain of was walking. Each step, each succession of steps, an accumulation that contributed to forward movement, while the sun, a pale companion, mocked us, withheld warmth. We had no way of knowing how high the mountain reached, how far we must go to gain its top. Or what we might find there. These upper slopes were devoid of life; even the shadow-beings I had passed below had ceased to haunt. Perhaps Burton's fortifications had stopped them.

The perspective changed, and several confused minutes followed before I comprehended; for an eternity, our view had been restricted by the ever-rising terrain. Now—I could see beyond, could see edges! To our right, the land ended, dropping into nothing. We crept as close as we dared, to view the broad beyond. The Unreasoning Forest smudged the horizon with green, a green that I longed to return to, despite its dangers.

Carson pointed. "That dark ribbon. How small the Everlasting Current looks!"

Here ended all grass, shrubs, even dirt, replaced by barren rock, a surface split by fissures and littered with boulders. The incline forced us to walk bent forward, often using hands for support. Snow blew sideways, whipping and squealing. A stretch of nearly vertical climbing left me beyond exhaustion; we flopped onto a concave rock, the first space large enough to support us. I pointed at a black eagle, its wings spread to catch the thin air. "A fine way to travel," I said.

I tried to say more, but my voice bled into a torrent of coughing. Carson handed me a water bottle. I accepted, then attempted a few whispers: "At the top, we'll find a sweet spring that flows down the far side, cutting an easy path for descent, and there will be raspberries and watercress to soften our hunger."

Onward, packs lighter, bodies weary. A moaning sounded . . . wind? . . . exhaling through a gap in the rocks. The pitch and intensity varied, and sometimes a high whistle combined with the moan, as if someone was tuning an enormous musical instrument. Then I heard it closer, softer, and in turning realized that it issued from Carson's lips. And . . . horrified . . . I slapped a hand over my mouth to cut off the sound that I too had been making. Dark-washed towers rose, fleshy towers that pushed skyward. Colors danced on the sides of the towers, sky-measured rainbow of black, red, and orange. The towers stretched pseudopods toward each other, embracing, joining. The moans, an organ chord blasting outward, drew us into a cold and wet embrace. We entered a zone where light had died. I stumbled and thrust a hand to break my fall. Rock-scattered footing had changed to sponge. After a few unsure steps across the sponge, I lost Carson. I called her name, my voice sounding thin and frantic in the moaning dark.

Defeated by the purple-dark, my lantern failed to ignite. Desperate, I pulled and pulled at the striker. All that it caused were brief flares. I tossed it aside.

The flares when I pulled the striker—a memory nagged.

Heavy snow fell and clung to me, a sticky casing that accumulated, slowing my already feeble pace. I tried to brush it off, but the snow resisted, adhering and thickening until it locked my arms.

I screamed but kept moving . . . couldn't let legs turn to plaster. The tumble of snow-spore-sludge dissipated. A wall of fleshy moss confronted me. Mine-worker bearers . . . Burton's park stewards . . . embedded . . . some visible only as vague shapes. The surface radiated heat and the sweet-bitter odor of feces. The wall curved; turning, I saw more wall, an enclosing cylinder, like the insides of the moss-pillars but the size of a great room. No indication of where I had entered. Above, stars glinted. Their familiarity sent me hope. Forcing myself closer to the wall, I peered into its depths, trying to identify the figures within. They linked, hand in hand, a chain of bodies that formed the frame on which the moss had built its structure. I needed to find Carson, rescue her if I could, if she had become part of this living wall.

Past the next park steward, I stopped in front of Belo. His chin tilted forward, and his mouth . . . his mouth wrapped around a pulsing moss-appendage. His eyes stood open, staring at nothing, blank and unblinking. I continued down the line. Everyone I passed was the same as Belo, even Burton, his features now devoid of the fervor that had possessed him. Then, another mine-worker, and Carson.

I thought I could cut her loose with the pickaxe but, unable to do more than wriggle my fingers, I had no way to get it. I looked around, hoping for something, an outcropping of rock, that I might use to scrape the stuff off. But the ground was uniform, flat. With my fingers, I probed the encrustations; the surface had hardened into a crust. Crust could break. I flung myself down. Though the floor was spongy, the impact caused fissures to appear in my carapace. Repetition loosened more. With one arm free, I cleared enough snow-sludge to reach into my pack. Pickaxe in hand, I slashed at the wall between Carson and the mine worker. The moaning changed tone, a staccato that could only mean alarm. I cut more. Chunks fell, a quivering pile. I peeled a layer away from Carson's thighs.

The wall began to shudder, and the linked bodies writhed. Something on the periphery caught my attention, a bulge about shoulder-high. It flowed toward me.

Frantic, I slashed at the wall. Another slab fell, and beyond lay darkness, the darkness of nighttime.

Then the bulge was upon me. It projected itself from the wall, a globe of moss-flesh on an arm-like stalk. The globe opened like a fingerless hand the size of my chest. It thrust at me. I dodged, then hacked at it. The hand pulled back, out of reach, and closed itself into a ball. The surface rearranged into eyes, mouth. And looked at me with a cruel caricature of Hays' face. I embedded the pick between the eyes. The Hays-head jerked it from my hand. I lunged to recover it and slashed again. The head drooped, sagging to the floor. Another slash severed it from the stalk.

I resumed my cutting along Carson's side, lengthening the hole. A breeze pushed its way in, cold and fine.

The floor rippled, pushing me against the wall. I recovered my balance and turned to look. In the middle of the room, the surface had puckered,

opening into a wide, mouth-like projection. The moaning grew louder
and faster, and the floor rippled again. With each moan, a plume erupted
from the projection-mouth, belching spores . . . choking-binding-dust—
spore dust. The flares when I pulled my lantern's striker. Now I recalled.
Some mosses were cultivated for their spores, for use in explosives.

Another hacking cut, and the wall parted. But a second wall-bulge
advanced, larger; it reached for me. I stepped back, then lunged toward
Carson.

The impact freed her. We tumbled to the outside. Behind us, within
the cylinder, the spore-plume continued. Some moss-spores fell around
us but most shot up, darkening the sky. The hands of those who had
linked with Carson reached toward each other across the gap where her
body had been. Moss-flesh expanded to fill the hole. I dumped out Carson's pack, scooped up the lantern, and ran to the moss wall. The lantern
ignited on the second try. I flung it in.

Flames spurted from the top of the moss structure, roaring anger of
flame and heat. The stench of singed hair choked me. My hair. I made
it back to Carson. The moss structure glowed, and shook. Carson
shook too. Gelatinous moss blocked her nose and the remains of the
moss-appendage filled her mouth. The moss-appendage was slimy, difficult to grip, but I dug my fingers in and pulled. A strip the length of
my arm came out. I flung it as far as I could, and cleansed my hands in
snow.

She gagged, vomited, and screamed, a drawn out wail. Flames subsided and the moss walls crumbled. Snow turned to hot mist. I held
her, for a peaceful moment. Then the mountain roared. A heave of earth
tossed us. I slid across land mimicking violent water, Everlasting Current whipped by maelstroms of summer. The air turned dark with flying
debris. Eyes shut against the grit, I reached to pull Carson closer. But
where was she? Lost again.

Moss-tentacles stretched me, dough-like, into a thin disk, and hurled
me skyward. I floated, and floating brought a peace unlike anything I
had known. Infinite shades of blue caressed me. But the blue acquired

heat; sparks cracked in blue membranes, stinging sparks. A spark lashed my back. Another dissolved the blue, leaving nothing but the scalding sparks. The current sped me onward. A roar filled my being.

And, later, I lay upon a gray-streaked land inhabited by hobbling shapes that carved individual paths, like river buoys each moving along a private current. I joined them.

VALLEY OF THE FALLING CLOUDS

Rex discovered the valley near dusk. On reaching the top of a ridge, his gaze cleared the rim of surrounding rock, and he cried out, yelping at the beauty that stretched below him, an undulating carpet of the darkest green. Over a pinnacle, a hawk hung silhouetted against the sky. The breeze blew cool against his face, and he took off his broad-brimmed white hat to let the wind trickle through his hair. Music from a creek below drew him down the steep slope through a gap in the rocks.

He had been rambling the back country for a week, following the blue winds of early spring, stopping when he felt the need, wandering with the randomness of thought. He had spent the past year and a half working on a ranch near Moonsocket, sharing a bunkhouse with a feather-collector named Montgomery and several others. On finishing a job, he usually moved on, but this time leaving would be difficult. He had grown to love the area around Moonsocket, the surrounding hills and ranches, the town with its willow trees and tin-roofed homes, the shops laid out along the river.

Most of all, he loved Apple Jane, the herbalist's daughter.

He made his way through a field of knee-grass to the creek heard from above. The water had sliced a curving trough through the valley floor and was lined with willow and oak. He took off his boots and backpack and sat on the bank to soak his feet. The swirling water chilled him at first, and silvery perch no larger than a half-dollar swam up to nibble at his toes, but as he gazed around at the hills and flowers, listening to the calls of the birds, serenity descended on him.

Rex had met Apple Jane because of his fever, contracted soon after moving to the area. The ranch boss took him to the herbalist for treatment, and on waking from delirium he saw a young woman with a blurry face sitting near him. When he smiled at her she ran from the room. He wondered how he could have frightened her. A few minutes later she returned with a cup of mint and goldenseal tea.

He remained at the herbalist's for several days, regaining strength, and Apple Jane took care of him, fed him, read to him. One morning, when she came in with a mug of steaming fruit-water, he told her that he was strong enough to get up and eat breakfast at the table. She helped him out of bed, and as he stood, with her strong arm keeping him steady, he had a vision of the two of them together, holding hands before a fire. Cautious, afraid of rejection, Rex hid his feelings.

Rex valued caution—it had kept him alive through blizzards, cave explorations, shipwreck, brownrot epidemics, and the war with the people who dammed the river above Moonsocket. A temporary worker with no great allegiance to the community, he had nevertheless joined the fight, helping to defeat the dambuilders and their beaver allies.

Though governed by caution, Rex didn't lack bravery. He had proved that in the war with the dambuilders. While the town council bickered over the chain of command, Rex led a company of wolves in a midnight raid on the dambuilders' headquarters. While the wolves drove the dambuilders and their beaver allies downstream, away from the headwaters, Rex ignited the dam with carbide from his caving light. "Let them stay downstream where they can't hurt us," Rex told the crowd that had gathered by the river to celebrate. Apple Jane kissed his cheek. He smelled the rosemary in her hair and wished he could know her feelings.

Moonsocket was a well-kept, logical sort of place, with board side-walks and a graveled main street. Founded originally by immigrants from Arcadia, its position on the banks of the Caslon River placed it between the larger towns of Alexander to the north, and the provincial capitol in the south, where the Caslon joined the much greater Zephyr before reaching the sea, and Moonsocket was able to take advantage of the river's bountiful flow of trade. It was a town similar to others that Rex had known in his nomadic life, and the aloofness of many of its residents did nothing to promote goodwill, but a fondness for the place grew in him. And was he not the defender of their homes? Yet he wanted no glory for himself. Though what did he want? Constant travel had served as substitute for wanting, but now the questions arose.

Rex sat, entranced by the water and the swaying branches. The quarter-moon floated over the hills, catching him in its pale luminescence. He wouldn't go back to Moonsocket, not yet, but he wouldn't move on to another job in another town either. Instead, he would dwell here for a time, alone in the valley. Solitude would be his guide.

Why Rex Stayed
1. He liked to look at hills.
2. Spring-fed creek.
3. Wild strawberries.

But such an action cannot be codified in this straightforward manner. Despite Rex's various wanderings and jobs (his lack of a permanent anchoring place), he considered himself a social being, and found easy friendship wherever he went. Restlessness does not equal a desire for solitude. This valley then, and his time here, represented a point between, an unlocked and unoccupied time, not permanent abode, not transit to a new job, town, or ship. Cloaked in the beauty of this pastoral scene, anything could be possible, even settling here for a longer time, even . . . a transition to permanence . . . asking Apple Jane to join him.

Rex's first viewing of the valley in morning light did nothing to change his mind, and he devoted the day to exploring. Across the creek, wild-flowers bloomed, pink, blue, and yellow waves. The creek flowed in through a thin gap at one end, growing wider and deeper downstream, where it disappeared below ground. Several oaks of great girth watched over the southern end of the vale. The land on one side of the creek stood about twenty feet higher than the other. The terrain on the higher side was rougher, but he found a flat area above the high-water mark, about midway through the valley. Among the trees, Rex planned the building and placement of a shack. He staked out its dimensions, picturing the walls rising around him, a protective shell.

Late in the afternoon, he moved his campsite to the place he had picked for his shack. He laid out his bedroll in the spot he wanted the bed to be and made a fire where he planned to build the fireplace. The creek provided trout for supper, and after eating, he stretched upon his bedroll, smiling at the stars. This is home, he said to himself.

Since leaving his parents' farm at fifteen, Rex had lived a restless life, taking various jobs and never staying anywhere long. As he lay under the stars, he thought about how he had never committed to staying in one place. Would he be able to settle here, or would something deep and unresolved push him away? The night wore on, but he couldn't sleep. The night noises seemed unusually loud, and the gentle stars that had glowed with such welcome now bored into him like a million pinpricks. He pulled the cover over his eyes and kept repeating to himself, this will be my home, my hope . . . home . . . hope.

Sleepy-eyed in the morning, Rex looked around at the creek and wooded hills. Yes, this *was* where he wanted to live, but he couldn't do much without building supplies and food. He needed to return to Moonsocket, should in fact leave immediately, unwise to delay the beginning of con-struction—now was the perfect season to begin. Though first, he spent several days scouting the slopes of the surrounding hills, making a list of useful plants so he would know what additional seeds he would need to buy from Apple Jane's mother. Though what would he say to Apple Jane?

The question occupied him all the way back to Moonsocket, and even after arriving, he found no answer. He decided to concentrate on what he understood best: building his shack. He would construct its walls from a combination of poles and clay-mud mixed with straw. The clay-mud he could dig from his building site and other spots along the creek. Furniture, he would build when needed. He hired a wagon and pack horses and asked Montgomery and some other friends from the ranch to help.

When everything was ready, they tethered the horses at the herbalist's house. In his head, Rex cataloged the supplies that were packed on the back of the nearest horse. Had he bought enough flour? He should get more—he didn't know when he would be coming back. Laughter and music came from the house next door. His companions laughed too, and entered the house of music and laughter. His stomach tightened as he walked up the path to Apple Jane's front door. She looked up from the sofa and smiled a soft smile, as though expecting him. She had tied her dark hair back with a green scarf, showing the scar on her forehead, a wound received as a child when she tried to pet a broken-legged bobcat her mother was treating.

"I smell like the desert wind blowing north out of Byzantium," he said.

"I know," she said.

He felt shy, but sat beside her. "The valley I found, flowers blooming, pecan trees, the creek, no one else near. . . . "

"It sounds magnificent," she said. He breathed in and out, in and out. He knew he couldn't keep everything inside, but still, he couldn't talk, couldn't open himself to her, not yet—soon—after a time in his valley. He touched her hand, where it lay on the sofa.

A week out from Moonsocket Rex began to worry about finding his valley again. He wasn't seeing the landmarks he remembered. Part of the problem was that when he came through before, he wasn't looking for anything, and the whole area was new to him. None of the people helping him knew the area either. All but one, a short, hairy fence carver named Virgil, were recent immigrants to Moonsocket.

They stopped to camp for the night near a spring; Rex made a fire, and Montgomery began preparing their dinner.

"It's somewhere near," Rex said to Virgil.

"My grandmother," Virgil said. "She heard stories from those who came before: 'To the north and west, across the jagged hills, lies a shadow.' Then something else about the valley of the wind's dominion. I don't know what that was supposed to mean."

"Maybe it's a weather pattern we should look for, something unique to the area, like a thermal gradient," Montgomery said. "In the morning, I'll study a hawk's flight pattern. That should tell us something."

Virgil had shot a deer earlier, and while the meat roasted, they discussed the peculiarities of weather. One of the others described a coastal town he had lived in where the wind always built delicate sand columns at points marking low and high tides.

The next morning, Rex awakened first and wandered out, following a stream. He tried to duplicate his mood from the day he found the valley, but thoughts of Apple Jane kept intruding. After his fever, just before he left the herbalist's house to return to work, Apple Jane had taken him on a short walk along the river south of town. She told him how the language of birds contained fourteen vowels and ten consonants. Lost in his reminiscence of Apple Jane, Rex didn't feel the ground rising until he looked at the water, now about ten feet below him. Ahead, the hills rose and he rose with them. Through a cleft at the top, his valley waited.

Montgomery and the others helped Rex unload, but the next day they took the wagon and horses back to Moonsocket. Alone, Rex began work on his shack. The labor helped him think, and as the shack took form, so did his ideas. He dedicated his work to Apple Jane, and the hope that she would someday join him. When he tired from setting poles and mixing straw with clay-mud, he dug out his garden, planted beans, cabbage, corn, and potatoes. He sifted the dark earth through his fingers, sniffing the rich clumps. He had grown up on a farm, watched by his three older sisters and a harried, ineffectual mother, until age seven or eight when his father forced him into the fields. While his father pushed an ox-drawn plow, Rex carried a pouch heavy with seed, breathing in the dense aroma of soil, animals, and his father's sweat. Once, he had stumbled, spilling seeds over the furrows. His father slapped him, hard, knocking him down.

All these years since leaving home, Rex had avoided the soil and its reminders of his youth. But now, in this valley, *his valley*, he spread his arms wide, welcoming all that the earth might give him.

He worked slowly, enjoying the spring weather. He would take many breaks, tramping through the valley and up the sides of the surrounding hills, hunting, fishing. During one of his rambles, he found, on a low ridge, a deposit of crumbly gray rock from which grew a mass of mushrooms—pasty-white tubes about the size of his index finger, with bulbous tops. He squatted in front of them and plucked one. A rancid stink erupted. Coughing, he dropped the mushroom and stood, backed away from where they sprouted. Everything flashed red—a sparkling red mist obscured the valley. He reached toward a nearby tree to steady himself, but in the dizzying red, his groping hand found only air; he tumbled from the ridge.

The cry of a hawk pierced the fog in Rex's head, and he opened his eyes. The violet sky of evening hid behind low-hanging clouds that reminded him of fanged jellyfish. He found himself sprawled at the foot of the ridge, now twenty or so feet above him. He had landed in a clump of thistles. Their spiny stalks lay crushed beneath him. His fingers burned where he had held the mushroom, and a throbbing rose through his body. He lay without moving, waiting for the throb to centralize itself. After a time, he wiggled his fingers and raised his forearms. On lifting his arms over his head, pain in his left shoulder made him cry out, and he reached with his right hand to probe the injury.

A squirrel chattered at him from a nearby rock, a high, grating sound that combined with Rex's other aches to make his head throb. "You think I've fixed myself bad, this time," he said to the squirrel. Though Rex was not the sort to talk to himself, he often held conversations with nearby animals, not knowing or caring whether they understood him.

"Well, maybe you're right. Let's see if I can get up." He bent at the waist, raising himself to a seated position, then drew his feet in and stood. His left leg gave way from the pressure, but he kept from falling by shifting his weight to the right. "Looks like I'm going to need your rock," he said, and limped toward the squirrel, which skittered away unquietly. Rex sat on the rock and extended his left leg, carefully flexing knee and hip. He had apparently fallen on his left side, bruising his hip and shoulder, though nothing appeared to be broken.

Later, after a stumbling, limping walk punctuated by several necessary rest-stops, he reached his shack and lowered himself into the cold-flowing stream without bothering to remove any clothing besides boots. There he lay, letting the water soothe his bruises. After a time, he heard a horse approaching from the south and scrambled out to see who was coming into his territory.

A man on a white horse rode up the valley. Rex waved. The man ignored him but kept coming in his direction. On reaching the half-built shack, horse and rider stopped. The man still hadn't looked at Rex. The man had long, gray hair tied back with a red bandanna. His face was beardless and lined from age or long exposure to the outdoors. When the man stepped down from his horse, Rex saw that he was blind.

"Nice valley here, but it stands in the wind's dominion." The blind man's voice rasped, sounding as though he had ridden far without a drink. Rex filled a cup from the creek and pushed it into the man's hands. The blind man drank. The horse drank from the creek and wandered off to graze. Rex waited for the blind man to continue speaking.

"Generations ago, seventeen brothers founded the city of stone as a monument to their mother, whose suffering in childbirth caused her death after the emergence of the sixth son, who forever blamed himself, though his brothers did not.

"The North Tower housed the offices of the prefect, a man renowned for his deeds on the battlefield and unsurpassed culinary skills. 'The hands of a true king hold the sensitivity of a chef,' says the proverb, but in a democracy, the prefect had no hope of attaining royalty.

"He pledged his support to the president, a woman both wise and beautiful, and he became her most treasured advisor, as well as personal chef.

"Such stories never end well. In the heart of the president's husband, a man adept in business but not the kitchen, jealousy grew. He arranged to send the prefect from the city in a quest for the fabled fungus that grows only from the detritus of clouds and causes red blindness if handled improperly. Alas, the good prefect never returned."

The blind man tossed Rex's cup into the creek and whistled. His horse trotted up to him. He remounted and rode up the valley toward the northern mountains. Rex watched him diminish with the distance. It wasn't until the next morning that he discovered how the blind man's horse had eaten all of the young pea shoots and greens in Rex's garden.

Rex thatched the roof, enjoying scents of preserved summer that rose from the reeds and rushes he had gathered. Despite the partial destruction of his crops, and the blind man's troubling tale, every morning when he woke and looked around, at the fireplace, walls, windows, rough table and chairs, he couldn't believe his good fortune. It was as though a long-closed gate had opened inside him. Everything felt cleansed, renewed. At night, the stars smiled down, approving of the elegance with which he had constructed his dwelling. The shack was a marvel of simplicity, well-suited to the rustic life he planned there. Of the shack itself, there was no particular item he valued more than another.

Always in the employ of others, he had never built for himself, and he found this activity had strengthened certain aspects of his will, as if the creation of his world here had also formed in him a new confidence. The only drag to this new sense was his expectations for Apple Jane. Having never fully expressed his desires to her, why did he think she would even be interested in moving to this lonely valley?

For someone like Rex, accustomed to the life of a wanderer, his shack and the land around it constituted his own nation, with himself as king, himself taking on the power his name implied. He would rule well, and as lone subject he would respect the king's wishes.

Apple Jane though, she was a town-dweller, immersed in life there. He knew from talk with Virgil that she had been courted by many: Dowling the baker, Lebkowsky the minstrel, who also ran a children's theater company, and several others. But Rex assumed, with a confidence new to him, that her truest feelings were for him.

His crops bloomed and fruited; he harvested, preserving what he could, by drying, brining, or storing in his root-cellar. Soon, he would need to return to Moonsocket for dried beans, flour, and other supplies. At the thought of that . . . Moonsocket and she who lived there . . . he froze. What did that mean, this immobilization? Days passed. He left his bed later each morning, unable to convince himself to rise and push through the summer hours. Moonsocket and Apple Jane—the two were entwined, tangled even. To the west, Virgil had told him, lay the town of Lamping, smaller than Moonsocket but without Moonsocket's extra complications.

He packed food for the journey and set off; on the way, he listed his reasons for avoiding Apple Jane, but none of them convinced him that he wasn't avoiding the prospect of disappointment.

Lamping proved to be a pleasant enough town, at a higher elevation than Moonsocket, with a well-stocked grocery. He bought a donkey named Evening and packed his supplies onto her back. The return to his valley . . . a thrill that overcame all doubt. "This is home," he said to Evening. "You'll find much grazing, but please stay out of the garden."

———

But Autumn brought destructive forces. A thunderstorm stalled over the highest peak, sending torrents down the valley. The wind pushed against his walls and forced itself through the window frames. Rex watched the creek, worried it would rise and carry him off. He assembled a pack of food and clothing and waited, ready to leave if necessary. An object scraped the side of his shack. The sound made him cringe—he couldn't stand the thought of something happening to the home he had worked so hard to build. He ran to the door to look out through the whipping, slashing rain. A tree with a long, straight trunk and flopping branches swept past.

When the storm finally moved on, Rex walked outside to a sunny day. The creek remained high. On the other side, where the land was lower, water pooled and eddied. A dead bear sprawled over the crown of a fallen tree. He wished he could get at the animal to slaughter it before the meat spoiled, but the water was too wild and high to cross.

The shed he had build to shelter Evening still stood, but the donkey was gone. He hoped she would find her way back.

Gray boulders littered the slopes of the hills to the southeast. The boulders hadn't been there before the storm. Perhaps the land had eroded, exposing bedrock. He walked up toward the boulders, his feet squishing the sodden ground. The area around the boulders looked undisturbed; the grasses, though flattened by the rain, remained rooted in place. Perhaps, dislodged by the storm, the boulders had rolled from the hilltop. Closer, he felt heat radiating from the boulders. They hissed and popped, emitting sharp jets of steam. The sizes of the strange boulders varied, though each of them was a near-perfect sphere. Their color and texture reminded him of clouds.

Deciding to wait for them to cool, Rex returned to his shack for flatbread and dried fish, which he ate in the meadow near the cloud boulders. After finishing, he approached the nearest cloud boulder. Its surface had contorted into myriad ruffles and lines, all running in the same direction. He touched it: still warm, and rough, like pumice.

Some of the boulders were coconut-sized. Most were much larger, large enough to crush his home. He carried one of the smaller pieces down to his shack. It had occurred to him that they would make fine building materials.

Another storm crashed through the valley in mid-afternoon and stalled. Forced inside by the weather, Rex sat at his table and began making a shirt from a flour sack. He didn't want to worry about cloud boulders, but the storm distracted him. Leaving the shirt unfinished, he built a fire in the fireplace. While the thunder, sharp and heavy, banged outside, he lay on the floor in front of the fire, staring at a knot in the beam above him. In the dim light, thick with the threat of swirling wind and rain, the knot coalesced into a face, a twisted face, the face of his father.

Why had he never noticed the resemblance? It angered him that his father's image had invaded the sanctuary of his shack. He closed his eyes, hoping that when he opened them again the light would have changed, casting off the illusion. He tried to replace the face with Apple Jane's, but his father kept pushing her aside. Like a bear, he stood over Rex, loud and hateful. Rex's cheek throbbed from the blow, and he pressed it into the soil, letting moist earth soothe him, but his father would not allow rest. He dug a boot into Rex's side, yelling at him to get up and finish the job.

Lightning crashed, a flash sensed through Rex's closed eyelids, followed by a boom that shook the walls of his shack. In the morning, his father's face had left the knot, but unease still gripped him. He went outside and circled the exterior, checking for damage. Walls, roof, windows—everything had withstood nature's barrage.

The storm had dumped broken clouds on a steep knoll about fifty yards from his shack. They were beautiful, all gray-white and steamy in the cool air. He heard a cracking sound from somewhere beyond them. On the slope of another, higher hill, a line of trees parted, their trunks snapped off by a wave of cloud boulders. He stared up at them, thinking they held no danger. The boulders slammed into those on the low hill, dislodging some. One massive boulder rolled toward the creek. Its momentum carried it into the air to crash on the other side. Another rolled down, closer. He could tell from the angle that it would miss his shack. Then it hit a tree stump and changed direction.

Accelerated by the impact with the stump, the cloud boulder rushed down the grassy slope. Rex threw himself into the clover and covered his head. The crash blew pieces of his shack into the air and over his body. He lay still, listening. A wall thumped to the ground. He counted to ten before turning to look. The chimney and one wall remained standing. The boulder had flattened everything else.

The back of his arms stung from splinter scrapes. He sat up, looking at the jumble of broken timber, straw, and mud, then at the hills around him, the red and gold autumn leaves, the creek. A honeybee settled on a flower near his knee. The broken cloud lay a few yards past the ruins. A dusting of crushed mud and twisted beams spoiled the meadow.

Rex stood and walked into the middle of what had been his shack. Such care he had taken in building: sanding, cutting, joining. He glanced behind him, up at the trail the boulder had plowed through the grassy slope of the hill, then sat among his dented tin plates, staring at his splintered chairs. After a time, he got up and built a fire in the fireplace. It would be dark in a few hours, and the nights had been cold.

While the fire caught, he sifted through the debris, stacking salvageable items in the corner between the fireplace and the remaining wall. Though he hadn't much of an appetite, he filled an iron pot with water, added potatoes and cabbage, and hung it over the fire. It made him sad to do it, but he pushed his shattered chairs into the flames. His bed had been crushed, and the mattress ripped open. Feathers, a gift from Montgomery, lay in clumps around it. He stuffed them back in and patched the tear with the material of his unfinished shirt.

Steam rose from the pot, and the gentle aroma of cooking vegetables calmed him. He lay down, staring at the sky where the roof had been. The stars had not yet emerged. In the west, the sky remained clear, but in the east clouds obscured the moon. Rex had always hated the selfishness of clouds, the way they camped around the moon. It wasn't fair how they kept people from enjoying its glow. These clouds, destroyers of his home—they taunted him, but he wouldn't let them win. He would rebuild.

Looking up at the night sky, he imagined what Apple Jane would be

doing. Probably sitting down to dinner with her mother. Maybe a traveler seeking medication had joined them.

Rex should have remained in Moonsocket, forced himself to talk to
Apple Jane. Now the clouds had wrecked everything. The vegetables sim-
mered until the fire burned down. He fell asleep without eating. A few
hours later, he woke from the cold, got a blanket, removed the cooking
pot from the hearth, and rebuilt the fire. Asleep again, he dreamed of a
shack made from dried heads of cabbage.

With no roof to block it, the morning sun woke him. Rex forced himself to sort the wreckage. He worked the morning through, working
without thinking, and as he worked he felt better. A new shack took
shape in his mind—planks this time, with two rooms, a floor, a wood-
burning stove, and a sink, with water piped from the creek. But he kept
looking up at the hills. What if the next storm left more cloud boulders?
No point in making a better shack if it was to be exposed to another
disaster. He would build a wall at the base of the hill to deflect cloud
boulders as they rolled down.

He began by carrying stones from the creek bed and broken shack
timber to the spot he thought most suitable for the wall. Then it occurred
to him to try cloud boulders too—he liked the irony of that, using them
to defeat their brothers.

As he walked up the hill to where the first boulders had appeared, a
cool breeze chilled his neck. In this valley, winter could strike early. The
weather might force him to leave and rebuild in the spring. He could
spend the winter in Moonsocket. His stomach jumped a nervous jump.
The thought of Apple Jane's smile, her dark hair, and the way she had
laughed when she made his wool hat. During his recovery from illness,
she had knitted it from yarn of deep brown and gave it to him when he
was ready to return to work. She had touched his head, measuring it,
feeling the contours. The touch—recalling it, the warmth and strength
of her fingers on his head—he realized that was what had made him
love her.

Rolling the cloud boulders, even the largest, took little effort. He levered them using a pole and smaller boulder, then guided them downslope. His wall would make Apple Jane proud. She would marvel at his resourcefulness, his ability to reshape his life from the wreckage. Thinking about Apple Jane made the work easier. His wall would protect the new shack. All he had to do was make it strong enough. He sang as he worked.

"Menelaus was a fisherman
Caught the pale moon in his net
He let it out and made a wish
That he would die a wealthy man."

A few yards from the base of the hills, he dug a shallow trench, shaping it like the prow of a ship and rolling the largest cloud boulders into it. He stacked more on top, fitting them neatly into the gaps.

When the sun touched the tops of the hills, he stopped for the day. After dinner, he lay by the creek watching the glint of fireflies darting through the clearing. On a night like this—who needed a shack? He closed his eyes. Degrading walls of falling embers in the moonlight falling embers falling embers falling stones. Wheels becoming wells becoming walls.

The next morning, Rex rose early again and began work. The breeze still blew in cool from the northeast, and he put on a heavier shirt. From somewhere beyond the hills a wolf howled. He hadn't had much contact with wolves since the time they had helped him defeat the dambuilders. Wolves were like that. They would appear if he needed them. But they couldn't help him make the wall or rebuild his shack.

When Rex was a child, his father had trapped a wolf cub and caged it in their barn. Its howls made Rex cry. He had crept out of the house at midnight and lifted the latch on the cage. The door swung open a little. The wolf pushed it out farther with its muzzle. It had looked at him

with large eyes, as though wary of a trick. Rex turned his back. The wolf
darted to the barn door. It stopped there, looking at him, then it was
gone.

Stopping to camp his first night after leaving home, he heard wolves
coming. He backed against the side of a cliff and waved his walking staff.
The wolves' eyes shined in the light from his fire. One wolf crept forward
and dropped a rabbit. He recognized the now-grown cub and thanked
it. The wolf howled back, joined by its companions. Rex knew that he
would be safe with them. The wolves showed him how to hunt, how to
sense the weather, helped him survive his first year alone.

Rex bent to examine some grayish residue at the base of his cloud
boulder wall, touching it with a fingertip. A powdery substance came
off, adhering to his skin. His eyes watered and he felt dizzy. He found
himself sprawled on the flattened grass, though he didn't remember
falling. A reddish mist fuzzed everything—hills, creek, the cloud boulders. He rolled onto his back and sat up.

At the base of the cloud boulders, half a dozen mushrooms had
sprouted during the night. Why here? The only place he had seen them
was in that deposit of crumbly rock.

A horrible sensation pushed at him, and he slipped his hatchet from
his belt. With the blunt end he hammered on a piece of cloud. It broke
into a gray powder identical to what he had found the other mushrooms
growing from. He put the ax back into his belt and looked at the hills
that had once seemed so inviting. Something in these solid clouds caused
the mushrooms to flourish.

The wind picked up, whipping the tops of trees. The breeze on his
neck felt colder than the day before, and it was getting darker. A wall
of clouds moved from the north, pushing their way over his valley. Fall
blizzard—that must have been why the wolves had howled. He stopped
working and ran down to his shack. He would have to erect a lean-to
against the remaining wall.

Knowing the unpredictable nature of these storms, he worked quickly, building a fire first. There were enough salvageable wall sections and roof thatch—he stacked them into a lumpy hut large enough to make a shelter for him and his salvaged belongings.

The first wet flakes began falling.

He slipped the wool hat Apple Jane had made him onto his head and sat by the creek watching the snow. Winter would be harsh in the valley.

Daylight faded, and the snow fell harder, forcing him to shelter himself under the igloo. He removed Apple Jane's hat and held it against his chest. The cloud boulders and the mushrooms they fertilized—this valley wasn't safe, not for him and not for Apple Jane. He had wanted so badly for this to be his home, but nothing lasted, nothing but the dream. He fell asleep holding the soft knit in his arms.

Cold air and weak sunlight woke him. He assembled a pack of food and left. Trudging through the snow, he could feel everything he had won in the valley draining from him, all the assurance and pride gained in building his little kingdom slipped out like the mist of his breath.

Atop the peak from which he had first viewed the valley, he looked down. The sun emerged from the wall of gray, casting everything once again in beauty. Snow in a smooth sheet covered the ground and the ruins of his shack. Only the chimney stood out from the snow. Smoke from his dying fire curled up into the clear sky. He turned away. On his return to Moonsocket, he would ask the herbalist what she knew of the mushrooms. Perhaps there was a way to guard against them. Though he knew there wouldn't be.

He walked south with Apple Jane's hat on his head and a heavy pack on his back. Past the valley, there was no snow. It was as though he had gone through a sharp break in the seasons, but the gentle weather only darkened his mood.

Four days later, he reached Moonsocket under a sapphire sky. All the shops were open, people everywhere. The crowded sidewalks bothered him. He had been alone for so long. A man nodded a greeting—someone

Rex had met in the war against the dambuilders, a former comrade in battle, but he couldn't remember the name, and that phase of his life seemed so distant he could barely equate it to his present condition.

At the herbalist's house Rex dropped his pack on the porch and knocked. No answer, and no one in back at the greenhouses either. He entered the house by the unlocked front door and flopped into an over-stuffed chair to wait. Tired, so tired, from the journey, from the frantic work on his wall, from the storm. He hadn't sat in a chair like this in so long, too soft for him, but the fire made up for it. This wasn't a bad way to live. If only he had come as visitor rather than refugee. Where were they? He tried to recall what they would be doing, but he didn't know the day of the week. He closed his eyes. And the cloud boulders rained down, smothering him. He reached out, hoping to find a way to lessen his pain—the loss of his shack, his life.

The sound of creaking porch-boards woke him. The front door opened. Apple Jane and a sandy-haired man came in together, holding hands. The man turned Apple Jane to face him, then kissed her. She saw Rex and pulled away from the man, as though embarrassed by Rex's sight of her with her new lover.

"I didn't know you were back," she said. She knelt by his chair. "You smell like the desert wind blowing north out of Byzantium." She kissed him, and her lips tasted of jasmine tea.

Once, the taste of Apple Jane's lips would have blinded Rex. The crunch, the tearing, awful crunch that the cloud boulder made on its impact with Rex's shack filled his ears with a darkening mist. Dark shapes of more clouds pressed against him, through which he clawed and slashed his way, gagging from air tainted by desolation.

Apple Jane sat on the sofa where he had pushed her, mouth shaped somewhere between the end of her kiss and an "oh" of surprise. The sandy-haired man now lay at Rex's feet, and Rex took pleasure in the slowness of the man's movements, and the way he clutched his face. Rex wiped the man's blood from his knuckles.

No indecision now, no inability to speak. "I came to say goodbye," he said. Apple Jane's mouth continued to hold that in-between shape. Rex walked out into the street, walked and walked, then something invisible struck him and he collapsed onto a nearby bench. But not from a physical blow. An amorphous "thing," an "it." He had been sitting so comfortably at the herbalist's. The fireplace, dried lavender scents mixed with sage and rose petal . . . then the "it" struck again, bashed at him, with a force that left him faint. A wall enclosed him, brick by brick, a wall of his own futility. Of course Apple Jane had never loved him, or had only loved him the way one loves sick and wounded creatures. And he, perhaps once, perhaps back then, before his shack, had been one of the sickly, needing healing and comfort. But since that time, he had encountered forces beyond what most could weather.

Across the street was Woolwright's Tavern. Honking calls made him look up in time to catch the slow, arcing flight of a troop of cranes. How would it be to join them, flap powerful wings against the air, pushing ever forward to the warm coast of the south and back again in the spring? They passed from sight, but he continued to stare at the clear sky. This is it, this street, this sky. This is what lies beneath the skin and gives a body strength. They knew the sky, these cranes, as he knew the earth.

He entered the tavern and sat at a table in the back, ordered dinner. He could still picture the flock of cranes, suspended in the evening sky like a mobile, and his mind rose to follow them.

PART THREE

in the undiscovered small town

IN SPRINGDALE TOWN

The lonely road is my companion
A faithful friend in times of pain
It serves me well in all my rambling
Through fire and snow and driving rain

I was not always lost and damned
Nor doomed to live a life disgraced
But darling Maggie, she did shun me
For a man of handsome face

(chorus)
Now the days, they pass in sorrow
For my lost love, no wedding gown
I last saw my Maggie dying
By the river's edge in Springdale town

—Traditional

1

Richard Shelling left his rented Santa Monica home on a weekend evening, with no particular destination other than away. Earlier that day, while attending a brunch at a television producer's beach house—he attended many parties—looking down from a balcony at the groves of his fellow actors, he heard a voice in his ear whispering "Away, take yourself away." He glanced at his companions, assuming that one of them had spoken, but, as usual, they were taking turns not listening to each other's stories. Shelling set his glass of rum punch on a table and left. At home, he packed a bag.

His impulse propelled him east, rather than north or south. On the edge of the continent, west was impossible without a ship, and he understood this to be a road trip. Besides, he had grown up and gone to college in the northwest. East signified new territory, and the exploration of it would fortify him, grant him insights into previously hidden realms. He drove toward Interstate 10, then to 15. In Barstow he stopped for gas and bought a road atlas and two compact discs of truck-driving songs; back in his car, he inserted the first disc and studied the atlas as sounds of horns and snare drum readied him for the journey. ✤ Las Vegas was next, and although he had no desire to see that fabled city, it stood between him and Interstate 70's uninterrupted cross-country pavement. Distance plus thought equals change, he decided.

✤ Various Artists, *Songs of Route 66: All American Highway* and *More Songs of Route 66: Roadside Attractions*, Lazy S.O.B. 1997 and 2001. This type of music has a certain nostalgic appeal for some. Oh, that open road, the wind in your hair. The feeling, however, loses something in its transcription to a compact disc player in a mid-size, plushy Japanese car that reduces road noise to a happy little hum and is not meant to be driven with the windows down. Still, there remains the satisfactions of the centerline, tires eating distance, and viewing the sky through tinted glass. ✤

First light of the new day found him a few miles short of the Colorado border. He had never driven into the sunrise, and the intensity of the light, the tactile pinks and yellows filtered through his caffeinated brain, thrilled him. Turning up the music, he sang to the dawn.

By the time he reached Massachusetts (after sleep-stops in Kansas City, then Ohio, where he left I-70 for a northern route), the highway miles had stripped his California shellac and softened him. The past fourteen years he had spent acting in assorted television programs, years he would have to describe as lucrative but unrewarding, and he found the appeal of a simple, rural life growing in him, coalescing into a picture of a farmhouse surrounded by open countryside.

Fields gave way to hills and low mountains, to billboards advertising ski slopes. A peculiar yellow-gray mist filled the hollows, and he powered up his car windows to block a growing chill. He thought he saw flashes in the mist, like a horde of fireflies. Where the road slid between a sheer rock face on one side and a ravine on the other, the mist thickened, and he couldn't see the road curving. He braked sharply and turned the wheel inward. His right front tire grazed the narrow shoulder, but he managed to straighten the car. He slowed to 25, then 20, then 15. A sign announced Highway 7, Springdale, five miles. At the intersection he turned right, hoping the new road would free him from the mist.

Springdale—the name tickled his memory. He had an image of a river, and a blonde woman wearing a thin, satin dress with a plunging neckline. She wouldn't let him near her; another man interceded.

Shelling bounced his right fist off the dashboard and laughed. That wasn't real life—Springdale was the name of the town in that sexy TV drama. He had three guest appearances on it, which he had hoped would develop into a recurring role. He laughed again. The road, that was it, driving too long, couldn't even keep memories of television appearances separate from reality. He needed to stop at a motel and sleep. No sense pushing things. Springdale then. The thought of visiting this real-world namesake of a TV town appealed to him. ✹

His highway intersected with another, and he turned left. The stone buildings of the town spread before him—town hall, schools, churches, shops. He didn't see the river till he passed the library. The water drew closer to the road, and half a block farther, Shelling pulled the car into the gravel drive of a riverside park. He lowered the front windows and turned off the engine. Woodsmoke and a hint of springtime growth flavored the air. The sign over Springdale Savings showed 54 degrees, cold to his California skin, but

✹ The material contained here does not reflect the views of the producers or writers of the show *Blake's River*, nor is it meant to be a speculation on any episode of the show that has been or ever will be broadcast. Although the name "Springdale" is used throughout, it does not constitute a representation of any actual Springdale, whatever its geographic locale, or the residents thereof. ✹

he left his jacket in the car and wandered toward the water, savoring the clean air and the music of the stream.

Later that afternoon, he checked into a motel on the south edge of town. From there, he could explore the area, though there wasn't much need—he knew he would stay. When morning came, with a dance of sunlight waking him through the motel windows, the first place he visited was the real estate office on Main Street. The realtor had reddish hair, one of those stiff coifs that could only be maintained with weekly visits to the beauty parlor (which they were still called in places like Springdale). She looked at Shelling carefully, as though judging whether he was worthy enough to buy property in her proximity.

"I was thinking a farmhouse," Shelling said. "When I was a kid, I visited my Uncle Nathan on his farm in Northern California. Uncle Nathan raised goats." Shelling paused as the realtor's left eyebrow rose, an arc that he interpreted to mean he had lost points on her worthiness meter. "Not that I'm planning to raise goats here," he added, hoping he hadn't damaged his standing with her.

Despite his assumed faux-pas, the realtor drove him to an 1890s farmhouse on the river, about five miles from town. Though he gave it a day's deliberation, he knew as soon as he saw the house and land that he would take it. He arranged to have his things shipped from California, and moved in as soon as the details of purchase could be settled.

In Springdale, Shelling knew no one, but anonymity pleased him. As though instinctively planning this new life, he had always used a pseudonym for television, so his real name meant nothing to the realtor, and his face—well, *everyone* looked like someone else. Plus, the show on which he had spent the most time was a futuristic drama set on some far-off planet; for three seasons Shelling had worn orange neoprene over his face and head. Only the most avid fans read the behind-the-scenes articles showing him without make-up. When the realtor inquired about his career, he said he was a computer consultant.

The first time he went to the hardware store, the woman working the cash register asked him if he was Patrick Travis, which sounded familiar, and the name nagged at him for days, until he remembered: the character he had played for his guest appearance on *Blake's River*. He couldn't believe somebody had recognized him from it, but then maybe here, in this real-world Springdale, people took a peculiar pleasure in following the dramas of the fictional one.

Shelling's new town pulsed; he exulted in the weekly paper, reading about the issues that gripped the residents, learning from the editorials, articles, and the police report. In the letters page, residents discussed radio towers, affordable housing, water quality, and traffic. (Surprisingly, for a town its size, the volume of cars passing through on Main Street proved excessive at times—especially during the tourist seasons—and a newly opened resort complex northwest of town inspired much debate.)❖

But even with these signs of life, as a newcomer to Springdale without local connections, with no job-place interactions, Shelling could not figure out how to meet people. He started classes at the yoga center (something he had always meant to do in California), and although the teachers and classmates seemed friendly, it was hard to engage them in something that moved beyond the site of the class, into a café or bar, the socio-emotional realm of deeper contact.

Conversation, a coffee with a friend or two, the spontaneity of a large group—he needed these things. Yes, he could, and did, talk to the various waitpeople, movie ticket sellers, fishmongers, but feared that they would think him odd, coming in day upon day, buying a coffee here, a sandwich there. Perhaps *he* should open a café, or a bookshop. Then the people would come to *him*. But proprietorship would put him on the other side, the server side, and a wall existed, the barrier between the served and those serving.

❖ We were urged by Anita Fulton Long (*Springdale Town News*, October 12, 1999) to "be a little kinder to all those big, bad property developments," but the denizens of those tombstone monuments need also be kinder to the pedestrians of our town. The garages of these new high rises house those metal monsters which mount a new daily death toll as they roam our downtown streets. Ms. Long is sure "everything will be okay," but that's what boosters also told West Lee, Smithville, and Fairmont, which now face mud, flood, and smog in Necropolis. Why not cage the "carbarians" and bury them before they bury us and write our cemetery epitaphs with high-rise signatures in our own city of the dead?

Conrad Walker Burns,
109 Grapevine Street. ❖

In the Japanese restaurant, he often spoke to Monique, the redheaded waitress. He learned about her art school background, her pottery; they had made vague plans for him to visit her studio, but he worried that seeing her outside her job would change the nature of their relationship, might commit him to a course of attempted romance, the failure of which would prevent his return to the restaurant.

Without local contact, he found himself calling Vuksek, his financial advisor, every day for chats having nothing to do with investing.

2

Why had I let myself come back to this . . . place? My train passed the big farmhouse north of town, then the duck pond. At least they've made some improvements, I thought, noticing a particularly robust mallard. Welcome to Springdale. After Deirdre and Michael's wedding invitation showed up in the mail, I let desk-clutter pile over it so I would forget. I liked them, I wanted to be at their wedding, but why did it have to be in Springdale?

A week or so later, during one of my straightening fits, I found the invitation stuck on the clip that was keeping together the brief on the drunk chef case. That was what I had been looking for—the brief I mean—because the case was going to trial in a few days. I picked up the invitation and stared at it, then taped it to my computer monitor. The next morning, I made a train reservation.

My ex-wife, Caroline, grew up in Springdale. We had moved there after I finished law school.

"Why don't you set up a nice country practice," she had said.

I should have known it wasn't a good idea to move to a town that served as the setting for a murder ballad. Three years we lived together there, the last of which she had been sleeping with that bastard Dr. Malcolm. Somehow, everyone else in town knew about it. Then the fight, the threats of lawsuit, disbarment. Three years isn't enough time to connect to a place, so leaving wasn't any trouble. I had come back once, to wrap up the divorce and sell our house. I hadn't planned to return.

Another couple of minutes and I would be there. I had brought a product liability journal to read on the train, but over the last twenty minutes or so, as the distance to Springdale shrank, I kept reading, over and over, the abstract to one of the cases. ⊕

Finally, I gave up and stuffed the journal into my bag.

It was turning out to be a bleached-fish kind of day. The sky had that rotten fruit look, all bruised bananas and sour lemon. I briefly considered taking the next train home. Instead, I picked up a car at the little rental place in the station. Like last time, I had booked a room at a hotel by the shopping mall, about six miles from town. No way was I staying any closer, not that there were many choices—the bed and breakfast or the old Drake Motel, with its sticky cabinets and fried insect smell. Most of the people in town Caroline had known her whole fucking life, and I didn't want to run into any of them today. There would be enough socializing at the wedding.

Michael had moved here with Deirdre about a year before I did, to teach at the college. Dee grew up here, a couple of classes ahead of Caroline; they had known each other of course, but hadn't been close friends. Michael and I had bonded over the newcomer-in-a-small-town thing.

⊕ A woman took diet drugs and died while attempting to lose twenty-five pounds for her wedding. Something to do while planning the seating arrangements for the dinner? "Let's put Uncle Martin with the Phillipses—whoops, just lost another pound." Some months before her death, she began to hallucinate conversations with an idealized version of herself. The counterpart's history included extensive training in dance and ice skating, culminating in an Olympic figure skating competition in which she won a bronze medal. The woman wrote in her journal: "There is a hardness to her, so lithe, so strong. Jealousy overcomes me. I want her body." ⊕

It's hard, with break-ups. Some friends try to be neutral, some take sides. Michael and Dee chose mine.

Enough of that. I was starting to sound like some damn country song. I have a pretty nice life in the city, a job at a good firm. I've progressed from the little country practice to big-time product liability law. It's this town—it brings things back. I don't like being a fool, but who does?

Springdale looked the same. These places always do. Was in the town charter or something: we will never change. Minor things, like a new café on Main Street, different name on the bank. I drove around, avoiding Pearl, my old street, but working my way toward it neverthe-less. Unavoidable, considering the size of this place. I crossed Pearl, but kept going toward the highway out of town. A block farther, I turned around. What would it hurt to drive past the house? Caroline didn't live there anymore.

The new owners had planted pines and maples in the front yard and painted the clapboard a buttery sort of color. It looked comfortable now, a place where people could live and be happy. All Caroline and I had ever done was buy a new refrigerator. Seeing the house all cuted up affected me more than anything else. So many things I had wanted to do with it. I had studied bunches of house and garden books, but we had never managed to find the time to decide what we would do first. Of course that made sense after I found out where Caroline's spare time was going.

Damn this bitterness. An artifact of my past, that's all. I left town by a back road, then cut across to the highway leading to my shopping mall hotel.

3

Although Shelling awakened with a headache and tingly fingers, the sensations faded, and he didn't expect the day, a Friday, to differ from the routine he had established since moving to Springdale several months ago. He spent the morning pulling weeds from his vegetable garden and sitting in the shade of his back patio, where he dictated his journal into a digital recorder, as he did every morning. It wasn't until afternoon, when he went into town for his yoga class, that he noticed the emptiness.

At the yoga center, though the door hung open and the lights were on, he found no students or teacher. He sat on the sofa outside the practice space and removed his shoes and socks, then entered the practice area, a rectangular room with a golden oak floor and a wall of windows—a calming zone in which he always found freedom from the grasping tentacles of chaos that followed after everyone.

He unrolled a mat and waited, sitting cross-legged facing the windows. Cloudless and blue, the kind of day that promised much—perhaps this time, after class, he would suggest lunch to some of the others. Usually, on finishing the hour-and-a-half sessions, he felt so exquisitely drained and limp that conversation proved difficult, and the opportunity for companionship slipped past him.

This empty room was odd though—someone, at least the teacher, should have arrived by now. He unfolded himself to his feet and walked into the closet-like office, then back to the sofa, where he sat reading a brochure for a weekend seminar with a visiting yogi. Next weekend, actually. Perhaps he would sign up for it. He read the brochure a second time, looked at his watch, looked in the office again, looked in the practice space to see if he had missed seeing a note, and put his socks and shoes back on. Outside, he crossed the parking lot to the food co-op, where he bought an avocado, some lemons, and a bag of organic potato chips. Aside from the young woman at the cash register and a man putting out produce, the store was empty.

He deposited the groceries in the trunk of his car and walked toward Main Street; while crossing the street in front of The Cook's House (a store selling upscale kitchen items), he decided to go to the Springdale Library.

The library occupied an attractive 1920s-era brick building with wood floors and high ceilings. Several afternoons a week, Shelling would come here to sit in the magazine section and look through various newspapers. On this visit, he paused in the foyer to look at a poster advertising the performance of three short Samuel Beckett plays at the college. He had never read or performed any Beckett. Off to his left stood a table of new books; straight through led to the fiction, he knew that . . . but where was the drama section? He thought to ask if the library had the featured Beckett plays.

Besides programs at the college, there were a few theater groups in town. Funny, his discontent with television had colored his entire view of drama. But why not enter the theatrical life here? Though he was hesitant to reveal his past, or rely on his background to secure parts in local productions, it was ridiculous to turn away from acting altogether. Perhaps instead of acting, here in Springdale he would direct plays, explore a more artistic vision, divorced from the business that had involved him for so long.

Finding no one at the front desk, he rummaged through the new books, picking up one with a painting of a sailing ship on its cover. He flipped through several pages, then several more. The text was not English. It so closely resembled English that at first he thought his eyes had blurred, mixing the words into random configurations. He picked up another book, and it was the same, words in a sort of near-English gibberish: "*Leth free, tor mousled, ol shan vetchy*," read the line at the top of one page, opposite a strange drawing of young women and people-sized cats wearing clothes. Shelling searched the library for another patron or employee, but found no one. At the circulation desk, he called out: "Is anyone here?" The ceiling, distant and white, mocked him. He found he couldn't breathe, could not force air in through the knotted thing his windpipe had become. A sudden wave of heat engulfed him, a magnified exhalation, as though he had become lodged in the exhaust vent of an immense furnace.

———————

4

I had just entered my room with the daisy-print wallpaper and started travel ritual number one ✢, when someone banged on my door. Not wanting to talk to anyone, I ignored the knock. If the hotel needed me, they could shove a note under the door. The knocking changed to pounding, a rhythmic thud, like some overworked drum circle reject. With each drumbeat, my irritation magnified.

"Okay, I'm coming," I said. I turned the knob, preparing an irate comment, but smiled when I saw Michael.

"Took you long enough," he said, pushing past me, followed by two men and a woman, all of whom I thought I recognized from my previous life. "Train ride okay? Should've let me know what time so I could meet you."

"I figured you would be pretty busy with the wedding."

"Well, we're out to have some fun. Not exactly a bachelor party. Drinks with some guys. And not even all guys." He pointed to the woman.

"I'm Sherrie—you handled my divorce," she said.

I nodded, although I didn't remember her. "I have to phone my office," I said, lying. "Then go over some notes on a case. I'll meet you later."

"Too much work," Michael said. "That's not the Patrick Travis I remember."

✢ Remove glasses, contact lens case, and contact lens solution from bag and arrange by sink, glasses to the left, contact lens case and solution to the right. Contact lenses were a constant source of irritation, but vision with them was so much better than with glasses. Eye drops made lens wear more bearable, though late in the evening, especially after a night of poor sleep, even drops were insufficient. Vision-correction surgery, the kind that reshaped the cornea, was an option, but the idea of cutting, even with laser rather than knife, seemed so drastic. And then the horror stories of people who had undergone the procedure, yet still needed to wear glasses, or had their eyes damaged, forever seeing the world as green and gray shapes flowing in and out of focus. ✢

They left. I waited half an hour, then went out to eat mall-food, one of those stupid chain restaurants that make you feel as if you haven't traveled. Springdale has excellent dining, but that was enough reunions for the day. I drifted around the shopping mall till closing. The anonymity comforted me.

5

Swells of oceanographic angst buffeted Shelling. A profusion of discolored velvety fur—pelts of beaver or raccoon—lined the street, softened his fall. Shelling had a beaver dam on his property, and he liked to sit near it, under the trees, losing himself in the sounds of his land. He planned to move a picnic table out there, or try fishing (if there were fish to catch), though he worried it might disturb the animals. But why was he lying in the grass outside the library? Shelling jumped to his feet, and hurried down Main Street.

Half a block from the library, he stopped, unable to recall the source of his agitation. That's what happens when you miss your yoga class, he thought. He would have appreciated an explanation for the cancellation. With his unstructured life, disruptions left him dangling. If not for the discipline of yoga, his transition to life in this small town would have been difficult; the practice relaxed and invigorated him, opened him to new experiences. Living in the Los Angeles area for so long, he had grown contemptuous of other places in the country, of small towns, of any place lacking big-city sophistication.

As he walked, he glanced into the windows of several stores, seeing a clerk behind the counter in some, and in others, no one. Not just the yoga center then; the town appeared to be shorn of people, residents and visitors alike.

He entered Frisell's Coffee Roasters, pausing in the doorway, as had become his habit, to allow the fertile aroma of the roast to permeate his lungs. Two young women sat on stools behind the counter. They

were laughing; as he drew near, he heard the one at the cash register
mention elephants, or maybe cellophane. The other laughed harder,
gasping, sucking air through the laughs. She hunched forward, cupping
her reddening face with both hands. Silver rings decorated most of her
fingers. Shelling recognized one with a raised zigzag design on a dark
background, from the jewelry store across the street. He had spent parts
of two afternoons there, trying on rings, assisted once by a bland-faced
woman and the other time by a well-manicured bald man, neither of
whom gave any indication of interest in talking to Shelling beyond the
requirements of their job.

"What's so funny?" he asked. Neither woman responded. The young
woman at the cash register asked the other to start a pot of decaf.
Shelling ordered a cappuccino and waited while the ring woman prepared it. The cash register woman held out a hand for money. A tattoo
of a dark bird, wings outstretched, decorated the underside of her wrist.
Shelling wanted to join their discussion, but saw no way to breach the
wall. He opened his mouth, preparing to tell the young woman that he
admired her tattoo; instead, he carried his mug to a table and looked out
the window at the empty sidewalk. The two women continued their
conversation as though Shelling didn't exist.

"There's an archival method, Albania or someplace," one of them said.
"They use numbered index cards to keep track of the tides."

"Are they suspended by fishing line, like in Greece?"

This emptiness, it haunted him: empty cafés, empty theaters, stores.
No cars passed through. Shelling drove around town, searching, up
Main Street and into the neighborhoods, but saw no one other than the
waiters, waitresses, ticket sellers, fishmongers, and shopkeepers at their
respective stations. He pulled his car into the parking lot of The Crow
Bar, a brew-pub occupying a former grain mill on the north edge of town.
The place was large enough to absorb ski crowds or summertime hikers.
This evening, neither were in evidence, though he did find the bartender
and two others, a man and woman.

Shelling felt a smile growing but shut it down. It would be a bad idea to appear over-eager. He would order a drink, wait for conversation to happen. The dark ale reminded him of winters spent in the mountains, in lodges surrounded by friends and strangers, all laughing and talking. Where were these people now?

The man at the bar spoke to the woman. Shelling couldn't place the extended syllables of his accent. "A man dressed all in black enters a white room. The only sound is the air conditioner, blowing through a vent in the ceiling." The man stopped and drank the last third of his pint. He motioned to the bartender for another. His hands were wide, with sausage-like fingers.

"How large is the vent?" the woman asked. Her voice was husky, as though from smoking, but Shelling saw no ashtrays near the couple. Her accent didn't match the man's.

"Doesn't matter. Just a vent blowing air." The bartender set a full glass down on a coaster; the man wrapped his thick fingers around it and lifted it to his lips to drink before continuing his story: "So, here's this man, dressed all in black in a white room. The room is rectangular, maybe four times deeper than it is wide. It's cold. The blowing air pushes against his hair. He takes out a black knit cap, the kind that covers his whole head except for the eyes and mouth. But he doesn't put it on. He's waiting for something, or someone."

The man tipped his glass and drank, finishing the beer in one deep swallow. He nodded to the woman, who picked up her purse and stood.

"What's he waiting for?" Shelling asked; they left without answering.

Shelling sat for a while, drinking his beer in small, brief sips and idly taking pretzel sticks from a bowl. The bartender moved off to shelve a rack of clean glasses.

When he first stopped here, on his cross-country drive, the streets had been crowded with cars, pedestrians. Or had they? It was as though he carried competing memories—a town alive with human contact, and this, the emptiness.

6

I dressed and drove to town for the wedding. Michael and Dee had decided to hold it in a mansion owned by one of her relatives. The place was a wreck—hadn't been lived in for years—wallpaper peeling, dank corridors leading off into uninhabitable wings, but it had this amazing ballroom, gilt molding, parquet floor, and a ceiling painted all in cherubs and naked nymphs. I stood in the back, apart from everyone. What a fucking waste, all this. Within a couple of years, either Michael or Dee—didn't matter which—would do something stupid, some fling with a co-worker or whatever, and that would be the end. People are predictable. Everybody starts out with the same well-meaning platitudes.

The woman who had come to my room last night with Michael and the others sat beside me. "Sorry you didn't make it out to the bar," she said. "It was a good time. Some of Michael's former students—I think they had all just turned twenty-one recently and were feeling way proud of it—showed up, and we had them going with stories about Michael's wild days in the merchant marines."

She waved to some people standing near the door. They came over and sat in the remaining three seats of the row. The woman introduced them, but the music started, freeing me from conversational obligations.

Dee and Michael appeared from opposite ends of the room, all smiley, and their smiles shamed me. I tried to feel better, or at least to hide my cynicism with an outward shine. Hard enough for them without all my negativity coming at them. And they looked great. Dee had bought some vintage wedding dress and shortened it to just below the knees. Michael was wearing a pink ruffled shirt and dark pants.

The wedding was a nice civil-ceremony with cosmic overtones; afterward we relocated outside for the reception. The garden was overgrown with brambly things, but they had cleared enough space for tables and chairs. I went through the hand-shaking line, then sat alone beside a ragged shrub with purple flowers. Late May here was always perfect. I had forgotten. Michael owned a canoe, and after his classes were over, we would take it out on the river. I had always assumed that after putting away enough money from my law practice, I would buy a canoe and a riverfront house. Okay, I could still do it, just not here, not in the way I had pictured things back then.

At least Caroline wasn't in town. Turned out she and Dr. Wonderful had gone to Spain for a month. From my spot by the shrub, I saw a familiar-looking woman talking to Caroline's best friend, that romance writer Skippy Brisbane. I definitely wanted to avoid Brisbane. That other woman smiled a lot when she talked, which looked odd next to Brisbane's sour face. Smiley-woman was wearing a flowered tank dress that showed a lot of leg. Maybe I had met her once. Maybe she hadn't been wearing glasses then, or her hair had been long. Several guys I used to play softball with came over, blocking my view of smiley woman. We traded life-triviality; I told them about lawyering and stuff in the city.

Then this man showed up, waving his hands in the air and screaming about broken hearts. He said that if the wedding wasn't stopped, he would "do something." He never said what he would do, just kept repeating the line. A woman standing near him said the wedding had already happened, and he grabbed her shoulders and shook her. That's when that fat cop I had nicknamed Scooter intervened. He maneuvered the man away from the guests and escorted him through the back gate.

Now I was feeling guilty for all that negativity I had radiated earlier, thinking I had somehow caused this. One of the softball guys said the screaming man had been Dee's boyfriend before she met Michael. Someone else said they had been engaged. I had wanted to hide, alone, by my flowering shrub, but more people joined the group around me. When I saw Brisbane and smiley woman moving my way, I slipped out.

7

Perhaps the emptiness had been forced on Shelling to balance his past. In his previous life on television, solitude had never been a factor. Even when a network cancelled a show, he found more work quickly; when a relationship ended, another started soon after. All of that seemed so far away now, relics. He wondered what some of those people he had known were doing. Though he owned a television, he hadn't turned it on since receiving his belongings from California.

Saturday morning passed without the situation changing. Shelling sat with his tape recorder as usual, though he thought he spoke with more determination and insight. "In the continuum of solitude, all beings are supreme," he said, then talked for a while about the consequences and benefits of geographic relocation. The recorder had a voice-activation feature; he clipped the unit to the waistband of his pants and moved out into the yard, where, with an unthinking determination, he dug out a broad swath of turf and turned the soil in preparation for sowing. He forgot to talk into the recorder until he had finished digging, then spoke of the seeds he planned to buy, the vegetables he would plant. And with his garden in mind, he drove into town.

Downtown Springdale consisted of Highway 848 (which, as it cut through the town, became Main Street) and the intersecting blocks between Hill Street and the turnoff where Highway 7 veered right to merge with Highway 23 and cross the river. Hill and Knight Streets ran perpendicular to Main. Various stores, offices, and restaurants lined Springdale's streets. Shelling had visited them all. The used bookstore and the Japanese restaurant were on Knight. One of the two movie houses was on Hill, occupying a former vaudeville theater. A new complex, built in a space behind the buildings on the west side of Main Street, housed the other theater. Though new, it had been designed in scale and style to blend with the surrounding buildings.

Shelling left his car near the newer movie house. On reaching the used book store, he allowed himself to be sidetracked from his goal of the garden shop. Entering, he had an odd twist in his stomach, apprehension, he thought, though of what? He laughed—nothing in a book store could hurt him.

The woman who ran the shop came out from the back, passing him without a greeting. Shelling roamed the store, flipping pages and looking at pictures in a few cookbooks, but none drew him. In the fiction section, a book protruded from a shelf; he reached for it, *Dead Language*, stories by Samantha Hidalgo. He had heard the name somewhere. The dust jacket photo showed a woman with short dark hair and squarish glasses. "A linguistic and phantasmagoric tour-de-force," the blurb said. He opened the book at random and read the beginning of a story. ✿

✿ Across the vale stood a circular structure, mundane in appearance, though around it was an area of desolation, circular like the structure, as though something radiated from it that killed everything within a certain distance. Some trees stood, bare, trunks brittle as dust, unable even to rot without the creatures that feed on rot. If a hapless traveler came upon it, and few did, the person would have felt an oppressiveness, as though their weight increased with each step closer to the structure. And the structure itself, blocky walls constructed from a green limestone prized for its use in building. The traveler, circling the structure, would note with surprise its lack of windows, and upon making the full circuit, would also come to notice the lack of a door. The traveler's gaze would drift up to the roof, a vault constructed so that each stone shared the weight evenly.

From the erosion surrounding the structure, the ruts along the south slope, and the lifeless earth piled higher along the northwest, one would surmise that the entirety had once been buried, and that the work of the elements over time was slowly revealing more.

All of this would lead an observer to ponder: what would drive people to build such a structure and bury it, creating what must have looked like nothing more than another hill in a landscape of hills. Though, one might assume, it would have been a hill as devoid of life as the area around the structure, which, if true, would mean that the piled-on earth, with nothing to hold it in place, had not lasted as long as its builders might have wished. ✿

Shelling paid for the book and left the store. Back at his car, he opened the passenger-side door and dropped the book on the seat. There he lingered, not ready to return to his empty house. Across the parking lot, the movie marquee beckoned. Shelling didn't like going to movies alone, feeling exposed and self-conscious, judged for his inability to find a companion, but Springdale had given him little choice.

The ticket booth was on the inside, to the left of the entrance. Shelling found it untenanted. A film called *The Painting of Kathleen Alice May* would be starting soon.

The theater smelled of corn syrup and stale popcorn. ⊕ Shelling walked toward the back, passing where the ticket-taker commonly stood. Ahead, the hallway stretched. No one came to challenge him. Continuing, he found the air began to thicken, first around his toes and rising, assuming the consistency of a thin oatmeal porridge, and it resisted his forward progress, pushing on his thighs and sucking at the soles of his shoes. Viscous air oozed and flexed to hinder his entry.

Perhaps a new security measure initiated because of the lack of present employees?

As the air thickened, it also darkened into an unpleasant, orangey brown. Shelling looked back over his shoulder at the line of fluorescent light fixtures, bright where he had entered, fading here. A glow framed a doorway to his right, from behind which came the sounds of a movie playing, but in

⊕ Savory snack and sweet snack share an origin in the humble grain of corn. Multiple processed products originating from a few raw materials have replaced the diversity once found in the human diet, forming the illusion of diversity. Food that once came from the region in which a person lived now journeys unimagined distances to reach the local supermarket (Though "local" and "supermarket" are terms of deep contradiction that indicate a separate societal malaise that will be discussed elsewhere.). Even with this bounty, many choose the pre-packaged route rather than assembling and cooking, and many of the new mega-groceries display their variety of produce more as a colorful decoration rather than to provide our dining and nutritional requirements. ⊕

the dark of the hall, Shelling couldn't read the sign showing the name of the film.

He traveled on, immersing himself in the shape of the hallway, more a shadow of a hall than an actual one, a shadow that clung to him, and he found himself embracing it, willing it closer, wearing it as a cloak. Even as the last, scattered elements of light skittered away, across the blackened carpet, still he continued. His eyes adjusted to the dark, seeing it as a blackness that shaped the world into figures, into objects of startling unfamiliarity, and in them he found comfort.

8

I drove back to my shopping mall hotel and sat on the balcony, which overlooked the mall's main concourse. The problem with solitude, sometimes, is what to do with it. For me, here, in this generic milieu, the options were few: read my legal journal, watch television (64 channels!), or traverse the corridors of the shopping mall in search of amusement. A movie theater anchored the far end. I considered going, but decided that seeing a movie would constitute a form of replacement solitude.

Three stories below, water flowed from a fountain in the shape of that famous cartoon penguin—the one with the new movie that was doubtless commanding two screens of the theater here. Benches ringed the fountain—I had sat on one last night after dinner. The water sparkled as if dyed with light. For the moment, the view's artificiality appealed. People ambled: young couples holding hands, families, tired office workers relishing their weekend, everyone buying things: movie posters, compact discs of the latest hit songs, jogging shoes, and sweaters. Shoppers paraded plastic bag emblems, allegiance to the brand.

The fountain's water-level rose. Waves began lapping over the sides of the basin. I figured something must have clogged the drain, though it should be a closed system—water in the basin pumping back up to exit from the penguin's mouth. So with a clogged drain, no water should spew.

Water splashed and pooled on the pavement surrounding the fountain. A child, maybe six years old, ran laughing into the growing puddle, splattering its clothes and head. The mother pulled it away, lifted it, and carried it into a shoe store.

I was hungry (I hadn't eaten enough at the reception), but didn't want to leave my balcony—the scene here entertained me more than any movie could have. I went inside and called room service for pepperoni and mushroom pizza with a salad. When I returned to the balcony, some man in blue coveralls, likely from mall maintenance, stood near the fountain. He held a mobile phone to his ear, perhaps observing the situation while someone elsewhere attempted to turn off the water. As the water converged on the bases of the surrounding benches, he was forced to take several steps back to keep his feet dry.

Surely by now someone would have figured out how to shut it down? My liability-law nature started coming up with scenarios. Obviously a problem with the pump's manufacture, though it could also be a question of improper maintenance.

Down at the other end of the balcony, the elevator door pinged. A man wearing the white smock of a kitchen-worker emerged, pushing a cart that carried a round tray with a lid—my pizza.

The pizza smelled pretty good, considering where I was. I opened the packet of blue-cheese dressing and worked it into my salad. The salad actually had more to it than limp lettuce. I speared a cherry tomato with my fork and ate it, then took my plate out to the balcony to continue watching the show.

Another blue coveralls man had joined the first. A man in a business suit called out to coveralls men . He trudged around the growing pool, keeping his glossy shoes far from the water's edge. Now a couple of inches of water covered the bases of the benches, and I wondered how much farther it could extend. There was a sporting goods store toward the other end of the mall, and I pictured its employees busily inflating rubber rafts for use in an evacuation. They would paddle through the stores, forcing their way through floating clothes and plastic toys. Someone would attempt to buy guns.

Closing time neared, and few shoppers remained in the area. Some clerks from stores near the fountain hung out in their doorways, watching. They jeered when the flow of water stopped, their voices drifting to my perch as thin echoes. I finished the pizza and wiped my lips. With the live entertainment over, I slipped inside and changed for bed.

9

Cold and dusty morning light filled Shelling's front room, a thick light, a light that promised nothing. It smelled of degradation, of decay. Shelling had no place here, the light said. But look around—were these not his things, had he not made his mark on the house, the garden? He refused the light's verdict.

The Briar Café had always been crowded on weekends. Shelling decided to breakfast there among his fellow townsfolk, away from the dismal light that had invaded his house. He reached the café at 8:45; no one was there but the teen-aged wait staff and the unseen cooks, though a few minutes after the arrival of Shelling's blueberry pancakes, he heard the chime of the brass bell from the door opening, then the sound of people being seated in the booth behind him.

"Ran around naked with the neighbor's horses?"

"Well, up until maybe seven or so. I was her babysitter, did you know that? And her parents' Tarot reader of course."

The first speaker sounded like Shelling's Great-Aunt Paula, grandmother's sister on his father's side; the other woman had a scratchy voice. Scratchy-voice had apparently been to a wedding the day before. Shelling ate his pancakes and listened to the women. He wanted to talk to them—the first non service-providers he had encountered since the couple at the bar, but he didn't know how to initiate it. They appeared to be giving him no attention. Obviously, the emptiness wasn't universal, or his presence would have held more significance. Indecision tore at him—he longed for conversation, but feared being rebuffed.

"I went to a CAMAG✣ retreat," Aunt Paula-voice said. "Down in Oakville."

✣ *Citizens Against Microbes and Germs* (sarcastically referred to as "Antibacteriolites"). Founded in 1988 by William Blankenship Morris, a wealthy homophobe. He started it in a paroxysm of AIDS-related hysteria, consumed by the notion that people (even Good people like himself) could contract AIDS through the skin. Among other things, he drafted the rules of hand washing and prayer (updated to incorporate advances in cleansing technology):

 ☞ Turn on tap; while waiting for water to reach optimum 65 degrees Celsius (149 degrees Fahrenheit), recite the blessing for mountain streams, then wet hands thoroughly;
 ☞ Soap hands (If in a public restroom, and there is only a bar of soap, not the pump-dispensed liquid variety, DO NOT touch it, water alone will have to serve.);
 ☞ Rub hands to make lather (While rubbing, keep hands above free-flowing tap to prevent vital lather from washing off prematurely.);
 ☞ Wash now-lathered hands front and back with a firm motion, being careful to scrub between fingers and under fingernails;
 ☞ Rinse hands well under optimum-temperature flow of water;
 ☞ Dry hands thoroughly with clean paper towel or air dryer (If neither is available—leave hands wet, but don't touch anything.);
 ☞ Alcohol-based hand sanitizers or gels, or antibacterial wipes are useful alternatives if soap and water are not available (such as after riding in a taxi on the way to a business meeting or before eating a meal on an airplane). ✣

"Did I mention the vegetables?" Scratchy-voice said. "They brought in tubs, growing I mean, limes, peppers, mangoes. Had 'em sent from California. Instead of flowers, you see." Scratchy-voice coughed, a tearing sound that couldn't have been painless. Shelling hoped that she had given up smoking, but he knew so many who continued despite onset of emphysema and worse. The names the women kept repeating—Caroline, Wadholm, Caitlin, and others—reminded him of something. Probably he had seen them in the paper. An event as big as this wedding—no doubt there had been an announcement.

Rainfall had begun on Shelling's way to the café. The sound of it pleased him. The season had been far too dry. Inspired by his new farmhouse (and the solitude), Shelling had planted a vegetable garden, which he kept expanding as spring progressed into summer. Broccoli, basil, tomatoes and, of course, carrot. Aided by a detailed do-it-yourself book, ✿ he installed a drip irrigation system, but a steady rain like this was so much better.

"Didn't shoot anyone," Scratchy-voice said. "Pointed at the sky and fired off two rounds. There's just nothing like the report of a Colt 45 Peacemaker."

"What year?" Paula-voice asked.

"Eighteen Seventy-four, with mother-of-pearl grips."

"Sounds like a presentation model."

Shelling paid his bill. On the way out, he paused beside the women's booth and smiled at them. Scratchy-voice was maybe seventy, with gray hair pulled back in a bun. "I don't need no more coffee," she said.

He went outside. Damn this place—

✿ Oscar Pitstick, *Make Your Garden! A Guide to Preparing the Perfect Garden Environment*, Pieczynski Publishing, Great Barrington, MA, 1997. One of those books that causes purchasers to consider themselves experts as soon as they acquire it, though it does contain some useful information and techniques. As with all guides and do-it-yourself manuals (sometimes called by the clever marketing term DIY), everything depends on the individual. Many people are incapable of following instructions, others excel. Innumerable dissertations have been written on the subject. Richard Shelling proved to be surprisingly (given his actor past) adept. ✿

nobody gives a thought to a stranger. What use, this river, this scenic vista of a town? He had thought . . . a home, he thought he had found a home. Nothing for him, no one. He slumped against the wall. His throat constricted; he coughed, and his stomach . . . as soon as he realized what was happening, he staggered to the parking lot side of the restaurant and vomited. Unbelievable—first time in years he had thrown up. In a daze, he re-entered the café and shuffled into the bathroom to splash his face at the sink. He swished water in his mouth and spat, then pulled several paper towels from the dispenser to dry his face.

Somewhat refreshed, he left the bathroom. The women were still eating. He stopped and leaned in close to Scratchy-voice, his hands resting on the edge of their table. "Hey," he said, using his best growl, the one he had developed for the wife-beating psychopath in that episode of *Precinct 10.* "I don't work here. I don't refill no damn coffee cup. Got me?"

Without waiting for a response, he spun around and swaggered out of the café, aiming himself in the direction of the hardware and garden store. Weekends there were always busy. Last week—had it been last week?—he had waited for the old guy . . . Frosty? . . . Smokey? . . . to finish showing some woman how to build window screens and help him, but he had given up and left.

Today, he went straight to the seed display. A man passed him, and Shelling looked up expectantly. Not a customer. And he refused to talk to any more shopkeepers. He selected packets of seeds: arugula, Boston lettuce, and acorn squash. After paying, Shelling found the exit blocked. The door had been propped open to admit the rain-cooled air, and a man several inches taller than Shelling and as wide as the doorway stood there, facing outward and talking to another tall man.

"But even that's a reaction," the big man in the doorway said. "I'm trying to reach cause, not effect." He had a long ponytail down the middle of his broad back and spoke in a deep voice.

"Excuse me," Shelling said, thinking more of passage through the door than conversation.

"But what makes a man start fires?" the other asked.

"Excuse me," Shelling said, louder this time.

"When I was in social work it was easy to feel defeated by the forces of nature," the big man said. As he spoke, he gestured wildly with his beefy arms. Shelling tried to squeeze through while the man's arms were up, but the big man brought a ham-sized elbow down on Shelling's forehead, staggering him back against a flashlight display. "What I'm trying to do now," the big man said, continuing, apparently without having felt his arm's impact with Shelling, "is formulate a working model of societal impulses. How everything comes together to form behavior."

Shelling leaned against the flashlight display, taking shallow breaths. He had dropped his seed packets on hitting the display, and they had scattered nearby. He left them. The faces of the men in the door pulsed and distorted, as if viewed through phosphorescent clouds. A humming sounded, starting low and rising to a cicada shriek. Clenching his eyes shut, Shelling propelled himself forward, smacking against the big man at about kidney level. The impact thrust the big man aside and threw Shelling to the sidewalk. Shelling pushed himself to his knees and crawled toward a sidewalk-bench.

Someone lifted him onto the bench and held him there. Voices echoed, and lights flashed orange and white. A diorama filled the hardware store's front window: in it, a model train rolled along tracks bounded by cornfields and into a town that mirrored Springdale, the stone church on one end of Main, the movie theater, river, shops. Minute figures flowed along the sidewalks. *There were the people!* His memories of the town, so jumbled—people walking, enjoying the quiet life here. Which town did he inhabit? The train stopped to disembark passengers, who joined the other pedestrians on the crowded streets. Two police officers, a man and woman, walked toward the hardware store.

10

I drove to the station in the rain. Between the car rental place and the ticket machine, the rain stopped, which I took as a sign. I decided to extend my visit. I suppose I was feeling sentimental, especially with Caroline away. After the rain, the morning sky turned lemony and wrinkled. The air changed from denial to promise.

The train station was behind the town hall, a brick, Victorian-era structure that also housed the police station. Scooter and a tall policewoman were escorting some guy in. I went to the bed and breakfast and booked a room for one night, remaining there just long enough to drop my bag on the bed and arrange my glasses and contact lens stuff by the sink. Back out on the street, I stood watching passersby. Mist floated on the hills behind town. I had always admired the houses up there, with their sweeping views. I liked height, liked the way the town sat in its nest of hills, with the river cutting through the middle.

A search for breakfast led me to the little café off Main. I aimed for an empty stool at the end of the counter. As I passed these two old birds at a booth, one of them glared at me. No idea who she was. Sitting on the stool next to mine, I recognized smiley woman from the wedding. She nodded a hello. I smiled, not wanting to seem rude, but seeing someone who maybe knew me, or at least knew Caroline, wasn't the way I had intended to start the day.

The waitress came to take the woman's order; she stared at me. "Weren't you just here?" she asked. I said no. She gave me a funny look and handed me smiley-woman's menu.

"The pancakes here are great," smiley-woman said.

"Thanks." I looked at the menu, then at her. She had one of those haircuts that showed off the neck, and she had a great neck. I tried to remember if I had ever met her.

"I saw you at the wedding," she said, a flat statement implying that her noticing me signified nothing special. "I guess you haven't been back here since the crap with Caroline."

"Hmmm," I said. This place . . . just couldn't escape things smelling of Caroline. At least Skippy Brisbane wasn't here too. Smiley-woman—she hadn't been Caroline's friend back when I lived here, or at least I don't remember her.

"I've never liked her much," she said.

Enough with all these people knowing my past. What was I thinking, staying another day? Endless prosecutorial miasmas shook me, tendrils popping and sticking like unwanted household knickknacks, objects discarded for the associations they held—the clay figurine with the twisted face, bought on a brief trip to Mexico with Caroline the summer before I entered law school, the shirts, many shirts, bought at her insistence, an attempt to remake my image into something fashionable. But I didn't jettison my entire past—it existed, deserved to exist, even the unpleasantness. I had saved the footed bowl. It sat on my office desk, holding wrapped peppermints (because Caroline hated peppermints).

⊕ Parker Duofold, circa 1930s, black body, gold nib. Not a pen to be trifled with. Fountain pens . . . the velvety way the nib slides across paper, the heady smell of ink . . . and the status, yet another way for people to flaunt money and pretensions. Fountain pen stores in shopping malls? Patrick Travis had glanced into one his first night at the mall hotel. Uncle Omar's shop had been a dusty old place, with counters and other fixtures dating back to a long-gone era. But no one knew more about pens. Few people like Uncle Omar left in this disposable plastic world. The old building was, of course, demolished, replaced by a high-rise complex not worth describing. ⊕

"We met at a party."

The woman's voice broke through my reverie, and I turned my face toward her.

"Don't remember whose party," she said. "You were there alone. Caroline was off somewhere, doing something. Maybe you came with Michael and Deirdre. We somehow got into a discussion about fountain pens."

A notebook lay on the counter near her plate, and beside it a fountain pen with a dark, enamel barrel streaked with green. Seeing the pen, I made the connection. "Right—Sammy Hidalgo."

My Uncle Omar had repaired fountain pens. As a child, he used to let me play with worn-out nibs and other parts. When I graduated from high school, he gave me an antique Parker. ⊕

I told her that I had read one of her novels after I moved away. She said she had finished a first draft of a new story early this morning and had gone to breakfast to celebrate. We chatted for a time, reminiscing about safe subjects from my years in Springdale, until her food came. Her three pancakes were spread on the plate, overlapping. She stacked them evenly and began cutting, first in half, then fourths, then eighths. The waitress brought my coffee, and I ordered pancakes too. The coffee here was good, some kind of organic shade-grown. There had been other ownership when I lived here, and I preferred this new version. I don't know when this up-scaling—The Change (as I called it)—had occurred, or why, but it was nationwide. I liked it. Sure, there's an air of pretension involved sometimes, but overall, the good coffee, microbrew beer, fusion cuisine, beats the crap out of blandness.

"I'm not one of these delicate women who can only order a salad," Sammy said. She pushed a forkful of pancakes around the amber pool of syrup and lifted it from the plate. "I was in L.A. last month, having dinner with some friends in a Thai restaurant, and all around me were these pretty little women with tans and tight asses, and I started speculating on how many salads are served per day out there. Greengrocer's wet dream."

"Is the total salad consumption in Los Angeles greater than the rest of the country combined?" I asked.

"It's a fight between New York and Los Angeles. The winner is awarded a bronze sculpture of iceberg lettuce to display in City Hall. The rest of the country is irrelevant." ✧

Pancakes arrived, all nice and buttery, with those crisp edges that are so difficult to achieve without the proper combination of fat and heat. I drizzled maple syrup over them (lots

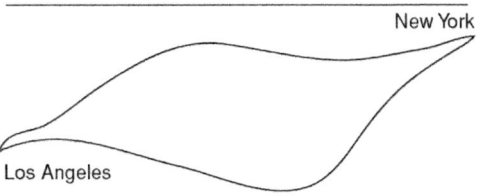

✧ Map of the United States (lower forty-eight) by body weight. From a model formulated by Drs. Silas Barndale and Jane Bricem in 1994, "Geographic Weight Distribution and its Lack of Effect on Public Opinion," published in *The Journal of Eclectic Dysfunction*, Vol. 12, No. 7. ✧

of it—Springdale's maple syrup is divine). Her talk of salad-eating had made me self-conscious—I didn't want to use so much syrup that she thought I was horsely, or so little that she sneered. Maybe I should order sausage. Though why did I care? I didn't have to impress anyone in this damn town.

Sammy gave me an incomprehensible look (and I could usually interpret facial expressions—had to for my lawyering).

"High fructose corn syrup," she said. "That's the other thing that sends me on a rant. We're given these competing and contradictory models to follow. Processed high-fat corn syrup food is pushed at us all our lives, but at the same time we're bombarded with images of skinny asses and sculpted bodies." She waved her fork at me, and a ribbon of syrup slid toward her fingers.

"If I followed the model that women are given, I would need to apologize to you for my eating pancakes and tell you that I'll have to spend all afternoon at the gym to work it off. Well fuck that."

Plates emptied, we remained at the counter finishing our coffee. The café had cleared out, and neither of us appeared to be in a rush. I tried to remember what, if anything, I had heard about Sammy. Besides her jacket copy. When I changed plans at the train station, I had been thinking how important it would be to spend some solitary time sorting out my memories of Springdale, which, as the weekend progressed, had slowly shed its malevolence. Sitting here with her helped, though I still wanted some alone-time to what—meditate on the sorry-ass conundrums that beset our society?

"Dee and Michael must be on their way to Barcelona by now," she said. I dropped some money on the counter and stood. She left with me. "What are your plans for the day then?" she asked. "Now that you've decided to be brave and stay a little longer in this terrible place." She smiled when she said that, an open, cheery expression that I found touching.

"Nice out now," I said, looking at where the sun burned through a few remaining skins of cloud. "If it had stayed rainy I would have probably caught the next train out. Maybe I'll take a taxi to the Josephine Rodgers House ✥ and see the gardens. It was great talking to you." I extended a hand to shake, and she gripped it with both of hers.

"Why not let me show you what's new around here since you left?"

Despite my desire for solitude, I found myself unwilling to cleave myself from her company.

✥ Josephine Rodgers kept a summer house in the area, the garden of which was famous for its splendor; however, during Rodgers's life, her partner, Susan Marcus did most of the gardening. After Rodgers's death, her conservative family refused to acknowledge Marcus's claims to the property and set up a non-profit foundation that paid several family members enough money for them to quit their jobs and move to Florida. ✥

"Or, I have an idea. It's not new, but it's someplace Caroline never would have taken you. Wouldn't have know about, actually."

11

When had Shelling last eaten? His stomach was a shrunken, leathery thing. He found himself in a narrow room facing two square windows set high, near the ceiling. No furniture but the wooden chair on which he sat, cushioned by a piece of folded burlap. A vent on the wall behind him blew air across the top of his head. Spiders had crafted nests in all the corners. From the windows, the entering light radiated a pinkish glow.

Lethargy gripped him. Shouldn't he demand to see a lawyer? He had acted in enough cop and lawyer shows—you can't shut someone up like this. Must be something in the white air of the narrow room that kept him from fighting. The vent stopped blowing. At first, the quiet pleased him. Each molecule of silence emerged, one after another. He pictured them waltzing in loose swirls of air, forming patterns more intricate than snowflakes. Untouchable, they swam, free of the clinging spiderwebs.

But after a time, Shelling grew tired of observing the dancing silence. He found himself longing to hear Mozart, a piano sonata to fill the empty spaces.

Now restless, he rose and paced the room, measuring it with his steps: seven steps wide and twenty-eight deep. Did it mean something that the room's depth was divisible by its width? He stopped in a corner to examine the spider webs, whorls of filament rising from floor to ceiling. When he had moved into his farmhouse, he found it full of webs—in corners, doorways, along the base of the kitchen cabinets—and he eradicated all as he encountered them. These, he left undisturbed, for they gave him something to observe besides the white walls and the door, a slab of green-painted metal with no knob.

Lost in his examination of the webs, Shelling needed several repetitions of a hollow clanging thump to register the sound. Suddenly filled with nervous energy, he rushed back to his chair, turned it to face the door and sat, trying to calm his heartbeat. Another clang, then a scraping sound from a mechanism inside the door, and it swung outward. A man in a dark blue uniform came into view outside the door. The top of the jamb obscured his face, and he had to dip his head and turn sideways to enter.

The man straightened. He had a russet potato of a face, and a dark blue helmet hung low over his forehead. "Come on now," he said in a rumbly voice. Though obviously some sort of policeman or jailer, he wore no visible gun.

"Where am I? What do you want from me? I won't be—" The policeman-jailer's unresponsiveness stifled Shelling's protests, and he decided to stay in the chair—would not go anywhere until the man answered.

Once, in fifth or sixth grade, Shelling's teacher had tried to send him to the principal's office, but he had refused to go. Despite her command, he remained at his desk, and when she tried to pull him away, he had gripped its sides so firmly she couldn't dislodge him.

"C'mon, no funny stuff," the jailer said. He moved behind Shelling's chair and tipped it forward, forcing Shelling to stand. The jailer was huge, well over a foot taller than Shelling—so large that Shelling couldn't see all of him without stepping back. He flattened against the wall, facing his jailer. He couldn't fight, not this . . . human monolith. The jailer motioned for Shelling to precede him. They entered a narrow hall filled with reddish light; twenty feet or so farther they reached another metal door, which swung open.

"Right turn," the jailer said.

This new passage ran straight, with the same red light and a worn, asbestos tile floor. Shelling tried to estimate the corridor's length, but the featureless passage numbed him. No other doors appeared, and they continued without pause. From behind, he could sense the bulk of his escort, and he labored to remain ahead of the man's heavy stride. The jailer's breathing echoed from the walls and ceiling, a living, writhing sound that encircled them as they walked, formed a path for them through the center of the hall.

Disconnected thoughts and observations flooded Shelling's mind. No other doors here, no rooms. Lost. Subterranean passage . . . ending where? This man, this jailer, his steps, his stride deliberate, each identical to the ones preceding . . . giant robot man . . . maybe only the one speed. Run? Can't run. Viscous atmosphere pressed, like the oatmeal in the movie theater. He longed to be back in his farmhouse bed. This passage bored through the heart of the planet. The walls closed over him, suffocating, so heavy with the weight of earth overhead, all the cities rivers mountains. . . .

Gasping, Shelling stopped, unable to take another step along the limitless path. Behind him, the jailer also stopped. The man's broad hands pushed against Shelling's back, and he cried out as he tumbled forward. Rough stalks pressed against his face. He heard a door clang shut, but when he sat up, he found himself alone in a cornfield.

12

"You ever have flying dreams?" Sammy asked. She pointed to the east, where a wave of passing rain clouds hung. "I become lost in the clouds every time. Can't tell up, down, whatever."

"So where are we headed first then?" I asked, though I was thinking of telling her I had changed my mind again.

"I grew up around here," she said. "I was gone a while, Waterloo College in Austin, stayed there several years after graduating. I got my first book published when I was in Austin. I guess I didn't want to come back here till I had some success. It's the kind of town that draws people back." She smiled. "So you better be careful."

I followed her into an alley between the rug shop and the Japanese restaurant. I had never noticed the alley before, but figured that it led through to the next street, the train station, fire house, movie theater. I was feeling kind of detached, and willing to be led. I had begun the day expecting to go home. Changing my mind about that led to meeting Sammy, so allowing her to guide me on an adventure seemed right. My whole point of staying was to face my past, prove—to myself anyway—that a town, this town, couldn't control me.

"Springdale is a great place," she said, somehow picking up my thoughts. "I guess you weren't allowed to see the best of it though. In a way, it's two towns. There are the bored would-be socialite types. Like Caroline and her friends. And an artistic and intellectual side, related to the college of course but not only people on faculty. It's more like an attraction anchored by the college, but extending beyond it."

"Well, I never saw any of that. Unless you would call Skippy Brisbane an artist. I think she has a computer program that assembles her romance plots." Sammy laughed and, walking close to me, slipped a hand between my bicep and my side. I asked her if she was working on a new novel. "Not to insult you by following a comment on Brisbane with a question about your writing, of course."

She laughed again and squeezed my arm, and my whole body tingled.

"I'm doing something quasi-historical," she said. "I'm more after mood than historical accuracy. It's about Diogenes of Lesbos." ⊕

⊕ Words emerge. Where they come from is a question that has mystified philosophers for generations. The Greeks used to sit under the twisted branches of olive trees and argue that words were given to humans by either whales or birds.

Some years before the Punic War, the members of the whale camp made the distinction that birds lacked the capacity for speech because their tongues were too small. The bird camp held up the example of parrots to disprove this. Mere mimicry, the whale supporters rebutted, not true speech. These arguments persisted throughout the Classical period. Eventually, a group of rebel philosophers, led by Diogenes of Lesbos, started its own city on a hill overlooking the Mediterranean south of Corinth. Diogenes of Lesbos was a charismatic figure, depicted always with a crow perched on his upraised right forearm and his left hand grasping the staff of knowledge. The Diogenines, as they came to be called, set up a multiracial, egalitarian community based on observations of the Pacific albatross. They learned to communicate with birds in ways never before accomplished.

The other group, those espousing whales, left only legendary data. At some point before the time of Alexander, they moved to the North Sea where they could live closer to the whales. Unprepared for the extreme temperatures, they froze to death, and all records of their research disappeared. Recently, an expedition sponsored by the National Geographic Society encountered what might be the remains of their settlement, located on a promontory in Norway.

Meanwhile, the bird branch has proved that Mozart understood the method by which birds transmitted language to humans. He was working on a piece that, when finished, would have enabled all humans to comprehend the complexities of language. Unfortunately, he died before completing this work, which took the form of a series of harpsichord sonatas. Incomplete, they serve only to show us what might have been. Future researchers may find a way to decipher his notes, which resemble the footprints of pigeons in the sand. ⁕

It seemed like we had been trudging along for some time. I hadn't worn the right shoes. They were a kind that looked like they should be great for walking but just don't have the proper support. I should get rid of them. Cost versus comfort. If I stop wearing them, my feet will feel better, but then I would be wasting something that I had spent too much money on.

The walls on either side remained a uniform red brick, but beneath our feet, the surface had changed from pavement to wood, a knotty pine with a gleaming finish, like a basketball court. The alley darkened, and I shivered. The air didn't feel any cooler, but it felt different somehow, tingly—that's how I would describe it. I looked up. Despite the gloom down here, blue sky filled the space between the buildings, and sunlight reflected off a low cloud, but the light couldn't seem to reach us. The cheery sky combined with the gloom around us reminded me of that Magritte painting, the one where the street is dark even though a daytime sky hovers over it.⁕

⁕ L'empire des lumières (The Dominion of Light) 1952, oil on canvas, collection of Lois and Georges de Menil. Magritte made sixteen oil and ten gouache versions of L'empire between 1949 and 1964. He believed that a painting does not express ideas, but has the power to create them. In a letter to Marcel Mariën, July 27, 1952, Magritte said: "The attempt at an explanation (which is no more than an attempt) is unfortunate: I am supposed to be a great mystic, someone who brings comfort (because of the luminous sky) for unpleasant things (the dark houses and trees in the landscape)." This reconciliation of opposites was a paradox typical of the Surrealists. ⁕

Farther on, the light increased; when I looked up again, the sky had vanished, replaced by a domed ceiling painted in abstract colored blobs, bright shades of red and orange, with black streaks. Somehow, we had entered a vast, circular space, illuminated by recessed lighting. A railing ran around the diameter of the dome at about second-story level.

I stopped. "Hey," I said. Sammy turned to face me. "Where the fuck are we?"

13

Shelling plodded through the corn for days or what seemed like days, unable to reach the edge of the field. At least he had food. The ears were mature and sweet; he stripped off the husks and ate as he went. But walking was a struggle. He found it difficult to maintain a straight path in any direction. What crazy hand had seeded these fields? No even rows here, everything random, as though planted by chance. And so early in the season—he had thought that this year's sweet corn wouldn't be ready until much later, deep into July or even August. He looked skyward. The clouds were that runny kind, but whatever breeze energized them didn't reach into his lonely cornfield.

He tried to keep the sun ahead. As a child, he had often tramped along a ditch near his house, pushing his way through tall sunflowers, slashing at them with a hunting knife. But he had known the ditch was near, a few feet to his left, and across it, the streets leading home.

At last, when the sun reached the top of a line of distant trees, he found a road. Roads like this crisscrossed the area, connecting farm, field, and town. He set off to his right, and after a hundred yards or so, a house appeared behind a tumbled stone wall. He decided to stop there and ask directions. A stone path, crowded by overrunning grasses and dandelions, led to the house, and when Shelling reached the front door, he recognized it as his own.

His door was unlocked as usual; he turned the glass knob and

stepped into his living room. Oh, home, his furniture, the two paintings by that California-based Russian artist that he had acquired in
L.A., the lingering scent of last night's tomato-basil-garlic pasta. He
flopped onto the sofa and sobbed. The day, its unknowable trials now
passed, folded down, but the familiar objects of his life supported
him. Sitting in his comfortable living room, that cell, the jailer . . . now
distant.

When Shelling opened his eyes, the sun had set. He showered and
dressed in clean clothes. Unable to remember why his car wasn't there,
he called the town's taxi service, and when a cab arrived, he told the
driver to take him to the Japanese restaurant. He remained silent all the
way to town. At the restaurant, he took a seat by the front window.
The empty dining room saddened him. He had thought, after seeing the
women at breakfast, after the day's ordeal, that he would find the town
revivified. Not this . . . continuation of emptiness.

Monique the waitress brought him tea. The unglazed teapot and mug
had a rough shape, more likely formed by hand than wheel. The warmth
of the mug seeped into his palm and flowed up his arm. "Are these
yours?" he asked. "I keep saying I want to visit your studio and never
do—is tomorrow afternoon good?"

The waitress's expression reminded him of the men at the hardware
store—distant, as though inhabiting a different world. She walked back
toward the kitchen, leaving Shelling to stare out at the street and the
darkened store opposite. At some point he heard another customer enter
but didn't turn around to see. What was the use? He couldn't stand the
thought of another snub, another cryptic encounter. A person, even an
outgoing person, soon succumbs, shrinks into solitude, even embraces
it. But that wasn't him, wasn't what *he* wanted. Where was Monique?
He thought that he had made some progress, attempting to set up an
appointment with her outside the workplace. That wall again. Things
had to be done in small steps, but the time involved, he didn't have the
patience anymore. He would tell Monique he was an actor. She would

want to sleep with someone who had appeared on television, who knew famous people.

Someone slid into the booth behind him; the cushion and frame creaked with the person's weight. A rumbly voice asked for tea.

14

Looking back the way we came, I saw no entry point, nothing but an unbroken curve of wainscoting that rose to chest-level and, above it, plaster walls painted a warm terra-cotta. I stood in the middle of the room, under the multicolored dome, while Sammy circled the periphery.

"What is this place? I didn't notice us going through a door. We were in the alley—"

"The transition is always subtle," she said. She kept walking, trailing a finger along the surface of the wainscoting.

This made no sense. We had been walking down an alley. Which must have led directly into this place. Since my arrival in Springdale, I had been preoccupied with my past. An autopilot kind of thing, and being so inward-focused, I hadn't been aware enough of my surroundings to notice where we were going.

"Here's something," she said.

She looked over at me, but I didn't move. Who was she, really? We had met, what, an hour ago? She pushed on the wainscoting, and a section swung away from her. It might have shut after we entered, but I didn't remember coming in over there. Sammy stood by the open section, waiting for me. I joined her.

"This is ridiculous. How could somebody who has never been here find their way out after the door closed?"

"This isn't the way we came in. It's the way forward."

I just stared at her, irritation building inside me.

"Patrick, I said I would show you places Caroline never took you. She's

lived in Springdale her whole life but knows nothing about this. Springdale's mysteries are well-guarded, to keep the unaware safe."

It must have been obvious from my face that I still wasn't accepting
anything; she smiled and touched my cheek with her fingertips. "Springdale is a complex town, a crossroads, and we're in its hub. We enter, we
find our way through. Maybe something we experience changes the way
we look at the world."

Sammy emanated a sincerity that I found comforting—a jury would
have bought it, no problem. So I buried my reluctance and smiled back.
Her explanation hadn't answered my questions, but if adventure beckoned, I was ready. This was adventure day, obviously, originating in that
moment, that precise alignment of cloud and sun when I decided not to
leave Springdale.

She stooped and passed through the doorway. I followed. Inside was
round, curved like a pipe; the ceiling was too low for standing erect. The
passage appeared to continue in a straight line, lit from a source I couldn't
identify. The indirect light had a misty quality, making it hard to judge
distance. A click from behind made me turn. The wainscoting door had
swung shut behind us. I pushed, but could find no way to open it.

"You can't do that," she said. "When you're in here, forward is the only
way to go. Come on."

I had no choice but to follow. My neck started to ache from walking
hunched. Sammy was only an inch or so shorter than me, so she didn't
have it any easier. My thoughts turned into a jumble; I found myself wondering what time I would be returning to the bed and breakfast. Those
places were often weird about their guest's hours.

"It's always different here, each time you come," Sammy said. "Sometimes these corridors run straight out to the cornfields. It's better when
the ceiling's higher. I feel like I'm walking on chicken strings in here."

Eventually, our pipe intersected with a cylindrical room, like a vertical
pipe, with a ceiling several feet over our heads. "This is way better," she
said as we straightened. I reached back to rub my neck with both hands.

"Let me," she said, and began kneading my shoulders. I could feel her breasts against my back. Her hair smelled perfect, some kind of mint and rosemary scent. ✥ I liked having her near. It was funny—aside from a brief conversation at that party back when I lived here, we had met only that morning, but I felt as though we had a connection that went deeper. I suppose that explained why I wasn't more anxious about this place she had brought me—I had some innate trust in her. And I wasn't anybody's timid waffle. I liked to explore.

"I appreciate you bringing me here," I said. "Wherever 'here' is."

She stopped massaging but left her hands on my shoulders. They felt warm there, strong guides. "We picked a good day," she said. "This place isn't always possible to find." She pushed my right shoulder and pulled my left, turning me around. Her face had a soft expression, thoughtful, and I felt that connection again. "I wanted to share some of the real Springdale with you."

✥ Aveda™, Mint and Rosemary Shampoo, with organic invigoration. Is this a pretentious choice? Could her hair not be equally well-served by the products shelved in drug and grocery stores or the natural brands found in the local food co-op? Connor Evans, proprietor of Kinetic Hair, would say that this brand, this particular formula, is perfectly matched with Sammy Hidalgo's hair type. Though he, of course, is not a reliable reporter. What would be the opinion of Caroline Miller, ex-wife of Patrick Travis and no friend of Ms. Hidalgo (for reasons having much to do with Ms. Hidalgo's status as an artist and with her Mexican-American heritage). Unfortunate that she's still in Spain, out of range of this discussion. ✥

"Sammy . . . I, I appreciate that. But this—" I waved my hands around. "It doesn't make any sense. These rooms and passages leading nowhere. Anyway, I guess we have to go back now." I hunched over and turned into the low corridor from which we had just emerged, but before I could go any farther, she grabbed my arm and yanked me back.

"You can't do that!"

She had a bark that I hadn't expected. She still held my arm, which started to throb. I shook her grip loose. "What's—"

"I told you before. You can only go one way." She rubbed my arm gently, as if smoothing out the spot she had held. "I hope I didn't hurt you." She moved closer and touched my face with her other hand. "This place is sort of a sophisticated funhouse. It has rules, though, and they have to be followed. The main rule is you always move forward. To advance from here, we have to find another door."

15

Shelling loved yellowtail the most, followed by tuna and salmon. Before finding consistent TV work in L.A., he couldn't afford sushi. Sometimes he would order a cup of miso soup and one piece of fish and make it last an hour. He wasn't a glutton, but now, with no financial worries, he wouldn't deny himself the pleasures. He had been thrilled to discover that his new town possessed such a fine Japanese restaurant. What was it Kinsey-Moore had said in her essay on gastronomy? "The path to flavor, though often blocked by under-seasoning, over-saucing, improper cooking, and so many more obstacles that it makes one hesitate, has at its end rewards ample enough to make all trials worthwhile." *

This joyful trinity: fine food, drink, and congenial companions was what made all the Hollywood crap bearable. Crazy how much money the people out there flung around, even to pay small-time actors like him. Though never in a starring role, he had always found consistent work and had invested his earnings well, never wasting money on ridiculous expenditures like sports cars and trendy Albanian clothes. He

* Ruth Kinsey-Moore, *The Lore of True Cuisine*, Williamson House Press, New York, NY, and Glasgow, Scotland, 1974, p. 123. Perhaps the best book on food and eating ever written. Dwarfish, frizzy-haired, and caustic, Kinsey-Moore would not have thrived in this era of telegenic celebrity chefs, though many of the current breed pay banal compliments to her legacy. *

had known others, friends from his early years, people who had shopped in the same thrift stores, but who, after "making it," spent everything they earned and more, a never-ending deluge that inevitably turned into over-extended credit and the forced-liquidation of expensive toys as soon as the sources of income dissipated for any length of time over a month.

Something heavy approached, a presence forceful and unavoidable. A hand landed on his shoulder, where it stayed, pressing with an insistence that caused him to look up, discovering beside him the massive blue-uniformed man who had taken him from the narrow room, and who was now holding his shoulder with a wide and formidable hand. The man beckoned with his other hand, and Shelling rose, abandoning sushi and contentment.

The man steered him up the street to a dim alley between the Japanese restaurant and the rug shop. Shelling stopped at the black maw of the alley. "What's this all about? I have rights, you know."

He tried to turn, but the man's fingers clamped onto his shoulders. Shelling refused to move. Let the man push him. Instead, the man slipped his hands under Shelling's armpits and lifted. Shelling squirmed, trying to break the policeman's hold. He swung his legs back and forth, kicking at the man, but nothing had an effect. The policeman-jailer kept walking.

Shelling had appeared in a short-lived television series starring that former professional football player, the one with the state of Texas tattooed on his scalp. The man's size and intimidating interactions with the rest of the cast had upset the delicate essence of creating the show. Once, for fun, the man had grabbed Shelling from behind, encircling his neck with a chokehold that he didn't release until Shelling began to pass out. The man had laughed his "huh huh huh" laugh, and what could Shelling do?

But this new situation was opposite. There was a peacefulness to being carried, as though the act stripped Shelling of responsibility. He felt outside himself, and imagined what it would be like to gaze upon

this scene—the dark-uniformed man carrying his burden (some recalci-
trant youngster) down the alley. The massive jailer transported Shelling
farther than he would have thought possible in this small town. Had
they perhaps left the town, penetrated some intersecting region acces-
sible only to this man?

At some point they must have passed into a building, though Shelling
noticed no transition from open alley to closed-in corridor, identical to
the corridor he and his jailer had traversed earlier.

16

Sammy and I chose opposite directions, but reached the moving panel at
the same time. This one opened to a closet with a metal ladder emerging
through a hole in the floor. We descended, Sammy first. The cold of
the rungs bothered me, and I had to concentrate on not going so fast
I trampled her fingers. The light in the tube grew dimmer the farther
we descended, though it appeared to follow us, illumining the nearest
rungs. Above, everything was dark; I didn't look down any farther than
the next rung and the top of Sammy's head. My shoulder muscles burned
from the effort. Sammy's breathing rasped, a heavy sound from deep in
her throat.

How much longer would this ladder to nowhere continue? The air
down here . . . thin . . . insufficient. The walls, the tube, constricted,
became difficult to squeeze through. Something grabbed my ankles, held
them. I tried to kick them free. I would not become trapped, not here,
not before seeing one last time the glitter of sun on water, hearing waves
caress the shore.

"Patrick!"

Who here knew my name? Not the others—they cared for nothing
but their own petty squabbles. This dream amber-trapped me, forced
its will.

"Stop moving. Breathe, Patrick, breathe." I became aware of Sammy's hands gripping my ankles. I looked down. She had hooked her feet and knees onto the ladder for support. "You were panicking," she said.

"I'm okay now." I must have sounded uncertain because she didn't release me. She talked, not really saying anything, but the sound of her voice soothed me, and she stroked my calf with her fingers. My breath settled, air sliding in and out of my tender throat. A few more breaths, and she slipped her hands from my ankles and resumed her descent.

I hesitated, though not for long. She kept talking; obviously she thought I needed help staying calm. Who had put her in charge anyway? A ladder. I could go down a fucking ladder without coddling. I knew how to handle myself pretty well, no matter the circumstances. I glanced down at the top of her head. She cared about me, didn't want me to injure myself. And she had brought me to this place to share an experience before I left town.

"Looks like we're nearly there," she said. "Somewhere, anyway."

Careful to maintain my desperate grip on the rungs, I leaned out, trying to see what lay beyond her, at the base of the ladder. There was a pinkish surface, difficult to make out in the dim light.

"Hold up," she said. "Looks like the ladder ends a few feet from the bottom. I'm going to grab the lowest rung with my hands and drop." She worked her way down rung by rung, then slid her right foot off, followed by the left.

"How far?" I asked, but she had already let go.

She cried, "Wheee!" and dropped, holding her glasses to her face the way a scuba diver holds the mask. Her feet met the surface. "It's spongy foamy—" Her legs, then her body, disappeared into the pinkish mass, cutting off the rest of her words.

I scuttled down the remaining rungs and, not wanting to drop directly over her, pushed off. The stuff met my falling body and pulled me in. It had a thin membrane that made a little "shoup" kind of noise, then I sank into a mass of translucent jelly. Before I could think, I inhaled. The stuff sluiced into my mouth and throat, but instead of choking, I felt refreshed, as though the jelly contained an oxygen-rich mix—a viscous, breathable swimming pool. I folded onto my stomach and swung my arms downward, attempting to paddle. The vat of jelly disoriented me. Light came from somewhere, maybe the jelly itself. Although I could see through the stuff, I had nothing with which to orient myself. The tube containing the ladder hadn't been more than three feet across, but I had no way of knowing the size of this jelly tank. I wanted to find a wall and gain comfort from its solidity. I tried a breaststroke, my version of one anyway. I had never been much of a swimmer, but this—with no worries about squirting water up my nose or having to match the strokes with my breathing—was kind of nice.

Stopping, I hung in the stuff and looked around to see if my swimming had brought me to anything recognizable. Off to my right I saw a shape darker than the jelly, and I set off toward it.

17

Shelling woke on his back. He had dreamt of an academic conference at a beach resort, where he spent his time at various lectures, the nature of which he couldn't remember. There had been something he was expected to do, prevent a group from being trapped or taken prisoner. Odd thing for him to dream. He had never been to an academic conference, hadn't even played an academic on television.

His nose itched; he reached for it, but discovered that he couldn't move. Padded straps locked his wrists and ankles to some kind of pallet or slab of plywood.

He rolled his head as far as he could in every direction. High on the wall were two windows. A whistling vent stirred the air. The room—he had been here before. His forehead and armpits were sweat-dampened. He needed to wipe the sweat from his face . . . couldn't . . . could do nothing. A wave hit, helplessness complete. He lay looking up at the plaster ceiling. Dry streambeds scored its surface, flowing around peaks and fissures. A desert, not without life, but the spiders stayed mainly in the corners, building their homes without disturbance.

He had known an actress who reminded him of a spider—something about her dark hair and long, skinny arms and bulbous elbows, the shape of her mouth when she spoke. He always thought she was trying to suck in the world. That show they had been on . . . a comedy. She had played the main character while he appeared in five episodes of the first and only season ⊕.

⊕ Linda Scales. Now the kickboxing partner of Ralph Ambrose in the syndicated action-adventure series *Poseidon's Quest*. It is doubtful that she would remember Shelling, having taken no notice of him during their time together on the comedy show, though this was not his fault—Scales was one of the most self-centered people in an industry of self-centered people. ⊕

Without those giant walnut elbows he would have found her arms alluring. Long arms attracted him—the smooth distance down from shoulder, along bicep, humerus, and tricep.

The lights in his cell brightened, a flash that overpowered his eyes with white. His pupils retreated, agonized by the unexpected intrusion; he covered them with his lids. A clang sounded, then a clicking-whirring. He blinked repeatedly, trying to bring the room back into focus.

His vision cleared enough for him to see the outlines of the windows, and as he concentrated on their shape, his pallet moved. The end where his head lay began to rise, a slow, ratchety pull; the whole pallet climbed the wall, lifting him upright.

"Adjustments, adjustments must be made. No one prepared, and so I must crank and strap, fill and elevate."

The speaker was a woman. Her voice soothed him, a musical tone not unlike that of Mindy, the actress he had lived with for six months, the one who had been a folksinger before getting a part in a movie about a folksinger, which led to more parts, even parts having nothing to do with folksinging. He had left her eventually, though he couldn't recall why.

His rising pallet was becoming uncomfortable as gravity pulled at his body, at the straps binding his wrists. He tensed to hold himself upright. At some point his eyes recovered, and he could see the woman. She was directly below him and bent over, fiddling with something at the bottom edge of his pallet, now several inches above the floor. When she straightened, the top of her curly red hair was about even with his waist. Behind her stood a low, wheeled platform; on its front was a metal rod topped by bicycle handlebars and a control panel, like a piece of exercise equipment.

She looked up at him, and he thought it *was* Mindy, but with hair red instead of blonde. Mindy though, she was six feet tall. Funny how he had thought of arms—he had loved to watch the movement of her arm when she strummed her guitar. He closed his eyes. She had written a song for him, "only one sky / sometimes in blue and sometimes gray." ⊕ Stupid to have left her. With her, here, this empty town wouldn't seem so bleak.

When he opened his eyes, the short woman had gotten onto the platform. Her hands rested on the chrome sides of the control panel. She pushed a button with her thumb, and the platform elevated, kept rising until her face leveled with his.

"Better, better," she said, and tweaked the joystick forward, then left, to maneuver herself in front of him.

Close, she no longer resembled Mindy.

⊕ "Only One Sky." Though actually written by Jack Hardy, released on *Omens*, 2000. Mindy Vaughn had lied. Why? Was it because she considered her own song writing to be inadequate and wanted praise from a man she admired? And Shelling—a few months later, he responded to her admiration by ending their relationship. ⊕

Her eyes were farther apart, or maybe less rounded, and her nose wasn't as pointed.

"And now we can attend to preparations."

Her skin was creamy, unblemished by mark or wrinkle, and her eyes were a soft blue-green. Surely this wasn't the face of a torturer? She lifted the ends of a belt from the sides of the pallet and buckled it over his chest, then pulled it tight.

Shelling gasped. "What is this? What have I done? Hurts . . . I won't be strapped—" He couldn't take in enough air to form words.

The woman wheeled her platform back a few feet. "Subject #17 has been secured for analysis." She leaned over the control panel and flipped a cigar-shaped plastic rod from its socket and pointed it at him. Holes covered its rounded tip. With a stubby forefinger, she reached down to push a green button. "Begin recording. How many faces do you have?" She looked at Shelling as though waiting for an answer. "How many?" she asked again.

He tried to speak, he opened his mouth, intending to offer something, but his outburst had drained him of words.

"Subject refuses to speak." She pushed the green button again.

He moved his head from side to side and mouthed "no no no," but she wasn't looking. What crime had he committed? This town, *his* town, he had thought, but if it *were* his town, it would not have conspired to keep him alone and helpless, would not have subjected him to the giant policeman and his partner, this crazed midget-woman with her straps and platform and buttons.

18

With the jelly limiting visibility, I was right over Sammy before I saw her. She hovered, facing downward. At first I thought she had lost consciousness, then her hands flapped, slow, water-treading strokes. She appeared to be watching something. I stroked downward. It took a lot of strokes to reach her. Either I moved half an inch at a time or she was way farther down than I had thought.

Sammy must have sensed my movement—as I neared her, she looked up and smiled. She turned onto her back and waved. She spoke, but the jelly absorbed the sound. I mouthed back. When I reached her, she pointed down at whatever she had been watching. Below lay the town, like a view from an airplane. Everything was there, church, town hall, houses, stores. Paperclip-sized cars moved along Main Street. She reached for my hand, and we hovered there, holding hands and watching.

"I want to get closer," I said, and mimed swimming. We kicked to propel ourselves lower. A man exited the hardware store and stepped into the street without waiting for a car to pass. The car jerked to a stop, and the man kept going. Farther up the street, several teenagers blocked the sidewalk in front of the record store. When I saw the café where Sammy and I had eaten breakfast, my stomach rumbled. Had that been this morning? It seemed so long ago. What a god-like sensation, floating over the town like this, so real I thought I could sweep a hand down and pluck a tree from its bed. Probably a video of the town projected onto the floor, with the jelly giving it a three-dimensional appearance. Releasing Sammy's hand, I stroked downward, then I reached to touch the floor. My fingers punched in the roof of a pickup truck. I jerked my hand back and looked at Sammy, who had followed me down. Her expression reflected my surprise.

We stayed at this lower level but kept our hands well away from the street and buildings. Someone emerged from the alley by the rug shop and looked up. It was that fat cop, the one I called Scooter because I couldn't picture him chasing anyone. He was looking in our direction, or at least at the area where we would be if we were really there instead of floating in a vat of pink jelly.

Then he raised his right arm and pointed his index finger straight at us. Sammy grabbed my hand and squeezed. My heart started thumping. "There's no way he can see us," I said. The jelly swallowed my words, but Sammy knew what I meant.

Scooter, as though aware he held our attention, slowly rotated his hand toward the alley behind him, and held it taut, like a weathervane in a strong wind. He held that pose for a while, as if making sure we understood his intent. Then he turned and walked into the mouth of the alley.

Sammy pulled my arm, then dropped it and stroked toward the alley. I followed. The buildings grew larger the closer we got to them, rising like the sides of a brick canyon. We swam through the canyon till we reached a wall that blocked the alley. Sammy touched my hand and pointed up with her other, then kicked her way skyward. We found an open slit of a window. Sammy went straight for it. She tilted her head to the side to make herself flatter and pulled herself in.

I waited until her feet were all the way through, then tried to copy her, but when I put my head into the window, I couldn't breathe. Worse than on the ladder, this crack, the world above, its magnitude sagging. I tried to pull out of the crack, but my head wedged. Sammy would have to come back to help push me free. I stopped moving, trying to think. What had she said earlier? Can't go back.

Closing my eyes, I concentrated on slow, even breath, and pushed myself in. My shoulders somehow flattened enough for me to squeeze through, and I tumbled onto a carpeted floor about two feet below the window. Sammy lay beside me. We had escaped the jelly. Right away the stuff started to dry out, congealing in my hair and face like gelatinous latex. I pulled it from my mouth. Bits of the stuff clung to the back of my throat, but they slowly dissolved. Exhaustion and exhilaration surged through me simultaneously.

"The town," I said. "Like we were there. That breathable jelly." When I got the stuff out of my eyes, I turned back to the window, which was larger on this side. Out there, the sky was a pinkish haze. I grabbed Sammy's hand. "What about that truck? I couldn't have—"

"I don't know. The whole thing was new for me too." Her face had a fixed-in-place look, as if she was trying not to be scared, and her fingers curled tight over mine.

We worked on peeling ourselves clean. Sammy had cleared most of the stuff from her head and neck. Bits of it dotted her nose, and strands hung from her glasses' frames. "You look like you've dumped a bottle of one of those facial mask things all over yourself," I said.

"Would you like a mirror?"

When I smiled, the stretch and crack of solidifying goo tickled my face. I ran my tongue over my lips, which tasted sweetish. A strip of the dried jelly stuck to Sammy's cheek; I reached to brush it off. She held my hand there and leaned toward me. Her lips tasted sweetish too, fruity-tart like a plum jam. She stroked my back, passing her hand from the base of my neck down and up again. I felt her lips on my ear, and everything tingled. She moved her hands to my face and held my cheeks. Her dark eyes . . . what were they trying to say? We kissed again, slowly, and I understood something I never had with Caroline. We don't need explanations for every action. Tenderness, warmth for another, don't have to be linked with anything other than their own existence.

I forced myself back. "Scooter—that's what I call that cop," I said. "He couldn't have been motioning to *us*."

"His name is Officer Stockman," she said. "Something's wrong. We'll have to keep going till we get to him, find out what's happening." She raised my right hand and kissed fingertips. "Later . . . later, can I take you home and cook you dinner?" We stood close, and the pressure of her strong thigh against mine reassured me.

The room had a normal door, with a panel of frosted glass and a metal knob. We went through it into a long hall. Ahead, something blocked the corridor.

Our movements felt disproportionate to the stretched-out passage, so that we walked and walked but appeared to grow no closer to whatever awaited us. As though afraid that speech would slow our progress, we remained silent. My calves began to ache, dull pain accompanying each step. We held hands, and I found the contact comforting. I knew that together, we would reach . . . then, with a suddenness that made me pause, the shape loomed close; a few steps farther it became Scooter. He stood motionless beside a wide, rust-colored metal door. His bulk filled the hall. At first, I thought he was asleep standing up, but when we got close enough for me to see into his eyes, I had the impression that his mind had turned inward, to run some deep mental process requiring an intensity of concentration that I wouldn't have thought him capable of mastering.

He turned his jowly face toward us, a movement so gradual that it gave me this crazy detachment, as if I watched him look at me from a vantage other than my own. He seemed to measure me with his eyes, dissecting every detail of my appearance. When he spoke, his voice rumbled and his words made no sense. "Thinner, hair different, but identical. One inside"—pointing to the metal door—"and one here. Both inhabiting where only one should." He looked at Sammy. "Do you comprehend?" She nodded.

"I don't," I said. "When we were in that jelly, I touched a truck."

He waved a broad hand, quieting me. "Two roads met here, and the force of their meeting sent waves rolling in widening curves, encompassing worlds." He shook his head, as though trying to clear it.

"Laureanno's Law?"✢ Sammy asked, and Scooter nodded. She looked at me.

"I'm not understanding any of this," I said. I needed to go outside, into sunlight. Scooter reached toward me with a tree branch arm and rested it on my shoulders. The contact warmed me; I hadn't realized I was shivering.

"Laureanno fits the circumstances," he said. His voice filled the space, embracing me with as much force as his arm had. "Only the one who belongs can remain. Expelling the other should regain the balance." I pictured his voice flowing down the hall and bursting out into. . . . I had no idea where the hall led.

Scooter lifted his arm from my shoulders and turned to the door. It creaked open at his touch. He stepped through and gestured for us to follow. Inside, a man lay on a hospital bed with the back part elevated so that he sat up. The tall policewoman I had seen around town with Scooter stood on the far side. Her gaze absorbed me the same way Scooter's had.

✢"What we regard as the real world is determined by the information our brain is able to process. If we depart our 'real' world, our brain, depending on the attributes of this 'unreal' world we enter, sees only those elements which correspond to our 'real' world . . . if our counterpart exists in this 'unreal' world (which would, of course, be 'real' for our counterpart), complications arise which stretch the proportions of the world in unforeseen ways." M. Laureanno, *Understanding Dimensions*, 2nd ed., Springer-Verlag, Philadelphia, PA, 1998, pp. 169–70. ✢

19

The giant policeman slipped into Shelling's cell, a silent arrival, unnoticed until his bulk commandeered the entirety of Shelling's vision. Two others hovered beyond him, a man and a woman, framed by the doorway. The giant policeman and the two newcomers approached the midget woman on her platform. The new woman looked familiar, but everyone he saw now reminded him of someone from his past, someone he had worked or slept with in California, and that was impossible; it needed to be impossible. His brain, rebelling at his treatment, had formed associations that, although they defied logic, served to give him an anchor in this otherwise disorienting experience. He looked at the other newcomer, expecting to be reminded of yet another figure from his past. But instead of a face, the other had a patch of glowing, blue-green mist.

Shelling twisted his body; the padded straps cut into his wrists. "Let me go," he said, surprised that his voice was working again.

20

Sammy peered at the face of the man lying in the hospital bed. "You're right. They are the same." She looked back at me. "Patrick has to be the right one. But how could the double have broken through?"

"What are you talking about?" When I stepped forward, it was my turn to gasp. The man on the bed had my face. Like Scooter said, hair, other bits, different, but still me. The man's pupils were dilated, and he jerked his head around, looking at each of us in turn, over and over.

Scooter approached the tall policewoman. She and Scooter were about the same height. He glanced at her notepad, then back to me. "What do you see?" he asked. I looked at him without responding. He waved an oven-mitt hand around. "This room, this person, what do you see?"

"A room. A man in a bed, hospital bed. He looks like me. What am I supposed to see?"

Sammy reached for my hand. "This can't be easy," she said. "I'm here. I'll help you."

"Help me what?" I pulled my hand away from hers.

"Only one of them can stay," the tall policewoman said. She spoke softly, but her husky voice carried.

Scooter nodded. "But which?" he asked her, not looking at me.

"This one." The tall policewoman pointed to the man in the bed. "He says he's an *actor*." She said "actor" as if it were an explanation, and Scooter bobbed his heavy head up and down in agreement.

Scooter turned to Sammy. "We brought him in earlier, but let him go. We felt the waves crossing, but weren't positive he was the signifier."

The tall policewoman came over to my side of the bed and stood between me and the other, extending an open palm toward each of us as though using them to probe our identities. She had her back to me, and when she spoke, she directed her words to Scooter. "This one, in the bed, he has a past, but his misplacement distorts his perceptions."

"And so he must be removed," Scooter said.

"Removed?" I said.

The tall policewoman lowered her hands and turned to face me. "Sent back to his world."

I looked up at her narrow face, trying to read it, looking for some sign of concern. I pointed to the man in the bed, who had stopped his erratic head-turnings and locked his gaze on me. "This person. He's somehow a version of me?"

Sammy stared at the guy in the bed for a moment, then came over to me. She took my hand again. "Your counterpart is an actor. That's his connection."

"*You* must perform the separation," the tall policewoman said.

"I don't know what you mean."

"Don't be stupid!" Her spittle brushed my cheeks. I started to yell back at her, but she grabbed my shoulders and pushed me against the door. The back of my head struck its hard surface, and I cried out. My vision turned yellow, black, and red. I flailed my arms but couldn't break her grip. A rush and confusion of voices filled the room—Sammy's, Scooter's rumble—then the tall policewoman released me.

Scooter spoke: "Please believe me. Officer Mercurio has never raised her voice or struck anyone in her life. The other's presence causes distortion. The removal must be done now."

My head throbbed. The tall policewoman, Officer Mercurio, her face was still too close. Her eyes, a dull brown, stared into mine, and I couldn't break contact, couldn't blink. She spoke, her voice low and soothing:

"Rare and marvelous though it is, a moment of exquisite alignment of script, cast, and performance can cause a new reality to emerge, inhabited by the characters involved in that moment. Of that moment." She said some other things, but I couldn't grasp any of it. At some point she stopped and turned away.

Sammy held a hand near my face, but didn't touch me. "You understand now, don't you?" she asked. "Not everyone here knows these things."

Officer Mercurio unsnapped her holster and withdrew some kind of automatic pistol. I knew nothing about guns. I took a step back. "No—I can't shoot a person."

She pulled my hand over the grip. "Must be the head. Move closer." When I didn't move, she gripped both my shoulders and shook me. "Only you can perform the restoration. Now."

"What happens if I don't do it?"

Scooter screamed in my face—"You're a fool! A base and ignorant man—you have no idea what forces are involved, the consequences we all live with, the powers shaping our lives."

Officer Mercurio put a hand on Scooter's shoulder and spoke quietly: "Officer Stockman is right. You don't know. That isn't your fault, none of this is your fault, but that doesn't change the circumstances. If *you* do it, no harm will come to your counterpart. The only other choice is for us to erase *both* of you."

I stepped nearer to my counterpart and raised the gun. It was too heavy for one hand, and its weight seemed to increase the longer I held it—a fell instrument of dire construction, I thought. The man in bed stared at me with my eyes, but I had the impression that what he saw differed from my vision of the room. Did he see a man, a man with his face, pointing a gun at him?

Holding the gun with both hands, I sighted down the barrel. "I'm sorry," I said.

I saw the bullet from both sides, its slow, straight path away from me but also flying into my face, so close now that I could read the letters on its tip.

The recoil threw me against the door. The other separated from me, and as he slipped away, I had a sense that he was returning to something. My head throbbed even more and my vision blurred. Someone removed the gun from my hand. Sammy's arms encircled me, and I took solace in her touch.

21

Shelling watched a black, circular body pass before a fiery
disk. The movement of the black
shape captured his attention. He couldn't
look away, and as he watched, he lost all
desire to try. Something—some warning he
had once read about direct viewing of solar
eclipses—flashed across his consciousness.
The black shape kept moving until it
obscured the fire, and in the ensuing
darkness a cloud of chilled air
covered him.

22

When my eyes were working again, I moved closer to the bed. I needed
to see what I had done. The man's head had exploded, painting the wall
in bone and blood. I gagged and tried to back away, but my knees gave
out. Scooter was there for support on one side, Sammy on the other. They
carried me into the hallway and lowered me to the floor. The reddish
lights of the hallway spun, forming whirlpools of virulent illumination
and color. I reached toward them, spinning too, floating up and out,
joining the evening air, where a pale moon hovered and trees sighed like
reunited lovers.

23

Danielle Saul was bragging to Shelling about the photographs that
she had commissioned from Crain, or some name like that, a famous
celebrity photographer whom Shelling had never heard of. He smiled
and nodded, the way people did in Hollywood. She had just finished
filming a movie that was scheduled to be the summer's biggest hit and
was expected to be her final step toward super-stardom. Shelling felt
detached from the conversation, from the party around him, which was
in the cliffside home of Rod Spender, the television producer responsible
for *Precinct 10*, *Gravity Man*, *Fresno Boulevard*, and many others. Shelling
had worked on several of them.

He left Danielle Saul and drifted into Rod Spender's "trophy room,"
the walls of which were covered with photographs, awards, and assorted
memorabilia (Duggal's battered helmet from *Gravity Man*, a Fresno Blvd.
street sign, a baseball uniform from some long-forgotten sports drama).
Shelling's attention wandered across the pictures, recognizing the original cast members of *Blake's River*, posing in the town where the opening
credits had been filmed. He couldn't remember the real town's name. On
the show, they called it Springdale.

The faces in the photograph, the buildings behind them—he had been there, and not solely for his guest appearances on the show. Another time, but when? Finding the photograph somehow threatening, he backed from the wall. What had happened to his house? The simplicity of his vegetable garden had given him such pleasure. He felt a sudden loss . . . intangible yet rooted deep within him. His eyes teared, but for what was he weeping? The patio doors stood open, and he stepped through them to the terrace. Crows called from a line of trees overlooking the ravine. He stared past them, toward a distant house, memorizing its shape as though it held a key to his future.

And beyond these hills lay the city, encircled by the arteries and veins that propelled the life-giving metal corpuscles onward. The edge of a continent crossed by more roads than could ever be traveled. Roads, the reflections of roads, railroads, paved roads, busses, cars, houses along the way—the center of the earth is paved and waiting for the first drivers to arrive.

"There you are." Rod Spender slung an arm around Shelling. "Looks just awesome from here, doesn't it?" Shelling agreed. "I've got something for you," Spender said. "If you're tired of masked aliens. This'll be more like playing yourself."

"I'd like that," Shelling said. "I might even use my real name."

24

I woke on a sofa in an unfamiliar room. Soft light came through the drawn curtains, a lacy, ivory-colored material through which I could see an overhanging branch and, beyond it, the street. A car passed, its lights sweeping along the wall. An odd mix of antiques and rough-made furniture decorated the room. The coffee table in front of the sofa appeared to have been constructed from wine crates: the words Cincque Terre appeared repeatedly over a logo of intertwined vines.

I sat up and rubbed my eyes. They were irritated from my contact lenses, a gritty tiredness that made thinking difficult. I reached into a pants pocket for my eye drops, but couldn't find them. After this . . . day . . . I'd had, all I wanted was my damn eye drops.

The groan came out before I could stop it. I held my breath, listening. I didn't want anyone to know I was awake until I knew where I was. Sounds emanated from another room—water running, then the clang of metal against metal. I got up. Taking care to keep quiet, I walked toward the noises. An arched doorway separated the living room from a dining room, and through the dining room door I could see into the kitchen. Sammy, at the stove, stirring something.

I pulled back, not wanting her to see me. I couldn't talk to her, not after. . . . How could she be cooking dinner as though nothing had happened? I crossed to the front door and turned the glass knob carefully, opened it just enough to squeeze my body through, and escaped into the evening air.

The area was familiar; Sammy had one of the houses overlooking the town. It would take me at least ten minutes to reach the bed and breakfast. As I walked, I kept expecting her to come after me. Next corner, I turned onto the street leading down to the town. The train station was between me and the bed and breakfast. I looked at my watch, which showed ten minutes past eight. There was an 8:50 train. By midnight, I could be back in the city, in my own bed.

I increased my pace, letting the slope pull me. I had no time to explain the situation to the proprietor of the bed and breakfast—what would I say?—or to retrieve my suitcase. I had only packed for a couple of days anyway. I could leave it. But I needed to pop out these damn contact lenses or at least put in eye drops.

Life on the street appeared serene, but in the faces of those who passed, I sensed knowledge of the events that had transpired in that funhouse, or whatever it was. These people . . . this town . . . repelled me. I wondered what would happen if that tall policewoman, Officer Mercurio, saw me. Or Scooter, that comical name I had once applied, now preposterous. A sense of unreality clothed the air. I couldn't bury the feeling that I was escaping something—that if I had stayed with

Sammy, eaten dinner, gone to bed with her after, I would have trapped myself in this town forever.

By the time I got to the train station, I still had fifteen or so minutes. I bought a ticket from the machine and went back out. I wanted to run, but I had to stay calm. Best not to be noticed. The bed and breakfast wasn't far. The foyer was empty. I heard voices coming from the lounge. My room was at the top of the stairs. I fetched what I needed and returned to the street in less than a minute.

By the tracks, I stood watching the steps up to the platform, obsessing on the notion that I would soon view, emerging from the top of the stairs, first the heads of Scooter or Officer Mercurio, then the rest of their bodies as they climbed each step, propelling them toward me to prevent my escape.

Only one other passenger waited, a man in a dark suit standing near the tracks. My position, without the anonymity of a crowd, exposed me to too much scrutiny. I walked farther down the tracks and selected a bench hidden by an overhanging shadow. I waited.

When the train came, it brought the relief of knowing I would soon be home. I boarded and chose a seat. A jolt of dizziness shook me. I slumped forward. That room, what I had done there—it all returned to me, and I watched, a flash of memory so real I felt that I was there again, though apart from myself. The shot, and that man—my doppelganger—the impact of the bullet with his head. His body twitched, rose a few inches, then settled. A glow seeped from him, pinkish like the breathable jelly, and the glow conformed to his features, aped the contours of his body. Where the head had been, the luminescence formed a replacement, solidified, then began to contract, shrinking and taking the body with it until nothing remained but a pink silhouette on the sheets. Then it too faded.

I stared out the train window, trying to see beyond the dark platform, to the town, to the maple trees and peaceful streets, Sammy's house. My fingers cramped, and my right arm spasmed. I relaxed my hand—I had been clutching my contact lens case. The raised L and R indented my palm. I unscrewed the caps and popped my lenses out, relieving my tired, gritty eyes, and with my glasses on, I resumed my vigil.

By now, Sammy would have noticed my absence. What was her role in this? She had given me some crap about living with the knowledge. And Officer Mercurio, what had she said—inconceivable that a character would fall out of its reality. At least I had been here to help send him back to TV land, or whatever the hell it was. But was that his reality . . . ? I jumped up from my train seat. Officer Mercurio, she had said my counterpart was an actor. That was supposed to mean something. And she said he had a past. Implying that I didn't?

Sammy wanted me to stay. And despite everything that had happened today, I trusted her. The train door swished shut.

"No, wait," I said aloud to the empty car.

I scrambled over and tried to pry open the door. "I want to get off." I drummed my hand on the Plexiglas window, yelling for someone to open the door. There had to be a conductor near. Pain shot through my hand—looking down, I saw I had torn my fingernails on the door. With a jerk and shudder, we pulled away. As we rolled out of town, the tangible darkness, with warm sticky fingers, invaded the train.

DARKNESS, AND DARKNESS

Darkness surrounded Newsome, unexpected dark—he hadn't meant to work so late. In the library basement, time passed unnoticed. He had been preparing course packets for next semester's classes, copying articles and applying for permissions, the steady, repetitive work that he preferred. Upstairs, the windows' nighttime clothing startled him—where had the sun gone? He stood near the reference desk, alone in a room emptied of clerks and patrons. Bare branches clawed at glass. He hesitated, reluctant to enter the dark, the resinous, grasping dark. At night, the streets change, their daylight veneer scraped off to reveal glutinous remnants.

Half of the campus and four blocks separated him from home, blocks filled with green walls of hedge and tree to snag the unwary. Lacking its students, the college was silent. He didn't like students, their mocking laughter and eternal youth, but their presence helped expel the dark.

Newsome had grown up around them. His father, an electrician, had worked for the college until his death. That death—a highway accident that also took Newsome's mother—was what brought him back to town. He had been living in a larger city, sharing an apartment, working in a pet store. Tired of cleaning the stank cages, he moved into his parents' paid-off house.

Tonight, the college was a blackened husk. Darkness penetrated his jacket with dismaying ease. The glow of the campus security building sneered at him, too distant for its light to help. He considered going there to complain—they were required to keep certain lights on, for safety. But he avoided the security people, many of whom he had known since childhood. Not friends then or now. Bookboy, they called him. As if that would hurt. His books held far more power than the ridiculous sports programs that mesmerized *them*.

He stopped, remembering a title that he had meant to bring home. Too late to return for it—the dark pushed him onward . . . home, now shared with his sister and her boy. Two months ago, they had appeared at the door. He couldn't prevent them from moving in.

"Our house too," she had said.

The death of his parents had saddened him (and he had never been particularly joyful). His response had been retreat, into himself, into his childhood home. The memories there were better companions than the people he encountered. Ghosts now—his brother, his parents. They deserved sanctuary, with him as curator.

Newsome's brother . . . at fifteen, the dark stole him, the deep dark that filled the old quarry outside of town. Dark in daylight, overflowing with black after sundown. His brother had gone there late, meeting friends. Newsome's parents thought he was in bed, in the room he and seven-year-old Newsome shared. Divers never found the body. Authorities speculated that he had become lodged under an overhang. The brother's disappearance cracked Newsome's youth, cracked his mother.

The sister was two years younger than Newsome, younger but more worldly. If promiscuity and worldliness were the same thing. O'Neill—one of the security guards—visited her, as he had in their youth, insinuating his unwanted bulk into Newsome's refuge. Despite all that Newsome disliked about his sister, he could have suffered the co-habitation, something he had been forced to do for her whole life, but the inclusion of O'Neill infuriated him. In high school, once O'Neill began "seeing" Newsome's sister, Newsome became the favored object of torment for O'Neill and his teammates. After graduation, O'Neill had played football for one of the small colleges in the area, expelled his junior year for never going to class. Now, football uniform exchanged for security guard, the tormenting continued.

Newsome had gone to college too, a small state school, graduating with a degree in biology. He had thought to become a veterinarian, but never pursued it further.

He crossed North College, leaving campus, but the street wasn't much brighter. Curtains drawn, people trapped the light in their homes. A streetlight flickered, died, crushed by the encroaching gloom.

Sensing motion ahead, he stopped. Writhing shadows blocked the sidewalk—he had nearly walked into them. He groped for his keychain flashlight, switching it on before freeing it from his pocket. Creatures made wholly from blackness roamed the night streets, stalking and devouring. Houses, closed and lighted houses, held them back, but one night, their gathered strength would crush all barriers. Last week, a storm had knocked out power, and three days passed before light had been restored. During those powerless nights, the darkness gained territory. A section of the town still remained dark. Explanations for the outage abounded, but solved nothing. Newsome understood why, and he suspected that others did too.

He stepped off the curb to bypass the shadows and continued along the middle of the street. These shadow-creatures grew ever more bold, pushing their bounds, taunting. Their touch would demolish him. In the street, starlight shone down, casting him in a fluid shield. The stars—once he would have thought them unreachable, immune, but even they would fall, when darkness began its final onslaught. Their dying cries would rupture the world; petrified dark would pour out, strangling whatever life remained.

Home wasn't far now. Who would he find there? Perhaps his sister and the boy were out, giving him a few moments of blessed solitude. Each time he reached home after work, each time he saw her car in the driveway, his irritation grew. She didn't have a job, though she claimed to be looking. And the boy—Newsome hated when she forced him to watch the boy on the nights she went out with her friends, presenting it as a fact without argument. Fortunately, the boy was accustomed to being ignored.

The shadows . . . their interference, their threats, had increased after her arrival. She had called soon after Newsome moved in. "Hi, it's sis . . . you visiting? I want to talk to Ma—it's time to make up, don't you think?" The way she spoke—a torrent of self-involvement—left no openings for comment, and it wasn't until after she had gone on about a daughter's need for her mother that Newsome was able to explain what had happened. She expressed shock, and Newsome believed her, had no reason not to, but he didn't trust her. And a few weeks later, she appeared at the door. Perhaps O'Neill had told her about their parents. The thought of living rent-free was too appealing to ignore.

The house was in his name. His parents hadn't known how to find her, hadn't talked to her for several years. They left everything to Newsome.

They had been frugal people and, in addition to the insurance settlement and the retirement fund, there had been a surprising amount of savings—from investment in several certificates of deposit bought when interest rates were high. His sister couldn't have known how much, but she knew their frugality as well as he, had disliked it very much, actually, as it prevented her from having the things she thought she deserved. Not trusting her, not liking her intrusion, her presence in the house, Newsome hid all financial documents.

Her behavior had been disappointing to their parents, but they cared about her boy regardless. They had even invited her to come back to live after he was born, after it became apparent that the father was absent. But she laughed at them. At Newsome, actually, the one who presented their invitation. "So they can control him the way they tried to control me?" she had said. Yet, here she was, pushing, claiming what she had long ago lost all rights to. What if he offered her something? Her fair share, he would call it. Then, if she wanted it (and she would), he would tell her that she had to drop O'Neill. Tonight, if he saw her, he would set it in motion. Surely he could engineer it. A proposition, some discussion . . . not mention O'Neill right off. Play her first. Like fishing . . . his father had been a fisherman—when the accident happened, his parents had been on their way to a rented cabin for a week of fishing. But fishing reminded Newsome of the quarry. He avoided bodies of water. They hid their contents too well.

Before his sister invaded his solitude, he had been content to spend days in the library, amongst the comforting strength of books, and evenings ensconced in familiar surroundings. Although dark had sometimes bled into his home, he was vigilant. He kept spare light bulbs in all rooms, plus powerful flashlights, even a propane camping lantern, which had shielded him during the power outage. His sister—perhaps the shadows had claimed her as a child, bent and shaped her but left her alive.

Thinking that he heard footsteps, he looked back. Darkness followed, darkness pushed him onward. More shadows waited ahead, grinding an impatient rhythm on the pavement. The temperature had dropped. Chilled, shivering . . . the icy shadows laughed—their laughter clogged the air, choking him. He fell to his knees. Nothing and nothing, nothing but helpless hopeless yearning. Maybe he would be the one to leave. Let her have the house. No—sell it. Let a realtor handle everything. He wouldn't miss the chill of dark, but the house . . . his mother's warm perfume . . . the mud on his father's boots after a fishing trip . . . his brother's baseball glove, bat, and scuffed balls . . . even his sister, before she lost her early joy—those bound him.

The darkness had incorporated Newsome's brother. On moonless nights his shadow walked the streets. One night, a few months after the . . . accident . . . he tried to return. A fragment of him surfaced, emerging from the black, seeking home. Newsome heard tapping at his second-floor window. A shape darker than the night sky clung to the

glass, too weak to lift the pane. Newsome pulled a flashlight from under
the bed, but in the light the shape dissolved, leaving oily residue in the
form of his brother's face

Newsome passed through an intersection to reach his block. Down the
cross-street, a figure stood, tall, wearing a long coat. Newsome ran. He
reached his house. Once inside, he looked out a window. The figure
passed, and Newsome recognized him. Henderson, the Spanish professor, who lived at the other end of the block. Jumpy, so jumpy that he
mistrusted anyone walking the nighttime streets.

Still gazing out, he realized that his sister's car was gone. On his way
in, he had been too rattled to notice. Newsome closed the curtains and
switched on lamps. The house had few overhead lights, but had a number
of lamps scattered throughout. He wished there were more. Despite
his father's electrical skills, he had never bothered to install additional
overhead light fixtures (the house dated from a time before those were
common). Newsome could do it, having learned from his father. He had
meant to do it. His sister's arrival interrupted renovation plans.

He slipped off his jacket and sat in his father's armchair. Shadows
seeped through the gaps around the front door and windows. They
whispered, the shadows, they clicked and hissed. The lamps lacked the
power to repel their advance.

Fewer shadows plagued the city he had been living in, and they were
timid, less likely to infiltrate. In darkness, they fatten and grow. Brightness had shielded the pet store, but the cages, great piles of steel and
feces . . . odor overpowered . . . cluttered future, stinking future . . . that
lamp by the front door—hadn't he turned it on? He stood and it sputtered to life. Its glow framed a splotch, an ink-like stain on the floral
wallpaper. Had the stain been there that morning? The wallpaper was
old, but his mother had kept everything perfect.

Seeking more light, he went into the kitchen, where an overhead fluorescent blazed. He fixed dinner and ate with the plate on the counter,
but nothing tasted right in the viscous dark. He tossed out the remains.

Upstairs, he shut his door so he wouldn't have to see his sister or the boy when they returned. He avoided her, he did, and she goaded him. She knew what made him react. She had laughed at him when he wanted help with Clarissa Hudgens. . . . Young Newsome had been afraid to talk to the girls his age. His sister's friends, younger, less intimidating, he thought they might be impressed by an older boy. He was sixteen; Clarissa Hudgens would be fifteen in a few months. But when he asked his sister . . . he learned not to do that a second time.

His bedroom window rattled, as if from a branch, but no trees grew near these windows. Dark, tactile dark. If his sister left, the darkness might subside. Bricks of rage assembled themselves around him. Why should he give up his chair . . . the lamp . . . his place to sit and read? And his book, the book he had been reading lay on the table beside the lamp.

He wanted to howl, sometimes to shriek. Walls, the house, its walls were to be his shield, but now they trapped him, held him while cracks and holes extruded shadows.

From the top of the stairs, he could tell that all the downstairs lamps were off. The dark poured upward like the quarry's black water. It splashed the stairs. The air stank of it, rotten rotten stink. He went back to his bedroom for a flashlight. The dark laughed at the light's thin and pitiful beam. But from deep within the laughter trickled his brother's trapped sobs. Newsome rushed down to reach the nearest lamp. Darkness tripped him. Somehow, he kept hold of the flashlight. He crawled to the lamp and switched it on. Black thinned, but he knew its withdrawal was incomplete; it would remain as long as his sister did.

Last to turn on, the light by his reading chair. He sat and took up his book. His book! He flipped pages—black, all of them black, charred by the dark into an unreadable slab. The black stained his fingers. Despair rose in a spiral that chewed through layers of dark, but the chewed dark assaulted him, plastering his stomach with tar, and in the tar, living in the tar, the one-celled creatures that gave the dark its shape; these creatures need no air, no food, and though they fear the sun, they had, over millennia, learned to shield themselves. Where was their counter, a sun-creature to devour the dark and shit it back into the world, tamed and subdued?

Darkness pushed him awake. He gulped for breath, as if he had just surfaced from deep water. Lights snapped back to life, but a resilient shadow clung to the ceiling. He dozed. A dream appeared, sunlit plazas—useless dream!—because at night the plazas abound with black-toed creatures that slither and jump, creatures that dissolve the flesh from anyone unwise enough to enter their domain. He dreamed of his sister, her dyed-black hair filled his mouth, choked him. The black-toed creatures nested in her hair, lounging and waiting. Voices penetrated his dream, foggy voices, whisper-dark voices. Footsteps brought the voices closer. He opened his eyes. His sister yelped and jumped back.

"Hey man, scared us," O'Neill said. "Sitting in the dark. Looked like maybe you'd passed out."

"Passed out," his sister said. "Biggy brudder passed out." She giggled. "Take me upstairs before I pass out, you." O'Neill put a hand on her arm and guided her up the stairs.

Newsome's father wouldn't have permitted such behavior. Though not a large man, he had been a fighter. He had never let anyone oppress or insult him—any individual. Institutions oppressed him, the school administration, the union, the hunting and fishing regulators, banks. . . . But he never would have allowed someone into his house who he didn't like, never would have allowed anyone to taunt him without retaliation. As a child, Newsome's lack of aggression mystified his father. "Don't you understand that fighting is important?" he would say. But he accepted it, accepted his son as a father must. Now, Newsome wished he had fought O'Neill, fought him as a teenager—but would that have changed anything, forced O'Neill to respect him? Only if Newsome had beaten him, and that had never been a possibility.

Newsome picked up the book and returned to his room, his childhood room. He lay on the bed. The house had three bedrooms. When he moved back, he hadn't wanted to take his parents' room. He went through their things and sold or gave away whatever he didn't treasure, but he hadn't touched their bedroom furniture or decorations. His sister claimed their room. She trampled Newsome's protest, and it irked him that she had a valid point—the boy needed his own room, and if the boy took her old one, the parental bedroom was the only remaining choice. Only choice while she lived there.

Now the book was clean, but he felt too drained to read. He turned off the main nightstand light. His lamp had two bulbs, one of normal wattage for reading, and one a faint blue, strong enough to keep the dark from reaching his bed. He always slept with the blue on and his door locked. But tonight, sleep was hard to reach. Dark fangs encircled him. Down the hall, shadows licked his sister's drunken body; they slid in and out of orifices. His fists clenched. Every time he thought about his sister, his fists clenched. The impact with her face would be satisfying—like a ball of pizza dough smacked onto the rolling board.

What drove this violence into his head? Not his way, not his way. Even his father, his cantankerous father, never struck Newsome or his sister or brother.

His sister cracked eggs into a bowl and beat them. "I sure gotta have eggs for my headache," she said. "Eggs and coffee, coffee and eggs. Can you go to the store? Almost out of eggs. I got a cocktail waitress job. Ralph's. Starts tonight. You'll have to watch the boy. I didn't have time to set anything up. He's at Darla's but she has to work tonight too. Don't think the job'll take. Not with those drunken assholes pawing after me all night. But biggy brudder says everyone has to work. Isn't that what you say?"

Darla was their cousin, a hapless woman married to another of Newsome's boyhood tormentors. But however hapless, she had no infection of shadow controlling her. Mornings transformed night-shadow into an imaginary beast. How could shadows, or even the memory of shadows, survive the daylight? They hid, somewhere dank and deep. His sister and the boy had arrived in the evening, having driven all day from wherever.

Encroaching dark flung them to his door. Perhaps, had it been daylight, he could have kept her out.

"Our parents left some savings," he said, speaking over the sizzle of her eggs. "I want you to take some and go find your own place to live. This is my house now." He looked out the kitchen window. Daylight suffers in winter, shrinks and hides; its return is never assured. Today, he would leave the library well before sundown.

She flipped her eggs. "How much money you think I need, biggy brudder? Rent ain't cheap, even in this ass-crack town. How much then?"

He gave an amount, but in telling knew that even if she accepted it, even if she moved out, once she had spent everything she would return for more. How to arrange things to prevent that? The combination, his sister and O'Neill, the combination was what he found intolerable. He thought he had passed beyond the era of childhood torment. He had left this town, traded it for the anonymity of the city. But once back, elements returned to their former configurations.

Piles awaited him when he reached his basement workplace, great stacks of books needing their bindings repaired—more preparations for the upcoming semester. How did so many books get so mangled? Newsome worked part-time, arriving most days after eleven; today, having made his offer, he had left home early. Her lack of answer ground at him. He hadn't even stated the conditions required. He wished he could grab her shoulders. Shake her. Force her to accept. But if he touched her—fury would explode, and the shadows would erupt, never to be stoppered again.

He didn't mind the piles. Some might call what he did drudgery, but the steady work calmed him. He glanced at books as he taped and glued. The usual ragged academic tomes, Roman history, economics, literary criticism. He flipped through an architectural history of the state. Next was a bound typescript by a sociology professor named Harold Borkins . . . dated 1952. An account of Borkins' years at the college. Newsome read a random page: "Blumenthal was named department chair.

To be expected. Their kind always sticks together. It should have been Evans." Then bits about classes, a list of books he planned to read for a scholarly article.

Newsome skipped ahead. A page, blank save for a sentence in the middle: "Walking home tonight, later than I had meant to stay out . . . the darkness . . . darkness stung my arm as I passed along a street without light."

The darkness—even then, the darkness attacked. And a few pages into the next chapter . . .

> "Cold air propelled me. My elbows brushed the walls! The passage had contracted, a gradual diminishing of space that escaped my notice until the fact of it became incontrovertible. The dark and cold air made breathing difficult. This basement, this basement corridor that I have traversed many times, now transformed to a funnel herding me, herding me where? Behind me, the library, ahead, Landon Hall and my office."

Newsome had never known of a tunnel between the library and Landon Hall, or any buildings.

> "Shall I press onward? In my office, Lenore awaits. I crave the opposite of delay; I crave to be with her already, to bury my teeth in the flesh of her youth.
>
> "Ahead, the ceiling lights flickered and dimmed, as if strangled by dark, a dark I had no desire to meet. I turned back the way I had come, preferring to journey aboveground, despite the mounds of snow and ice-clothed sidewalks."

The chapter ended, and the next covered more mundane items, school administration politics, local politics. But later, darkness returned.

> "Evans knocked on my front door last night. I hadn't seen

him in over a week, had, in fact, taught his class on Thursday due to his absence. He stood before me, blinking. The street lights flickered.

"'Evans!' I said. 'Where have you been? Blumenthal wants your head! The Jew bastard actually had to teach a class.'

"Blackness seeped from his pupils; cloud-like tentacles coursed through iris and into the whites. The brightness of my living room appeared to disturb him. My lights—I had hired Newsome, a young electrician from the college, to install (at great expense) fluorescent lighting in all my rooms. This type of fixture appears to be less susceptible to whatever is interfering with standard bulbs.

"I didn't want to invite Evans in. In the protective glare of my living room, I waited for a response. He reached as if to shake hands. I started to reciprocate, but recoiled. His palm was blackened, charred-looking. I slammed the door in his face and turned the lock."

Florescent lights! And installed by Newsome's father. At home, only the kitchen had them. He would add more.

"I returned to the underground passage—why would I after my recent experiences? I had not intended to, but as I walked toward the library's exit, I spied Blumenthal and quickly turned around. Had he seen me, he would have buried me in the minutiae of departmental matters. And, Lenore again waited in my office.

"This time, the passage has changed! Brightness, so much brightness that no shadow dares appear. . . . "

The writing became more erratic, repetitions of grocery lists, names of students, and one graphic account of sex with the student named Lenore. He made her paint her breasts and stomach black. That was the last chapter. It ended with: "darkness and darkness and darkness—will these shadows never fade? I go to them. I grow weary of hiding."

Newsome got up. Where would the entrance be to a tunnel, and . . . would he find the brightness, the anti-shadow that Borkins described? He checked every door in the basement, to closets, offices, not caring what the few people working down there might think of his activities. In the boiler room, he found a door blocked by cardboard boxes. He moved them and turned the knob.

Damp steps led down. At the bottom, a small room ended at a wall, brick and mortar splotched with oily-dark residue. Passage sealed, an attempt to trap the shadows? A dank breeze pushed at him. The wall had gaps! He looked around the boiler room for tools, finding a long screwdriver and a hammer.

Fearing that he would attract attention, his hammering was tentative at first. Even so, the mortar flaked off with little effort. A brick thumped to the floor on the far side, and he hammered with more force. Dust and chips flew. A shard gashed his cheek. He dropped the screwdriver and banged away with the hammer, covering his eyes with a forearm. More thumps. The gap looked crawlable.

He returned to the boiler room to retrieve a flashlight he had seen in the drawer where he found the screwdriver. Once through the hole, he turned it on. The beam caught a wall switch. He tried it, and overhead lights flickered on. Dead bulbs outnumbered the living, but there were enough for him to turn off his flashlight. Shadows clung to the walls, the regular kind, harmless in the light. The walls curved, like a giant pipe. Perhaps other tunnels joined. Borkins had only mentioned going to Landon Hall.

Water dripped, forming a miserable stream that trickled along the pavement. Floating, floating, he hovered . . . no walls now, not constructed walls, a world-artery. World-blood coats the shadows, clings to them, traps them, and once trapped, they take on a blanket of sediment, hardened glop that stinks and clogs. A shape projected from the sediment. Closer, the shape formed a body . . . Borkins . . . skull-face locked in the fright of the dead, resting now in the muck of solidified shadow.

Trickles combined, one stream joined another, growing a broad and sluggish river, a river thick with shadow, more shadow than water, conduit of a great shadow beast. A body floated past, then another, victims of the endless dark. Miles separated Newsome from the opposite shore, but he spied details on the far-off bank, a city, a white and crystal city that repelled shadow. And in the city walked figures clad in bright colors, more yellows and blues than he had ever seen. How could he reach them? He came upon a stone wharf and, moored to it, a barge that could fit maybe a dozen people. From the opposite shore, a chain ran through a box on the barge and around a pulley mounted to the wharf. Newsome stepped onto the barge. The box that the chain went through had a crank on one side. He turned the crank. The barge moved! Cranking, cranking, he entered the flow. But the shadow-water rebelled. The barge tipped one way, then the other. A third tip flung him into warm, sinuous water. He went under, fought to the surface, fighting the shadow-water's grasp. Never much of a swimmer, not like his brother, but . . . his brother . . . lost to shadow-water despite his skill. Pattern of stroke, this leg, that arm, breathe, keep face clear of shadow. His arm struck the barge's chain. He pulled himself along and onto the wharf. Shadow-water squealed but released him.

A voice startled him. His body jerked at the unexpected sound. Something shook him. He focused; the voice became clear.

"Bookboy, sleeping on books." O'Neill, with a hand on Newsome's shoulder. "Bookboy's sister needs him at home. Time for her to go to work. Kid needs babysitting."

Newsome sat at his desk, books and binding-repair tools spread across its surface. When had he returned to his desk? The city . . . he needed to reach the bright city.

"Come on." O'Neill pushed him. "No time for walking. Get your shit. I'll be outside in my truck."

A mound of rubbery darkness lay under Newsome's desk, shadow-residue that had dripped from his clothes, his skin. He pushed a pencil at it. The material quivered and stiffened, resisting the pressure. He left it and hurried outside. In the truck, O'Neill lectured him about being more considerate of his sister's needs. "The world is unkind to single parents," he said. Newsome wondered what television program gave O'Neill the insight. O'Neill seemed oblivious to the shadow-dark and also unaffected by it. Darkness needs cleverness, and O'Neill was decidedly unclever.

His sister's screech greeted him and he forced himself to respond. "I'll take care of the boy tonight," he said. "But that's it. You fix things." He retreated to the kitchen, to the safety of the fluorescent light. The boy had eaten. Newsome fed himself.

Throughout the night, Newsome felt oddly at peace with the boy. They worked on a puzzle for a while and watched television. The boy's joyfulness repelled shadow. The boy wasn't like his mother. His father's genes, whoever the man had been. Perhaps she didn't know—one of the many who enjoyed her company. A life of proximity to her would ruin the boy, joy or not.

He helped the boy prepare for bed and lay beside him reading aloud. The boy's room had none of the shadow-oppression that sickened the rest of the house. Calm seeped into Newsome. When had such calm last touched him? Glow of calm like summer mornings. He forced himself to shift to his own room. Outside his window, the night-shadows taunted him. Distrusting his senses, he no longer knew which shadows were benign and which were the opposite. Newly acquired calm fled his body, leaving dusty bitterness. He closed the curtains, turned on the blue light, and went to sleep. In sleep, he begged for calm, for light—a blaze to burn the shadow away. Shadows glowed red, then white, then yellow, and with a shriek, disintegrated.

He took a flashlight to work, setting off before his sister awoke. Snow had fallen overnight. Few tracks marred the snow-carpet, and the pillowy whiteness gave comfort. Down in the library basement, someone had leaned a sheet of plywood against the hole in the brick wall and replaced the boxes. He pulled everything aside and crawled in. But no shadow river flowed, no city glistened from the far bank. He walked an endless tunnel, a tunnel inhabited by dust . . . carcasses of burned and banished shadows.

The tunnel spiraled downward, through layers of darkened crystals and green wafers. Thickened air resisted his intrusion. A final spiral revealed a cavern that stretched out of sight in all directions, a subterranean bubble over which the town sat. Ladders, rows of them, extended to the far-off ceiling; many were broken, sheared off at various points. On one of the intact ladders, a figure moved. His sister came into focus. He concealed himself behind another ladder. She appeared oblivious to everything but the rungs under her hands and feet. More people appeared on the ladders. He recognized Henderson, the Spanish professor from his street, Nosey Ninny, from the grocery store, and others, many others. No one descended the ladder that sheltered him. His sister reached the cavern floor. The ladder to the left of hers was broken about five feet up. He concentrated on remembering its position. Her ladder came—he was sure—from his basement. He would ascend and block it from above.

More people left their ladders. They moved deeper into the cavern. He joined them, keeping behind his sister. No one spoke. All walked slowly, calmly, as if strolling their neighborhood.

The cavern narrowed, narrowed so quickly that Newsome didn't comprehend the narrowing until the walls pressed him into contact with the others. An odor permeated from them, an odor of dark, a thick, wet scent that clogged his nostrils and caused a tingling on the back of his tongue. The crowd carried him forward—not the subterranean river that he had sought, but one just as entangling. Overhead, passed a black shape that he at first took for a bat, but it more resembled a jellyfish, though without dangle of tentacles. It shimmered in and out of sight, dark on a dark background, and he became aware of more of them, crowding the air. Newsome tried to turn, but the body-tide bore him onward, bodies packed too tight for him to break free. The creatures howled, a shadowy noise that faded and rose with their shimmers. And they had faces, human faces, or at least impressions of them, eyes, noses, mouths, and the mouths—they were the source of the shadowy howls!

The passage opened into a larger space, not as vast as the ladder room, but large enough for the press of bodies to loosen. The ceiling rose too, and into that vault the jellyfish-faces flowed. Newsome was glad to have more distance from them. The others moved forward. In the larger space, he was able to remain in the rear. He could make out a dark shape on the floor ahead; closer, it proved to be a pit. The first to reach the pit leaned over and vomited downward, spewing darkness. Another followed, and another. They formed a line on the edge. The shadow-odor worsened, a choking stench that twisted his guts. Breath held, he backed away, backed and turned . . . ran out of the vault-room . . . breath, more breath, but he couldn't lose the shadow-stench. He ran toward the ladder room, but the corridor brought him back to his starting point.

Darkness covered the hole that he had torn through the rotten brick. He kicked—the darkness quivered like the black pile that had collected under his desk. Screaming, he kicked and kicked, kicked himself to the floor. He lay in the dark dust. Laughter reached from across the wall, O'Neill and his sister, triumphant. Let them laugh, let them think the darkness had defeated him. He would find a way through the ever-shifting passages.

But everywhere he turned, a wall confronted him, old brick sealed by impermeable tar. Batteries drained, his flashlight dimmed to nothing. He crawled across the blackened floor, down a chute carved from bones of darkness, ever downward to a place where light had never lived.

NEW NEIGHBORS

Brown carried his stir-fried rice noodles and steamed pork bun from Grand Sausages up the five flights to his apartment and ate amongst the boxes of his life. This place, container of memories, would become memory too; its map would move into new compartments, its interior objects into a new locale. Eleven years, four rooms, two fire escapes, a bathtub in the kitchen, the bathtub where he first had sex with his recent ex-wife—the sensation of her soapy body still haunted him. But even with the soap memory and all the others to push him onward, he wasn't actually giving up the apartment. His friend Danvers was subletting.

The movers were Danvers and the crew of hefty youths who inhabited the cigar store downstairs. Their leader was Eddie. He volunteered the use of a truck: "My dad's a trucka," he said, and they settled on a price.

The majority of Brown's possessions were books, many boxes of them, which he had packed with care to prevent shifting. He worked with books, collected books. A book was the reason he had picked his new town, Springdale.

Brown finished his breakfast. Danvers arrived, then Eddie and his two stout friends.

"We found us a good spot for the truck a couple a doors down," Eddie said. "Malcolm saw some guy leave, and put garbage cans there till we could take it."

Moving progressed. The only issue arose from the crew pushing book boxes down the stairs. When Brown stopped them, Malcolm-the-parking-spot-finder said "They're just books." Carrying so many heavy boxes from the fifth floor wasn't something the movers had expected. They called in two more friends. Disallowed from pushing, Eddie and company set up a chain, one person at each landing. Eventually, everything was loaded. Brown rode in Danvers' car. Eddie and two others followed in the truck. They set out for Springdale.

Springdale! The name conjured unlimited mystery. He had first seen the town referenced in a manuscript he copyedited, an encyclopedia of vanished colonial towns. The book described Springdale's setting as "a jewel of Western Massachusetts, where a sparkling river chuckles past rocky banks." Debate over the location of this jewel fueled his curiosity. Research followed. At the library, he found a travel guide from 1902 that listed Springdale's various natural attractions, with no reference to its having been abandoned. A map showed the town's location, a two and a half hour drive north of the city. No modern maps showed anything.

Intrigued, Brown convinced his wife to go with him for a weekend of exploration. Then, as often happened, she found an unexpected theater obligation. He picked up the rental car and set off on his own, driving north with the 1902 book and a new road map. The morning was a cold, gray December, but the impending adventure cheered him onward. Past one of the towns shown on the new map, he stopped at a roadside diner for a late breakfast (late-breakfasting being something he particularly enjoyed).

From the diner, he took a small county road not shown in the 1902 book but appearing to flow in the right direction. The road entered a valley with a steep bank on one side and a creek on the other. In places, the bank came near to overhanging the road, giving the impression of a tunnel. This part went on longer than he would have thought possible; his new map showed nothing like it. A cassette tape ended and reversed to play the other side. The overhang receded, cattle pasture emerged. Brown felt his breath pass more easily through his body. Buildings began to appear, antique store, car repair shop, veterinarian—obvious signs of a nearby town. Then, railroad tracks, a small green sign read Welcome to Springdale, and the road became Main Street. He found parking in front of a store called Fudburry's Toys.

Springdale. He had found Springdale.

The sky had taken on that burnt-metal look, and the temperature had dropped. Cars and pedestrians flowed past. A snowflake drifted along its private air current, then another. On the opposite sidewalk, a large, blue-suited policeman paused and glanced at him. Could they identify strangers that easily here?

He locked the car and crossed the street toward a two-story brick building with the sign Springdale Guest House. Inside, a woman about his age, with dark, curly hair, stood behind a counter.

"Yes?" she said, and waited.

"Is there a room available?"

"Well that's certainly possible, but I'm on my way to the dentist. Can you come back?"

"It's snowing."

"Okay, I see what you mean." She opened a registration book. "Looks like we're empty. You can have number 3."

He retrieved his bag from the car and left it in the room. Accumulating snowfall couldn't keep him from exploring. He found a local history center and perused exhibits. He bought a book in a used bookstore.

Now, a year and a half later, he was moving there.

Brown and Danvers met Eddie and crew at the roadside diner. Brown had sensed that Eddie wouldn't be able to reach Springdale without him.

Two months ago, Brown had borrowed Danvers' car and went to find an apartment to rent. Getting to Springdale took most of the day. Roads that he thought went there didn't. He had to return to the diner and follow the same overhanging route.

They parked in front of his new building and unloaded; a second floor apartment eased the work of book box carrying. Eddie and his assistants left. Danvers planned to spend a couple of nights, helping him unpack. Brown's apartment was in a two-story house near the river. He had windows on four sides—a luxury after tenement living. From the apartment, he could walk to the food co-op, but the larger grocery stores required a drive. Before leaving, Danvers took him to a car dealer in another town, where Brown bought a well-worn but operational model.

Again, Brown sat alone amongst his belongings. A house . . . apartment building . . . is alive, a creature with needs, desires. Its inhabitants influence this life—a sick building is symptomatic of the inhabitants' issues. A building that houses a rapist, a molester, can never feel peace. Brick rots and crumbles, mold and decay invade. Effects are subtle, but worsen, as the more sensitive and wholesome residents leave. The balance tips, buildings collapse into ruin. There were times, as Brown's marriage worsened, that he feared he was damaging his building. Part of the reason he decided to move was that he wanted the building to heal.

Boxes emptied, shelves and cabinets filled, walls took on their ornamentation. The apartment had one bedroom, a kitchen large enough for his table (and no bathtub), living room, and a comfortable little study off the living room. Now that Brown had moved in, the town felt different. Feeling unsettled was expected. He gazed out his windows at mud and crocuses. Moving to a new place had always been difficult. An operational phone helped. And a delivery truck brought a 600-page botany text to copyedit, giving him the comfort of routine.

He had wondered how to receive deliveries . . . whether he *could* receive mail, deliveries. The town wasn't on maps! The address that the woman at the rental office gave him was for Berkshire County.

This town . . . its absence from maps, the differing accounts of its existence—he had expected it to be smaller, a remnant or two of colonial times plus a gas station. But downtown Springdale wasn't that much smaller than Great Barrington, though Springdale was more compact; once away from the center, the town dissipated into farmland and forest.

He worked, he explored. His neighbors remained elusive. In the city, people maintained aloof distance, even from neighbors, but he had managed to get to know many of the people in his building. Three or four, anyway. He had expected neighbors here to be open and friendly. Perhaps they had all been at work during the unloading of the truck and didn't know that he was there. Between bouts of unpacking, he had gone downstairs to examine the mailboxes in the entryway, which must have originally been the house's parlor. From there, stairs led up to his apartment. A door to the right of the stairs had a blue plastic A nailed to it. According to the mailboxes, Michael Bullock and Cynthia Walters shared unit A, with Amy Simpson in B; the leasing agent had said that apartment B was in the rear.

Later, Brown discovered that the house contained an additional resident.

Leaving early one morning to breakfast on almond croissant and cappuccino at Frisell's Coffee, he heard a woman's laughter coming from A. Thrilled to have the silence broken . . . eager to see another face . . . to meet someone, someone in Springdale besides leasing agents or grocery store clerks, he paused, thinking of knocking, but sudden shyness prevented him; he had to satisfy himself with a moment of personal interaction at the bakery.

His building had a covered front porch with wrought iron chairs and a small table. He decided to sit outside on nice mornings, hoping to see someone leave on their way to work. The first two days, no one passed, but the next morning, as he sipped his coffee and read the *Springdale Town News*, the front door opened and a woman came out. She had dark skin and short frizzy hair. She saw him, looked away, then back. "Oh, I thought you were someone else."

He told her his name. "Apartment C, as of six days ago. You're the first person from the building I've seen."

She looked toward a man passing on the sidewalk, then back to Brown. "I'm on my way to work—why don't you stop in for a glass of wine later . . . six-ish? Unit A. We should be home."

"That would be great," he said.

The simplicity of interaction, chemicals released, the body glows, flows, finds the means to move forward, survive, thrive; in the movie version, the triumphant song rises over a montage of domesticity and sunshine, friendships cemented and expanded. Expectations abound, but real-life rarely contains such clarity.

At 6:11 (not wanting to be too early), bottle of wine in hand, he left his apartment and descended the stairs. At Brown's knock, a blond-haired man a couple of inches taller than him opened the door. "Hey, come in. I'm Michael." They shook hands. Brown gave him the wine. The living room walls were painted dark yellow. Brown's were white. The realtor had told him he could repaint, and he intended to. A woman sat on a sofa the color of roasted beets. "That's Amy," Michael said. "Have a seat, and I'll get you a glass of wine."

Brown said hello to Amy and sat in the armchair opposite her. The room was dim, illuminated only by candles on the coffee table and a nearby cabinet. Amy picked up her wine glass and sipped, looking at him over the rim. Judging, perhaps. He felt judged, but that didn't mean anything. He was the new tenant. They would feel compelled to judge. Though judgment made conversation awkward. He squirmed in her gaze—inwardly only, he hoped. The staring couldn't have lasted as long as it felt. Such things rarely did. But duration can never be measured properly until it ends. Would this end? Eventually, she would need to blink.

"Cynthia and I have been friends since our freshman year of college," she said. "We're close." She looked away, toward the scent of toasting bread.

Michael returned with a glass of wine for Brown, the unopened bottle Brown had brought, and a corkscrew. Cynthia carried in a tray of bread and cheese and sat on the sofa next to Amy.

"Now it's time to interrogate our new neighbor," Michael said.

Expecting something like that, Brown had worked out what to say . . . tiring of the city, the split-up with his wife. The subject was difficult to talk about. Not the feelings of it, exactly, but how much to express. He had learned that people don't like hearing excessive personal details too soon, and the definition of *excessive* varied.

The evening's conversation moved along to less personally controversial subjects. He learned about their careers. Cynthia and Michael taught at the college, history for her and literature for him. Amy was a graphic designer for the *Springdale Town News*. She said that they could probably use a part-time copyeditor, if he wanted to work outside the house. Which he might. He went to bed with a pleasing sense of contentment. Meeting neighbors, sharing drink and story, gave him attachment, the antidote to displacement, pushing him along the gradual path toward his new home becoming Home.

And with home comes the welcome mundane. Laundry, for example. His new building had a washing machine and dryer in the basement. An incredible luxury after eleven years of carrying his clothes down his stairs and two blocks to the laundromat. The day Brown looked at the apartment, the leasing agent had only taken him to the top of the basement stairs. An odd scent floated from the darkness. Basements should smell of dampness and underground, he thought, though he didn't know enough about them to be an authority; whatever he knew, he had absorbed from copyediting or his old proofreading job. Something from a book. But he thought that this odor was more animal than dirt.

The agent flipped the light switch and nothing happened. "Again? I'm going to have to bring in an electrician. The bulbs keep burning out. Well, the washer and dryer are down there to the right of the stairs."

Remembering the issue with the bulb, he put a flashlight on top of the

pile in his laundry basket. And, not unexpectedly, the light switch provided nothing but continued darkness. The smell that propelled itself
toward him was somewhat doggish, though he didn't think any of his
fellow residents had a dog, didn't think pets were allowed at all, though
perhaps they were. He turned on the flashlight. Its beam shaped a path
down the stairs—stairs with no railing. A railing would have made him
more comfortable, but the stairs were of a decent width. He found and
loaded the washer.

Back in his apartment while fabric rinsed and churned, he prepared a
sandwich. The cutting board was in a drawer second from the bottom;
light bulbs were in the bottom drawer. He took out a bulb and left it by
the door. Even if he chose to remove his bulb from the socket when he
was finished and bring it back upstairs, having light would ease the job
of washing. Sandwich eaten, he descended, bulb in hand. He unscrewed
and replaced the burned-out bulb, ascended to the switch, and . . . light!

He hadn't explored the basement, previously. Couldn't have. Not easily, with his small flashlight. Even with a bright bulb, the room held too
many shadows. The floor was concrete. That much he had known via
flashlight, and was pleased to see. Dirt floors were disturbing. Aside from
the fact of being dirt (and therefore dirty), anything (or any *one*) could be
buried. There had been windows, once, four of them, now obscured by
plywood, thereby increasing shadow-retention. He pulled at the wood,
but nails held firm. Shelves and cabinets stuck out here and there, metal
units rooted to the floor and others with wall mountings. They displayed
basement kinds of things, old paint, crusty tools, dark jars of something
canned long ago and forgotten. He opened a cabinet drawer, finding a collection of dowels in various sizes. Handy items, dowels. If you were the
sort of person who used things like dowels. Perhaps here, he would be.

The drawer below the dowels held treasure, compartments filled
with bits of hardware: tiny valves, square iron nails, brass fittings, pulleys, copper wire, and many unidentifiable others. Even the identifiable
were mysterious—valves to what? for example.

Had his neighbors made similar investigations? Technically, everything down here belonged to the building's owner, but Brown doubted

whether that person, whomever it was, might miss a few odd bits of hardware. Hardware that he . . . she . . . whomever . . . was unlikely to know existed. These items were not of recent manufacture. That much Brown knew, or at least supposed. He picked up a piece of hollow metal about the size of the last joint of his pinky finger. The metal was in an elbow shape that ended at a circular hinged piece. He put it in his pocket.

With his clothes tumbling in the dryer, he ascended the stairs. At the top, he turned off the light, planning to retrieve the bulb later, after it cooled.

Having no weekend plans and no desire to continue his copy-editing work until Monday (separation from the job being an issue of working at home), he packed a bag and drove toward the diner; from there, on to the nearest town with train service to the city (tracks passed through Springdale, but no train stopped). Two nights in his old apartment (sleeping on Danvers' fold-out sofa), seeing friends and visiting favorite restaurants and bars proved restorative. Friends promised to visit him, but people rarely left the city except in the hottest months. He expected to have many guests in July and August. Perhaps more than he wished.

Springdale days continued. Brown cooked beans, more than one kind, having bought them bulk at the food co-op next to the yoga studio. He had never considered himself to be a bean-maker, but now was the time to expand. Beans are nutritious and economical. He worked, as usual, but also began integrating himself into town life. He tried a beginners yoga class. Alice, the yoga teacher, was a gentle creature with long brown hair and a fiancé named Stuart who did not appear to share her mild nature. (At Brown's second class, with only one other student present, Stuart insisted that Alice shouldn't bother teaching such a small group because they could instead get an early start on wedding-related errands. Another student arrived. Stuart left. Alice taught the class.) Perhaps Stuart had other qualities. Perhaps Alice would be unhappy with him. Who could tell? Human relationships are difficult to predict.

Brown had hoped that neighbor wine invitations would become a regular occurrence. Likely, he should have already invited the three to his apartment. He wrote invitations for that evening and put them under doors, then went to buy wine, cheese, bread, and roasted artichoke hearts. Which are always useful to have, even if on one's own. No one came; he drank wine and ate cheese. But the next morning, he found a note pushed under his door: Michael, asking if he would be interested in going to hear a band that night in another town. He was. Despite the long drive. Desperation is never charming, but he did desire companionship, and nearer than his friends in the city.

Michael drove the curvy roads and told Brown about his classes at the college; the college was, apparently, a harmonious environment. Students were content, faculty and staff were treated well. Brown tried to concentrate on their route, thinking it different from what he recalled of his own drives. He wanted to talk about the mystery of Springdale, his difficulty finding the town. He hadn't, during the wine visit. Perhaps *in Springdale*, one doesn't discuss such things. Now they were miles away. "How did you find out about the job?" he asked, as a way of working toward the topic.

"Oh, an ad in some journal or other. Must have been, but I don't remember exactly. I was at Central State. I liked it okay there, but it's always good to look, right? And if I hadn't, I wouldn't have met Cynthia."

"Clearly the correct decision then," Brown said.

"C. and Amy were sharing the apartment. This guy Devlin was in the back unit. Upstairs where you are was a yoga teacher named Chandra; she had lived there for years. Devlin wasn't at all appropriate for the building. Amy moved into his place. I moved in with Cynthia. By then, she was pretty sure I understood."

Brown understood the dynamics of apartment building tenancy. If that was what Michael was talking about and not some sexual configuration. People often did talk about such things, though Brown didn't.

They turned off the smaller road to a larger one and entered a town. "I'm curious about the want-ad or whatever . . . it referred to the college,

I assume, but did it say anything about Springdale? I ask because I've found Springdale to be somewhat intangible. Even our mailing address omits the name."

He told Michael about the scattered and conflicting references and his eventual search. His eventual successful search.

"I suppose Springdale is there when needed," Michael said. He laughed, as if dismissing whatever mystery Brown was attempting to present.

However, Brown agreed. Had to agree. Springdale had certainly been there when needed and, despite his newness, he already felt something for the town, something elusive (like the town), comfort, acceptance—as if the town had accepted him, or had started to.

Another laundry day. The move had disrupted his schedule, and he wanted to catch up, empty the hamper. In addition to normal accumulations, he had bought a set of sheets and several towels. He had to be frugal, of course (he was always frugal), but the cheering effect of a few additions was worth the expense.

Like last time, he screwed in his bulb. He loaded the washer, turned it on, and started up the stairs. From somewhere below came a click, like a deadbolt shifting, and a shuffle of footsteps. A man-shape emerged from a back corner . . . to the light . . . reached up . . . unscrewed the bulb. Brown froze, blind in the sudden dark. A bolt clicked again. The whole procedure had taken seconds. Trying not to lose his balance and tumble, Brown reached around to his back pocket for his flashlight. Silly, the stairs were sturdy *and* wide enough. With light, they presented no challenge. In his flashlight's reassuring glow, the ceiling fixture was empty. That animal-mustiness was stronger. Emanating from the bulb thief, he supposed.

Back in the sunlight of his apartment, he wondered how the man had been able to remove the hot bulb without being burned, without visible flinching. When he went to transfer his clothes to the dryer, the beam of his flashlight again caught the fixture. The bulb was there. He tried the switch. Nothing.

The man . . . the bulb taker . . . had emerged from a cloud of dark. Brown looked for a door, though the flashlight was inadequate for a detailed search. Was a moving panel obscured by a metal shelving unit? That was the only possibility. A possibility that verged on impossibility. Didn't it? Though, why? People lived where people lived. Whoever he was, he must have a reason for choosing a dark basement.

Later, Brown walked the exterior of the building, looking for evidence, perhaps an outside door, a vent, something. The bulb taker—Mr. Dark—might be at this moment standing (or lying) beneath Brown's feet. But . . . however Brown might accept the man's choice of living arrangements, where those arrangements conflicted with the rest of the tenants, accommodations must be made. Brown and everyone else needed light in the basement. Assuming that the other residents used the washing facilities. Which, it turned out, they didn't.

Breakfast had used the last of his bread; he went to the food co-op for a fresh loaf and a few other items. On the way back, he saw Cynthia. They walked the rest of the way together. She said that she came home for lunch on days when classes, meetings, and office hours permitted. Brown asked about laundry.

"Oh, we use the laundromat in town. It's easier, newer machines. Less intrusive."

She was unimpressed with his city laundromat history.

"The laundromat has air and light, it's next to the café. What more do you need? I know you'll think so after you try it. It really *would* be better if you stay out of the basement."

Well then. She spoke with such finality that he was afraid to contradict or say anything about Mr. Dark. But the anti-laundromat idea had rooted. He called the leasing agent and talked with firmness and determination. He recommended a new light fixture, fluorescent tubes. Brightness, the basement needs reliable brightness, he said. A safety issue. The stairs have no railing, but he didn't have a problem with that as long as he could see without having to wave a flashlight while holding a laundry basket. She acquiesced, and two days later, he saw from his front window the arrival of a van, white, with red lettering:

MacLeod's Electrical. Two people emerged, a smallish man with a red cap and gray beard, and a woman, taller than the man, with dark hair emerging from her red cap.

As the day was pleasant, Brown took his work down to the front porch, hoping that he might overhear something. The pair were some minutes in the basement. They left the building and crossed the porch.

"Where to next, Dad?" the woman said. They got into the van, the man on the passenger side, and drove away.

Toward better lighting, Brown hoped. But how would Mr. Dark react? Perhaps with sabotage. He should warn the electricians. Assuming that they returned. Which they didn't, not that day. The following day, he took the train to the city for a meeting with a new client, ate dinner at a Korean place he liked, and took a late train back. Sitting in the train, looking out at passing town and country, it occurred to him that the city had begun to feel alien. Springdale, though it had grown in familiarity, was also more alien than not. Where did that put him? He needed to belong somewhere. He *wanted* to belong to Springdale. Why not? His things were there, shoes and all. Indeed, as his car's headlights picked up the landmarks indicating that he approached the town, a pleasant upwelling came to him. Surprised, he smiled.

The electricians had returned. Looking out from his front window, drinking morning coffee, he saw the MacLeod's Electrical van. Its back doors were open, but no one was in sight. Working downstairs, he assumed. He decided to investigate, though not immediately. He showered and drank another cup of coffee, ate a small bowl of yogurt and granola. Brushed his teeth.

He had enough dirty clothes for a small load. Best to make his foray under the guise of laundry. His flashlight proved unnecessary. They had hung work lights from nails in the overhead beams. Warm light enveloped the basement. What would Mr. Dark think of that? The grind of a drill erupted from the far end. He had heard it while upstairs, muffled, but hadn't understood what it was. The dark-haired woman was drilling

through a thick beam. Was that safe, putting a hole in a beam? He supposed it must be. She would know. *He* certainly didn't.

He set his basket on the washer and approached her. She had finished
the hole and was preparing to drill into the next beam. There was a
line of holes (and sawdust) leading to the back of the basement. A wire
dangled from the ceiling near where the holes started.

"Is it okay to run the washing machine?" he asked. "I can come back
later."

"No problem," she said. "It's a different circuit."

She spoke with a quiet sort of authority that he found attractive. He
thanked her for the work. He wanted to talk to her more. Needed to,
really. Not just because of her attractiveness. That helped, yes, but more
because his Springdale still lacked human contact. He had his neighbors,
his yoga class, but more was necessary.

He asked about the wiring, pointed to the holes and the dangling
strand. She explained about the breaker box, switches, and wiring.
The wire was old, the switch was old, the fixture was old. They were
installing new. The work sounded simple, yet exciting. He told her how
nice it was to have the machine so close. "I'm sure that sounds kind of
silly, but I left the city so I could have a few more comforts. I love the city,
but it beats you down."

He wanted to say more, but the stair treads squeaked; Brown turned.
The electrician—Dad—carried a long flat box on a shoulder. The box
had a picture of a light fixture.

"More light down here will be great," Brown said. He loaded his wash.
When he went down later to transfer clothes to the dryer and again to
take them upstairs, clean and dry, the pair were still working. The fixture was in place, and a bright new yellow wire ran along the ceiling
through the holes that the dark-haired woman had drilled, but as yet no
new light brightened the basement. At some point in the afternoon, he
looked out the front window; the van was gone. Curious, he went to the
basement stairs. The new switch did nothing but flip from off to on. Perhaps they would finish the following day. Perhaps Mr. Dark had already
sabotaged the new fixture. Not needing to wash, he forgot about it. If

they returned, he didn't see them. Meanwhile, on a trip to the hardware store to get a nice ocean blue paint for his bedroom walls, he also bought a slim, keychain flashlight. Something useful to keep in his pocket.

He was due back in the city. A book publisher had hired him to copy-edit the promotional text for their catalog. They preferred him to be in their office for however long the work took to complete. This would be his third time. Part of why he had sub-let his apartment to a friend—housing wasn't an issue. He decided to stay an extra day and go to a new exhibit at an art gallery.

One slice of unpleasantness reminded him that the city may be large, but its size diminishes to a small town when you inhabit a finite set of locations—he saw his ex-wife, twice. Once from behind (funny how when you know someone well, you can recognize them from any angle); he crossed the street and turned up another, avoiding her. But the next day, in Union Square, there she was, with her new man, walking toward him. He had no time to turn. And decided that he didn't want to. Instead, he greeted them as if they were distant relatives he hadn't seen since a mutual cousin's wedding six years ago . . . and moved along. Still, he didn't enjoy the encounter. Who would? But such things are unavoidable. And yet, the encounter—its memory—stuck to him. Even on the train and ensuing drive. Chasing him. Unfortunate (one of her words)—he didn't want a fresh memory of her invading Springdale. A fresh memory . . . though it might carry pain . . . that particular pain couldn't hurt him. He smiled. He reset. He was on his way home. To Springdale.

He went to dinner with Cynthia and Michael. A Japanese restaurant, which was very good. He had passed it in his acquainting himself walks but hadn't tried it. Dinner conversation . . . generalities . . . life in Spring-dale, laundry. He mentioned the electrical work, and . . . they weren't pleased.

"Remember, I told you that the laundromat is better?" Cynthia said.

"Yes, there's no benefit to on-site washing, not when you consider all factors," Michael said. "Centralized resources are much better. We don't *all* have to own washing facilities. That's the kind of thinking that leads to consumerism and waste."

Brown disagreed. "Use of the laundry is part of the rent we're paying. The facilities *already* exist. It's not like I'm buying a washing machine for my apartment. There's no reason to pay more to go to the laundromat. And I'm sure the landlord agrees, or they wouldn't have approved the electrical work."

"That's a lot of disruption," Michael said. "They can't start a big remodeling project without letting us know. At least a note in our boxes."

"They're about finished," Brown said. "And you didn't even notice. So you can't really call it a disruption." He smiled, realizing that his words might sound taunting. Though he *was* annoyed with their attitude. Neither returned his smile. They glanced at each other, then back at him. Michael was the first to speak.

"Well, no matter, I'm sure the situation will be resolved without conflict."

Cynthia nodded in agreement.

They knew about Mr. Dark! Brown didn't want conflict either, but no basement dweller could keep him from using the laundry facilities. Did Mr. Dark even pay rent? No point continuing the topic. Talk drifted into music and other things, though none of them spoke with much enthusiasm. The check came. They paid for dinner and walked home.

Brown didn't need to do laundry yet, but the next morning he went to check the light and found it still inoperative. Contractors were so unreliable! They carried jobs near to the point of completion, then abandoned them for some other client. He sat at his table to work, but the lighting situation irritated him too much. His concentration vanished, which irritated him even more. The leasing agent didn't answer the phone; he left a message. Irritations piled upon irritations! Perhaps he would call the electrician himself. He looked up the number but decided there wasn't time before his yoga class. He packed shorts and a tee-shirt into a bag.

The class smoothed his irritations. He had known it would. After, he went into Frisell's Coffee. The electrician woman was in line ahead of him. She smiled a greeting, but he didn't think she remembered how she knew him. He reminded her where they had met, or at least talked—they hadn't exchanged names, that day in the basement, though he would like to. And did. Suzanne was hers.

"How's the new light working out?"

He hesitated. What she said implied that they were finished. Her turn to order came. He was afraid that she would get her coffee and leave before he could respond. He touched her arm. "I'm sorry, you asked about the light. It wasn't working this morning, or any other time I've checked. Something must be wrong with it."

"Oh . . . well, I'll drop by later and have a look. Sorry about that. The manager should have called me." She took her coffee cup and left.

He walked toward home with his coffee and a muffin. On sighting his building, that gentle lift . . . the contentment . . . homey warmth— feelings that continued to surprise. Springdale, his place in it. Cynthia and Amy appeared, walking toward him. Expecting a moment (at least a moment) of conversation, he paused. They didn't say hello. They didn't stop. Whatever he had planned to say fizzled. Had he somehow offended them? Because of the basement? He walked up the steps, angry now, anger pushed him into the building. He opened his mailbox. A check had arrived, an overdue payment for a large job. Therefore, a large check. Payment improved his mood. He settled in to work. And did, for some time, then didn't. He sat. Sitting didn't help. If he couldn't work toward the next check, why not go out and deposit the current one?

He tried some banter with the teller, a young man named Tim. With no success. Tim seemed preoccupied. Not his usual perfunctory friendliness. Maybe he didn't approve of basement illumination either.

After the bank, Brown kept walking. Home . . . that home feeling . . . it would return. He assumed it would. He hoped that it returned when he returned.

The street perpendicular to Main, a short block that contained a rug store, the Japanese restaurant, other businesses . . . had there always been an alley after the restaurant? He turned into it, thinking he would circle back to Main, cross, and keep walking toward the river. It was a nice alley. No garbage smell, no garbage. Not wide enough for vehicles. The alley extended farther than expected. Well, why had he expected anything? The architectural configurations of downtown Springdale hadn't been well studied. But did alleys commonly have a roof? This one did, now; before, it hadn't. Something that looked like a roof. A ceiling, anyway, from his perspective. Though he knew one couldn't exist without the other. Not easily.

His alley turned to the left. He turned with it. Onward is always the best direction. As the alley was now more like a hallway, it was not unexpected when doorways materialized. Numbered doorways, some with nameplates: Anderson's Creations, Claxton, Inc., Mendelson and Associates, Witcover Dentistry, but as he went on, the names became less legible. Or, perhaps his eyes grew tired of reading. He sometimes over-used them in his work.

He passed a door open to what looked like a motel room: bed, chest of drawers, nightstand, and a repellent stench of alcohol. Curtains covered the lone window, blocking light. Broken bottles, many (many!) broken bottles littered the floor.

Another hallway intersected. A crossroads. He turned left again. The carpeting here was a dull brown with a much-worn pattern of delta symbols. Dark patches showed in places where white paint had cracked and peeled. The overhead lighting (florescent tubes in box fixtures, every twenty feet) became less dependable. Once bright, they were now a dim and dusk-like wattage. For reassurance, he put a hand in his pocket and touched his new flashlight.

His side began to hurt. He had been walking too fast. No need, not really—no reason for hurry. This evening, he might have to work late to keep up the number of pages-per-day to make his deadline. But he was accustomed to that and, living alone, he had no one to interfere with his work. Hadn't, for much of his marriage either. When his ex-wife was performing in a play, he was obligated to attend, but not every performance.

The lack of windows bothered him. What if he opened one of the doors and looked in at whoever worked or waited? When a sign looked interesting enough. Not a dentist, certainly. Perhaps a travel agent? He had once considered becoming a travel agent but was unsure how to go about it. Is there travel agent school? He could have asked a travel agent, but hadn't, or at least hadn't yet. And probably wouldn't, though changing careers was still an option, wasn't it? He supposed that he didn't want to copyedit books for the rest of his life. A job that had more interaction with other people would be nice. Depending on the other people, of course. Perhaps a job at Springdale's college. They must have an office where available jobs were posted and applications turned in. Or the job at the newspaper that Amy had mentioned. Assuming that she would still recommend him.

The sign on the next door he passed: Wilkenson Properties—that was the name of the leasing agent for his apartment. Though not the office he had visited. Unless a back entrance. The door was unlocked. He went in. The lighting was worse than the hallway. The waiting area was rectangular, with three unlabeled doors and no receptionist desk. Olive-painted walls. No window. One metal chair with an orange seat cushion. Definitely *not* the office he had previously visited. He knocked on the leftmost door, then (after no response) moved to the middle. At the third door, he tried the knob, which turned, but the door wouldn't move. Rather, it moved but didn't open; something cushiony but heavy blocked it. He pushed harder. Something that moaned too, a sleepy moan. A napping horse or giant dog. Unlikely, but what other explanation could there be?

The other doors were locked. He upended the metal chair and turned it sideways so the backrest was against the jamb of the blocked door. He pushed until there was enough of a gap to slip the backrest in and use the chair as a lever. The door opened with a pop. Opened into darkness. He took out his flashlight. Its beam showed more hallway and no large animal. The ceiling had the same light fixtures, but he didn't see a switch on either wall. Someone should call an electrician. Had Suzanne the electrician gone to look at the basement yet? He hoped he saw her again. This lonely walk had him thinking about companionship. Which he didn't think he would get from his neighbors, not anymore. What was she like, away from her wires and circuits?

His neighbors. He tried not to let irritation overpower everything. Mr. Dark—they were only protecting his preferred environment. If the leasing agent hadn't mentioned the laundry facilities, he never would have gone down there, never would have encountered Mr. Dark. Reconfiguring his expectations might be the best thing. If he was to continue living in the building, in Springdale, he needed to have friends. Needed to have friendly neighbors. Would they be satisfied . . . forgive him, if he proclaimed his commitment to the laundromat?

Something gave way under his feet. He stumbled, then sprawled backwards onto his bum.

The flashlight beam hadn't caught a short flight of stairs. When he got up, pain shot through an ankle. He tried a few tentative steps. The pain wasn't excessive, but the fall took away his nonchalance, his exploratory vim. There had been no one else in this endless alley-corridor, no way to get help. What if his injury had been more severe? He sat on the steps, turned off the flashlight to save the battery, and rested. Dark . . . the darkness here had no limits. Mr. Dark may have the best solution . . . calm in the dark . . . peaceful, yes? But impractical for everyday life, which includes laundry.

He decided to return the way he had come. From the side-alley to here had felt like a journey of hours, but he knew that if he went back, only a few minutes would elapse. Travel always feels longer in a new direction with an indeterminate goal. He turned on his flashlight and got up. His ankle throbbed, but he could walk. Still no horse or dog blocking the waiting room door. From this side, the knob didn't turn. He knocked, paused, knocked again, harder, then harder still. And waited, but not for very long. No choice then but to go forward. Surely, by now, he was close to something.

———————

Choice is a vague word, an even vaguer concept. Is there really ever a choice? In anything? He hadn't chosen to have his wife leave him for her director, unless, in choosing to be with her, he had chosen all ensuing possibilities. Had he chosen to be with her? Had he chosen his Springdale lodgings? He knew better than to explore this avenue of thought. Didn't he? For a long time, after his wife left, the only feeling he had, for anything, was indifference. That passed, as much in life passes. What was his current all-encompassing feeling—choice? Moving forward into the unknown?

Which consisted of more dark hallway, and dark hallway no longer signified as unknown. No, he knew dark hallway, and dim hallway. Though he preferred bright hallway and no ankle pain. Having a new flashlight, with new batteries, was a comfort.

A slight shift in the air . . . sudden depth . . . space.

He stopped and swept the light around. A few feet ahead, the hallway ended; a cavern swallowed the beam. Cautious, he tilted the light downward and approached the cavern. The hallway floor dropped away. He stood at the edge. The bottom was . . . ten feet down? Hard to be sure in the fuzzy darkness. But he thought he could lower himself, grip the edge where the hallway ended, and drop feet first. Leaving the flashlight on, he slipped it into a pocket. The glow through his jeans was reassuring. He lay on his stomach, feet pointed toward the gap, and slid toward the edge.

For a moment, he hung, then let himself drop. His feet hit bottom, jarring his ankle, and he fell on his back. He must have cried out when he fell. People often did. He lay where he landed. At some point, he realized that he was moving. Not on his own. Someone *moved him*, pulled him by his feet. Someone with a familiar sourness. His head caught on jagged sharpness. He yelled and kicked. The puller dropped his feet; his ankle sent him more pain. Hands lifted his head; not the sour-smell, a perfume he recognized. Then a sharp pain made him yell again—something was pulled out of his head. The sour-smell leaned in close. The stench nauseated him. He flailed his arms. From behind, grunts . . . words? The dark muffled everything. He sat up, then tried to stand. His ankle gave way.

On his knees, he felt in his pocket and pulled out the light. Its glare blinded him. Was that Michael . . . Amy? Her perfume, buried under the sour one. The shadow-shape of Mr. Dark batted the light from his hand. It clattered onto the floor and died. Sourness overcame him. He screamed, gagged, tried to scream again. Sounds blasted from above . . . explosions . . . lightning . . . storm-battered, he persevered. How long had he traveled, shipwrecked . . . living off seaweed and clams dug from damp sand with broken fingernails? He crawled, collapsed, crawled farther. A washing machine came into focus. Footsteps. Voices. One voice.

"Hey, are you okay?"

His eyes adjusted. The electrical lady stood over him. Suzanne—that was her name.

"What the fuck *was* that?" she said. "Something was down here, on top of you, then it disappeared. Smells like a . . . I don't know what." She helped him stand.

"I hurt my ankle," he said.

"I found a loose connection at the breaker box, fixed it, came to try the switch and saw whatever I saw." They started up the stairs with her supporting him. "You've got a lot of blood on the back of your head."

"Can you help me to my room? I'm on the second floor." He pulled out his key.

She settled him on his sofa. He touched the back of his head, winced at the pain and the bloody palm.

"I'll go down to the truck for my first-aid kit."

He closed his eyes till she returned. She dampened a cloth and wiped the back of his head. "Looks too jagged for a nail. Some scrap of metal, but it's not that deep. The head bleeds a lot. I've had to patch up a lot of cuts, working on old houses. I'll wrap a bandage around your head so you don't get blood on your pillow. You'll need to soak your shirt in cold water to get the blood out."

She gave him a glass of water and a couple of pain-killers. "Anything else I can do before I go?"

"Ice maybe? For my ankle. There are plastic bags, bottom drawer, next to the light bulbs." She looked worried, he thought.

"You'll be okay? You really ought to get a tetanus shot." She put a cushion on the coffee table for him to use as a footrest and helped him wrap his ankle.

"I'll call a doctor tomorrow," he said.

"I can stay a while longer, if you need me to."

"I'm fine. I just want to sit here for a bit. Thanks." She rested a hand on his knee for a moment, then turned to go.

"Oh, Suzanne, could you turn off the overhead light on your way out? That switch by the door."

Alone, he sat amongst the shadows of his apartment. His eyes adjusted to the dimness. The throb of his head receded. From outside, a streetlight cast its glow. He thought about closing the curtains but was too comfortable to move. Comfort was important, here and in the basement. Down there—Mr. Dark—he was part of the building. It was a good building. Brown wouldn't disturb it. Everyone deserved a home.

SPRINGDALE LONGITUDE AND LATITUDE

Once upon a January, 1999. Somewhere in Western Massachusetts. Alone. The kind of drive that extends far beyond actual time or mileage. I happened to stop at a roadside diner for lunch. The road might have been Route 23. A waitress pointed me to an empty booth and brought me coffee. I sat and listened to the conversations around me, pocket-notebook on the table and too close to the coffee, which dripped over the rim of the cup and attacked the notebook, granting an unwanted travel souvenir. I can show it to anyone who doesn't believe me.

At a nearby booth, a man and woman, around the age I was at the time, talked about people they knew and had just seen (where, I didn't catch, but let's say it was a wedding, the back yard of a house on a wooded riverside). Several years ago, the woman had an affair with the groom, during his previous marriage (though she wasn't the woman who the previous wife found out about, that was someone named Matilda).

They paused conversation long enough to give their orders to the waitress: bacon-lettuce-and-tomato sandwiches, one with French fries, the other with onion rings. I looked at the menu. Fried chicken would be nice, but I didn't want something so substantial for lunch.

The groom they spoke of was a reporter for a local television station. His new wife worked at a bank, a relationship manager, whatever that is. "Can you imagine anything sadder than waiting to take over an anchor spot on the local news?" the woman said. "Those guys never retire. They just get more and more fossilized."

"He's going to have to move to a larger market. More jobs."

"Male anchors, of course. Women have to disappear *before* they start aging."

The waitress brought them drinks and turned to ask what I wanted. I said grilled cheese with onion rings. A nicely made onion ring is a wondrous thing. For those unfamiliar with the delicacy, here's a basic recipe: Slice an onion latitudinally (taking root end as south, green end as north); pull apart the rings; dip rings in batter or dip in milk and then in flour or bread crumbs, then fry. A deep fryer is best, but pan-frying works. And some history: *New York Sun* May 29, 1910, pg. 195; New York Public Library's Susan Dwight Bliss collection.

> "A novelty that progressive New York restaurants are intro-ducing with great appreciation from their patrons is one that can be reproduced at home without difficulty—French fried onions. In flavor and appearance they bear little relation to the usual breakfast dish, and which, moreover, are possible to many to whom "for the stomach's sake" the others are impos-sible. The sweet Bermuda onion is used for this new dainty. It is cut thin to resemble French fried potatoes. Before cooking dredge with flour. Fry quickly in a wire basket in hot deep fat until crisp, brown, and free of grease. Very delicious as an accompaniment for beef steak, or, in fact, good with almost any kind of red meat."

With the intrusion of plates, their talk slackened but didn't end. Lis-tening, I became confused, realized that I had been mistaken. They weren't talking about people they knew; I recognized the names: from a television show I had watched in a motel room the previous night.

The show was one of those ensemble-cast things, with inter-connected stories and intersecting groups of characters. Actually fairly interesting the way it's put together. There's the sad musician—a bass player for a successful band who fled the city with his photographer wife who's now his ex-wife; her new husband, who runs a store that sells and installs miniature trains for amusement parks or the yards of the wealthy; her restaurant-owner brother; the guy who runs a small high-tech company; the African-American woman and her Anglo husband, who both teach at the college; there were other ethnic minorities shown, but they didn't have much to do in the episodes that I saw. I had read about the show and was able to pick up enough while watching. This was before DVD, before streaming or downloading, so it wasn't easy to watch missed episodes.

Well, I thought (smugly), don't these people have more interesting things to talk about than TV drama? And why do they discuss it in such detail and from within the milieu? I talk about TV shows and movies, but as a writer, interested in story. I don't natter about how Daryl treated Betty at the company picnic, or the ordeal that Malone was having with his landlord that might cause him to move his toy store to a new location. The woman was surprised to hear about Malone. The man said that he had been to dinner with Malone on Wednesday, and learned everything directly from him.

Curiosity replaced smugness.

From their talk, I had figured out that the man worked for a real-estate company and the woman was an assistant principal at the high school. Springdale High (which was the name of the town on the show). The man asked, "Anything crazy happening at Springdale High?" That's how I heard the name. She said that the hole kept getting darker.

There was nothing remarkable about their conversation, no philosophical or political insights. The man kept talking about local real estate; I couldn't tell if the woman was interested or polite. If I hadn't just stayed up too late watching three episodes in a row, instead of reading, writing, or sleeping (all of which would have been more useful), I might not have noticed them at all, not understood or recognized the names of the place where they lived or the people they were talking about.

They finished their sandwiches. I asked for my check. Paid. They did likewise, and left, getting into a small hatchback car. The woman drove. I followed.

I was living in a town in Western Massachusetts called Great Barrington, and though I had explored many roads in the area, the one that the pair took was unfamiliar. On one side a creek flowed, and on the other loomed a hillside. Loomed is a boring, overused word that writers often spill onto the page when confronted with a tall physical object. Recently, a friend, when reading proofs of his upcoming book, was appalled at the number of times he used "loomed" or "looming." But in this particular description, loomed is accurate: the hillside wasn't merely steep—for long stretches it overhung the pavement like half a tunnel, reducing the already-weak light to the flavor of dusk.

Why did I follow? I didn't *know* that they were driving to Springdale. Normally, I don't believe that TV shows are real.

The year that I spent in Great Barrington wasn't my best or my worst. It constitutes a minute fraction of my life (one-fiftieth, to be almost exact). Something life-changing happened while I lived there (but not while I was there). Mostly, I was alone. I worked at home, with once-a-month trips to Manhattan to work at the office of one of my clients. I knew few people there, and those I did know included a married couple who are the two quietest individuals in the world (and therefore less able to introduce me to others). I had never lived in a small town, and I didn't know *how* to live in one, didn't know what kinds of things a person should do to meet people and construct a life. Trips to the grocery store or a restaurant became anticipated social engagements. I didn't have much money and couldn't eat in restaurants often enough to get to know the staff. I tried a few new things: a full-moon hike, yoga, but talking to people in the class afterwards turned out to be difficult: the activity made me too tired, but also too peaceful. Inward centered? So I wrote a man-alone story about a guy named Brown and a levitating head that appears in his living room.

While I liked Great Barrington, I considered it transitional, a place to stop and consider my life while looking for a more permanent place. I had been thinking about Northampton, because it was larger, with more things to do. Northampton was slightly farther from New York, though closer to the interstate. I considered Seattle, but the idea of all the miles between was too daunting.

The looming road continued for longer than I thought possible in that direction. The road pointed south, toward Connecticut, which shouldn't have been far. In the gloom I could have missed the Welcome to Connecticut sign. There wasn't an obvious border, no river, for example. On the car stereo, a tape ended; I let it reverse to the other side. Writing that . . . after the years . . . it's hard to remember what it was like, playing cassette tapes in a car. I would tape new CDs to hear in the car (as I had done with LPs before I switched). A CD player for the car was a luxury I couldn't even think about buying. Though I remember an album ending, I don't remember what it was or what it switched to on the reverse. (Here is where a real memoirist would insert a meaning-laden choice from that year, say _____.)

The hillside receded, replaced by a cattle pasture. I felt able to breathe again.

I began to see buildings, an antique store, car repair, veterinarian— obvious signs that I was approaching a town. I crossed a set of railroad tracks. The highway became Main Street. A sign announced: Welcome to Springdale. Downtown reminded me of Lee, a town near Great Barrington where I had found a decent Mexican restaurant. The people I was following turned right onto a cross-street, then into a parking lot. I eased my car to the curb. The building where they stopped had a sign that said Wilkenson Properties. The man left the car and entered the building. Were the couple involved romantically? Openly? I saw nothing furtive in their behavior. It had occurred to me that they had chosen a remote spot for a reason, but if so, they would have arrived separately. The woman backed the car and turned to exit. I decided not to follow.

No need. I pulled away from the curb and drove around to find a parking place.

Some of this is fuzzy. Memory is an untrustworthy creature. What is certain: I left the car and walked around. One of the first things I saw was a used bookstore, called Riverside Books. In I went. The two used bookstores in Great Barrington had brochures listing all the used bookstores in the area. I didn't recall this one being in the brochure. What a luxury that now seems. Back then, working freelance, pre-child . . . I could drive around with no goal other than exploring used bookstores and whatever else I saw along the way. Riverside Books was nice, with the right kind of musty paper smell. I found a hardback of Angela Carter's *The War of Dreams*, which I decided to get even though I already owned and had read it in paperback as *The Infernal Desire Machine of Doctor Hoffman*; also, an intriguing-looking book called *Undiscovered Countries* by someone named Gerald Ubder (the cover showed a woodcut illustration of a stylized flying machine over what looked like a village in Medieval Europe). I know I bought it, I know I carried it out of the store, but I can't recall what happened to it and have never found a reference on the internet or library database.

At the cash register, I tried to chat with the proprietor, a light-haired youngish man wearing eye glasses that had wooden frames. I'm not good at small talk and am easily put off by people who don't offer much communication. Maybe I was too exuberant. "This is a great store!" "I even want to buy things that I already have!" And so on. The man totaled my purchases and bagged them.

I set off to explore further. I passed a toy store called Fudburry's, a closet-sized pizza restaurant, another real-estate office. A sign at the entrance to an alley-like space between buildings said Sublime Junk, with an arrow pointing alley-ward. Through the window, I could see an orange lamp, the shape of which made me think of an onion, some decorative plates, a purple vase with dried flowers. A bell on the door announced my entrance. The front room had junk and also not-junk, though I didn't find anything sublime. At the counter, a woman with gray hair pulled back in a bun nodded at me and looked down. She was working on a jigsaw puzzle of a seaside town.

A back room had kitchen items. I picked up a rusty, one-egg-sized cast-iron skillet. That would be easy to clean and re-season. You can never have enough cast-iron skillets. The bell clanged to announce the entrance of another patron; voices mingled, one clearly the shop-owner's, the other also female. I browsed my way deeper, setting aside a pile of things: mugs, the skillet, a framed and completed paint-by-numbers farmhouse, enameled camping plates, a lamp with a wooden sailing ship for a base. In the back, a cupboard showcased teapots and vases. I picked up a ceramic rooster with a pink tongue, red-orange body with a few lumps shaped and painted as stylized feathers, and oversized yellow feet on an oval base painted green. The signature on the bottom looked like Ortega. The whole thing was about the size of my forearm, from elbow to wrist. There was something loud and fun about it. I'm always looking for things to decorate my writing space.

"I want that," said a voice behind me.

Memory drips, swirls, calcifies. The voice was of the woman I had heard talking to the proprietor. I turned . . . recognized her . . . TV show. An artist who teaches art at the college, played by an unfamiliar dark-haired actress. I thought she was good. I liked how she looked, too, and had seen her mostly naked, having sex with a visiting artist before he left town. And here she was—but which *she*, actress or character?

"I do too," I said.

"You can't. I've been coming to see it all week. I needed to think about it, visualize where it would go and how it would interact with other objects." She reached toward the rooster but stopped short of trying to take it from me.

"Same here. Not the coming to see it all week part, but visualizing its placement. I'd like it for my writing space, on my desk, probably to the left of the computer monitor. Maybe even use it in a short story."

"Well, you can't. I've already claimed it and the owner's my friend. She wouldn't have sold it to you even if I wasn't here."

She was about my height, with green eyes. Knowing something about her . . . did I know something about her? "Are you an artist?" I asked.

Her head dipped, the slightest of nods, a nod that said she was unwilling to move the subject away from her goal. "I thought so—the way you talked about visual space, your determination. What media?"

"Painter, mostly. Some collage, some illustration. I teach at the college here. But . . . I need that." This time she touched the rooster, wrapped fingers over its head.

"Fine," I said. "It's yours. But how about buying me a cup of coffee to make up for my loss?"

She took the rooster and held it against her breasts. Her body relaxed. "Okay, sure. We can do that. I was going to Frisell's next anyway. I have to teach class in an hour."

Her name (she told me—but I knew from the show, too) was Regina Spangler. I told her mine. The place she took me, Frisell's, was back on Main Street, on the side where I had parked. Before joining her, I returned to my car to put lamp, books, and other purchases in the trunk. She was still waiting for a cappuccino; I ordered one too. Music played. I recognized the singer but was unfamiliar with the album. I asked the woman who took my order. She said that she thought the owner had picked it. Regina and I sat at a square table, her back to the window, me facing. Across the room, a loud-voiced group had put two tables together. Regina waved to them. An older woman sang part of a show-tune. A man walked past, and the singing woman invited him to join them. An old man told a corny joke and everyone laughed.

Springdale seemed a friendly place, friendly to those who were already part of it. Not to strangers passing through, but what place is? I might return, spend a night and explore further, go to a bar or two, restaurants.

We talked. I told Regina about my writing, my frustrations with finding publishers for my stories. I explained how my writing doesn't fit magazines that publish fantasy and science fiction *or* literary journals. At that time, I had only had two publications, in very small literary journals, and my bread story was forthcoming in *Back Brain Recluse* (except the magazine went under before they could publish my story, which finally appeared years later in *The Third Alternative*). I didn't know that my day's adventures would become my first book.

This feels stupid and clumsy-worded; it's hard to stain the page with my own dialogue. Also, I could tell that I had lost her interest. It's one of those things that's hard to describe. Eyes don't really glaze over, for example. But if you have any kind of sensitivity (if you're not someone who talks and talks regardless of whether the receiver of your words cares to hear them), you can tell when someone isn't interested. Words become harder to launch into the space between you and the other person. The voice feels like it's failing, fading.

Hoping that I wouldn't sound desperate, I said I would like to see her studio. I should add, here, that part of my reason for leaving New York involved the end of a relationship, an end that hurt a good bit less at this point than it had six months previously but still hampered my ability to speak to women I might be attracted to. Regina said, sure, sometime, yeah, but she had to go to her class now. Did that mean I should ask for her phone number, try to set up a time I could see her work . . . see her again . . . but did I want to? She was a person, not a character in a television show. Muddled, I looked down at my coffee cup, and when I glanced up, she had vanished.

I flung my chair back and stood. The opposite side of the street, now visible through the window no longer blocked by her body . . . buildings gone . . . all I could see were trees interspersed with tall grass. The loud group had also disappeared. The rooster remained. I picked it up. Walked to the door. Which stuck, then popped like the release of a pressurized container. The outside air prickled my throat. No one else was on the sidewalk. I ducked in and out of empty shops, working my way down the street. Sunlight was fading from that winter-gray haze of sky that defined New England—I never got used to the winter sky there. In comparison, my part of Ohio feels like the south. But . . . my car! It was the other way. I turned around. I didn't hurry, but I wanted to be near it.

When I was a block closer to where I had parked, I sensed movement behind me. I eased toward the building and turned to look. Two people. One tall and heavy, one thinner but about the same height. Blue uniforms. Why did I assume that they were looking for me? Walking, getting closer. The larger one was male. They glanced into each shop they passed but didn't go in. I needed them to go in. How else could I move, reach my car? But what was wrong with letting them see me? I hadn't broken any laws. The rooster was still in my hand. True, it hadn't been mine to take; grabbing it had been a reflex, retaining it an act of . . . desperation? I moved, not quickly. I didn't look at them.

No more than three steps later, voices called out for me to stop. I took another step, looking back as I moved . . . a beefsteak hand gripped my elbow. How had they reached me so quickly? The man-cop was immense; his companion less so, but she blocked my path. She looked up into my eyes. Her gaze stopped me as much as the man's grip.

Long ago, I had an unpleasant experience at school. In my arithmetic class, fifth grade, I think. There were three fifth grade classrooms. Each class spent most of its time in its main classroom, but split into mixed groups for English and arithmetic, based on skill level. These classes might be in your own room or in one of the other rooms, with that room's teacher.

This particular day, we were supposed to be doing long division. I couldn't find my pencil. I accused the girl next to me of taking it. She might have been teasing me earlier. She might have been the girl who had stabbed my finger with a pencil some weeks previously. Likely, it was that girl. The teacher wanted to know what I was doing, wanted me to get to work on the assignment. I said I couldn't find my pencil. She said: *I have a pencil.* That *has* to be what she said. But what I heard was: *I have your pencil.* How did the teacher get my pencil? My child-mind couldn't process. She wanted me to come to her desk and get the (my!) pencil. I refused. I didn't trust her—how could I?

I don't remember what she did. I suppose I must have sat at my desk doing nothing until the class ended and we went to lunch. In the lunch-room, as we lined up to return to class, the teacher tried to make me go to the principal's office. I refused. Back in my regular classroom, the principal came in. He tried to make me go to his office. I wouldn't. I grabbed my desk's metal post. He pulled my arm but couldn't dislodge me. He left.

I didn't understand why I was being harassed for losing a pencil, or for the teacher having taken it. My impulse was to pull in, turtle-like, and wait for the threat to pass.

Toward the end of that day, my class went to the school library (a place I was pretty fond of). While the class was leaving, the principal entered, carrying a wooden paddle. He kept me from leaving. Once the other kids were gone, he made me bend over to be paddled.

No one ever talked to me about it. I don't remember the principal saying anything. No one ever asked why I had refused the teacher's offer of a pencil. That's public education, at least in Texas, at that time. Maybe it's different now. I don't want my daughter to be treated like that.

The way I was feeling . . . my confusion at the situation . . . the sudden appearance of authority ready to blame me for . . . what? . . . brought this memory back. I wasn't going to go with them. I'm not violent. I haven't been in a fight since I was fourteen, but I didn't want that big cop's beef-steak touching me.

I slammed the rooster's base onto his hand. He howled and let go. The woman jumped on me. Blindly, I swung the rooster, connected. She fell. I ran. Distance increased. Not from my running. Pavement stretched. Their bodies distorted . . . giant hands reached toward me then snapped back, as if I had reversed a telescope to the wrong end. The nearby buildings dissolved, increasing the distance between me and the cops. They walked away from me, woman-cop . . . changed, taller, now the same height the beefsteak cop, and . . . between them, they dragged a limp body.

Have you ever been surprised, disoriented, when you see a photograph of yourself taken from behind, especially if you hadn't known you were being photographed? Imagine a video instead, and you get closer to what I experienced.

More buildings faded. I reached my car and got in, finding immediate comfort in the metal enclosure. I started the engine. As I eased into the roadway, the sidewalk transformed into grass. I drove. Trees, trees and river, replaced the town. I crossed a bridge. The sun was behind me. I drove, waiting to intersect with a larger road, a road I recognized.

I got back to my apartment around 7:00 p.m. I lived on the bottom floor of a two-story house that was a short walk from the center of town. The owner lived upstairs. Her son and his girlfriend lived in an apartment in the back. I opened the car door. The rooster was on the front passenger seat. I reached for it, got out, and pulled my overnight bag from the trunk, leaving the books and other things for later. I set my bag and the rooster near the door and flopped onto the futon-sofa. I looked around, bookcases, front door, windows, rooster. Home. How long did I sit there? Isolation, smothering isolation, filled the room. I wanted to hear something, the owner, moving around above me or coming down the stairs with her dog, a beagle whose name I've long-forgotten, or her son, his girlfriend, their dogs . . . hounds . . . I got up. In darkness, I walked downtown. Finding myself at the movie theater, I went in. I didn't care what was showing. But no one was in the ticket booth, or concession, no one else in the lobby. I sat, unable to leave, hoping another person would soon appear. I took out my notebook and began a story of a man lost in Springdale.

ACKNOWLEDGMENTS & STORY NOTES

Thanks to the creative writing teachers and journalism professors who got me started with words, especially Peter LaSalle and Zulfikar Ghose. Carol Emshwiller. Clarion West class and instructors of 1997. Editors who published the stories, including Giancarlo Malchiodi, Chris Reed, Gavin Grant and Kelly Link, Mark Rudolph, Andy Cox, John Klima, Eckhard Gerdes, Deborah Layne and Jay Lake, Jonathan Strahan, Keith Brooke, Nick Gevers, and Peter Crowther. Blurbers, Jon Langford, Steve Rasnic Tem, and Lisa Tuttle. Too many stories with too many readers over too many years for me to remember everyone who gave me feedback. Melissa Tinker for recent stories; Nancy Jane Moore for most of the ones in here. Always, every story, Rebecca Kuder.

Tales of the Golden Legend

The bread story. The title comes from a René Magritte painting of flying loaves seen through a window. In 1992, I went to a major Magritte retrospective at the Menil Collection (Houston, Texas), then mined his imagery for many stories, most of which were unpublishable messes. The painting's title refers to a medieval book on saints, but I didn't know that when I wrote the story. Soon after I moved to New York City from Austin in early 1995, I took a writing class with the late Carol Emshwiller. I had read some of her short stories and met her through mutual friends. She gave the class several writing exercises, in viewpoint, dialog, place, etc., some of which became the various sections of "Tales of the Golden Legend." The story was accepted for publication twice, first by *Back Brain Recluse*, but the magazine folded before publishing it, then by Andy Cox of *The Third Alternative* (since renamed *Black Static*).

Suspension

In 1997, I attended Clarion West, an intensive, six-week writing workshop in Seattle for writers of science fiction/fantasy/horror—also for writers like me, whose work isn't genre sf/fantasy/horror, or realism. The workshop plan is to write a new story every week and submit it to the group for feedback. Each week, a different writer or editor leads the workshop. The other participants and that week's leader critique the stories. Clarion has the reputation of starting and ending careers and marriages. My Clarion experience made me doubt whether my fiction belonged in the genre. Some instructors agreed; one said it was too bad I wasn't alive in the 19th century because my writing might have found a better reception then. Another suggested that I attend Borges lectures in New York (where I was living at the time) to see if I could meet publishers there. But I also had great and encouraging teachers like Nicola Griffith, Lucius Shepard, and Michael Bishop.

"Suspension" was the first story I wrote at Clarion. I had been thinking for a long time about a story based on the four-armed man in Magritte's painting "The Sorcerer." Also, I had been reading Samuel Beckett's prose and went to several Beckett plays; his work is filled with sedentary characters: people trapped in bed, in piles of sand. One day I was walking West on Grand Street, Lower Manhattan; up ahead was a very large woman. Seeing her, I wondered what would happen if she slipped and fell. How difficult would it be to lift her? That thought led to a man in the snow, which then combined with the Magritte painting, a giant, four-armed man in the snow. I named him Quatrain Brauner (Quatrain for his four arms and Brauner for surrealist Victor Brauner).

The first draft was third person with excessive attempts at humor. After Clarion, I changed it to first person, and to help me with snow-bound philosophizing, I read Friedrich Nietzsche. I've forgotten what exactly I got from the Nietzsche or even which book it was. There are times (too few) when I find the perfect thing to be reading while writing or revising something. Some thought or feeling or concept gets incorporated into sentence structure or becomes an image or scene. "Suspension" first appeared in the very excellent 'zine *Lady Churchill's Rosebud Wristlet*.

Indifference

One night, I was reading Harlan Ellison's collection, *I Have No Mouth and I Must Scream*; when I read: "The Form of the Habit she had become still drove him to one side of the bed," from the story "Lonely Ache," the idea for "Indifference" flowed into me. I put the book down, went to my desk, and started writing. The story references an unpleasant period of my life that had occurred a few months earlier. Brown's helplessness echoed what I had felt; I, too, was once puzzled by the appearance of coriander seeds. The head, like the solidified clouds in "Valley of the Falling Clouds," appeared to me fully formed, from whatever neighborhood of the subconscious holds such things. The story was published in the debut issue of a 'zine called *Full Unit Hookup*.

The Secret Bag

Death and shopping bags from the Chinatown stores I frequented. I once met a then-girlfriend's dying father in a hospital room with a view of the

Rocky Mountains. The story was published in *The Journal of Experimental Fiction.*

The Baker

Connected, obviously, to the bread story. I started writing this in the class I took with Carol Emshwiller in 1995 and finished it in 2016. It's something I would pull out and work on between other things, stop, think about, do something else, go back, and so on. Eventually, I reached the end. I wrote the last section under the influence of a nearly forty-four minute piece of music called "Rules of Play" from the album *Rules of Play*, by guitarist Doug Snyder and drummer Bob Thompson.

The Green Wall

I don't remember where I got the image of a rain forest projected on a wall. Or a portal to a rain forest appearing on a wall. Whichever it is depends on how you read tales of the fantastic. Part of what inspired "The Green Wall" was the short fiction of J. G. Ballard. I wanted to evoke some of Ballard's obsessional mystery, and his fiction is full of mirages and phantom images. The wall was the wall outside my apartment window in New York. Perhaps I was stuck for something to write, looked out the window, and said: what's out there?—oh, a wall, maybe it has a rain forest on it. The Feast of San Gennaro takes place every autumn in Manhattan's Little Italy and is little more than an excuse for fairground attractions, beer, and sausages. It isn't much fun to experience as a resident of the neighborhood.

The art gallery in the story is based on a real place which no longer exists and shall remain unidentified, but anyone familiar with the New York art world knows a Hannah Rezinsky. Publishers are kittens compared to gallery owners. I'm glad I never worked for her nor was one of her artists, but I liked her just fine. When I began working on my novel, *The Painting and the City*, I decided to use the sculptures I had described in "The Green Wall" for the art of the main character, Jacob Lerner. Because "The Green Wall" had not yet been published, I added something about Jacob Lerner to the story and referenced Hannah Rezinsky in the novel (which takes place some years after Lerner has moved on to much more stable representation). This story first appeared in *Polyphony* 5.

Travels Along an Unfurling Circular Path

After graduating from college with a degree in journalism, I worked in a bookstore, did public relations and an employee newsletter for an engineering company, and proofread for a typesetter. Somewhere in there, I took additional undergraduate classes: computer science, anthropology, and creative writing. I wrote a very early version of this story for a creative writing class taught by Zulfikar Ghose, a fine and extremely unknown writer. In the computer science lab, while procrastinating from working on my programs, I would play a text-based game. You would type "look to the right" and the game would generate a description of whatever was in that direction. I wanted to write a story with a similar feel. It became my first publication, appearing in 1996, in the debut issue of an annual called *Excursus*. And, years later, I turned it into a much longer and different story, which John Klima published in *Electric Velocipede*.

Sidewalk Factory, A Municipal Romance

This story includes several pieces of flash fiction dating from various periods. The oldest short-short (from approximately 1990) is a fictional press release about a new factory for making sidewalks from hats. In 1996, on a plane from New York to Texas, I opened my notebook and out came a lecture by the great Professor Fenster. Wandering New York's Metropolitan Museum of Art one day, I came upon The Temple of

Dendur, unexpectedly, having had no idea of its existence. The temple formerly stood on the left bank of the Nile River; it was disassembled during the building of the Aswan Dam and reassembled inside the Metropolitan. I sat on a bench near the temple and imagined an event from the temple's history.

The final factor that helped me build the story was the death of Kurt Vonnegut. Several years earlier, a friend had given me a copy of *Mother Night*, which I had missed during a Vonnegut-reading frenzy in my early twenties. I didn't read it till after Vonnegut died. Reading it made me want to try political satire. I combined the various flash fiction elements and wrote more around them, curious to see where it would go. When I begin a story, I usually don't know much about it. I have an image, situation, place, character. I write, the story emerges, sometimes easily, sometimes not. Once I had the short-shorts lined up, "Sidewalk Factory" came together fairly easily. I thought of the Lord Mayor dispatch sections as a tightening noose, going from light to dark, from absurd to sinister; the municipal worker begins as a happy oblivious citizen who learns to reject his beliefs.

Mountain Story

Driving along through rural Ohio one day, I wondered what would happen if a mountain materialized. Originally, I wanted to write something like J. G. Ballard's "The Drowned Giant," but it came out more like an Edwardian travel narrative. The story is a thematic companion to the political satire of "Sidewalk Factory."

Valley of the Falling Clouds

In June, 1996, I went to the Kerrville Folk Festival, a yearly music event in the Texas Hill Country, a land of cedar, prickly-pear cactus, and heat. The festival has been going on since 1972. It lasts three weeks, with crowded outdoor concerts on weekends and smaller concerts during the week. Some people go just for the weekend concerts, some stay a few days, and others camp out for the entire festival. There's a tradition of elaborate campsites that groups set up in the same place each year. Musicians who aren't official performers go to play their songs in the campgrounds and hang out with friends. It's like a science fiction convention but without the boring panels and pontification; also without a bar, but there's no lack of drink.

While sitting outside my tent, under a tarp, smothered by heat, I had an image of solidified clouds rolling down a hill and crushing someone's house. A story unfolded about Rex, his longing for Apple Jane, the herbalist's daughter, and his departure to the wilds beyond the town of Moonsocket. I tried to have the story begin with the cloud boulders rolling down the hill and crushing Rex's shack, then jump back and forth in time. Jumbled mess. It was one of the stories I submitted to Clarion West. The fifth week, tired, not getting anywhere with a new story, I revised it, re-arranging things in chronological order. Based on feedback, I removed assorted details. A few years later, more confident about what belongs in a story I write (what makes a story my story and not someone else's), I put everything back. Because of its origins at a music festival, the story has various song references woven into it, "wind's dominion" from Butch Hancock, the name Rex and "blue wind" from Townes Van Zandt's "Rex's Blues." The story used to end differently, but life changes made that ending impossible. It was the first of several stories I had published in the excellent *Polyphony* anthology series.

In Springdale Town

Inspired by Jonathan Carroll's novel *Land of Laughs*, in which a children's book author has written a town into existence. My original concept of Springdale was its creation from a perfect episode of a television show set in a town with that name. Springdale is difficult to find and sometimes unsafe to leave. Springdale is different things to different people.

I moved from New York City to Great Barrington, Massachusetts at the end of 1998. I had never lived in a small town, knew few people there, and worked at home. You could say I was lonely. One evening, I went to a movie theater; the door was unlocked but no one was inside. I sat in the lobby and started writing about a man alone. I had with me a pocket notebook that the acclaimed and esteemed Paul Di Filippo made me buy. PS published *In Springdale Town* as a book in 2003, and it was reprinted in *Best Short Novels* 2004, edited by Jonathan Strahan.

Darkness, and Darkness

This story emerged from reading *The Best American Noir of the Century*, edited by James Ellroy and Otto Penzler. Two stories, "The Homecoming" by Dorothy B. Hughes and "The Hunger" by Charles Beaumont, struck me by the way the authors used the idea of things hiding in the dark or looking different in the dark to add tension to the story. Additionally, I admired the anthology's older stories for their economic language and style. I wanted to write a story that used darkness and was tight like the best of the stories in the anthology. And I wanted to make the darkness a more literal threat. Nick Gevers published it in *Postscripts* 36/37.

New Neighbors

Brown from "Indifference" moves to Springdale. Where else would he go? I had considered using this scenario for a story that the artist Lisa Snellings asked me to write for a series of chapbooks and possible anthology that she was planning. Her idea was to create art and give the art to a writer to use as inspiration for a story. Greg Ketter of Dreamhaven Books published three chapbooks before the project fizzled, *Strange Birds* by Gene Wolfe, *Strange Roads* by Peter S. Beagle, and *Strange Light* by Larry Niven. My story would have been "Strange Neighbors." Years later, I decided to write it. One of my inspirations was the fiction of Robert

Aickman. Long ago (1984, I think), I was washing clothes in the laundry room of an apartment complex in Austin, Texas. The apartments surrounded a courtyard. The laundry room took up a section of courtyard, opposite the door to an apartment. A light outside the laundry room had burned out. I put in a new bulb. Later, I watched a man open his door, reach into the sconce to unscrew the hot bulb, and retreat, bulb in hand, into his apartment.

Springdale Longitude and Latitude

I wrote this as an afterword to an ebook of *In Springdale Town* published by Keith Brooke of *Infinity Plus*. Some of it is true.

Story Credits

"Tales of the Golden Legend" (*The Third Alternative* #30, Spring 2002);

"Suspension" (*Lady Churchill's Rosebud Wristlet* #8, Fall 2001);

"Indifference" (*Full Unit Hookup* #1, Spring 2002);

"The Secret Bag" (*The Journal of Experimental Fiction*, Winter 2003);

"The Green Wall" (*Polyphony* #5, Fall 2005);

"Travels Along an Unfurling Circular Path" (*Electric Velocipede* #10, Spring 2006);

"Sidewalk Factory: A Municipal Romance" (*Psychological Methods To Sell Should Be Destroyed*, Electric Velocipede/Spilt Milk Press, Spring 2008);

"Valley of the Falling Clouds" (*Polyphony* #3, Fall 2003);

"In Springdale Town" (PS Publishing 2003);

"Darkness, and Darkness" (*Postscripts* #36/37, 2016);

"Springdale Longitude and Latitude" (Afterword to Infinity Plus ebook edition of *In Springdale Town*, 2012);

"The Baker," "Mountain Story," and "New Neighbors" appear here for the first time.